The Love Child

The Love Child

Fiona Hill

G.P. PUTNAM'S SONS · NEW YORK

To TJ, who reads me

1

"I know you do not particularly care for criticism," said Lady Louisa Bridwell, reaching as she spoke for a round bonbonnière on the parcel-gilt table before her, "yet I cannot but account it the most unutterable madness to have invited so many people down this year. Will you hand me that box of comfits?" she added, her plump arm failing of its goal.

"Are you afraid they will eat up your sweetmeats?" inquired her hostess, in a voice whose stridency did nothing to mitigate the unkindness of her remark. "You needn't be; there are sufficient for all appetites."

"It is entirely astonishing, Sarah," Lady Louisa rejoined placidly, her tongue wrapping round a confection of an especially satisfying flavour, "how proof I am become against your sharpness. I do not mean to say, you know, that it ever discomforted me much; but there was a time, in our girlhood, when you succeeded in producing a disagreeable twinge or two in my conscience."

The lady thus familiarly addressed made no reply; rather she trained a faintly sceptical gaze on the other, the tip of whose tongue was now engaged in probing (with imperfect discretion) certain recessed regions in her mouth where a trace of the interesting lozenge might yet linger.

"Don't look at me that way!" Lady Louisa cried out, when at length she perceived her hostess's steady regard. "I protest, you make raspberry taste like vinegar."

"You ought to drink vinegar, you know," her companion advised her, "and eat very little. Otherwise you will fall prey to the gout."

"I beg you will not be so silly," her ladyship returned uneasily. "Females are never goutish."

"They may be," the other observed. "However, I will be quiet if you like."

"Oh, you needn't be that!" Lady Louisa exclaimed, as if horrified. "One might easily languish away altogether down here, were it not for a little conversation."

"And that, my dear, is why I have invited so many people this year. For precisely that reason."

"Now you are teasing," was the instant objection. "You could never languish away, under any circumstances, I am certain. You are always reading, always writing; you have your embroidery and your household accounts . . . I never knew anyone so industrious, who might so easily be idle. Sometimes it positively frightens me!"

If this were meant for a compliment, its recipient did not acknowledge it. Instead she fell again to observing her interlocutor, or rather to appearing to observe her interlocutor, since she did not look so much at as through her. Such a stare might be deemed very rude in another person; in this it was accepted without demur. It was the powerful gaze of a powerful lady—the Duchess of Karr, in fact, and very few were those who cared to judge her. It will have been observed that Lady Louisa Bridwell made one of that élite, but she dared to join them more from a consciousness of her own ineffectuality than from any desire to command or to correct. The duchess was serenely aware of this circumstance, as she was aware of most things, which was as well for the defenceless Lady Louisa. Yet in her own way, perhaps, the latter too understood what position she held in the duchess's private, very personal ranking of society: she was tolerated for her agreeableness, and otherwise regarded much as one regards the blindfolded player in a game of blindman's-buff—which is to say, was whole-heartedly, though not cruelly, laughed at. It was a feeble, inelegant position—but it was a position. Whatever her understanding of it, Lady Louisa made few complaints.

The duchess entertained her guest, on this occasion, in an apartment known as the Rose Saloon from its being hung with rose-coloured silk. A suite of parcel-gilt mahogany furniture was disposed within its walls, the most prominent piece of which was a large, high cabinet in the Chinese style, its transparently-paned doors revealing an exquisite collection of miniature cups and saucers in cloisonné enamels. A long scroll suspended opposite to this cabinet, lettered in Chinese characters and with a water-colour representing a waterfall and some tiny trees, encouraged the Oriental effect of the furnishings, as did the floridly-carved, marble-topped table which Lady Louisa's hand (as the reader will recall) could not quite reach.

The Rose Saloon was but one of innumerable apartments within Grasmere Castle, the principal estate of His Grace the Duke of Karr. There were in addition libraries and sitting-rooms, breakfast and dining parlours, the conservatory, the ball-room, the bed-chambers . . . in short, a bewilderment of nooks and spaces. The castle had not, as was the case with numerous other ancient residences in the neighbouring hills of Nottinghamshire, been permitted to fall into decay. On the contrary, the fortunes of the noble family of Karr had been consistently so felicitous as to permit of the addition to Grasmere, in each succeeding age, of every modern convenience and refinement—and since this process had been in continuance some three or four hundred years, there were many refinements indeed to be found there now. At the date with which we concern ourselves, the castle had yet a rather Gothic air, very satisfying, perhaps, to viewers in whom the appellation "castle" might conjure up fancies of towers, pinnacles, and iron-worked fronts. There were indeed towers, and a myriad of spires and narrow chimneys whose grey stone pierced the sky, effecting an impression which even the least romantic of critics must freely have admitted to be sinister. The duchess, though she had no taste for brooding drawing-rooms or mysterious studies, had yet always retained quite a fondness for the ominous exterior of His Grace's ancestral home, and did not endeavour to brighten its almost morbid aspect. The interior, of course, was something else again; there she had striven always for elegance and comfort—nor had her effort been in vain. The friends and acquaintances who wintered with her in Nottinghamshire—and some made an annual routine of it—could expect to find their personal quarters cheerful and spacious, and the common apartments warm and eminently habitable. The massive gates, emblazoned on either side with the arms of Karr, through which one entered the drive to Grasmere, were opened to them by an obliging porter attired in the blue-and-gold livery of the house. Everywhere, as they proceeded, such liveried gentlemen were observable; on arriving at the porch, they found themselves attended by the most willing footmen, the most discreet and serviceable butler, and these attendants were no scarcer nor less useful within the castle than without it. The duchess believed in comfort for her guests; she had frequently been shocked by the paucity or impudence of servants in the houses she had visited, and she had early taken the resolve that no visitor to Grasmere should be so uncomfortably imposed upon as that.

The other buildings of the estate were no less efficiently and conveniently managed than the castle itself. The kennels, housing a number of terriers, five-and-twenty setters, and a dozen blood-hounds, were maintained by a competent and trusted keeper; so also were the stables and the carriage-house, through the means of which any number could ride or drive; a small dairy was contained within the park, which was the source of the purest cream and butter anyone might desire. Game-keepers roved the woods that bordered the park, and closer in to the castle were gardens where vegetables were cultivated, orchards, succession houses, herb-beds, and a fine, formally-terraced flower garden, complete with a hedge maze. Grasmere had been built upon the slope of a gentle incline, so that the front, as one approached, reared up imposingly above the land before it; a stream, substantial enough to reward those anglers who visited it, separated the church-yard from the central grounds. The small, stone-work church stood above it on a knoll.

In all, Grasmere Castle presented a brilliant example of an English country residence. Its mistress, though perhaps not an inviting woman herself, was yet determined that her home should be hospitable in both the manner of its offering and the abundance of what it offered. Its master, an avid sportsman, willingly saw to the keeping of its grounds; moreover, his respect for his name and its history encouraged him to take an interest in his tenantry, and particularly in their education, which had resulted in a contented, orderly population both at Grasmere and in the local village. With such a picture in mind, the reader will soon perceive that it was not the fear of anyone's "eating up her comfits" which prompted Lady Louisa to make the remark we overheard at the beginning of this history; it was not, evidently, any fear of loss of ease or comfort at all. It did not proceed from any of these selfish motives, nor was it made quite at random. It had to do, in fact, with the perpetuation of this happy, generous race of land-owners; it had to do, more particularly, with the Duke of Karr.

Timothy, the Most Noble the Duke of Karr, was not the husband but the son of the lady whom we have already had the pleasure of meeting. The husband of this last, the present duke's father, had passed away some years before, the victim of an apoplectic temperament and a good deal too much wine. He was survived, of course, by the dowager duchess, and also by the eighth duke (his only son); he had no daughters. While the eighth duke, a vigorous man of some five-and-thirty years, made an admirable successor to his father in many ways—he was, for example, conscientious, good-humoured, capable, and intelligent—he had yet one flaw of perhaps critical significance. This flaw it was which so concerned Lady Louisa; this flaw it was which concerned the dowager duchess yet more. Very simply, His Grace the Duke was yet a bachelor, a condition which may reasonably be considered to constitute a serious fault in the head of so illustrious a household.

The duchess at least accounted it a serious fault: in the course of nearly a decade, she had presented to him several score of candidates for his bride, among them ladies both thoughtful and gay, slender and plump, dark and fair, biddable and independent. None of them suited Karr, apparently, for he continued his state of singlehood still. The duchess was not a woman to press, and she had begun her campaign mildly, with the introduction to her son of some two or three young ladies one season in London, and a discreet suggestion; in recent years, however, she had begun to grow quite alarmed. Her son manifested a more and more marked resistance to the notion of wedlock—it had become, in fact, a proverb among the London *ton* that unlikely events should take place "the day after Karr takes a wife"—and she could discern in his behaviour no indication whatever that he felt the least disposition to alter his views. She reasoned with him; remonstrated with him; refused, during one season, to speak with him: still the obstinate gentleman persisted in his contrariness. The only eligible party he seemed at all able to tolerate was a Lady Henrietta Helms, the daughter of the Earl of Marland. This rather sober young person, though in most other respects the soul of prudence, was yet rumoured to have turned down (on the basis of His Grace's slim encouragement, the gossips said) quite a handful of advantageous offers from other interested gentlemen. And yet the duke had not actually done her the honour to request her hand; she therefore continued to sit upon the shelf, at the age of twenty-two, growing slightly dusty and (it may fairly be supposed) just a trifle anxious.

Her Grace was highly partial to the possibility of a match being effected between her son and Lady Henrietta. While not precisely the sort of person to whom she felt herself personally drawn, Henrietta was of impeccable birth; she had an unexceptionable manner and a certain narrowness of ideas, of originality, which might not be wholly undesirable in the prospective holder of so valuable a position. At least Karr appeared to accept, if not to appreciate her. He had a habit of responding to his mother's hopeful queries regarding each newly presented young

lady with but a single word: Lady Alice? "Insolent." Lady Margaret?
"Insipid." To the interrogative, "Lady Henrietta?" which she had put to
him, the duke had replied, "Quiet." This epithet, while hardly enthusiastic, was yet the most promising of any he had previously uttered, and
it was with this fact in mind that the duchess included on her winter's
guest list the names of the Earl of Marland, his lady wife, and the happy
Henrietta.

"I can see perfectly why you take care to invite Lady Henrietta,"
Lady Louisa was saying, the duchess's uncomfortable gaze having in-
duced her to return to her initial point, "but the rest of them are mere
distraction. I like distraction," she added, "but I don't see how it can
further the achievement of a match. Particularly when you have asked
someone so distracting as the Contessa di Tremini! Really, Sarah, it is
errant foolishness."

The duchess smiled indulgently at this. She was a handsome woman,
statuesque for all her sixty years, with the dark eyes and straight nose
she had handed down to her son. The smile she now gave revealed an
even row of teeth behind her thinning lips; it creased her cheeks but it
did not lift them, nor did it add a light to those dark eyes. She had had a
genuine smile once, but she had lost it somewhere, evidently. Lady
Louisa had not seen it in some thirty years (the two women had been
acquainted since childhood), and if she did not miss it it was only because she had forgot it ever existed. It had been, once upon a time, a
delightful smile.

"I was obliged to provide for your amusement, now wasn't I?" she answered at last. "A moment ago you confessed, I believe, a fear that too
much solitude might prove fatal. Such a demise would be most grievous
to me—and most awkward."

"Sarah—" was the only reply, uttered in a tone in which reproach and
disappointment mingled ineffectually.

"Well, if you must know, my dear," the duchess took up more expan-
sively, "I asked them all down because *I* did not care to die of boredom.
Timothy is very interesting, I am sure, to his companions, but he and I
have long since exhausted the discourse of which we are capable alone.
And Lady Henrietta—well, a girl whose chief quality is her entire willingness to do, think, and say as she is told is not the sort of conver-
sationalist I cherish."

"Don't you care for Henrietta?" the other asked, with startled
naïveté.

"Of course I care for Henrietta," said Her Grace, placing a disagreeable emphasis on the word care. "She is an excellent girl, a very excellent girl. The point is, simply, that the persons for whom I care are not the ones whose company I most enjoy."

Lady Louisa took this in thoughtfully. "Does that mean you do not care for me?" she inquired finally.

"Not at all, my dear. It means I do not enjoy your company." And as if to prove the truth of this assertion, the duchess rose on her words and wandered toward a window. "Where *is* Karr, after all? He promised to be here for dinner, and it is nearly six already."

A long, pale shadow washed the room, curiously bleak for the light of early autumn. The Duchess of Karr gazed through a wrought-iron grille onto the park, and the stream and the church beyond. She could not hope to see her son, who was due to arrive tonight after a fortnight passed in London, through this aperture; yet she gazed, pensively, silently, her inexpressive back turned toward the room. The duchess was rather addicted to gazing.

"You will regret the Contessa di Tremini," Lady Louisa said, after a pause in the conversation which was painful to her. "Remember, I warned you."

"The Contessa amuses me. She is so thoroughly, so gracefully, so bountifully foolish."

"She has never seemed foolish to me," her ladyship objected. "Or if she is, I wish I could be so foolish. Her life appears to be completely made up of pleasure."

"That is precisely what I mean, Louisa," the dowager replied, turning from the window and pacing the length of the small saloon.

"Oh," said the other, her pudgy, unclear features relapsing into their habitual expression of submissive, slightly puzzled, resignation. "If we dine at seven, I suppose I must go and dress. I wonder where Sir Isaac can be?"

"I daresay he is at billiards with Mr. Faust," the duchess suggested. It was a plausible notion, since Sir Isaac Bridwell divided his waking hours almost evenly between the dining- and the billiard-table. That Mr. Septimus Faust should be with him was almost as likely an hypothesis, since he was the only other guest to have arrived at Grasmere as yet. Though he did not play at billiards with the devotion, indeed the passion, Sir Isaac did, it was probable that the latter had persuaded him to play that afternoon—for if he had failed to persuade him, he would have been left with neither food to eat nor billiards to play, and then where would he have been? There are certain eventualities so desperate that, faced with them, the weakest of men become strong, and the most inarticulate, eloquent.

Lady Louisa accepted her friend's surmise with a murmured "Oh," and rose (selecting just one last comfit to fortify her) to quit the room. She accomplished her exit using her wonted gait, a singular commingling of a shuffle and a flutter. She minced along, her feet never really quite leaving the floor, yet with such a bounciness in her plump figure as she took each step, that her progress gave the impression of being almost airy. In this manner she had bounced through life, from her father's house to her husband's, and in and out of her friends' homes; in this manner she would trip and bounce to her grave, no doubt, and into that mansion wherein there are so many houses. She was as incapable of causing pain as she was of desiring to do so, and was, all in all, a very good soul.

The reader has been led to suppose that she left behind her, as she went, but a single lady. To perpetuate such an illusion would be to do a grave injustice to Miss Lotta Chilton, a person of seven-and-twenty years who—for all she had been silent this past hour—was yet very much present in the Rose Saloon. She sat in a deep window-seat at the foot of a long, elaborately-paned window in the northern wall of the apartment; in one hand she held a slender needle—in the other, a piece of filagree half-completed. By her side on the wooden seat was an ivory case, from which she drew from time to time a tiny silver bead; this she threaded through with her needle, and so worked continually, serenely, at the unfinished piece. Her dark hair, smoothly combed and coiled in a massive plait at the nape of her neck, gleamed a little in the fading September day; her white morning dress, trimmed with ruches at the bodice and hem, and ornamented with a long sash, dipped low at the back to reveal shoulder-bones of flawless delicacy, and a pure white back. Her face, now bent to her work and half in shadow, manifested a very pretty symmetry. The complexion of her countenance was not so creamy as that of her back; rather it seemed nearly transparent, like a glaze applied to fine porcelain to enhance the clarity of its colours and the daintiness of its work. Blue eyes, oval in shape and set wide apart, abundantly fringed above cheeks whose colour shone with pale radiance through their gossamer glaze, a tiny, straight nose and full red mouth—these and other features equally delicate, equally fine, conspired to make up a face as pretty as it was open and fresh. Her figure, when she rose (and she was on the point of rising) might be observed to be slender and lithe; her carriage was elegant, even proud, and her step light and

quick. Such were her observable attributes; one might even observe, if
one did so carefully, something of her more inward traits. She worked, it
is true, at her filagree—serenely, I have said. Yet perhaps she evidenced
not quite so much serenity as detachment. She worked continually, but
she was not absorbed by it. On the contrary, she listened most acutely to
the voices round her; she heard their words, she noted them—maybe she
even judged them. Certainly she was not unconscious of them, for after
Lady Louisa had left the room, she addressed the duchess thus:

"I do not wish to interrupt your thoughts, Your Grace, but ought I to
disappear?"

The duchess, who had reseated herself, turned toward her interro-
gator with a look of tentative surprise. "Disappear? Can you?"

"I can from His Grace's range of vision," Miss Chilton returned with
a smile. She set her work down and crossed the room to the arm-chair
recently vacated by Lady Louisa. "I am not sure if you wish me to meet
him, or when," she explained.

"Oh, indeed!" said her employer—for such the greater lady was—"He
has not met you. I had forgot. I wonder what he will make of you," she
added more musingly.

"I trust he will allow me to remain what I am," said the girl, with a
pertness many *grandes dames* would not have welcomed in their hired
companions. The duchess, however, had engaged Miss Chilton precisely
because of her tendency to candour; the acquaintance had been in existence barely a week now, but it had already proved very interesting to
both parties.

The Duchess of Karr elevated, then dropped, her dark eyebrows. "He
has an unfortunate habit, I must confess, of allowing all young ladies to
remain what they are. No doubt you are right. Now tell me why you
suppose you ought to disappear—or is it that you prefer to?"

"On the contrary," Miss Chilton rejoined, in a sweet, musical voice
distinctive for its clarity, "I should by far prefer to remain. I have been
five years with my Lady Elsworth, as Your Grace may recall, and my
Lady Elsworth lived hideously retired. I have a great curiosity to know
your son; I own it freely. I should even like to sit to dinner with you,"
she ended, with a laugh.

"Then you shall," the duchess said abruptly. "I am sure there is nothing so dreadful in it, and it will greatly please me to hear some fresh
conversation."

Some of the colour drained from Lotta Chilton's pretty cheeks.
"Madam, I hope you do not mistake me. It was mere pleasantry."

"I am aware of that," the other observed tonelessly. "It will teach you to be careful in your jokes; some of them may come true."

"Like wishes," Lotta mused.

"Very much like wishes," said the duchess. "Does the prospect of dining with us alarm you? I have no wish to induce an indigestion in you."

"No repast taken with Your Grace could disagree with me," said Miss Chilton.

"Your stomach may not be so gallant as your sentiments," the duchess cautioned her.

"If it is not I will know the reason why," was the answer.

"Very bravely spoke," the duchess commended. "Now run off and find something suitable to wear. I suppose you have something?"

The colour of Miss Chilton's cheeks returned somewhat more precipitately than she could have wished.

"I shall send my dresser to you," said the dowager.

"Your Grace is much too good," cried Lotta.

"If I hear another pretty speech from you, I will turn you off without a reference. Remember, that is not why I engaged you."

Miss Chilton had been on the point of offering to stay in the Rose Saloon until another attendant had been found for the duchess, but this speech checked her, and she simply curtsied and departed. Her employer, who really had had a good deal more of chivalry and kindness in her life than she cared for, was more satisfied by this behaviour than she could have been by any other, and fell to gazing at the Chinese scroll in silence. Her long white fingers trembled and moved in her lap as she sat alone, but they moved to no purpose; she merely stroked her right hand with her left, then her left hand with her right, and again the right with the left. It was an indication of impatience; Timothy stopped away too long.

A knock at the door disturbed her at length. She turned, hoping to see her son enter, but was disappointed. The gentleman who came in was not the duke but rather Mr. Septimus Faust, the erstwhile opponent of Sir Isaac Bridwell. Mr. Faust was a tall, nervous gentleman, a pale and healthless man, who had yet a certain grace about his angular person—if one could but disregard his most obvious deficiencies. These were several: his nose was exceedingly long, and irregular; his cheeks and eyes were sunk into deep declivities; the carelessness of his dark, long curls was, alas, completely unfeigned. He slouched and lounged about, continually crossed his long, skeletal limbs into awkward and uncomfortable-looking configurations, spoke in riddles, and slurred his words. And yet his dark eyes were of an extraordinary beauty; they shone from within their hollows with a deep brilliance neither hard nor ironic but seductive, intrigued, compelling. He was a man of sudden delights and passions, who absorbed insatiably the nature, the air, of everything and everyone round him. He was exquisitely greedy, if such a thing may be.

At three-and-thirty Mr. Faust had achieved no great fame or success; he had done nothing with the modest estate he had inherited from his father except live on its income; he had, in brief, no claim whatever on the attention of so exalted a personage as the Duchess of Karr, nor on that of her son. If he was sensible of this fact, however, he never showed it. It seemed as natural to him that the dowager duchess should take him up as that farmers should farm and gardeners garden. His manner toward the lady was free, friendly, and whimsical; he regarded her in some sort as his patroness, though no such official relationship existed between them. He did have some claim to patronage, being the author of numerous odes and satires, the composer of some dozens of ditties, and the painter of multitudinous canvasses; however, to say that these had promise, and ought to be encouraged, was like saying that a patch of wild strawberries had promise, and ought to be cultivated: the resultant fruit might be sweet, but it would not be grateful. It and Mr. Septimus Faust were better left to the forces of nature.

On the occasion of his entrance to the Rose Saloon, Mr. Faust (for no apparent reason) put a slender hand to his prominent white temples and produced, in greeting to his hostess, a deep salaam. "Ah, Madam—" he intoned. "The eye is not satisfied with seeing, nor the ear filled with hearing." Upon which he drew a chair up near to her and seated himself on it. "How does my lady today?" he asked, adding an outrageous, familiar grin which revealed, behind crimson lips, two rows of crooked teeth.

"Do not quote Ecclesiastes at me," directed she, but smiling faintly nonetheless. "I know more of vanity than you will ever do."

"Ah, yes," he agreed; "but does that entitle you to refuse new prophets of it?"

"The privilege of refusing prophets belongs to everyone; it need not be won by experience."

"Your Grace is more accurate than comforting."

"If you are in want of comfort you may apply to Sir Isaac Bridwell.

Or to his lady wife. Or to Miss Chilton, for that matter. Comfort is to be had in abundance from any number of sources—but not from me."

"Ah, yes, Miss Chilton," said he, catching at the name. "Comfort from her would be a delicious thing indeed. Hyper-delicious, one might say."

"If one were fond of such affectations of speech."

"One is fond of all affectations, verbal and otherwise."

"And is one fond of Miss Chilton?" she inquired rather sharply.

"One has had so little time to know her," he answered, as if apologetically. "Tell me something of her; her complexion is a glazier's dream."

"And what, pray tell, of your own dreams, Mr. Faust?"

"Miss Chilton," he insisted. "Tell me about her."

"Very well. You have seen, I think, what is most interesting about her—I mean her person and her manner. Her history is not intriguing, unless I have been misled. She was born, I believe, in Italy, and orphaned when still an infant. An English family then residing in Florence, the Chiltons, took her in. Mr. Chilton teaches languages. He was, at the time, teaching English to Italians; after some years, the family removed to London, where Mr. Chilton taught Italian to the English. The girl grew up with the other daughters of the house; at a certain age she hired herself out as companion to a Lady Elsworth, who died some years later. Thence she came to me. That is all I know," she added, as Mr. Faust appeared to wait for more.

"Who were her parents?" he asked.

"Her parents? She is legitimate, if that is what you mean."

"That is only half what I mean. Such a beautiful flower as Miss Chilton does not generally grow without some toil and trouble; I am looking for the sand and rocks in her soil."

"Mr. Faust, you are quite romantic."

"It is one of my least offensive faults."

"In any case, I do not know of any great mysteries or hardships attached to Lotta Chilton's case. I believe her father was a member of the petty nobility of Italy. Her mother, I suppose, was a girl of the district."

"It is disappointing," Septimus was at last obliged to admit. "However, Florence is very suggestive, and I will undertake to compose a more suitable background for her in my imagination."

"As you like," said the duchess. "At all events, she is entertaining. She is very quick-witted, and keen of observation. She has already

begun to imitate my gestures—whether to flatter me or to improve herself, I hardly know. I suspect her of cherishing ambitions."

"Ambitions?" he echoed. "This is good. If not a past, then at least a
future. Do you mean she schemes?"

"She would like to, but she has scruples. She is jealous of power, but
she would not usurp it."

"Do you mean she envies you?"

"I mean she esteems me."

"This is very good. But I am sorry for those scruples."

"If an unscrupulous character amuses you, wait until you have met
the Contessa di Tremini," the duchess suggested. "To her the aura of
Italy clings also, and I assure you she is not burdened with any undue
moral freight."

"But is she beautiful?" he asked.

"She is very beautiful. Not so young as she was once, perhaps; none
of us is. But indisputably a beauty."

"Then I await her arrival with impatience. When may I expect to
meet her?"

"Tomorrow, I think. Yes, tomorrow," the duchess affirmed. "Until
then I must ask you to hold your interest in Lotta in check. I have not
done with her yet."

"I will try to hold in the reins of my fancy," said he, "but alas, they
are but frayed and fragile ribbons. Restraint has always been my
weakest point."

"And excess your strongest, I suppose," the duchess observed, with
some amusement.

"Excess my very strongest," he agreed, starting suddenly from his
chair and repeating his salaam on these words. He was about to quit the
saloon when a knock, immediately followed by an entry, caused him to
hesitate. This, at last, was the Duke of Karr; he entered in all haste, still
sporting the riding-breeches and muddied boots which attested to his recent journey, and strode at once across the circular Turkey carpet to his
mother.

"Madam," said he, bestowing on her white hand a dry salute; "I hope
I find you in the best of health?"

"Never mind my health; where have you been?" she said in accents
of irritation, adding irrelevantly, "Mr. Faust is here."

"Good-day, Mr. Faust," said His Grace, shaking this gentleman's
hand with a hearty vigour which that emaciated limb seemed scarcely
able to support. He had met the less illustrious man before, and did not

care for him overmuch, but a policy and habit of hospitality forbade his being otherwise than cordial.

Mr. Faust responded to his host's greeting with equal courtesy, and stepped back to observe him. He was by far too much fascinated with human nature and character to bother actually to dislike someone; however, the Duke of Karr was so very different a man from himself, it was impossible for him to feel any of his habitual empathy for the great nobleman—he could merely, as I have said, observed him. What he saw was a gentleman of about his own height, but who probably weighed nearly half again as much as himself. His Grace was robust, and visibly muscular; his garments, though now in disarray, were of the fit, quality, and elegance one would expect on so exalted a person. His dark eyes and straight nose, imparted to him by his progenitrix, were complemented by a high, handsome brow, a strong mouth and chin, an unfashionably swarthy complexion, and a healthy mass of chestnut hair. The style of his coiffure was somewhat remarkable, having been more common in the previous century than in this: it was dressed in *ailes de pigeon,* the bulk of his locks being secured at the nape of his neck by a white muslin riband. If it was not the most modish of fashions, however, it was certainly very well suited to His Grace: he looked at once strong, attractive, and intelligent. Dandies might demur, but Mr. Faust thought his host's coiffure very wisely chosen.

The duchess had repeated her irritable query as to her son's recent whereabouts, but Karr seemed to refuse to respond in kind. "I am desolate if I have delayed dinner," said he, with a good deal of manner. "I stopped in Melton Mowbray to collect Mr. Longstreth and Mr. Remington. I trust you don't mind their arriving a few days early?"

"Of course I do not mind; I only mind your arriving late. Dinner need not be delayed, if only you will go and dress."

"I sent Longstreth and Remington upon that very errand," said he, referring to two of his intimates. "I only stopped down here to allay any anxiety you may have had regarding my fortune on the road, and to receive your gracious welcome—dear ma'am."

The duchess, who was not given to being anxious about such commonplace events as journeys from London, knew she was being teased but would not smile. "I assure you, my heart *was* racing before; but it is now calm, and you are thoroughly, exceedingly welcomed—so do go on, won't you, and dress? I am beginning to be quite hungry."

The duke bowed and departed, taking Septimus Faust with him. "She's furious with me," Karr confided, as they strolled together down a lofty corridor, and up a wide, spiralling stair-case. "She told me to look in upon the Earl of Marland—and particularly, upon his daughter—when I passed through Hertfordshire, and she knows I did not. I did not tell her as much, you understand, but she guesses it from my silence just as well. She is very shrewd, you know; I do not believe she has ever been duped."

"Ah," cried the other, "in that case I shall stop trying to persuade her that *I* am her son, and you a mere imposter. I wondered she did not take the bait," he added musingly. "It had seemed such a good idea at its inception."

The duke laughed, and assured his fanciful guest that any other duchess would have been certain to have believed him. They parted at the top of the stairs, the duke proceeding to his vast suite of private chambers, Mr. Faust to the turret-room he had begged of the duchess—for the notion of a room with but a single wall had taken his fancy, and he swore to her he could not sleep in any other sort of place.

2

"I do not care about the *chasse*," Lady Anne Stanton was saying to her husband. "I do not care if you killed one *hundred* head of game; I do not care if—"

"But that is just what we did," Lord Stanton interrupted eagerly. "Seventy-three pheasants, fourteen partri—"

"My dear Walker, I have just told you I do not care!" her ladyship insisted. "Now I have sent for Amabel and she will be here in a moment; I wish you will help me speak to her."

Lord Stanton shrugged off his shooting-jacket and resigned himself to the obvious: he was not to be given the satisfaction of boasting about the success of his day. He tossed his jacket onto a chair—one of many in the spacious suite of chambers assigned to the Stantons by Her Grace the duchess—and set about loosening his soiled cravat. His lady wife was preparing to dress for dinner; in a moment he would repair to his own apartment to do the same. It might have appeared more reasonable, in light of these circumstances, for his lordship to delay the removal of his jacket and cravat until his valet had come to him with suitable replacements; but my lord was a restless man, an industrious man, and he was rarely still. Consequently his fingers worked busily at the stubborn knot while his wife addressed him; even after the cravat had been untied and flung aside with the jacket, Lord Stanton walked briskly up and down the room.

In spite of this superfluous activity, in spite of the interrupted character of their speech, in spite of their being only temporarily in residence here, the scene had a very tranquil and domestic look to it. Lady Stanton, an attractive (if somewhat faded) woman of forty-two, sat before her glass while her abigail combed out her long, dark hair; his lordship, an equally pleasant-appearing gentleman, strode familiarly about the chamber; their daughter, presently under discussion, would soon appear; and their son, though not now in evidence, was never entirely absent from either of his parents' minds. The Stantons were fond and sober guardians to their children, and they held one another in affectionate esteem as well. If Lady Stanton spoke, on this occasion, with insistence, it was not so much because her husband irritated her as because she was concerned for the welfare of her daughter. This young lady's future, as her mother now pointed out, was not nearly so securely settled as it might have been.

"We have stopped here nearly a fortnight, Walker," Lady Stanton said after dismissing her maid for the moment, "and if Wyborn's attentions to her now are any more particular than they were when we arrived, it is more than I can notice. That really is too bad, you know; she will soon be eighteen, and eighteen is too old to be hoping for matches that will never materialize."

Lord Stanton considered this. "I understand you," he answered finally, "but I do not see what there is to be done. She cannot throw herself at him, and he must know by now she has set her cap for him."

"I am certain he knows it, but he draws neither away from her nor toward her. He stays, so far as I can discern, at exactly the same distance. It is too bad," she repeated.

Lord Stanton had not yet replied when a knock on the door sounded and Miss Amabel Stanton came in. "Did you send for me, Mamma?" she asked, shutting the door behind her and advancing some way into the apartment. "Papa, what a sight you look!" she added, as her father came forward to salute her.

"Shooting, my dear," he explained. "I may look disarranged, but I assure you, the birds we bagged today look a good deal worse for the encounter."

"Did you shoot quite a lot of them?" his daughter inquired politely.

"Quite a lot! I should say so! Why there were—"

"That's very pleasant, Papa," his daughter cut him off gently. "What did you desire to see me about, Mamma?"

Lord Stanton sighed a little. "Your mother is concerned about the Marquess of Wyborn," he told her. "We both are."

"So am I, indeed," said Amabel. Her countenance, which was round, soft, and very sweet, took on a troubled look as she seated herself on the edge of her mother's bed. "I do try, you know," she said as if to defend herself, "to engage his attention; but it never seems to come to much."

"No one doubts of your trying," her mother assured her. "We are only perplexed as to his—his intentions."

"Does he address himself to you frequently?" Lord Stanton asked.

"More frequently, I suppose, than he does some other ladies," Amabel replied, in her soft, pattering voice, "but he would be obliged to do that in any case, no matter who I was. The duchess always seats him next to me at table, you know."

"Yes," her mother rejoined thoughtfully. "It is rather good of her, I think. She knows why we accepted her invitation, and agreed to stop so long; and though she never specifically mentioned Wyborn, I knew she would see to it he came down too. She is a great diplomat, when she chuses to be."

"Unhappily, it is not within her power to constrain him to stay forever," Stanton observed. "Probably he only means to shoot here for a few more weeks; then he will be off, and out of our reach."

"Did his lordship join your party today?" Lady Stanton interrupted him.

"Oh, yes; he never passes up an opportunity for sport."

"And he said nothing to you of Amabel?" his wife pursued.

"Not a word. Amabel, when he addresses you . . . is he agreeable? Familiar, perhaps?"

"No more so, I fear, than any gentleman must be. I *am* sorry," she added anxiously, her blue eyes clouding. "Perhaps I have no gift for capturing husbands. Perhaps he simply does not like me."

"If he did not like you he would not have called in Mount Street so often," said Lady Stanton, referring to their residence in London. "No, I am certain he thinks of you—"

"Only he does not know quite what to think," Amabel finished somewhat despondently. A silence ensued, during which Lord Walker Stanton paced the room even more rapidly than he had done hitherto.

"There is nothing to do but to wait it out," he announced finally. "It is impossible to approach a man in such a case without leaving behind the bounds of propriety."

"Amabel could encourage some other gentleman," Lady Stanton suggested hesitantly.

"In an attempt to make him jealous? Thank you, no. My daughter is not in so desperate a case that she need resort to machinations of that order. What the marquess regards above all, I think, is dignity. Fortunately, that is a natural trait among us; this is hardly a time to abandon the habit of decades."

"Very well," his wife responded, apparently neither injured nor offended. "If you are concerned with the dignity of the Stantons, however, I think you had best keep an eye on Chauncey. He is the one who most imperils it."

"Chauncey?" Lord Stanton checked his perambulations and looked at his wife in surprise. "How?"

"How?" she echoed. "Have you failed to notice? By his preposterous infatuation with the Countess Tremini, of course. It is a perfect outrage."

"Chauncey dangling after the contessa? Whatever for? She is twice his age and more."

"So is my lord the marquess twice Amabel's age," his wife reminded him. On this Lord Stanton exchanged a glance not entirely gentle with her ladyship; there had been, once upon a time, some disagreement between them as to whether or not Amabel (if and when she married Wyborn) could ever be happy with him. Lady Stanton felt he was rather too old for her; her husband insisted this factor was superficial and insignificant. Miss Amabel, being entirely the most biddable of girls, had accepted her parents' final decision without a murmur, but Lady Stanton continued to harbour some reserve regarding the advisability of the match. The glance between husband and wife was meaningful, though brief. When it was dropped Lady Stanton continued, "I do not think Chauncey behaves on any political motive. He is simply fascinated with her."

"I can't believe it," Stanton declared.

"Watch him tonight at dinner," she recommended with a tiny shrug. "You will believe me then."

Lord Stanton, clearly not convinced, quitted his wife's chamber some moments later to place himself in the competent hands of his valet. He conjured up the image, as he dressed, of the Contessa di Tremini, asking himself all the while how his son, a mere stripling of sixteen, could fancy himself in love with such an object. To do her justice, it ought to be mentioned that if one were, for example, condemned to live perpetually with an image, the Countess Tremini's would not be at all the worst to chuse. Even Lord Stanton, conservative though he was, could not entirely dislike the figure he now invoked: though doubtless some years older, even, than his wife, the contessa appeared to have found twenty-five so pleasant and flattering an age that she declined ever to pass it, opting to remain rather in constant communication with some myserious spring of youth. Her figure was womanly to the point of voluptuousness, yet it never (as happens so frequently) grew matronly or blowsy. Her cheeks retained, as if by magic, the firm fulness and rosy tint of girlhood; her eyes, an extraordinary violet in hue, were as arresting as when they had first rested on an eligible gentleman; and her warm mouth had lost none of its allure. No wrinkle disturbed the snowy purity of her complexion; no tinge of grey dared trespass on her dark, glossy head. She was English by birth, but had dwelt so long in Italy that a soft intimation of that warmer clime had crept, as if for safekeeping, into the rich, deep inflections of her voice. Widowed these past five years, she was a demon for play; beyond that, however, Lord Stanton knew nothing against her.

If it was no great hardship to summon up the contessa in imagination, it was certainly not painful to behold her in reality. Lord Stanton, along with the rest of the numerous party by this time assembled at Grasmere, had the happiness to do precisely this some half an hour after his conversation with his wife and daughter, when the duchess received her guests in a vast, square drawing-room and prepared them to go in to dinner. Lady Rowena di Tremini entered—one might have suspected, on purpose—last of all the visitors; thus her entrance and appearance were the easier to observe. She flew rather than walked in, seemingly borne on some capricious, compelling breeze, and hastened at once to toss dazzling smiles on everyone and everything. The brilliance of her smile was matched, though not exceeded, by the brilliance of the emeralds which everywhere adorned her. A cut stone glinted from her throat, from the raven thicknesses of her hair, from the third finger of an elegant, flawless hand. She wore their glory with perfect unconsciousness, allowing the gems to sparkle and glow in what light they might catch, declining, as it were, to know them. Her rich green velvet gown, on the other hand, was evidently not so proud: it knew the emeralds intimately, complemented them marvellously, whispered to them in low, familiar tones. Yet this striking conspiracy among her ornaments did nothing to distract from the (presumably) less artificial attractions of the contessa: the light of her eyes rivalled triumphantly the light of all else, and the grace of her every movement held sway supremely.

"Good evening, my dear Karr—Your Grace," she breathed and curtsied; "Miss Chilton, you are prettier than ever—" (Miss Chilton had continued to dine with the guests, to the astonishment of a few of them, for all the world as if she were one herself)—"you must tell me some time how you manage your complexion. Miss Cawley, Lord Cawley," she went on, moving away from her hostess, "I am delighted to see you looking so well. We must have some whist tonight, Lord Cawley, I really insist on it. Ah, and Mr. Faust, my most intriguing friend," she concluded, alighting finally near Septimus; "your bow is the most gallant in England. How do you do it, I wonder, without bursting into laughter?"

"You consider my bow ridiculous?" Mr. Faust inquired, without resentment.

"I consider it—satirical," she corrected. "It is so deep."

"It is the same; you consign it to the realm of the amusing."

"If wit is amusing, yes. I deem your bow to be witty."

"In the tradition of high comedy," he pursued, "or low?"

"In the tradition of sarcasm," said she.

"In that case, my most honoured friend, I must accuse you of contradicting yourself. You say my bow is deep; you say my bow is sarcastic. This, dear countess, is entirely impossible: what is deep cannot be sarcastic, nor what is sarcastic, deep. I must beg you to clarify your remarks."

"My remarks would not be in need of clarification if you did not, yourself, insist on confusing them." The contessa lifted a luxuriantly plumed fan from her side and spread it out before her. She was a shrewd woman, but she did not excell in such banter as this. She needed a moment to think. "Mr. Faust," she said at last, "I will set you a riddle."

"I adore a riddle," said he.

"All the better. But I must caution you, I have reason to believe you will find this one difficult."

"Lay on, MacCountess."

"What, Mr. Faust, is both deep and sarcastic?"

"Is that the riddle?" he asked, disappointed.

"That is the riddle. And if you can give me no better answer than my own, you must admit it to be your bow, sir."

"Stop a moment," he said, as he saw her preparing to rise. "Your ladyship sets me a puzzle indeed, but I believe I have an answer."

"Have you? How very tiresome of you."

"Your ladyship did not tell me I must not be tiresome."

"I will take care to do so in the future," she smiled. "Quickly, what is your answer? The duchess is beckoning to me."

"His Grace the duke, is the answer," said Septimus Faust. "His Grace is both things."

The Countess Tremini laughed, but she reproved her interlocutor, "Mr. Faust, I said *what*—not who. Karr is not an object, but a person."

"Ah!" he cried, casting a pointed and amused glance at Miss Lotta Chilton—who, in turn, was gazing on the duke. "That depends entirely on who observes him. For you, madame, he is a person; for others . . . he may be anything we chuse."

"Mr. Faust," said the other, rising at last, "you are a wicked man. I like a wicked man, but your insinuations are too oblique for me. I must go to the duchess; pray excuse me."

With this she moved away from him, leaving him (as he often was) reflective. But if he thought on the contessa, he was not the only one. The Honourable Chauncey Stanton—with a fixity even his father could not ignore—had indeed kept his blue eyes fastened upon her ladyship from the moment of her entrance into the drawing-room. He took no pains to conceal his stare, nor the admiration within it. Perhaps he felt his youth (and his consequent ineligibility) excused him; perhaps he forgot to think of concealing it. In either case, he stood alone in a corner, heedless of the people nearer to him, dropping a steady and hopelessly enamoured regard on the unsuspecting contessa. Master Chauncey was at an unenviable stage in human development. He was awkward, and gangling, and the skin on his upper lip showed that dark downiness which heralds, rather unbeautifully, an incipient entry into full manhood. I am sorry to record that the mouth beneath this significant lip was, though its owner knew it not, just perceptibly agape. If dignity were an invariable mark of the Stantons, this boy was not his mother's son.

Dinner was a gorgeous affair. Grasmere Castle was equipped with a variety of plate and porcelain so extensive that no setting was repeated, on the duchess's table, within a given fortnight. Tonight the dishes, blue and green in colour, floral in design, and embellished with a silver tracery, were graced (as the courses and removes followed one another) with a number of the pheasants we have previously heard of, a collection of other fowl, a soup reputed to be Russian in origin, boiled rice and potatoes, vegetables, *ragoût à la Françoise,* fricandeau, saddle of mutton, roast beef, boiled turkey with celery sauce, all manner of sweets, creams, and fruits—in short, such a collection of viands and delicacies as is not too often met with. Twenty-five sat to dinner, a like number attending them. Burgundy, Champagne, and Hermitage flowed bountifully into and from Her Grace's crystal goblets, hinting at what plenitude should serve the gentlemen when the ladies had departed . . . and yet, in spite of this wonderful array, so pleasing to every sense, my lord Stanton had eyes and ideas only for his son.

The behaviour he observed in that young man was not pleasant to him. Chauncey might be callow, but he was devoted: neither meat nor drink could distract him from his self-appointed vigil. Though he sat at some distance from the contessa, his eyes never left her (which steadfastness, combined with the superabundance of sauces and red wines, had an unfortunate effect on his white cravat). By the time the ladies withdrew from the table, Lord Stanton had already framed the opening paragraph of the lecture he meant to read his son. It would be impressive, and very sober, oratory.

Lady Stanton, meanwhile, received the honour of the Contessa di Tremini's conversation when the ladies had regained the drawing-room. The countess had shown little interest in her previously (the countess as a rule favoured gentlemen over her own sex), and she had no clear idea why the more beautiful lady chose, on this particular occasion, to sit so very near to her; however, it was not in her nature to tax her mind with questions overmuch, and she merely concluded that the contessa must have her reasons. In this she was correct: the contessa had a perfectly logical reason—to wit, the fawn settee on which Lady Stanton had seated herself was the only piece of furniture in the room whose colour neither swallowed up nor blazed against the green of her gown. This reason, as the reader will have perceived, was entirely trivial; the conversation which ensued between the two women appears, no doubt, equally trifling—and yet a part of it unquestionably belongs to our story.

The countess began it. "Lady Stanton," said she, smiling beautifully, "am I right in believing that lovely young girl belongs to you?" With the faintest movement of her fan she indicated Miss Stanton, who sat with a few of the younger ladies near the fire.

"She is my daughter," Lady Stanton returned, also smiling.

"Ah, she is very pretty," said the contessa. "One can scarcely credit your being her mother—you look too young."

"I am quite old enough, I assure you," the other said pleasantly; she did not share the countess's vanity with regard to age. "I have a son too; perhaps you have noticed him. He has certainly noticed you."

"A son as well?" the contessa echoed, as if this were another wonder. In a way, it did surprise her: childless herself, and with no great love of infants, Lady di Tremini was constantly astonished at the number of women with patience enough to raise children. "Which gentleman is he? Where did he sit at dinner?"

Lady Stanton told her, but the countess failed to recollect him. "I fear it would quite break his heart to hear you say so," Lady Stanton told her, with a gentle laugh. "He admires you most ardently."

"Does he? How very kind in him."

"He is only sixteen," Lady Stanton hastened to add.

"His first infatuation, then," the countess suggested.

"I believe it is."

"You would be amazed to know how very many young men do honour me with their first *tendres*. Not that I pride myself upon it; not at all. To be quite candid, I think it has as much to do with the exotic qualities of an Italian name as with my own attractions."

"You are too modest."

"No, indeed. Young men at their first encounter with romance are extremely impressionable: a name will win them as easily as a face. I have known boys to fall in love with women they have never seen, merely on the strength of an appealing appellation. Besides, they enjoy my being a widow—it saves them the potential trouble of duelling; and the fact of my being twice as old as they seems to comfort their more fanciful anxieties."

"I understand you lived long in Italy," Lady Stanton remarked, not caring especially to enter into a discussion of adolescent fancies, and reverting therefore to what seemed the safer topic.

"Very long; longer than anyone need live there," she agreed.

"You found it tiresome?"

"Anyone who stopped there as long as I did would find it tiresome," said the contessa. "Even the natives. Have you been there yourself?"

Lady Stanton paused a moment before she replied. "Many years ago," she said finally. "I hardly recollect it."

"Would I could say the same," the countess remarked, rather obscurely. "I beg your pardon—did you say you were at Florence?"

"I did not say," the other replied, with a curious stiffness.

"Isn't that odd? The name Florence just popped into my head," the countess told her. For a minute she said nothing. Then, "*Were* you at Florence?" she inquired.

But her interlocutor had grown suddenly restless. She had been gath-

ering her skirts during the contessa's long hesitation, and now sprang up
from the settee with unwonted abruptness. "I beg your pardon, Lady
Tremini; I think my daughter looks for me. I'm dreadfully sorry . . ."
So saying she rushed away, leaving the countess by far more pensive
than she was customarily. It may be noted here that if Miss Amabel
Stanton was looking for her mother, she must have had eyes in a most
singular location.

Lady Stanton returned to the fawn settee some while later, with the
intention of explaining her erratic conduct to the contessa. By this time
the gentlemen had regained the drawing-room; small parties were being
assembled for whist and billiards, and a cluster of men (gallant, but
mostly of middle age) had gathered about the Countess Tremini. Her
popularity was such that Lady Stanton could not gain her side; in consequence, she delayed her explanation (which would have been rather
vague in any case) and gravitated toward a less dense grouping of guests
which had for its center Miss Jessica Cawley. This group was more
obliging: the gentlemen, visibly flushed with wine, lost no time in es-
tablishing her in a comfortable chair and providing her with tea. She
had then the benefit of their conversation which, though she herself said
little, was as animated and bright as any discourse might be that had the
Cawleys for participants.

Miss Jessica Cawley, a dark-eyed, lively woman of some nine-and-
twenty years, was an authoress—one of those scribblers upon whose
lace-capped and banded heads so much disdain has been so liberally
bestowed. She had always been possessed of a preposterous imagination,
and when her first few seasons had come and gone without bringing her
a suitor intriguing enough to justify even half her fantastic whims, she
turned to writing and created her own. In story and setting she favoured
the Gothic (it was why she had agreed to pass the entire winter at Grasmere—the castle had utterly won her over), but her style had none of
the fatuous romanticism one might have expected. On the contrary, it
was diligently satirical, and she did not hesitate to parody, in her novels,
quite recognizable eccentricities of the people near her. In fact, Mr. Algernon Longstreth, who at the moment we meet Miss Cawley was offering her a biscuit, had figured very plainly as the villain's foppish, sentimental brother in her most recent effort, which had been published in a
small edition and thoroughly read by the *ton*. It was not a flattering portrait—they never were—and Mr. Longstreth, as he drew the plate away,
might have been observed to have been staring at Miss Cawley and
thinking very hard. Miss Cawley caught the look, but it did not discon-

cert her. Though pretty, she was not vain, so his stare did not make her conscious; though the author of a clever, accurate insult, she was all boldness—so his stare did not make her afraid. Besides, she had known such a quantity of young men already, with such a variety of emotions in their breasts! She had kept her singlehood through choice, as all the world knew—she was not a beauty, but her irresistible manner and perfectly charming smile had brought her plenty of offers. Even now her friends pressed her to marry; she begged them to desist, but they pressed her. There was only one man in the world who did not disappoint her (probably because she had so few expectations of him), and this young man was her brother.

Lord Roger Cawley was, as I have noted, among the young people Lady Stanton now joined. He sat at some little distance from his sister, quieter, more pensive, even graver than she, yet by any standard a most amiable and pleasant man. He was his sister's senior by some years, and had long been her guardian, both their parents having died in a coaching accident when Jessica was sixteen. Like Jessica, Roger was dark and of no great height; unlike her, he was actively interested in innovative agriculture, the quality and administration of justice in rural districts, and the impact of the French Wars on the English economy. He was so good, however, as generally to spare his sister the necessity of discussing these topics with him; in fact, he rather admired her less serious turn of mind, and wished, though without rancour, he could be as diverting in society as she was. He quite encouraged her unconventionality, and was not among those who thought she ought to marry. He, of course, must take a bride sometime or other—there had to be an heir to his father's title; but if Jessica was as happy now as he believed her to be, he had no quarrel with her chosen way of life.

"Do you mean it is as close as Nottingham, and yet no provision has been made for us to visit it?" Miss Cawley was demanding as Lady Stanton sat down. "What a dreadful oversight!"

"I am sure Their Graces had no idea of your being so interested," a young gentleman, Mr. Cosmo Remington by name, answered. He kept a house near Nottingham himself, and so was in a position to respond to her. "Goose-Fair is a great occasion to the peasantry, but it is not, in general, much frequented by the *ton*."

"What do you call it?" cried Jessica, with an incredulous smile. "Goose-Fair! Oh, now I am certain we must go there."

"Pr-properly, it is called the great October Fair of Nottingham," Mr. Remington informed her. "Goose-Fair is but a local name."

"It is by far more attractive than the other," said Jessica. "I, for one, shall adopt it immediately, and use it exclusively. Why shouldn't we go? Roger, will you take me?" she added in the same breath.

Her brother nodded his assent.

"Karr can tell you all about it, no doubt," Mr. Remington continued. "Really, it is only a country fair like any other."

"Somebody fetch him," Miss Cawley directed, fairly bristling with enthusiasm. Mr. Longstreth departed upon this errand, found the duke in conversation with his mother at the other end of the drawing-room, and returned with him presently. "My dear sir," Jessica addressed him reproachfully, "I understand you have been keeping a secret from us—but we have found you out. Whatever, if you please, is Goose-Fair?"

The duke, striking an easy pose, smiled affably at his accusing guest. "Dear ma'am, I assure you I had no intention of creating mysteries. Goose-Fair is simply a yearly market at Nottingham, attended chiefly by farmers and merchants, and having mostly to do with the trading of cheese and horse-flesh. Do you long to go to it?"

"He makes it sound so tedious!" she complained, appealing to Cosmo Remington. "Make him talk about the jugglers and the beasts. There *are* jugglers and beasts," she told the duke, with more than a hint of impudence.

"I confess it, there are," Karr replied, with an expressive lift of a single dark eyebrow. "Wombwell's Menagerie visits it every year; companies of comedians, discordant bands of musicians, and hawkers of every sort of cheap ware abound there. If you are seriously interested in going, I do believe some of the gentry drive there for the gig-fair—"

"The gig-fair?"

"The later portions of it, when the trading is over," he explained. "If you like I will engage to find a window for you in town, whence you may observe it."

"I do not wish to be a spectator!" she exclaimed, much dismayed.

"Perhaps you wished to sell some cheese, then?" he inquired.

"Roger, challenge that man to a duel," she said, with mock pride. "He insults my dignity."

"My profoundest apologies, madam," said Karr, bowing.

"Your apologies are accepted, sir. But in the future, kindly remember that I do not deal in cheese. I peddle books, as you ought to know." This speech was delivered in such a tone of rigid solemnity that it caused all its audience to laugh.

"You ought really to consider, Miss Cawley," the duke took up again in more genuine accents, "how little you would like being jostled among that mob. With your gown and your manner, beggars would cling to you all the day through; the gipsies might even try to run off with you."

"I will go in disguise," she answered.

"You will like it none the more," he warned. "It is the rudest of entertainments."

"We will all go," she announced, as if she had not heard him. "It will be a most memorable excursion. When do you say it takes place?"

"Four days from now," Mr. Remington told her. "The caravans have already begun to arrive, no doubt, and the horse-fair begins tomorrow."

"And it lasts how long?"

"Two days," she was told.

"Very well; we go on the second. My friends, prepare your costumes. Anyone who does not look thoroughly rustic will be excluded from the party."

"Miss Cawley," the duke enjoined her gently, "I really think this is most ill-advised. The dangers attaching to such a project are too serious; I should not like you to expose yourself to them on a mere whim."

"Your Grace, you are a perfect host, and you have done your duty very nicely. I am cautioned; we are all cautioned. But as for abandoning the scheme—never!"

"Miss Cawley, truly—"

"If it frightens you, you need not come," said Jessica, who was by far too addicted to her independence to retreat before a mild advisement.

"It is not, of course, a question of that. I will come if for no other purpose than to protect you."

"In that office, or in any other, you are most welcome," said she. "But you must be more careful in your disguise than any of us: the people may recognize you by your face."

Lord Cawley, who had said nothing hitherto, now thought it might be wise to interrupt his sister. "Jessie, really, if His Grace feels you will not be safe . . . It is too much to insist upon imperilling yourself while you accept his hospitality."

Jessica considered this for a moment; she held her brother in very high esteem. She ended, however, by rising, going to the duke, and taking his hands in her own. "My very good sir," she murmured to him, with a melting look which could not fail to be persuasive, "I regret extremely if I cause you anxiety. It is my last intention. And yet this fair must be so very delightful—and I cannot bear to observe where I might participate. Please, is there no means by which your most admirable desire to protect me may be reconciled to my wish of entertainment?"

The duke foresaw disaster; but the more immediate sight of this agreeable young woman, her heart set on having her own way with the earnestness of a child, presented a nearer and more affecting vision. "Madam," he said, "it is beyond me to resist such entreaty. We will bring with us some of the footmen—and if the ladies will promise to stay always near the gentlemen . . . I truly cannot resist," he broke off with a laugh, kissing her hands before he let them drop. "She looks as if she would cry, were I to say no," he remarked, feeling somewhat silly at having been moved by a pleading glance before so large a company.

Miss Cawley set up a shout of joy which attracted the attention of the other guests; in no time the excursion had been explained to all the company, and places within the party offered to everyone. To those who had not been present at the inception of the scheme, and who had not witnessed the obtaining of Karr's consent to it, it seemed but a feeble attraction; even Lady Stanton, who had herself seen everything, felt the excursion more suitable to younger spirits than her own. In the end, the group which chose to go was comprised almost entirely of those people who had been gathered round Miss Cawley in the first place: her brother, Mr. Remington and Mr. Longstreth, Karr, and Lady Henrietta Helms. Lady Henrietta was, as the reader will recall, the woman whom the dowager duchess hoped to see replace her as mistress of Grasmere. She had chanced to be sitting beside Lord Cawley when the scene sketched above took place, and though she said nothing, was listening carefully. The duke's rôle was of particular interest to her; being of sober judgment, she was somewhat surprised—even shocked—that Miss Cawley should persist in a plan so obviously discomforting to their courteous host. Nonetheless, she wished to go if anybody did; she would take counsel with her parents before committing herself, but only their permission, and not their encouragement, would be necessary to her.

The sole exception to the rule I have observed—that only those originally near Miss Cawley chose to accompany her to Goose-Fair—was Miss Lotta Chilton. She, neither too elevated in rank to be unfamiliar with country fairs, nor too elevated in years to be unattracted by them, most heartily wished to be one of the projected party; unhappily for her, her status among the company at Grasmere was so hazy as to prevent her putting herself forward for the purpose. The duchess, who was near her when they heard of it, caught the gleam of longing in her young companion's beautiful eyes, but she declined to encourage it. Lotta felt, quite properly, that the general invitation did not include her;

she must wait for a special one, and she soon perceived that the duchess did not mean to extend it. Within minutes, therefore, she resigned herself to stopping at the castle, even rebuking herself inwardly for regretting the necessity. The dowager had been excessively liberal with her already; she must guard against becoming presumptuous.

Her delighted surprise, consequently, may well be imagined when the duke himself arrived to rescue her from disappointment. He was feeling generous and benevolent, as one sometimes does after making a concession to another's happiness, and had caught (not, perhaps, entirely by chance) the single interrogative glance she had cast toward his mother. He had also caught the dowager's pointed lack of response, and the unequal interchange drew him toward them.

"Miss Chilton," he began, his dark eyes arresting her bright ones, "I hope you will favour us with your attendance at Nottingham."

She smiled, but tilted her glazed complexion away from the candlelight and replied, "I am afraid I must disappoint you, Your Grace."

"You mean my mother disappoints *you*," he corrected, continuing, "Madam, surely you can do without Miss Chilton's services for a few hours. I admit her conversation to be charming, but I must also point out your own considerable resources in the matter of solitary amusement."

"You press for a precedent which may be foolish," the duchess said, looking straight at him and not in the least abashed at approaching the matter so publicly, and so bluntly.

"I do not mean to press at all," he answered evenly.

"Miss Chilton is in my employ," the duchess said significantly.

"I am sure no one doubts that."

"On the contrary, they are all too conscious of it," she returned, with a dry laugh and an ironical intonation. The outrage some of her guests experienced at having to dine with a hired companion had not escaped her notice, and she had been deeply, though silently, scornful of what she deemed their narrow-mindedness. This scorn, which she now remembered, influenced her suddenly. "She may go," the dowager pronounced. "See she is well taken care of."

"Ah, madam! You may be easy on that head." The duke turned to Miss Chilton (who had endeavoured to be as invisible as possible during the preceding dispute) and smiled down upon her with an unexpected sensation of warmth. Miss Chilton—he noticed it as if for the first time—was really astonishingly lovely! It would be a pleasure to ensure her security, and he told her so.

"Your Grace is too good," she murmured.

"The goodness is all on your side," said he.

"Miss Chilton was right," the duchess broke in sharply. "You are much too good, Karr; much too good. You will learn the error of it someday."

"I will think of you when I do, madam," he replied very simply. "Miss Chilton," he bowed, and went off alone to see to the diversion of his guests.

These fortunate people, with all the facilities of a great house at their disposal, were—if at all uncertain what to do—bewildered rather by the abundance of possibilities than the lack of them. A party of gentlemen, led by the gallant Sir Isaac Bridwell, had already departed for the billiard-room. A few of the younger people were endeavouring to establish a table for Speculation, in which venture they sought the aid of Mr. Chauncey Stanton; he was loth, however, to quit the side of the Contessa di Tremini, who was in the act of persuading Sir Francis Olney to play at whist with her. The Duke of Karr entered into this scene, comprehended its visible and invisible aspects—the invisible ones being that Chauncey was infatuated with the countess; and that the countess entreated Sir Francis so specially because, and only because, his fortune was known to be such as could withstand deep play—and with swift and expert diplomacy arranged his guests in the most natural and suitable order. He introduced Lady Anne Stanton to the game of whist, trusting her to keep the stakes within reasonable bounds; encouraged the Speculation players to avail themselves of the vacant Rose Saloon (thus sparing Chauncey the necessity—and even the possibility—of gazing helplessly across the room at his heart's desire, and in consequence freeing his mind for the enjoyment of the game); and went off himself to minister to the welfare of Lady Henrietta Helms, who sat alone in a corner of the drawing-room, leafing through a large album. He chose this last occupation for himself not so much to gratify his own desires as to pacify his mother the duchess, who had been glaring alternately at him and at Henrietta these past ten minutes. Karr knew the meaning of that glare, and feeling he had crossed her with regard to Miss Chilton, moved himself to oblige her in this matter. Lady Helms, not inquisitive as to what good fortune had sent him her way, welcomed him sedately—she did everything sedately—and proceeded to engage him in a discussion of Alexander Pope.

Lady Henrietta's parents, Lady Madeline Olney, and Lord Wyborn having assembled at a table for the purpose of playing Cassino; Jessica

Cawley entertaining her set with a new enthusiasm—amateur theatricals, this time; and the duchess surrounded by her companion, her childhood friend, and the ever entertaining Mr. Faust, all was quiet enjoyment among the inhabitants of Grasmere Castle for some while. Now and then an excited cry of victory filtered into the drawing-room from the Rose Saloon; occasionally Miss Cawley, in her spirited efforts to fire the imagination of her friends with the idea of representing Congreve on an improvised stage, forgot to modulate her voice and became distinctly audible to everyone; but for the most part, a tranquil hush (in deference to the whist players) reigned in the large, square apartment. One expected the silence to be interrupted, of course, at some time or other—but certainly no one expected it to be broken in quite the manner it eventually was. Moreover, the person who disturbed it was among the least likely to commit so abrupt and startling an act—and yet it must be recorded that before even an hour had gone by, Lady Anne Stanton was generally and irrefutably heard to scream aloud, on the shrillest note imaginable, and immediately afterwards was seen by all the company to faint.

3

It was an extraordinary thing to do, and the confusion which followed Lady Stanton's swoon was equally extravagant. Footmen ran hither and yon, bearing flames and feathers and vinaigrettes; Lord Stanton was fetched from the billiard-room, and a doctor from the local village; Amabel Stanton held her mother's right hand, and Chauncey her left; the duke insisted on carrying the stricken lady up to her chambers himself; and speculation as to the cause and nature of her attack monopolized the conversation of the guests for at least an hour.

"Perhaps she saw a ghost," Mr. Algernon Longstreth suggested in a low tone to Miss Cawley. They hardly knew the Stantons, and were therefore free from any too great anxiety. "She certainly looked pale enough."

"Don't be ridiculous," Jessica whispered.

"The castle *is* haunted, you know."

"Of course it is—and so, I may add, is your brain. By nonsense, I mean."

"Miss Cawley!" he returned, as if indignant. "You don't mean to say you disbelieve in ghosts! Not when you yourself have created so many—!"

"And whose ghost might she have seen, pray tell?"

"Why, Robin Hood's, naturally. Or perhaps Friar Tuck's."

"Mr. Longstreth, may I ask what connection you imagine exists between Lady Anne Stanton and a very ancient legend?"

"Hush, please, Miss Cawley," he exclaimed, though still in a whisper.

"If you run about calling Robin Hood a legend *here,* he is certain to come and haunt you too. Don't you realize we are in the thick of Sherwood Forest?"

"Certainly I realize it. I have also been to the Tower of London, you know; and I assure you, it did not prevent my saying all sorts of nasty things about Lady Jane Grey."

"Miss Cawley, you have lived most dangerously!" he remarked, with eyes made round for the purpose. He bent his head, with its careful clusters of brown-and-gold curls, down to her ear. "Robin Hood's Larder is not five miles from here," he told her.

"And what, if you please, is Robin Hood's Larder?"

"My dear! It is an oak tree, a thousand years old: Robin Hood used it as a cache for his spoils. It has a hollow trunk, you know," he added, as if this might be of special interest to her.

It wasn't, however. "Mr. Longstreth, I am growing mighty weary of hearing about Robin Hood," she said warningly. Her exasperation, though, was partly feigned; she actually liked Algernon very well, and did not mind his teasing.

"Pray, I pray you," cried he, with an impatient gesture as if to make her be still. "If the ghost has been here, he will hear you."

"But there are no such things as ghosts!" she objected finally.

He gazed at her unhappily. "Oh, my dear ma'am. This is a most hazardous heresy. I had thought, from your novels, you were better educated in spiritual matters. I must beg you, for your own safety if for nothing else, not to blaspheme so persistently."

At this, and at his mock solemnity, Miss Cawley had at last to laugh. More serious discussions, meanwhile, were going forth round them.

"She showed no sign of weakness while you played?" the duke was inquiring of the Countess Tremini. He had left Lady Stanton to the care of her family and the doctor, and now felt it was his duty to discover, if he could, what had so overset her. "She said nothing of feeling ill?"

"Nothing at all," the contessa told him, after a pause during which she had closed her gorgeous eyes as if trying to recall every detail. "She seemed perfectly well—in fact, she was winning."

"Oh yes," Sir Francis Olney seconded. "She was my partner, you know. She seemed quite able to concentrate."

The duke turned to Mr. Ralph Hightower, who had been the fourth player at her ladyship's table. It would be useless to sketch Mr. Hightower for the reader: he was the sort of gentleman who, though one sees him a thousand times, never creates an impression of any sort. Hundreds of people had cut him by accident, simply because they did not recognize him on second or third encounter; he was constantly being mistaken, too, for someone else. He seemed to have no age, no features. He was distinctive, in fact, only for his utter lack of any distinction. Because he was immediately present, however, the duke remembered him on this occasion, and addressed him, "Did you observe no indication of failing in Lady Stanton?"

"None at all," said Mr. Hightower. "We had just finished up a trick; Lady Tremini gave her her new hand . . . she looked over the cards and —you heard the rest. Perhaps it was a bad hand, but I must say that *is* taking things a bit hard."

"I doubt it was that, Hightower," Sir Francis said in a friendly tone.

"No, of course not," Karr took up, addressing himself, chiefly. "But I wonder what it could have been. I do hope our dear Lady Stanton is not out of health."

"If she is, it was dreadfully sudden," someone offered.

At this point the duchess, who had moved noiselessly over to where this little group stood, intervened. "We may all hope Lady Stanton will be recovered tomorrow; the doctor has just told me there is no constitutional disorder that he can discover. In any case, she will have the best care; and since there is nothing, at least, to be done for her at present, I may invite you to listen to Miss Chilton play at the harpsichord. The music will not penetrate so far as Lady Stanton's chambers, and Lotta plays extremely well."

Lotta did play well, and most willingly too. She ran through a number of songs by Morley and Arne, singing in the peculiarly clear, sweet tone which also distinguished her speech. The harpsichord was situated in the Oval Saloon, a small apartment which was really not so much an oval as a modified rectangle in shape; most of the guests drifted in and heard an air or two, but Lady Stanton's mysterious collapse preoccupied them, and they presently drifted out again to rooms where they could chatter more easily. One who visited the Oval Saloon and did not soon quit it was the master of the castle himself. Though the episode concerning Lady Stanton was, of course, unfortunate, it had had for Karr at least one bright result: Lady Marland, Lady Henrietta Helms' mother, had been so distressed by the incident that she felt the need of retiring at once, and she had taken Henrietta with her. Since Lady Marland was known to be vapourish, her host had no real fears for her health; and the reprieve from Lady Henrietta's grave, sensible aesthetic was most welcome. He took a seat, therefore, on the cream-and-gilt sofa nearest to the instrument, giving himself up thoroughly to the pleasure of watching Miss Chilton's graceful hands glide up and down the keyboard. After a time they found themselves alone in the saloon. Miss Chilton completed the song she was playing and turned to the duke.

"Do you sing, Your Grace?" she asked. There was a timidity in her voice which she did not use when she addressed the duchess—though this was a more magnificent person, in air and manner, than her son—that did not escape Karr. He wondered if she were frightened of him, and hoped she was not.

"I sing a little," he told her, "but not so charmingly as you."

"I suppose I ought not to invite you to sing with me." She pushed aside a sheet of music and leafed through a few others.

"Why not? Are you afraid I will embarrass myself?"

"I am afraid you will embarrass me," she answered swiftly, and then looked a trifle conscious. "I suppose I ought not to have said that."

"Why not?" he repeated. "It is very uncomfortable to have invited someone to perform, and then to be unable to enjoy the performance."

"Or even to thank him," she agreed.

"If you gave me a very small and quiet part to sing, I might engage not to embarrass either of us," he said. "And you needn't thank me anyway."

"If I do not thank you for singing, I must for something else," she replied, turning her face away from him as she selected a page of music. Her voice resumed that timid note which it had lost for a moment.

"Shall I ask you what that is, or wait until you tell me?"

"Why, for speaking to Her Grace in my behalf, of course," she responded, as if surprised at his not knowing it at once. "It was excessively kind in you, sir, and I am grateful."

"I did it as much for my own pleasure as for yours. More, in fact," he added, without intending to. Miss Chilton had the most curious effect on him: she was such an odd blend of artifice and spontaneity herself—it seemed to encourage him to say more than he meant to. "I only hope it will not end unhappily for you: I pushed my mother rather far, I think, and she is not fond of being pushed. When she is angry she blames the nearest object, and you are more often near to her than I. You mustn't mind her if she scolds you."

To this Lotta made no reply. She merely indicated to him which part he was to sing and again put her hands to the keys. They sang together for half an hour, the duke much more ably (he was a modest man) than he had led her to believe. Lotta curtailed the exercise herself, saying she must return to the duchess; Karr escorted her to the drawing-room, where another game of whist (the contessa would have found a fourth if she had been obliged to enlist the butler himself) was in progress. Near mid-night the ladies retired. Most of the gentlemen sat up to supper and enjoyed a prolonged bout of drinking. Lord Stanton, naturally, stopped with his afflicted wife; Sir Charles Stickney, likewise, declined to sup: he had only just married Lady Dorothea, and they were quite nauseatingly inseparable.

Lady Stanton reappeared among the guests at breakfast, and from the circumstance of her husband's being dressed for shooting, the company gathered that her indisposition had been only temporary. She did look rather pale, however, and fairly jumped when the Countess Tremini inquired—with a very pretty concern for one accustomed to have little to do with women—how she did. Lord Stanton might have been observed to look a little grave as well, but this perhaps was on account of his son's behaviour, and not his wife's. In any case, he did go shooting; the other inmates of the castle dispersed to their duties or diversions, exactly as they chose—to billiards, to walks in the park, to the practise of music and the writing of letters. At two nearly everyone reassembled in the dining-room, where a plentiful nuncheon had been laid out informally on a number of small tables. When this repast had been taken the company adjourned to the drawing-room. There they divided into parties of three and four: it was the hour for excursions of a minor sort, and numerous equipages for driving, and horses for riding, had been drawn up before the great porch of the castle—a courtesy invariably provided by the duchess for her guests. She herself no longer rode, and drove out only infrequently; she took her air and her exercise in the terraced gardens of Grasmere, Miss Chilton by her side. The others, however, were free to go—and did go—to Stirnby, the nearest village; to the stone church across the stream; and on pleasure drives with less precise destinations. Mr. Algernon Longstreth, who strolled into the drawing-room in company with Mr. Remington, suggested this particular afternoon that a visit might be made to Robin Hood's Larder—Miss Cawley, he felt, might be especially interested.

"And why should I be interested in that?" she asked.

"You seemed interested last night," Mr. Longstreth said. He was looking rather well that day, in a rustic belted jacket and sturdy top-boots, which comfortable attire (though he could never have been convinced of it) suited his slender, compact frame quite as well as more formal wear. Mr. Longstreth did not have a very great deal of hair—and he

would have less in a few years, being now only thirty or thereabouts—
but he did his best with what he had. He was fortunate enough to own a
pair of quite beautiful grey eyes, and his nose, though crooked, was delicate. He was also blessed with a very pleasant grin, by far more in tune
with the common taste than was Mr. Faust's. Mr. Faust's grin seemed as
much a baring of his teeth as an agreeable appeal.

"I do not recall being interested," Jessica contradicted him, in spite
of the attractive smile he produced. "In fact, I distinctly recall being
bored."

"But you will love to see it," he told her.

"Will I?"

"Ah, indeed. It is full of history and romance. For a tree, it is very
Gothic."

"I should like to see a Gothic tree," she owned, but not as if she expected to see one.

"Then you must come. Cosmo and I are going—aren't we, Cosmo?"

Mr. Remington signified agreement by a nod of the head. He had
been, in his extreme youth, afflicted with a stutter, and therefore took as
many opportunities as possible of answering questions by nods.

"There, you see?" Algernon continued. "And how dull we should be
without a woman to accompany us! But perhaps you do not like to be
the only lady. Shall we invite . . . hmmm . . . Shall we invite Miss
Chilton, for example?"

Miss Cawley smiled, but said, "Not for my sake, if you please. Miss
Chilton is, I am sure, the kindest of gentlewomen—but very frankly, I do
not care for her."

"I th-think she is obliged to stop with Her Grace, in any case," Mr.
Remington put in.

"All the more reason not to ask her," said Jessica, satisfied.

"My dear ma'am, I hope you are not among those who object to Miss
Chilton on the score of rank," Mr. Longstreth murmured to her.

"Of course it is not that," she answered truthfully. "Let us only say
she is too pretty. Find someone less handsome than I."

Algernon assented to this, but wondered at the same time why anyone should take Lotta Chilton in aversion. The answer, which he did not
guess, was that Miss Cawley and Miss Chilton were, in some superficial
aspects, quite similar: both were bright, candid, spontaneous creatures,
and though Lotta was obliged (by reason of her position in the household) to suppress herself a good deal, Jessica had yet sensed the resem-
blance and—as often happens in such cases—held it against the other

lady. Mr. Longstreth did not question her closely; if he had, she would have discovered herself unable to say on precisely what basis her dislike was founded. At least, however, she was sure it was not a matter of rank.

"Miss Cawley," he said to her, after scanning the faces near them for a moment, "you place me in a difficult position. Now that you have stipulated our fourth must be less pretty than yourself, the invitation I extend will hardly be complimentary to its recipient."

"Mr. Longstreth, I hope you do not mean to pounce upon someone and cry out, 'Come! You are not so attractive as Jessica; you will answer very well!' Just chuse someone and ask her. Chuse someone older than myself, if you like."

"Lady Louisa Bridwell?" he suggested.

"Certainly. She will make an excellent chaperon."

Mr. Longstreth excused himself and went off to solicit the attendance of this lady. Anything called a larder could not fail to intrigue her, and she accepted with alacrity. Besides, she knew that if she stayed the duchess would ask her to walk into the gardens, and she despised walking. A seat in a plumply cushioned carriage appealed to her much more, and she was accordingly established in just such a seat not ten minutes later. The coachman, who had lived all his life at Grasmere, knew very well the location of the ancient oak, and in no time they were rolling out through the heavy gates of the castle.

"You know, dear gentlemen," Miss Cawley said when they had been travelling some little while, "I think, after my having been so kind as to accompany you to this—ah—tree, the very least you can do in return is to help me to represent 'The Way of the World.'"

"My dear ma'am," Mr. Longstreth replied; "forgive me if I cannot help suspecting that all you really wish to do is to play Mrs. Millamant yourself."

"It is a name more suited to the Countess Tremini, perhaps," she answered; "but yes, I admit I should like to play her."

"And who will you have for your Mirabell?" he pursued, ignoring her rather uncharitable allusion to the pleasure-seeking countess—it was not, at any rate, uttered in a spiteful tone, or with a malicious intention.

"Why yourself, Mr. Longstreth," she exclaimed, fixing him with an exaggerated look of appeal. "Surely you would not disappoint me—!"

"Never in the world," he was obliged to say. "I must caution you, however, that I am a very poor player."

"Oh, cautions, cautions! I hear altogether too much of such things at

Grasmere." Miss Cawley's spirits lifted—they had never been depressed in the first place—as she talked of the delights of Congreve, and assured her companion he should not regret having accepted a rôle in the projected performance. She chattered on and on about it, attempting to persuade Lady Louisa and Mr. Remington to assume rôles as well, and wondering if the duchess would be so kind as to have a platform built for their stage. She was still prattling when the coach drew to a halt, apparently in the middle of nowhere. The driver descended and informed the occupants of the carriage that he could proceed no further; the remainder of the journey must be made on foot.

"On foot!" Lady Louisa echoed, with genuine dismay. "My dear Mr. Longstreth, you did not mention this."

"I beg your pardon, ma'am. I thought, since we were going to visit a tree, you would understand . . . However, there is no need of your going any further. I say, Cosmo—"

"I will stay with Lady Louisa," Mr. Remington anticipated him. "Frankly, I don't care above half for Robin Hood."

"Shh, please! His spirit may be near us."

"Really, Algie—" Mr. Remington began, in accents of mild exasperation.

"Hasn't he become a fiend about it?" Jessica agreed. "I never heard anything so tiresome."

Mr. Longstreth maintained his dignity. "Belabour me as you like," he said. "Call me and blame me as you will. Only don't, for heaven's sake, disturb the rustic hero."

"You *are* doing it a bit brown," Jessica muttered, as he helped her down from the coach. The driver was to guide them to the Larder, since Algernon himself had never been there; the three of them consequently set off down a little path, leaving Lady Louisa and the obliging Cosmo to amuse themselves as they could.

"The devil fly away with this troublesome tree," Miss Cawley ejaculated when they had walked some ten minutes. "Where is it, after all?"

Algernon was about to launch into another lecture on the inadvisability of petulant denunciations, but the coachman forestalled him. "Just a few more yards, miss," said he. "It's up about here somewhere." He then wandered ahead a bit, as if making certain of his direction.

"I'll lay a pound he's got us lost," Jessica whispered.

"No such thing," her companion replied, moving suddenly off to the left of the path. "Here it is—this must be it," he cried, rushing up to an enormously lofty tree, and sticking his head at once into the hollow in its massive trunk. "Oh dear—it isn't much," he said a moment later, turning to face her. "Of course it has a history, but it is, after all, only an old tree. I'm awfully sorry; I dragged you all the way out here, too."

"Oh, I don't mind," she said carelessly. She walked round the oak, trailing a hand along the rough bark, and arrived at the hollow opening. "I think this is very jolly," she went on bracingly; she hated disappointments, and had suddenly determined to like the Larder very much.

"Oh, well," he answered listlessly. "Just a tree with a hole in the middle of it."

"No, indeed! It's a capital tree," she insisted. "It must have made a famous hiding-place; just think of all the things that have been stashed in here."

"Only game, I should think. Rabbits, or deer. It is called his larder, you know."

"Yes, but he must have used it for other things as well, don't you think? Jewels, and gold, and—my goodness, what's this?" she exclaimed suddenly. She had put her hand into the cavity, and had been rummaging about, tapping the interior walls and so forth, while she spoke. At this point she removed her hand and drew out with it a small object, thoroughly encrusted with dirt.

"A stone?" Mr. Longstreth suggested, without enthusiasm.

"Not at all! Look, it's a . . . an—" She rubbed the thing, whatever it was, in the folds of a handkerchief. "Mr. Longstreth," she said, very slowly; "it's a ring!"

"Yes, yes; I confess I was foolish to bring you all the way out here—it is not necessary to impress that upon me now."

"Mr. Longstreth, a ring!" she repeated, holding it up before him.

Algernon refused, however, to look at it. "Are my apologies not sufficient?" he persisted, his eyes on the ground. "I beg you will not tease me any more."

"Mr. Longstreth!" she fairly shouted, grasping his hand and forcing into it the treasure she had found.

Now he could not help but listen to her. In the palm of his hand, just as she had said, lay a heavy gold ring—a man's ring, though without a seal. "Damme," he breathed softly, examining the trinket. Dirt still clung to it, but the antique sheen it would reveal when it had been polished could already be guessed at. "Damme," he repeated, "it *is* a ring—and a century old at least, I should guess."

"A century!" she scoffed. "More like five or six, my dear sir. I'll lay a pony Robin Hood himself wore it."

"Ah now, merely because the ring was in this tree does not mean Robin Hood put it there! More likely some gang of marauders—some modern gang, that is—"

"I *know* Robin Hood touched it; I can feel it fairly vibrate," she interrupted him, rolling the ring about slowly within a half-closed hand.

"Let me try," he said, reaching for the ring.

She handed it to him. "You won't feel anything," she warned him. "Your senses are too dulled for such fine tremors."

"Perhaps you are right," he agreed, suddenly depositing the ring in a pocket of his jacket. "I sensed nothing."

"What have you done with it?" she cried at once. "Give it to me."

"Oh, no, Miss Cawley, I think you had far better let me keep it for you. I'll engage for its safety."

"I found it—I want it," she insisted, flaring slightly.

"Really, Miss Cawley," he admonished, turning back down the path toward the waiting carriage.

She ran after him and caught at his elbow, grasping it firmly. Her bright, pretty features had gone quite hard with anger. "Really *what*, prithee?"

"Really you make too much of it." He looked down at her, as unruffled as she was excited.

"Mr. Longstreth, I will thank you to give me my ring," she forced out, from between clenched teeth.

He stared at her a moment longer, then gave a laugh. "As you like, ma'am. I only thought that if it *did* have some historical value, you would prefer to be relieved of responsibility for it."

"I am not frightened of responsibility," she replied, taking the ring he finally offered to her. She slipped it on to the first finger of her right hand—it was made for the last finger of a much larger one, but fit very well what it now encircled—and surveyed it with proprietorial satisfaction.

"It is a little large for you, but comely," he said.

"Kindly keep away from it in future," said she, still miffed.

"Ah now, Miss Cawley," he remonstrated, while—the coachman following them—they retraced their steps to the road, "if we are to play Millamant and Mirabell, we must learn to deal better with one another."

"Come to think of it, you will make a much better Witwoud. We will ask the duke to act Mirabell's part."

"Have you designs on the duke, then?" he cried.

"Had I any on you?"

She was angry, but not so much so that her temper had not disappeared by the time the carriage began its homeward journey. She showed her golden treasure to Mr. Remington and to Lady Louisa as proudly as any bride who ever displayed a similar token to admiring friends, and chattered gaily about the deep inquiries she intended to make into the possible history of the prize. "You know, s-some people do think Robin Hood lived in Yorkshire," Mr. Remington informed her after a time. He followed this pronouncement with a broad wink to Mr. Longstreth—a wink that, in spite of its broadness, Miss Cawley did not notice.

"Fustian," she retorted at once. "Everyone knows he lived in Sherwood Forest. And how could the Sheriff of Nottingham have known him, if he had not?"

"That is a very pertinent question, ma'am. And yet, they do persist in believing so."

"I don't care what they believe," she said stubbornly—she could be stubborn, indeed. "People believe in all sorts of nonsense. Mr. Longstreth believes in ghosts."

"Don't you?" asked Cosmo, surprised.

"Not another one!"

"But madam, surely—!"

"But sir, surely not! Lady Louisa doesn't believe in ghosts—now do you, dear ma'am?"

"Oh, my dear," said this lady; "I am not quite positive whether I do or I don't. I thought I didn't, but last night I heard something that sounded so much like one, I think I may after all. I was dreadfully frightened. I was obliged to awaken my abigail."

"Poor girl," exclaimed Jessica. "Not but what I am certain you are an excellent mistress most of the time, my lady, but what you heard was without doubt only the wind."

"So I told myself!" Lady Louisa agreed, her pale, watery eyes opening wide into her pasty complexion. "Yet the more I listened, the more certain I became it was more than that. Even my maid thought she heard something."

"New places are always attended with new noises," Miss Cawley advised her. "I myself sat up writing half the night last night, and I heard nothing at all."

"Perhaps you were in another wing," her ladyship suggested plausibly. "Where is your bed-chamber?"

Mr. Algernon Longstreth, had anyone observed him, might have been noticed to listen very attentively for her answer. "In the corridor above the library—on the east side."

"Well! That explains everything," said Lady Louisa. "I am at the other end of the castle from you. The spirit probably saw your light burning, and passed you by."

"My dear Mr. Longstreth—Mr. Remington," appealed Miss Cawley, "do, for her own sake, reassure Lady Louisa that no ghosts frequent Grasmere Castle."

"But that would be prevarication," said Algernon gravely, while Cosmo nodded vigorously. "I am sorry to disoblige you."

"Oh—goodness!" she finally exclaimed, quite frustrated. "If there is a ghost, I hope it haunts *you*."

The gentlemen appeared undaunted by this threat, yet they gave no sign of doubting its possibility. Jessica concluded that she had stumbled, by chance, on three very superstitious individuals; she forgot the matter altogether by the time she reached her brother. She exhibited the ring to him, and recounted the circumstances of its discovery, a performance she repeated (for the benefit of the general company) after dinner. It was roundly marvelled at, and wondered over—no one except the duke, in fact, appeared to question her theory of its origin.

"One would think it would have eroded a good deal more in the course of so many years," he suggested. "Should you like me to send it to Nottingham, to have it examined by an expert?"

"No, thank you, Your Grace." She had grown extremely attached to it; she held it up now so that the smooth old gold gleamed in the candle-light. "I mean to wear it myself, always. When we go to Goose-Fair, perhaps, we will have it appraised."

"I doubt the jeweller will keep regular hours during the fair."

"Then we won't. Anyway, I don't want to part with it," said she capriciously.

"You understand, madam," said Mr. Longstreth, who stood near them, "that if you do wear the ring—and if it does have something to do with Robin Hood—you encourage his spirit to visit you."

The duke stared in unmistakable surprise at his old friend and shoot-ing-companion. "Algie—" he began, in a tone of reproach.

A quelling look was all he received for reply, but it sufficed to stifle him. In a short while, these two gentlemen departed together for the billiard-room, where Karr's unvoiced question could be answered; the other guests floated here and there, discussing what on-dits had been culled from the most recent London papers, arguing heatedly about politics, and playing at whist and piquet. Lady Madeline Olney, who made no secret of the fact that she constantly cuckolded her husband, flirted strenuously with Roger Cawley; while Sir Francis Olney, equally careless about the small matter of marriage vows, sat up past three playing cards with the Countess Tremini. This lady was so beautiful, thought he, as to make losing money almost palatable—and lose it he did, until she finally took pity on him and suggested they retire. "After all, it is quite late," she remarked, to spare him embarrassment. With this she feigned a yawn—a gesture which was, with her, not a loose and homely gape, but a sweet, deliberate stretching of full pink lips, till they had achieved a perfect O. Mr. Septimus Faust, who had also played with them (on the winning side, which was very fortunate for him, as he had no money to lose) observed the deep, delectable stretch, and approved it. The contessa was suffered to quit her companions in spite of their profound appreciation of her charms, and pursued her solitary way upstairs.

There was no incident of note, during the evening, but one: when the countess arrived at her chamber she discovered waiting for her there a note, sealed but not franked. "I don't know when it came in, your la'ship," said her sleepy abigail, "or how. It may have been when I was at dinner; for I'm sure I saw no messenger."

The contessa told her it made no matter, and presented her elaborate coiffure to be unpinned and prepared for bed. While she bent her head to her handmaid's fingers, her own broke the seal of the missive she held, and she scanned the page with a face full of interest.

"You shall receive what you desire," was all the letter said; "but I must have more time. Please do not be cruel. A courier departs for London tonight."

There was no salutation, and no signature. The hand was plain, dark, and legible, of a sort which might have belonged to any educated person. The contessa read the brief message thrice; then she put it away. On her lips was a very pleased, very genuine, very satisfied smile. It lingered on her mouth till she had gone to bed, and even while she dreamed.

4

"Well, I can't think it's very considerate!" Miss Jessica Cawley exclaimed at breakfast three days later to the gentleman on her left.

"Remington," said Algernon Longstreth—for it was he whom she addressed, "Miss Cawley can't think it's considerate."

"Sh-she ain't obliged to," said Remington. "It ain't considerate, anyway."

"There you are, Miss Cawley," parroted Algernon. "It ain't considerate."

"Couldn't you put her off—just till this evening? Today of all days!"

"A fellow can't put his mother off," Mr. Longstreth informed her. "It isn't good form. Besides, she only stops with the Stepneys this one day; then she's off to Scotland."

"Invite her to stop here," Jessica suggested. "Karr won't mind at all, and she's certain to enjoy it."

"But then she couldn't see Captain Stepney."

"Wouldn't she rather see you? You are her son."

"She'd rather see us both," said Algernon. "And Mrs. Stepney too. They came out together, at the same ball."

"Well, it didn't do Mrs. Stepney much good that I can see," Jessica replied crossly. "She appears to have married Captain Stepney, and to have got stuck out here in Nottinghamshire forever. Don't they pass the season in town?"

"No," he said simply. "That's why my mother must stop with them, and not here. They don't see each other all year. She hasn't seen me in months either," he added reflectively.

"I can scarcely deem that a hardship," Jessica returned, with customary impudence.

"There's no understanding a mother's love," said Longstreth.

"Precisely." Miss Cawley fell in silence to buttering a piece of toast, out of which she took a few slow bites. "Well," she continued at last, "it is your misfortune more than anyone else's. You will just miss the fair altogether. I hope your mother appreciates it."

"No doubt she has made such sacrifices for me, in her time," Algernon replied calmly. "Anyway, you will go and tell me all about it, won't you?"

"It isn't the same as if you came," she persisted.

"Oh, Cosmo will look after you," he said carelessly. "And Karr will see to your safety, and Miss Chilton will amuse you. She is quite diverting, in truth."

"Perhaps," was all she would say.

"If you don't care for her company, you may keep near to Lady Henrietta," Algernon suggested.

"Worse and worse," murmured Jessica, who had already heard as many of Henrietta's platitudes as she cared to listen to. "I shall stay with Roger all day, and ignore everybody else."

"Don't you like Mr. Remington?" that gentleman's friend inquired.

"Not much," she muttered, but immediately smiled at Cosmo and placed a neat hand on his arm. "I only said that to be perverse, you know," she informed him, smiling charmingly. "I adore to annoy Mr. Longstreth."

"Yes, yes; no matter."

"Mr. Remington, would you do me the kindness to play Petulant in 'The Way of the World'?"

"Ah, th-that is something else!" he cried. "It seems to me I have sufficient rôles to play already," he added, with a sidewards glance at Algernon.

"I beg your pardon?" asked Miss Cawley.

"He means he is obliged to act as my shooting-companion, don't you, Cosmo?" Mr. Longstreth interrupted hastily. "Mr. Remington loathes shooting, really—thinks it's cruel. But I make him come out with me. He has such a capital way with the dogs."

"Yes, yes; that's what I meant," Mr. Remington agreed.

Miss Cawley looked suspicious for a moment, but soon forgot about it. "I can't think why you do such favours for Mr. Longstreth. I am sure I would not."

"Miss Cawley, why don't you invite Miss Chilton to act in your play?" said Algernon, who did not care for the turn the conversation was taking. "I think Cosmo will agree to join you if you do."

"Mr. Remington, you don't mean to tell me you've conceived a *tendre* for her!" exclaimed she.

Mr. Remington looked in confusion from the lady to Algernon. "Certainly not," he replied, after a moment. "Don't know why you said that, Algie."

"I said it because it's true," he pursued. "Do you think I'm such a widgeon as not to have noticed how you look at her?"

"Algie!" he repeated.

"Go on," Mr. Longstreth said, addressing Miss Cawley. "Invite Miss Chilton to play Foible, and let Cosmo play Waitwell. You'll see if I am right."

Mr. Remington, by now, was blushing furiously. "Miss Cawley prefers that I play Petulant," he objected, with some dignity.

"It makes no difference. How will it be if you act Fainall, and she Mrs. Marwood? She will make a much better Marwood; there is something so very—artificial about her."

"Miss Cawley—" Cosmo began, and stopped.

"Then it's settled," she went on eagerly. "I'll ask Lotta today, and if she agrees we are almost ready to begin."

"Has Karr agreed to Mr. Mirabell's part?" Algernon asked, surprised.

Jessica shrugged lightly. "I'll ask him at the fair. He'll accept."

"Miss Cawley is confident," a voice behind her suddenly broke in. Jessica started slightly and twisted round in her chair to behold the duke himself, who had come to discuss the details of their projected visit to Nottingham.

"It is one of the qualities we most admire in her," she agreed, after a moment, speaking of herself in the third person. "And she does have her heart set on your playing Mirabell; you will, won't you? It would be too dreadful to disappoint her!"

The duke smiled. "For the moment, pray allow me to occupy myself with the gratification of your earlier desire. We will think of the play later; just now I should like to know whether you prefer to return in time to dine here tonight or to stop at an inn."

"Oh, an inn will be much more exciting, don't you think?" she said, appealing to Cosmo. "And you shan't come," she added to Algernon.

"Miss Cawley is confident and cruel," murmured Longstreth.

"Ah yes, your mother. You must convey my compliments to her," Karr told him. "A most amiable woman. I am very sorry she is too pressed to stop at Grasmere."

"I am not," said Jessica. "I still think her timing is most hideously inconsiderate. And now, if you gentlemen will excuse me, I must go and transform myself into a fragrant country lass."

"My mother has charged her dresser with the errand of gathering suitable clothes for your masquerade," Karr informed her as he escorted her to the door of the dining-parlour. "You will find them in your room."

"Ah, now *your* mother—she is a woman I can esteem! I trust *she* has no silly friends stuck away so inconveniently."

"You are very hard on Algie," he remarked.

"I like him very much." With this frank, if paradoxical, admission, Miss Cawley took leave of him, proceeding alone to her chamber, where she and her abigail contrived a fairly rustic disguise for her. The only tell-tale signs of her true condition were her delicate hands—far too white and soft for those of a peasant—and the ring she insisted on wearing on one of them. When she descended again she found Miss Chilton and Lady Henrietta similarly garbed and waiting for her in the Rose Saloon. The gentlemen entered some moments later, and it was a great amusement to her to see Mr. Remington, who usually affected a high degree of fashion, reduced to blue worsted stockings and a coarse cloth coat. His Grace, always a sturdy, comfortable-looking man, wore his rude attire more easily than did her brother or Cosmo, yet Jessica found most fault in his appearance.

"You mustn't leave your hair bound in that fashion!" she cried. "Everyone will know you in a minute."

Karr looked at her in mild surprise, and asked why.

"Surely you must realize you are the only man in England who still ties his hair back in such a manner," she exclaimed. "It won't answer."

The duke considered this. "Well, I can't crop it just for today," he mused; "and it certainly would look most singular to wear it in no fashion at all."

"If I may say something," Lotta intervened, all eyes turning to her as her clear voice sounded, "there will be many, many gentlemen at the fair with just such coiffures. Miss Cawley is habituated to London, and refers to the current vogues there, but in the country—well, they do tend to lag some decades behind town usage. His Grace will be much less remarkable than Lord Cawley, for example."

In spite of the other lady's having solved the difficulty, Jessica glanced at Miss Chilton with some displeasure. She was honest enough, however, to own that she had been wrong, and tried not to dislike Lotta for correcting her. "Then we are all prepared," she said. "Are the carriages waiting?"

"Quite," Karr replied. "And you have caused four footmen much happiness by making it a part of their duties to attend Goose-Fair."

"Four! Why, that is sufficient to protect a whole academy of schoolgirls."

"I think it very kind of His Grace to provide so bountifully for our security," the ever-loyal Henrietta put in.

Jessica rolled her eyes in exaggerated dismay. In the face of such stolid gratitude as this, even Miss Chilton's company was preferable. "Shall we be on our way?" she suggested, and made sure to place herself in a different coach from that which Lady Henrietta was to occupy. As a result, she found herself the neighbour of Miss Chilton, and this chance proximity resulted in an alliance between the two ladies which might otherwise never have been achieved. Cosmo Remington was also in their carriage (as well as a footman who did his utmost to appear to hear nothing) and at first Miss Cawley tried to address her remarks solely to him, but Cosmo insisted on drawing Lotta into the conversation until Jessica could no longer avoid speaking to her herself. In an astonishingly short while the two ladies found so much to say to one another that it was Cosmo who was excluded from their colloquy, and found himself instead nodding and smiling ever and anon at the self-effacing footman.

"But isn't it charming to be rid of those thin slippers and thin gowns for once!" Miss Cawley exclaimed to her fellow masquerader. "I daresay I pass half my days fretting over a scuffed shoe or a ripped hem. And one is forever chilly."

"Indeed, one pays a higher price than seems possible for the luxury of fashion," Lotta agreed. "When I was still in the school-room I died for a chance to wear silk and sandals; but now that we are better acquainted, I should give anything to be in stout, short frocks again."

"Oh, yes—and imagine wearing skirts so voluminous one might keep a pocket anywhere. I abhor to carry a reticule; I forget mine everywhere."

"Do you! So do I, indeed. I lost one once and was half a year finding it. I had given it up entirely, and then the housekeeper discovered it inside the works of the pianoforte."

Miss Cawley gave a laugh. "Did no one notice the tone of the instrument had gone?"

"Certainly they did. They thought it very sad, and lamented over the quality of modern workmanship, and the destructive properties of wet weather. It was a very ill-managed house anyway; things were constantly being ruined and discarded. It never seemed to occur to my lady to repair anything."

"Really? And where was this, Miss Chilton?"

"At Bellevue, in Surrey. I was employed there before the duchess was so kind as to engage me."

The meaning of employment took on a new dimension for Miss Cawley. "Poor Miss Chilton," she exclaimed, with genuine sympathy. "How dreadful to be obliged to stop in a harum-scarum household."

Lotta shrugged off this hardship, and smiled. "Quite candidly, the house-keeper's bad habits did not distress me nearly as much as the bad habits of her ladyship's nephew. *He* had such a collection as would provide sermons for a country curate every Sunday for a decade! And I am sorry to say that my distaste for him was not at all reciprocated."

"He was attentive to you?"

"Attentive! He was a perfect plague to me, since you ask. I have received slavering kisses from him wet enough to drench a bonfire, and water the flowers near it besides. He would grab me here, and hug me there, and offer to carry me off forever—! It was the horridest thing I ever had the misfortune to encounter."

"Could you not tell his aunt?"

"Ah, but she doated on him! He was her jewel, her darling, her faithful lamb. She'd have turned me off without a character."

"Poor Miss Chilton," Jessica repeated.

"Oh, I dareswear there are worse fates," Lotta said cheerfully; "only I can't recall any of them just offhand. Anyway, if you should wish to use a lady's companion in one of your novels, I'll be more than glad to tell you the harrowing realities of the situation. It would give me great pleasure to unburden myself for once."

"As it happens, the book I am now writing is about Grasmere Castle. Everyone is in it—slightly altered, of course. I delight in teasing people, and it is so easy to do so by turning them into characters."

Lotta smiled. "Unhappily, the duchess offers me no such dilemmas as did my last employer. Besides, she has no nephew that I've met—and if she did, I rather doubt she would doat on him."

"No doubt you are right," Jessica agreed. For a time the carriage rolled on in silence; then Miss Cawley leaned over to her neighbour and continued in a low tone, "I do adore Her Grace, you understand—she is a most perfect hostess, and a delightful acquaintance . . . but don't you find her manner toward her son just the tiniest trifle," she took a long pause, "chilling?"

Miss Chilton thought for a moment, then answered in a whisper. "When I first saw them together, I supposed it was merely the formality of a great house. But as the days went on, I began to wonder. I certainly should not care to have *my* mother treat me so! She deals with him as if he were her secretary, or attorney. An old friend to the family, perhaps —but not at all like a son."

"Precisely what I have felt," the other hissed. "We are awful even to mention it when she has been so hospitable to us—to me, at least—but one can't help but notice. I wonder if it is painful to Karr?"

"It is an intriguing question. I watch him sometimes when he is with her, but his face tells nothing. He speaks of her with respect, but also lightly. One thinks of him as being quite open, you know, and . . . frank; and yet if one comes to consider it closely, he is quite as reserved as she. It is impossible to get anything out of either of them—anything entirely sincere, I mean."

"And yet they are not insincere."

"Oh, no! Not at all."

Miss Cawley meditated for a minute, then spoke. "Perhaps we are unfair to them, after all. To what, really, are we comparing them? To some romantic notion of what mother and son should be—to a fairy-tale, I think. My mother died young, but even so, I saw a good deal less of her than I saw of my governess. Not every woman has the patience to be doating to her children—or the dulness, either."

"Indeed, you are quite right. I never knew my mother, and though Mrs. Chilton was a very pattern of partiality to me, I sometimes think she exaggerated such kindnesses expressly to compensate my loss."

"Then Chilton is not really your name?"

"No, though I have used it so long I never think of the other. My father's name was Lodovico del Silandro; he was Italian. The Chiltons took me in while I was an infant. Both my parents died very young." She gave a little laugh so that Jessica would not feel she had blundered into a painful topic, and added, "The Chiltons treat me so perfectly as if

I were their own, they would be horrified to learn I could speak of anyone else as my parents. My youngest sister has never been told we are
not blood kin."

"Ah, my dear," murmured Jessica, growing fonder of Lotta by the
minute, "you are a perfect heroine for a romance. So extraordinarily
pretty, even I delight to look on you—and such mysterious origins!"

The other laughed again. "So far as I know, one may not earn one's
keep as the heroine of a romance. However, if you are prepared to offer
wages for the position, I will gladly accept it."

Miss Cawley answered her laugh and the conversation turned to other
things, becoming general enough to include Mr. Remington again. He
was glad to rejoin it, for what Mr. Longstreth had intimated that morning about his regard for Lotta Chilton was, if exaggerated, largely true.
He did find Miss Chilton exceptionally interesting—for her looks, her
manner, and even her disadvantaged status in the household—and the
question of whether one might reasonably marry her had come into his
mind more than once already. Jessica returned to what was becoming an
obsession with her, the notion of performing "The Way of the World,"
and with very little effort persuaded Miss Chilton to act Mrs. Marwood's part (providing, of course, that the duchess consented). Mr.
Remington blushed even more deeply than he had at breakfast when
Lotta was told that her opposite, Mr. Fainall, would be played by himself; but Lotta obligingly pretended not to notice his discomfiture, and
they all arrived in Nottingham in high spirits.

It was a bright, crisp October day. Nottingham had been transformed,
as was proper for a Goose-Fair, into cheerful confusion, a mingling of
Astley's, Tattersall's, Exeter Exchange, and a Turkish bazaar—chiefly
the noisiest and most vulgar parts of each. Jessica enjoyed herself hugely
from the moment they arrived there (they prudently left the carriages at
some distance and came to the fair afoot), demanding that Roger buy
her this gaudy trifle, and that useless bit of stuff, and distributing
freshly-purchased gingerbread to all the party. They discovered themselves somewhat under-dressed even for this occasion, the local gentry
having turned out in all their finery and scorning even to nod at the
unrecognizable ducal presence. Lady Henrietta appeared distinctly uncomfortable, and clung very close to His Grace's arm, but Miss Cawley
skipped ahead of everyone else, dragging a not unwilling Miss Chilton
with her, and crowing delightedly over every new curiosity. If the rudely
admiring stares she and Lotta attracted from the young farmers they
passed troubled them, neither showed her unease; on the contrary, they

marvelled together at dancing harlequins, carved rosewood work-boxes, incredibly discordant bands of musicians—at everything, in short, that offered. It was a little difficult for Lotta at first, since her less than exalted rank might have led her companions to suppose she was now in her natural element, quite at home with rough, crude country diversion. For the others it was clearly a spectator's visit to what almost amounted to a foreign land and populace, but for her—she was afraid (and ashamed to be afraid) that they might think her as naïve and foolish as the simple folk round them. After a time, however, she assured herself that no one was likely to dwell on the subject so finely except herself— and if they did, it was mere priggishness on their part, and not to be regarded. She made up her mind to enjoy herself extremely, and from then on made a very pretty picture at it, her cheeks rosy and her lips curved in a perpetual smile of pleasure.

The duke did not fail to notice her unusual gaiety; he soon forgot his dark forebodings about the excursion and joined in the general jollity of the day. At a stall kept by a positively huge merchant, and his even huger wife, he purchased three bunches of ribbons and offered them to the ladies. Lotta and Jessica accepted them eagerly, threading them among the flowers which already adorned their heads, and allowing them to stream out behind them as they skipped along the crowded streets. Lady Henrietta, unfortunately, had some difficulty receiving the gift in the spirit in which it was offered; the poor girl knew she was not as lithe and slender as Lotta, nor as pert and bright as Jessica—in fact, deprived of her careful, elegant gowns, she looked positively homely. The knots of ribbons, she knew, would not flow gracefully from her hair, but rather hang there awkwardly: the more she pretended to countrified simplicity, the more she looked simply countrified. She pinned the ribbons to the waist of her skirt, and hoped the day would not last too long.

Unhappily for her, it became not only a very long day but also one she could not entirely approve of. They came, at length, to the end of the principal street, where a small stretch of smooth lawn had been transformed, by the young people of the district, into a sort of outdoor ball-room. A young fellow with a wooden flute and a second man with a small drum provided an endless round of country airs, and Miss Cawley —naturally—could not bear to look at them without dancing herself.

"Oh, Roger, please," she begged, extending a hand toward her brother, "I *must* dance. Come, come," she added, as he did not move.

"Jessie, my dear, perhaps it would be best if—"

"I never saw such a high stickler! Mr. Remington, won't you oblige me?" Mr. Remington hesitated, and Miss Cawley amended, "No, you dance with Lotta. His Grace will do me the honour, won't you, sir?" She grasped Mr. Remington's hand on one side and took up Lotta's on the other, pulling them together until they could hardly refuse without creating even more embarrassment, then took hold of the duke's arm for herself. Henrietta stayed behind with Roger, too dismayed at Jessica's inconvenient insistence to say anything, and watched with growing unease as the foursome entered the dance. Apparently there was nothing Miss Cawley would not do for amusement! She kicked her heels about, clapped her hands, swung arm in arm with men she had never seen before (and could not have been presented to if she had) for all the world as if she were a farmer's daughter herself—and a very forward one at that. Miss Chilton was slightly less exuberant, but nonetheless a spectacle, and Henrietta felt certain that (although he hid it very well) the duke was dying a thousand deaths of embarrassment. The footmen stood behind her, largely enjoying the sight of their employer's unwonted abandon, and only wishing they might join the dance themselves. They were not in livery, of course, and one young Nottinghamshire girl tried to induce one of them to partner her, but they knew their posts even in all that confusion, and held fast. Mr. Remington, meanwhile, acquitted himself very handsomely on the smooth lawn, and was gasping for air just as eagerly as the three others when they finally returned to the verge of the grass.

"Well, I hope we have had enough of that," Lady Henrietta murmured to Lord Cawley, as the others rested, laughing at one another's exhaustion.

"Are you fatigued, madam?" Cawley inquired, forever as polite as his sister was impertinent. "I shall suggest we go directly to the inn."

"Ah, not on my account," poor Henrietta forestalled him. Nothing appealed to her more than the idea of a speedy retreat from the scene, but she did not care to spoil the amusement of the others—even if their behaviour did suit their costumes far better than their true estates.

"If not on yours, then on mine," Roger Cawley answered gallantly. "I think my sister has seen sufficient of Goose-Fair—and you may be certain *I* have."

She smiled at him gratefully while he went off to consult with Karr and the others. Jessica called him a great boor for insisting on departing when they'd only just come, but her brother prevailed. The small group set off down the street toward the carriages, Jessica trailing sadly after them. They had nearly achieved their goal when an incident took place that went at first unnoticed by anyone but Lotta: Miss Cawley was several yards behind the company now, gazing longingly back now and then at the revelry they were leaving, when a miserably bent woman—evidently a gipsy—accosted her and drew her aside. Jessica was not at all opposed to the notion of having just one more adventure before going home, so she stopped with the woman and spoke to her. Lotta watched them from a little ways off, confident that no mishap could occur while she kept an eye on them, and much diverted by Miss Cawley's evident absorption in the gipsy's words. She had given her hand to the woman, and was obviously being promised a long life filled with happiness, when all at once an unmistakable look of alarm settled on her features, and she stared at the gipsy in good earnest. Miss Chilton drew near them until she could hear what was being said, and was nearly as startled as Jessica.

"You have stolen this ring," the crone was saying, in a deep voice thick with foreign intonations and harsh accusation. "Where did you find it? Where?"

Miss Cawley said nothing; she was too surprised.

"Where did you steal it? It belongs to the gipsies; it has always belonged to the King of the Gipsies. Give it to me!"

At this she recovered her voice. "I will not," Lotta heard her say, quite distinctly.

"You will not! You—wicked girl! You steal and stand there, brazen in your guilt. Much evil will come of this—to you and to everyone," the old woman muttered.

"Who are you that you dare to accuse me?" Jessica suddenly flared up, forgetting her humble disguise. The gipsy's head and most of her face were covered by a dirty scarf, over which a deep hood was thrown. "Show me your face, my good woman; I'll take you to a magistrate for this."

But the gipsy only drew her cloak more closely round her, laughing with a sharp, unpleasant bark. "Very well, keep it, my young lady. My young lady is so proud, so proud of her pretty bauble! We will see how she likes it when its spell begins to work." Before she had finished this speech Miss Cawley had pulled away from her, and had begun moving toward Lotta. The gipsy continued to call names after her, but she ignored them.

"Filthy woman," she said, gaining Miss Chilton's side. "Fancy a woman like that abusing *me!*"

"She was certainly horrid," Lotta agreed, "but you must recall she had no reason to believe you were anything but a plain country girl."

"Even so," Jessica replied, her voice trembling slightly, "I *would* take her to a magistrate, if I had got a better look at her face. As it was I could barely see her nose, what with the dirt streaked on her skin, and her hood and scarf." Miss Chilton had offered her an arm to lean upon, and Miss Cawley availed herself of it eagerly: the incident had been quite nasty, and had shaken her considerably.

"Should you like a vinaigrette?"

"No, thank you. I shall be right as a trivet in a moment," she said. They stopped for a moment (the gipsy had run off and was out of sight) while Jessica endeavoured to calm herself, inhaling deeply and saying nothing. "A perfect witch," she breathed at last.

"Absolutely." Miss Chilton saw the others looking back for them from the carriages, and signalled that they would join them shortly.

"But I wonder how she knew about the ring?" Jessica took up. "That it wasn't mine, I mean. Not that I believe it belongs to the gipsies, or any of that nonsense."

"Perhaps she saw how ill it fit you, and guessed you had found it," Lotta hazarded.

"Perhaps. Doubtless," she amended. "What else could it have been?"

"What else indeed?" said Lotta. Miss Cawley had recovered herself almost completely by now, and they began again to walk toward the coaches. "It occurs to me, however," Miss Chilton added, "that that woman may really be a lunatic. If she believes in her delusion—that the gipsies own the ring—she may try to follow us home, perhaps, and harass you again. It might be best to let His Grace put it away safely for you, just for caution's sake."

"Pooh," Jessica dismissed her. "There was nothing mad about her; she was only greedy. Everyone seems to want me to part with my ring, but I won't. I won't be frightened by a silly old crone like that." She was, as the reader will have seen, feeling quite herself again, and rather embarrassed at her temporary lapse into fear.

"Well, my dear young ladies," Karr welcomed them as they finally regained the carriages, "I have no desire to match wits with a professional prognosticator, but I will say I foresee some dinner in your immediate futures. Won't you step inside?" He helped them into a coach and climbed in himself afterwards, having permitted himself the luxury of assigning Roger and Cosmo to the task of diverting Lady Henrietta. On the way to the inn where they were to dine he pressed Miss Cawley for the details of her fortune; Jessica repeated what the gipsy had told her before seeing the gold band (long life, prosperity, and a husband with grey eyes) but concealed what had come later. Miss Chilton noticed the omission, of course, but refrained from saying anything in deference to Jessica's wishes. No doubt her new friend preferred to say nothing to Karr for fear he would (as might have been wisest) insist on taking her prize away from her.

The inn proved to be ancient and comfortable, though the table was somewhat grudgingly laid. The poor inn-keeper did not know what to make of this party, which looked so common yet arrived in ornate, fashionable vehicles. He knew the duke, and had some suspicion this fellow might be a relation of his, or even the duke himself; but Karr said nothing, submitting to be called plain Sir and demanding no more than ordinary attention. Had he been certain they were Quality their meal would have been very different; as it was, he showed them hardly more deference than he would have shown the local apothecary, or a visiting merchant. Jessica distinctly enjoyed watching Lady Henrietta's countenance when a servant referred to her as "Missy." Jessica, it will have been noticed, had a streak of mischief in her which sometimes slipped out of the bounds of charity.

No other incident of note occurring, the small party quitted the inn, entered their carriages once more, and pursued their way home to Grasmere. Mr. Longstreth had arrived before them, and greeted them on the porch only to be told (by Jessica) that he had not in the least been missed. "You would have been quite *de trop,*" she informed him. "We were perfect as we were."

"Ah, then it is well I did not disappoint my mother," he replied. "At the Steptons' I was not *de trop* at all, but just precisely what was needed."

Miss Cawley gave him a sharp, quick look. "I thought you said their name was Stepney."

"So I did," he agreed, almost immediately. "What of it?"

"Just this moment you said Stepton!"

"Did I? No, I'm certain I can't have."

"But you did," she insisted.

"Cosmo," Algernon appealed, "did I say Stepton just now?"

"Not at all," said he, in the act of having his coarse coat removed. "I d-didn't hear it, if you did."

"There, you see? Cosmo didn't hear it," Algernon told her. "Perhaps you are tired after all your merriment."

"I'm not tired," she objected. She never admitted to fatigue.

"Then perhaps your ears are playing tricks on you. That often happens to people who are haunted by spirits."

"Not that again!" she groaned.

"That?" he inquired innocently. "Do you mean to say you *are* being haunted?"

"Oh, for heaven's sake. Only by you, my dear Mr. Longstreth. Your conversation grows more spectral by the day: I see in it ghosts of what I saw an hour before, and hear the most tedious echoes."

"I am dreadfully sorry. I hadn't realized I repeated myself so much. Tell me about your day; that way neither of us will be bored."

Miss Cawley postponed the account requested until after she dressed herself in clothes more suitable to her surroundings. She did, though, meet Mr. Longstreth later, in a snug little sitting-room near the Rose Saloon. They were alone, so she was at liberty to embellish the delights they had seen and the adventures she had had to her heart's content. She told a glowing story, but when she reached the episode of the gipsy she stopped, as she had with Karr, before mentioning the antique ring.

"And that is all she said to you?" Algernon took up. "Just longevity, prosperity, and a husband with grey eyes?"

"Don't dwell too much on those eyes," she broke in, challenging his own. "I know an hundred men with grey eyes. It needn't mean you. Anyway, I don't think of marrying."

"My dear, no more do I!" he exclaimed, causing her to colour—a very rare event for Miss Cawley.

"Well, anyhow . . . I don't see what's wrong in such a fortune. What should she have told me?"

"I only thought that since we know you are well-to-do, and have every reason to expect you will live to a ripe old age, and are perfectly aware you may have any gentleman you chuse for a husband, it doesn't seem much of a fortune."

"You are too critical," she told him.

He ignored this. "Besides, if you won't believe in spirits, what can you make of palmistry?"

"I make nothing of it; I only allowed her to read my hand because she seemed set on it. It was amusing."

"Sounds dull to me."

"It wasn't. Anyway, I don't wish to speak of it," she added, as the memory of how disagreeable the gipsy had become returned to her.

"Very well, we shan't," he assented.

They sat for a little time looking at the fire in the grate, neither of them speaking. Jessica felt somehow that she ought to leave, but it was really rather pleasant, being in company yet not obliged to talk. She reached for a magazine on a nearby table and began to leaf through it when Algernon interrupted her.

"There is a story I think you might like to hear," he told her. "Do you mind if I ring for Frant?"

"Of course not. Why do you wish to?"

"It is his story," he said, a trifle obscurely. Frant, who had been born and raised at Grasmere and served Her Grace as head-butler for decades, appeared presently and inquired what was wanted.

"Mr. Frant, I think you will recall the conversation we had yesterday, regarding the Earl of Huntingdon."

"Yes, indeed, sir," the butler replied, still standing in the doorway.

"Would you be so kind as to come in and repeat it to Miss Cawley? She will like to hear it."

"It really is not necessary, Frant—" Jessica began to say.

"Sit down, please. Be comfortable," Algernon interrupted. "Just tell her what you told me."

The butler sat, a little nervously, on the edge of a small settee. He settled his hands, frail with age, on his knees, looked uncertainly from Longstreth to Miss Cawley, and began. "The Earl of Huntingdon was an outlaw," said he, "whom people round these parts believe to have taken on the name Robin Hood, and made himself into a hero."

"Ah, Mr. Longstreth, why do you torture me so?" Jessica exclaimed, with mock agony.

Frant was startled. "Shall I continue, sir?"

"Pray do."

"If the lady doesn't care for it—"

"Never mind the lady; she doesn't know what she cares for."

"If you say so, sir. Anyhow, the story is that Fitzooth—that's the earl's family name, miss—dined one Christmas Eve with the master of Grasmere. Of course, the castle has changed a great deal since then, but there was a Grasmere even in those days. The master, so they tell it, offered his guest a fine dinner, a seat at the top of the board, music to soothe him and dancers to entertain him—everything, in short, which the master of a castle could offer to a visitor in those days. Fitzooth ate and drank and enjoyed himself heartily, toasting master and mistress, and all their children; for though he mistrusted the rich he was willing, at Christmastide, to forgive for a moment and accept his host's hospitality.

The ladies retired, but the gentlemen sat awake till far into the night, drinking cup upon cup of wine and wassail. One by one they dropped to the floor, sleeping and—my lady will excuse me—drunk, until only the host and the outlaw remained. 'Well,' said Fitzooth, 'I suppose we must follow the lead of our friends. Where is my bed?' But the master surprised him. 'You have no bed,' said he, 'save a bed of new-fallen snow. Go from here, and lie upon it.' Fitzooth understood he had been duped. His host's hospitality lasted only until he was thoroughly intoxicated and spent. Then he was to quit the fireside, and trudge through the snow and mid-night to shelter.

"Fitzooth knew he had been played for a fool, but he forbore even then to repay the cruelty in kind. On another night the master would have got his due, but on the eve of our Saviour's birth—no. The guest left as he had come, alone and with his honour intact, but betrayed. That's all there is to the story, miss," Frant added, looking into the fire.

"Ah, Frant, you wrong me!" cried Algernon. "What of his ghost?"

The butler assumed a low tone, and leaned toward the gentleman. "I thought perhaps you would not like to frighten the young lady . . ."

"On the contrary. Or rather, she is incapable of fright. Tell her, tell her," said Longstreth with a smile.

"Very well, then. It is said that the ghost returns to Grasmere every year at Christmastide. He walks in the picture gallery—the banquet hall that was—and looks for the man who betrayed him. Yet still he forbears to harm him, being still a man—or rather, a spectre, as you might say—of honour."

"Did you make this poor man go through that whole story only to end with this?" Miss Cawley inquired.

"Do you believe in the ghost?" Algernon asked him, ignoring her question completely.

Frant had stood and begun to go to the door, but he checked himself at once. "But of course I do, sir. Everyone does. There's no question of believing, sir; you may hear him yourself, if you like. We all have—all the staff, I mean—though once was enough for me."

"Mr. Frant, you can't be serious," Jessica objected.

"Begging your pardon, miss, I am quite serious. There's no need to fear it—it never hurts a soul, as I say. Only it is a bit crawly, hearing those great footsteps and feeling that chill. I was twelve the last time I cared to listen, but I haven't forgot it."

"Really, Mr. Frant—" she began.

"Thank you, Frant," Algernon broke in. "That will be all."

The butler took one final glance at Miss Cawley, bowed his greying head, and retired. There was nothing in his manner, or in anything she knew of him, to suggest he was superstitious; on the contrary, he was a very gentle, well-spoken, deserving old man. In one of the under-maids Jessica could have comprehended such an unswerving belief in what could not possibly be, but Frant (who probably knew more of Grasmere than Karr himself, and had more to do with the household than the duchess) presented a puzzle.

Still, she shrugged and said lightly, "These old tales die hard. It was a curious story, however."

"You do not believe him?" Mr. Longstreth inquired.

She looked annoyed. "Certainly not. Don't you recall—he said the last time he had heard the ghost was when he was twelve years old. That is fifty years ago or more, I should guess. We heard only the testimony of an excited boy, whether Frant himself chuses to recognize that fact or not."

Mr. Longstreth regarded her and shook his head sadly. "I worry for you, dear Miss Cawley; truly I do. With your blasphemy, and your ring . . . I only hope it brings you no evil."

Evil! There was that word again. Jessica sprang up and shook out her skirts briskly, giving a nervous little laugh. "Mr. Longstreth, if you are half as silly as you pretend to be I can only hope that *you* will stay out of trouble. If you do, it will be through no virtue of your own."

Algernon refused to laugh with her, but eyed her soberly. It was all too foolish, these vague warnings and whispers of misfortune; she curtsied to him in silence and started toward the drawing-room, where the others had gathered. Finding herself a bit tired, however, of a sudden, she changed the direction of her steps, repassed the door of the sitting-room, and went unannounced to bed.

5

"I trust your mother has not been revisited by her affliction," Lord Wyborn intoned in the emphatic accents he appeared to think appropriate to an earl—an earl, moreover, whose person, rank, and fortune made him one of the most eligible *partis* in England.

"Oh, no, sir," said Amabel Stanton, frightened lest the imposing gentleman on whom her hopes (one might almost say, despairs) were pinned should suppose ill health was a part of her inheritance. "She is quite as strong now as ever—very strong. We are very strong," she hastened to add.

They sat together in the Rose Saloon, alone. There had been others before: after dinner a number of the company had gathered there to discuss the most recent news from London, the results of the day's shooting, and to make up parties for amusements. Little by little they had removed themselves to other parts of the castle—first the love-stricken Stickneys, then the Contessa di Tremini, then Septimus Faust. Amabel had held her breath at each departure, praying more and more fervently that somehow, by whatever miracle or act of God, Lord Wyborn would decline to join each departing group until only he and she remained. Her suspense mounted: now only Mr. Hightower was left with them. Would he never go? Did he even think of going? Perhaps he meant to stop there all night. It certainly seemed to Miss Stanton that he had been there an age already, making desultory conversation with Wyborn and herself, and humming just audibly while he tapped the arms of his chair. Go, go! She hardly dared stir herself, fearful that even the suggestion of restlessness might cause Wyborn to leave the saloon. Helpless, she glared at Ralph when he was not looking at her and smiled feebly when he glanced her way. Surely there was no other gentleman in the world so thick-skulled as he. Could he not see how urgent it was that she be alone with Wyborn? Was he blind, or an idiot? At last, eons (it seemed) since dinner, Mr. Ralph Hightower bethought himself of billiards, and rose. "I rather think I'll join Sir Isaac and the others," said he. "Care to join me, Wyborn?"

Ah, no! Not all this waiting for nothing! please, please decline to join him. She fairly squirmed while Hightower lingered.

"Thank you," said Lord Wyborn, and took the longest pause anyone ever had taken before he continued, "but no. One can tire even of billiards, and I believe I've had sufficient for now."

Miss Amabel Stanton felt she would shriek for joy (she did not, though). Her relief was overwhelming—but then a new tension began. Now she was alone with him; he had chosen to be with her; it could not have been accident. What would he say to her, and she to him? Ought she to address him first, or wait? If she did the former he might think her forward; if the latter, dull. Her breath became laboured and irregular; it seemed terribly stultifying in the beautifully hung saloon. She thought of her vinaigrette, and would have liked a whiff very much, but that would look so odd. She did nothing but wait, and endeavour to maintain a semblance of calm.

And now finally he had spoke. He had asked her a question—a rather bland question, it was true, but that was far better than if he had suggested they join the others in the drawing-room. And she had answered, and apparently he was not totally disgusted with her yet. Poor Amabel felt her entire family depending on her to marry Wyborn; it was not that they had no money, or no position of their own, but Lord Wyborn had been chosen for her, pointed out to her: it was the first, the only thing her parents had ever asked of her, and she felt she must die if she failed. If only his lordship would offer for her!

"You are fortunate," announced the remarkable, eligible man. "Ill health is a great burden upon a family."

Amabel's soft, round face strove mightily to match Wyborn's serious expression. "Oh, indeed—a very great burden! I should never dream of being ill," she added absurdly, in her eagerness to please him.

"I am certain you would not," said he.

There was a silence. "Oh, never," she repeated faintly.

"Your father shoots very well," said Wyborn at last. "Your father is an excellent shot. An excellent man."

"So he is, indeed. I am of the same opinion. One must be."

"Certainly *you* must. He is your father."

"Precisely! He is my father."

"Miss Stanton," the earl began, breaking off to clear his throat loudly and rising from his chair.

(Dear God, don't let him leave! thought she.)

"Miss Stanton," he repeated, stationing himself near the mantelpiece and regarding her steadily. He was a very large man, with dark hair turning to silver at the temples, a raw complexion, and an alarmingly concentrated light in his heavy-lidded green eyes. "Miss Stanton," he pronounced once more.

"My lord?" she dared to answer.

"Miss Stanton, I have taken the liberty of hoping—albeit silently—that you might do me the honour to become my wife."

Ah! there it was! Yet he continued to speak.

"Your beauty, your gentleness, your fond obedience to your parents all recommend themselves to me. Moreover, I am satisfied to reflect that an alliance between the house of Wyborn and your own family is not altogether incongruous. On your mother's side you are a Baddesleigh, and though I have not the happiness of being acquainted with the earl your grandfather, I know the name to be ancient and impeccable. Your father, of course—as we agreed even now—is an excellent gentleman. I have hesitated to address him on this subject as yet—otherwise than obliquely, I mean—until I might broach it to you. If you will permit me to hope, I will discuss the matter with him; if you chuse to disappoint me at once, however, it will be as if I had never suggested it. Can you give me an answer now? I am not afraid to wait, though naturally to be kept in suspense would be painful."

Could she give him an answer? Amabel was not the least taken in by his pretensions to ignorance: he knew what her answer would be, and knew also her father's certain acquiescence. It seemed awfully flat merely to say yes—but then it had been a flat proposal, too. She tried to think of a pretty speech.

"My very good sir," she commenced, not daring to look at him, "you do me a most valuable honour. Perhaps I ought to blush, or hesitate, but I would not for the world subject you to needless discomfort. I will be most happy to become your wife—if, as you say, my father has no objections."

It was unpleasant for her to maintain this charade but she assured herself it would soon be over. The chief point was that he had offered for her, and she had accepted: now it was but a question of formalities. Her thoughts, heady with relief, were interrupted by Lord Wyborn's coming toward her from the fireplace and reaching for her hand.

She gave it him. "My dear Miss Stanton," he said, kissing it lightly and making a shallow bow, "you give me great joy. Let us hope every future question between us will be determined with so much accord and candour."

He had straightened himself again and stood looking at her as if for some sort of response.

"Indeed," was all she could think to say. "Let us hope so."

In a little while they separated, she to apprise her mother of the long-awaited good tidings, he to seek out her father. Little more had been said between them, and certainly nothing more done. The question had been asked, answered, settled. Neither lady nor gentleman had smiled once during the entire interview.

Meantime, a great deal of smiling was being done in a smallish apartment not far away, an apartment known as the study—although no one, it seemed, ever pursued any scholarly researches there. The smiles belonged half to the master of the castle, half to Lotta Chilton. They had met after tea in the Oval Saloon, where Lady Henrietta Helms was playing a very precise rendition of an air by Mozart, and had departed (one after the other) as if by tacit agreement, to meet again in the apartment mentioned above. Lotta had left first, and sat, when the duke came in, once again engaged with her filagree. She made no pretence, however, of being surprised at his having followed her out from the Oval Saloon. Rather she looked up and smiled, nodding to his slight bow, and proceeded with her work in silence, as if it were as natural as could be that Karr and she should share the pleasures of a cosy fire and an unhurried, unnecessary conversation.

"Your fingers work busily," Karr remarked after a time, "but not so busily as your mind, I sometimes think." His brown eyes rested upon her, deep with interest and bright with curiosity.

She favoured him with a rather mysterious smile, saying nothing.

"I was only pretending to make an observation, you know," he took up again. "Really I was asking you a question."

"I know you were," she replied serenely.

"Won't you tell me?"

"Whether my mind is so well employed as my hands?" she said. "I never tell secrets unless I am certain of a comparable return."

"My hands being utterly idle, I hope it would be superfluous to inform you I am thinking faster than they are moving."

"I said a comparable return, not an identical one," she pointed out. "You are inquiring into my character; I should like leave to inquire into yours."

"You have leave, Miss Chilton."

"Very well, then: yes, I may say I think a good deal more industriously than I thread beads. My mind is never at rest, and only very rarely occupied by less than three subjects. Also, I hear music."

"That is Lady Henrietta," he said, with the very faintest hint of irony.

"I meant, I hear music whether Lady Henrietta is playing or not. Generally, in fact, more music when she is not."

"Ah, you are unkind!"

"Do you believe me to be so?" she asked, with a fresh smile—this one broader and yet even more mysterious than the last. The candle-light lit up her fine eyes and transparent complexion; it glinted in the thicknesses of her plaited hair and fell on her bare white shoulders.

Karr hesitated. "Not everyone is so musical as you. Lady Henrietta's proficiency cost her great efforts."

"And I think she ought to be rewarded for those efforts," Lotta said promptly; "but I do not think we ought to be punished for them."

"Ah, you *are* unkind," he repeated, with new emphasis.

Miss Chilton put her work aside and fixed him with a clear eye. "Your Grace," she said, "do you enjoy Lady Henrietta's playing?"

Again, he paused. "No. Not particularly."

"And has anything I have said been otherwise than true?" she pursued.

He thought. "No," he agreed reluctantly.

"Then why do you take me to task? Lady Henrietta is a very worthy person: she is not in need of my kindness, nor have I any need to be cruel to her. My remarks regarded her playing only, which we have both admitted to be not to our tastes. I am not unkind; I am only frank. Harsh, if you like."

"I shouldn't like that at all."

"No more should I." She took up her filagree again and said nothing for some moments. "It is time for my question," she said at length; "I have earned it."

"I will answer it, so it be comparable to mine."

"It will be. I should like to know, Your Grace, how you enjoy being the Duke of Karr? Is it a boon or a burden? We are told in church—at least I was—not to envy the great, for their lot is as onerous as ours. Is it?"

"Damme, I wish I had asked you a more difficult question!" he exclaimed. "This is hardly fair."

"Will you cry craven, then?"

"No, I won't, Miss Chilton," he said, standing on these words and advancing a little ways toward her. He quite towered over her in this attitude, and his strong chin looked very firm indeed. "You are extremely inquisitive, aren't you?" he asked.

"My answer first," she stipulated. "If I like it, perhaps we shall have another exchange of queries."

"Indeed. To be the Duke of Karr, since you ask, is both a boon and a burden. It is like everything else in this world, neither entirely pleasure nor entirely pain. It is like, as a wit would say, a woman."

"It is like, as I should reply to that hypothetical wit, a man. Fortunately, there are no wits here."

"Certainly I haven't any," he murmured.

"But how is it good, and how ill? You don't go into particulars," she objected, returning to her question.

"Did you?"

"There are all too many points of interrogation in this little talk," she complained after a minute. "It is beginning to sound like a court of law."

"At the risk of exacerbating the situation, may I ask you if I have told you yet how utterly exquisite you are? If I did not, it was gross oversight."

Lotta began to colour, at first slowly, then very rapidly. "Thank you," she said, working furiously at her filagree.

"Ah, if I had known you turned from a compliment—! You are like a flower that closes when the sun burns too brightly."

She was genuinely embarrassed, but she contrived to speak lightly in spite of it. "You, then, are the sun?"

"Miss Chilton, you are unkind!" he exclaimed for the third time.

"I thought I had dissuaded you of that," she said, looking up and beginning to feel more comfortable. "If I am unkind, you are obstinate."

"To that I must plead guilty. If I did not confess it, my mother would prove it for you. All the evidence is on her side, I fear."

Lotta held his gaze with her own for a long minute, as if balancing between saying something and holding her peace. She weighed, judged, spoke at last. "Lady Henrietta?" she hazarded finally.

His firm mouth tightened at the suggestion, and he stared at her just as fixedly as she had at him. Finally he nodded. "My mother is nearly in despair."

"Think of Lady Henrietta's mother!" she laughed.

"You are at liberty to take it lightly, but I assure you the situation grows graver every day. Twice I have been on the point of addressing Lord Marland," he commenced, and checked himself suddenly.

"You feel you have said too much."

"Much too much."

"So do I," she agreed, and sat wordless for a while.

"But when it comes to that—" he began, looking at her bent head, her white shoulders, the sheen on her blue satin gown—"I am in need of a confidant," he ended at last. He started to walk the length of the room, turned as he reached one panelled wall and headed back again to the other.

"You may rely on my discretion," she said. "I have been accused of many things—unkindness, most recently—but never of indiscretion."

"Yes, but . . . it isn't as if I couldn't talk to Longstreth, or Remington—or any of them. All my intimates are here; even an older man might answer the purpose; more experience, you know . . ."

"But those are men," she said quietly. "You need a woman."

He paused in his pacing and looked at her strangely. "Yes, come to think of it, I do. I'm not certain why it is, but I do."

"Then talk to me," she suggested, still softly, but with a sensible intonation. "I know most of it anyway."

"Doubtless," he returned. "It is no wonder your eyes are so very, very large. You must see many things with them."

"I see you are not happy about the future Her Grace anticipates for you."

"Then you see more than Lord Marland," he said, almost bitterly. "He, I sometimes think, has already written and franked the announcement for the *Gazette*. He only waits to send it away."

"And your offering for his daughter is a mere technicality," she guessed.

"Precisely." Karr stalked the room moodily now, his aspect more meditative than she had ever seen it.

"It is a very reasonable match," Lotta pointed out judiciously.

"Yes, it is a very reasonable match. And Lady Henrietta is a very good woman, a gracious woman, a gentlewoman in manner and rank. Marland was a friend to my father long before I was born, and the connexion would make my mother very glad. It is a very reasonable match," he repeated, then added abruptly (and rather loudly), "but I don't *want* a reasonable match!"

"Of course you do not."

"Of course?" he echoed. "Why of course? By rights I ought to—after all, it is all for my own happiness and comfort, for the sake of my name and my children. I am too old, don't you see, to be pouting and rebelling, like a school-room miss who does not care for to dance with her childhood playmate."

"You are very hard on yourself."

"It is my duty to be hard on myself."

"It is no one's duty to be harder than is necessary," said Lotta Chilton. "It is only a formula for unhappiness."

He glanced at her, puzzled. "Then you think I ought to disappoint Marland—after all that has been done, and is expected?"

"I did not say that," she replied swiftly. "I said only that it is foolish to do what is disagreeable simply on the principle that what is disagreeable must be right. I might observe, however," she continued after a moment, "that you speak in terms of disappointing Lord Marland. Do you not fear to disappoint Lady Henrietta?"

"Oh, Lady Henrietta—" he spat out, as if in disgust, then looked at her with as much surprise as if it had been she who said it. "Heyday, what am I saying?"

"I'm not certain," she answered. "What are you saying?"

"I *can't* feel that way about her," he exclaimed, aghast.

"Can't you?"

"Can I?" He turned away from her once more and paced about, knocking a doubled fist against the panelled wall as a ruder man might strike his own head. "Things do not seem to be growing any clearer," he stated at last, returning to the chair he had originally occupied.

"It depends on what you wished to see."

"I'm afraid I don't follow you," he said.

"Suppose you were looking for a painting," she suggested, "in a dark hallway. You have an idea where the picture hangs; you hold up your candle and pass through the corridor. When you reach the spot where you expect to find it, you hold up the taper to the frame—only to find that it encloses, not the picture, but a mirror. Imagine how baffling it might be to encounter your own image of a sudden, rather than the portrait you expected. It would seem almost as if nothing had been illuminated—since what was illuminated was not what you wished to see."

He sighed. "Miss Chilton, you are becoming distinctly philosophical," he said, sounding almost annoyed. "I had hoped you would be practical."

Lotta considered. "Sometimes one must be one to be the other," she concluded. "I apologize if I seem not to be helping you. Perhaps you ought to sleep on the matter."

"I have slept on nothing else these past two weeks," he said darkly. "It makes a most uncomfortable pillow."

"Lumpish?" she suggested, smiling.

"Just hard," he replied, and lapsed into silence.

Lotta fell to silence too, and when (a few minutes later) Lady Louisa Bridwell poked her head into the doorway of the study, she found there no conversation to interrupt. She was excited, and entered the room on a rather peculiar step, something between a hop and a leap. The sight of her plump figure sailing thus jerkily into the apartment attracted the attention of both its occupants, and they looked to her expectantly.

"News!" she cried. "Great news!"

"And what is that, Lady Louisa?" asked Karr, bowing.

"Miss Stanton is to marry Wyborn," she fairly shouted in reply, then immediately lowered her voice and repeated in a whisper, "Miss Stanton and Lord Wyborn—they are betrothed." She stood beaming at Karr, then at Miss Chilton, as if she herself had arranged the happy event expressly to please them.

"That is very well," said His Grace, smiling politely. "I must find him and felicitate him."

"And I may go and wish her happy, I suppose. She will need it."

"Miss Chilton, what do you mean?" inquired her ladyship. "Do you not think they will be happy? Her Grace is simply ecstatic!"

"My mother, ecstatic?" the duke echoed. "Impossible."

"Well, not ecstatic then, perhaps," she conceded, "but very satisfied."

"Not entirely indifferent, you mean," said Karr, who had naturally known Lady Louisa since he was in leading-strings, and therefore saw no reason to be indirect with her.

"Karr, she did interest herself in this match, you know," said her ladyship somewhat reproachfully. "Really, I don't know why you imagine your mother to be so cold-hearted."

"Don't you really?"

"Ah, my dear—" she began, a trifle despairingly. "In any case, she is certainly much interested in *your* marriage. She says very little, but I know she thinks of it constantly."

His Grace exchanged a brief glance with Miss Chilton, as if to say, "You see?" "I do not doubt it," he said aloud, after a moment. "Will you ladies pardon me? I shall go seek out Lord Wyborn."

Lady Louisa stood in the middle of the study, fidgeting noticeably. "He's such a dear boy," she remarked after a time to Lotta. "I've never known him to be unreasonable, except about his marriage. You don't mind my talking to you this way, my dear; it is only—it quite over-sets me to see Her Grace out of charity with him. She says nothing, as I told him, but I know how her heart must ache. You don't understand it now, of course, but when you have a little boy of your own you will."

"Have you a little boy?" asked Miss Chilton, tilting her head to one side.

Lady Louisa stared at her blankly. "No. No, I haven't. But that only makes Karr all the more dear to me," she told her.

"I see," said Lotta, smiling to herself.

"You know it is a *very* good connexion, especially for the Stantons. *Her* family is all very well, but he—he never had much property, you know; never will have. It is all on her ladyship's side. I am even a trifle surprised Wyborn came round. Why do you think little Amabel will be unhappy?"

Lotta hesitated, then replied gently, "I fear the achievement of a fortunate alliance is but slender comfort for a young girl about to marry a man twice her age. I imagine Lord Wyborn must seem a very great personage to Amabel—quite frightening, in fact."

"Oh, yes," said her ladyship, toying with the fringe on her gown and blinking nervously at Lotta; "but all young girls are frightened of their husbands. It doesn't mean anything; you oughtn't to regard it. She'll be over that in a moment."

"Were you frightened of Sir Isaac?" the logical question came.

Her ladyship's eyes rounded themselves in another stare. "I? Frightened of Sir Isaac? Why goodness no—who could be?"

"But then—"

"It only makes me all the more certain Miss Stanton will soon cease to be intimidated by her betrothed," Lady Louisa anticipated her. "And now, Miss Chilton, I really must go. There are so many people to be told, so many festivities to be thought of—! You will pardon me," she added over her shoulder, taking herself off with that strangely shuffling flutter which seemed so natural to her. Miss Chilton made as if to follow her, but changed her mind: tomorrow morning would be time enough to communicate her felicitations to the happy couple. There were many drawbacks to being the least significant personage in the party at Grasmere, but there was also an advantage, she thought, in being frequently forgot.

She was correct in supposing no one would notice her lapse in courtesy; all the parties involved in the impending nuptials had had quite enough of congratulations by the time they retired to their chambers. The duchess, pleased (as Lady Louisa had reported) by the knowledge that the Stantons had got what they came for, insisted on contriving an impromptu ball, to take place on the following evening, in honour of the betrothal. Amabel herself was soon fatigued by the exercise of receiving everyone's best wishes, and of having to glance at Lord Wyborn as if she loved him—or really, even knew him. Her brother, poor young fellow, had received instructions to the effect that he must welcome Lord Wyborn into the family with words as polite (Wyborn was a correct man) and warm (Wyborn was a lonely man) as any he could summon. These instructions came from Lord Stanton, of course, who had already made clear to his son his displeasure at Chauncey's inordinate admiration of the contessa: that interview had made Chauncey even a bit more frightened of his father than he already had been (and he had been quite frightened), but this new commission utterly terrified him. Though he did not feel too young to gape at the contessa, he did feel a good deal too young to be charged with such a heavy duty (as it seemed to him); he passed an hour and a half alone in his chamber framing the sentences he would speak to the earl, then found—on emerging at last—that his lordship had already gone to bed. The embarrassing failure then had to be confessed to his father, and Chauncey retired feeling very much mortified, as well as extravagantly ill-used.

The children asleep, Lord and Lady Stanton were at liberty to speak to one another privately, which they accordingly did in the comfortable suite of apartments they shared. The gist of their talk, however, was not at all what one might have expected—nor was their tone exultant. Lady Stanton, indeed, appeared distinctly anxious; and her husband was nearly as edgy as she.

"Naturally it is a relief," said her ladyship, clarifying, "Amabel, I mean. But I can't help thinking about—"

"You ought to try," Lord Walker Stanton interrupted her.

"But I cannot," she emphasized. "What can be taking so long?

Joseph ought to have sent word today—he ought to be arriving tomorrow. Perhaps we should send again. Matthew might go . . ."

"Another day, another day. Patience, my dear," Lord Stanton recommended. "Joseph will return. We have only to wait."

She regarded him fretfully. "And then?"

"And then we hand the money to her, and all is secure."

Lady Stanton was silent for a moment, gazing at her own pale hands.
"I think we are being naïve. Why should she leave us alone, when she has
us treed so perfectly?"

"Those were the terms we agreed upon," he reminded his wife. "She
promised to leave us alone."

"I should be happy to leave here tomorrow," said her ladyship after a
pause. "I very nearly fainted again today."

"It would solve nothing to depart," he said reasonably, over his
shoulder. He was pacing up and down the room, as he frequently did,
while he talked to his wife. "In fact, it is probably better to be present,
where we may keep an eye upon her."

"And she upon us. I wish she did not know about Amabel and Wyborn. It makes it all too clear what a position she puts us in. At another
moment one might endeavour to—" she breathed deeply, "—to brave the
scandal . . ."

"Never," said he, striding ever more rapidly. "It would mean the loss
of everything, all rank, all happiness for the children. I admit, a freshly
arranged match seems to make it all worse, but I should have yielded to
her under any circumstances."

Lady Stanton sighed.

"We have nothing to do but hope she keeps her word," said her husband, alighting beside her at last and passing an arm round her waist,
for comfort. "And in the interim, we may be glad for Amabel."

"I suppose," she answered listlessly.

They rested there a moment. "You haven't received anything more
from her, have you?" his lordship queried, as if it were a startling after-
thought.

"Nothing since she dealt me that note," she returned. "Do you think
we should leave another letter for her?" she added. "I asked her for
more time, but she never acknowledged the request."

"What does it matter?" he shrugged. "Another note more or less . . .
Though perhaps it will be best, in principle, to commit as little as possible to paper. Things are bad enough as they stand."

"Ah, yes, they are," she sighed again. She held herself very still against him for a moment, then shuddered all at once and began to cry. "Oh, Walker, I am so ashamed, so sorry! If it had not been for me, my folly— I ought never to have accepted you, after what had passed . . . Only it seemed so cruel to have to suffer all one's life for—!"

Lord Stanton attempted to hush her at every word, but they continued to spill out.

"My father was certain—I was certain . . . no one else could have known. I still can't believe she knows! How could she? How?"

"Perhaps . . . My only guess is that she met—ah—him, once," said his lordship. "That he told her, for some reason. If so, he was a wretch."

"Ah, God, who was he? It is all so long ago, I hardly know. I was so green then, a green girl—and even when I met you—or I should never have accepted . . ."

"I knew what I was doing," he said, a trifle sternly. "There is not need for you to take yourself to task. For what is happening now I am as responsible as yourself. I knew when I married you. There were no secrets, and I do not feel misused."

"You are so good," she fairly sobbed, burying her face on his shoulder and clutching at his familiar form. "So good," she whimpered. "I am ashamed."

But Lord Stanton could not let this pass, and he assured her again— and again and again, as it turned out—that she was no more to blame than he. When she had shed very, very many tears, and been reassured a dozen times, her remorse at last subsided somewhat, and permitted her to enjoy some hours of sleep. Lord Stanton did not quit her side all night, and his unfailing kindness and devotion to her were all that seemed good in a life otherwise filled with terror and regret.

6

"Then you *will* build a stage?" said Miss Cawley the next day, leaning earnestly toward the duchess over a small table where the remains of a nuncheon were still visible.

Her Grace raised her heavy eyebrows, a sign that she was amused. "Why is it so significant to you?" she asked, in a voice as sharp and crisp as the tiny pleats in the bodice of her forest-green morning gown.

"Oh, it is not so significant," Jessica lied carelessly, adding a little, indifferent-sounding sigh for the sake of verisimilitude. "I only thought . . . with so many people in the castle, and winter drawing on so very rapidly . . . I only thought it might be diverting."

"Who taught you to appear disinterested in the things you want most?" the duchess inquired. "It is not like you. Have you been taking lessons from Miss Chilton?"

Miss Chilton, who was sitting beside her mistress during this tête-à-tête, looked up at her with an expression of inquisitive surprise. "I beg your pardon, Your Grace?"

"There is no need to beg my pardon," said the great lady irritably. "Finish your roast beef."

This sufficed to hush Lotta, though she did not do as she was bid. In a moment a footman arrived to remove the half-emptied plates, asking the duchess, as he went, if anything else was wanted.

"No," she said, then, "yes. We shall want a stage in the ball-room. Tell Frant to arrange it."

"Ah, madam, you do my heart good," cried Jessica, springing up from her chair and running round the table to her generous hostess. The duchess, who did not care for spontaneous demonstrations of affection, stiffened as she guessed her young guest's intention, and held out a white hand to forestall any embracements. Miss Cawley took the hand and kissed it—though she knew it had not been extended for that purpose—and proceeded to embrace Miss Chilton. "It will be a famous performance, you'll see," she promised. "Oh, and won't Cosmo Remington be pleased. He is too timid to pay you his addresses on his own; this is his perfect opportunity."

"Cosmo Remington?" the duchess pounced. "Has he taken a fancy to Lotta?"

"I should say so," Miss Cawley told her, as she pursued her way back to her seat. "Who could not, however?" The duchess was silent for a moment, prompting Jessica to add, "Don't you like it?"

"Like it?" she murmured vaguely. "'How does Miss Chilton like it? That is what interests me."

Jessica's pert head tilted to a sharp angle, and her eyes brightened. "I don't know," she confessed. "How do you like it, Lotta?"

Miss Chilton, feeling somewhat uneasy at the presence of her august employer, paused before answering, "I am indifferent to it, chiefly. Though it occurs to me to hope Mr. Remington does not mean too much by it. If he felt a serious—regard for me, for example, it might be awkward. However, I trust it is only a brief interest."

"But why, Lotta?" Jessica asked. "He is very sweet—really, a very sweet man. And there is nothing to impede a marriage, you know; he's only a younger son, after all." These words, she felt on considering, had come out a bit brusque, and she tried to correct their effect by adding, "Not, you understand, that you aren't fit for—for anyone, but . . ." She concluded, too late, that there was nothing to be said to temper the sad reality.

Lotta smiled, aware at least of Jessica's good intentions. "You may say it," she assured her. "I am not sensitive about it. There is not a gentleman at Grasmere whose family would not be distressed to hear of a betrothal to me—and I can't blame them a bit. My origins are genteel at best—and that is only their superficial aspect. Beneath that, they may almost be said to be unknown."

"But you told me your father's name—" Jessica began to object.

"But I did not tell you my mother's. The Chiltons never told me, either."

"You did not ask?" the duchess caught at this.

"It seems very odd, no doubt, but I did not. I toyed with the possibility, at one time, but concluded it was best to leave the past where it was. I am certain the Chiltons felt the same; that is why they never mentioned it." Lotta looked from one lady to the other, as if hoping one of them would assure her they did not think her behaviour peculiar.

No assurance came, however. Instead, there was a lull in the conversation, after which Miss Cawley took up again the topic of the play. "Karr has agreed to play Mirabell, you know," she informed that gentleman's mother.

"Has he?" she asked in surprise. "I hope you will make Lady Henrietta Mistress Millamant, then."

Jessica heard her and coloured. "I was to play Millamant," she said in a low tone.

"Indeed?" said the duchess, the dark brows rising again.

"Not because of—what you think," Jessica defended herself, her colour dying down a bit. "Only for the diversion of it."

"If it is all the same to you, then, give the part to Henrietta. Or let Karr play Fainall, and Henrietta Mrs. Marwood."

Jessica's blush rose once more. "Mrs. Marwood is given to Lotta."

"And Fainall to Cosmo Remington," the duchess guessed. "I see."

Jessica frowned for a moment—pouted, would describe it more nearly —before she resigned herself to the inevitable. "Very well, ma'am," she conceded. "Since you have shown yourself so generous in the matter of a stage, I suppose it is only courteous to allow you to distribute the rôles as you will. I will make a list of them," she said, rising and crossing to a small escritoire in a corner of the apartment.

"You make a grudging gift," Her Grace observed, though without refusing it.

"Yours are not entirely free of consequences either," Jessica retorted, referring to the stage.

"My heavens, she is impertinent!" exclaimed the duchess to Miss Chilton. "You ought not to associate with her; you are bad enough as it is."

Again Miss Chilton regarded her with surprise. "I am sorry if I have displeased you," she offered.

"Dear, dear, one worse than the next. Where is Septimus? He is the only person I know who neither weeps nor hisses at a criticism."

Lotta still desired an explanation, but she knew her place. "Shall I find Mr. Faust for you?" she asked.

"No—no," said the *grande dame,* idly plucking the petals from a conservatory rose which adorned the table before her. The petals fell on the white cloth, scarlet and rather pretty; but she soon swept them away and contradicted herself, "Well, yes after all. Tell him to meet me in the study, in half an hour. You are at your leisure until dinner-time."

Lotta was not quite certain, but she guessed this last pronouncement meant that she was not to return to Her Grace after she had completed her errand—whether she wished to or no. She accordingly stayed away while the duchess and Miss Cawley wrangled over who was to play whom in "The Way of the World." Jessica told her later, though, precisely what had happened. The duchess had decided her son had too many obligations to take so large a part as Mirabell's, and had consigned to him the part of Waitwell. Henrietta was opposite to him, of course. Jessica had been obliged to return to the initial notion of using Long-streth for Mirabell—it was all the same to her, really . . . though she had liked the thought of Karr as the hero. Miss Chilton and Mr. Remington were the only ones, herself excepted, who had remained in the places agreed upon on the day of Goose-Fair; the duchess insisted upon letting Faust play Witwoud, and Jessica came upon the happy idea of letting her brother Roger play Sir Wilfull.

"But he is such a clown," Lotta protested. "Poor Lord Cawley!"

"Oh—pooh," said Jessica. "It was that or Petulant, and I will not have my brother playing a fool's fool."

"Who will play Petulant, then?"

"Do you know, I was in agonies over the question; I could not think of anyone. Then it came to me—Hightower!"

"Hightower?" Lotta Chilton repeated.

"Yes—Ralph Hightower. You know him, surely. The gentleman with the—well, he is not too tall, but not short either . . . and he has rather a—well, I don't know what to call it—" the other floundered.

"Oh, Mr. Hightower! Of course, I remember him."

"I am so glad you do," said Jessica, with authentic relief. "I had no idea how to describe him. Anyway, he will play Petulant, and little Amabel Stanton is Mincing, and as for Lady Wishfort—" she paused as if about to deliver the *coup de grâce.*

"Yes?" Lotta prompted.

"And for Lady Wishfort, Lady Louisa Bridwell. Don't you think so?" she asked with a grin.

"Ah, certainly! Exactly! But did Her Grace agree to that?"

"Without a murmur. She has no compunction whatever about sacrificing the dignity of her friends to her own amusement."

"And then, Lady Louisa has not a very great deal of dignity to sacrifice," Lotta smiled.

"Precisely." Jessica sat hugging her knees—the two young women were in the little sitting-room which opened off her bed-chamber—and looking dreamily off into space. "There is only one problem," she said at last. "I have no Mistress Fainall."

Miss Chilton thought. "Lady Madeline Olney?" she suggested at last.

"I'm afraid so—if she can be persuaded, that is. If it is not she, it must be the Contessa di Tremini, and I have a terrible conviction I should regret such a choice."

"She is very beautiful," Lotta pointed out. "She will double the enthusiasm of the audience every time she faces them."

"I know, I know," said Jessica broodingly. "I only think . . . first of all, I wonder if she will agree to it. She has not said she would be in the play, that I know of."

"Give her a pretty costume. She'll agree."

Miss Cawley smiled. "Very true, no doubt. But even so . . . she will make a very curious Mistress Fainall. She would do better in your part. I think she is deceitful," Jessica confided of a sudden.

"Do you? How?"

The other lady frowned at this. "I can't say. Just somehow."

"In other words, a baseless suspicion."

"Not entirely baseless," said Jessica, taking no offense at the implied stricture. "I have some experience in reading human character, you know, and there is something in her eyes . . . in her gestures . . ."

"As a good Christian, I am obliged to suggest you would not see that 'something' in her eyes if they did not shine so brightly, nor in her gestures if they were not so graceful."

"You accuse me of envy?"

"You accuse her of duplicity."

"And I accuse you of high priggishness, the worst crime of all," cried Jessica, but without malice. "You are very good, aren't you, under all that prettiness and candour?"

Miss Chilton smiled mischievously. "Are you disappointed?"

"Not disappointed so much as . . . Oh dear, not disappointed at all: let us confess it at once. I am not wicked enough myself to welcome wickedness in others. I should like to be," she added.

"It is a pretty romance," Miss Chilton agreed.

"But we always come to good in the end, don't we? That's the way of it, with women like us."

"And grow to be very old maids, with sharp tongues and a universal reputation for hearts of gold."

"I fear it; I fear it."

They looked at one another in silence for a moment. "Do you truly believe you will never marry?" Miss Cawley asked finally.

Miss Chilton gave a mock yawn, which she pretended to try to conceal. "I truly believe," she said, after a long pause, "that this is a sort of discussion I am grown too old to indulge in. If I *do* marry, it will have to creep up on me; certainly no one is going to arrange it."

"Lots of people try to contrive marriages for me," Miss Cawley told her. "In London. It is quite hideous of them. Thank God the duchess has no turn for such things; it is one thing I honestly admire in her."

"And my dear Miss Cawley," Lotta said, somewhat archly, but softly too, "am I to pretend to believe you don't care for Mr. Longstreth? If I am you need only tell me so; I won't tease you about it. But it does stretch my credulity something beyond its usual limits."

"My dear—" the other replied, on a note where discomfort and displeasure mingled. "My dear—you are to believe it."

"Very well, then. I shan't mention it again." She sounded as if she would keep her promise, and indeed she meant to. Miss Chilton was not overly fond of being teased herself, and she never inflicted such taunts as she was capable of unless she was certain the other party enjoyed it. Besides, she felt she and Jessica *were* too old to be giggling and guessing like school-room chits. The subject of romance was, consequently, dropped, and the problem of Mrs. Fainall returned to.

In the end it was offered to the contessa, who accepted it with only a tiny flicker in her violet eyes to indicate her awareness that Miss Cawley did not like her, and gave her the part merely for lack of alternatives. The others were informed of their rôles—or wheedled into accepting them, as need was—and given manuscripts to study until the stage should be built and rehearsals begun. Amabel Stanton was delighted with her part, small though it was, and ran off directly to tell her mother of her impending debut on the boards. She found Lady Stanton in her suite of chambers, in the act of clasping a bracelet round her wrist.

"I'll do that for you," said Amabel, for her mother was evidently nervous and could not work the tiny spring. Miss Stanton conquered it in a moment, and gave her mother the news.

"That is very pleasant," said she, but rather uneasily. She went to her

glass and smoothed her curls a trifle, evidently meaning to leave her
rooms in a moment.

"You seem distracted, Mamma. Is anything troubling you?"

"Nothing, my dear. I am tired."

"I hope you won't be ill after all!" said the dear girl, wandering
aimlessly round Lady Stanton's canopied bed and toying with a few ob-
jects on her writing-table. "What's this?" she said after a moment. She
held up a large packet, something like a letter, not franked but evidently
much handled.

"Leave that be," her ladyship commanded sharply—far more sharply
than she ordinarily addressed her daughter. Amabel dropped the packet
immediately, but tears started to her eyes at the uncommon harshness
of her mother's tone. "I am sorry," said Lady Stanton, regretting her involuntary severity. "It is nothing of significance."

Amabel wondered why, then, it had provoked such a reaction in her
parent, but she did not pursue the subject—she never pursued troublesome subjects—and she obediently sat still upon the bed. "You *are*
tired," she said, after a moment.

"Yes, I am, my dear. I will rest later, but now I must ask you to—"
she hesitated and checked herself. "Is Chauncey in the play?"

"I don't know," Amabel answered, suddenly feeling she had been a
neglectful sister. "Shall I find out?"

"Yes, do that," said her mother, with unmistakable relief. "Go on; I
shall find you downstairs in a moment."

"If he hasn't got one, I shall beg one for him," she told her mother as
she left the room. "The Countess Tremini is to play Mrs. Fainall, and I
know he will die if he is excluded." On these words she was gone. At
another moment her mother might have asked her to stay until she had
thought out whether it mightn't be best, all things considered, for
Chauncey to stay out of the performance, but she was far too distracted
now even to think of it. She gave herself a final glance in the mirror
when Amabel had gone, forced herself to breathe deeply several times,
picked up the packet, and quitted the chamber. Once in the corridor she
looked—rather furtively, one might say—up and down it, then turned
and followed its length to the landing of a flight of stairs. She climbed
the steps and passed again through a long hallway, until she reached a
door with an ivory handle. Breathing rapidly in spite of her efforts to be
calm, she knocked softly.

"Yes, my lady?" said the abigail who answered.

"Your mistress—" said Lady Stanton.

"My mistress is downstairs, I think," said the maid. "Shall I—?"

"Give this to her," Lady Stanton broke in, thrusting the packet rudely into her hands. "Mind you give it to her. Do not forget it. It is very important."

"Yes, madam," said the wondering abigail. "And shall I say it was from . . . ?"

"Never mind that. She will know." Lady Stanton found she could not say more; she felt a dangerous vertigo creeping upon her, and hastened away to her own apartment again, where she lay down upon the bed at once. "That is done," she said to herself, aloud. "All done. Dear God, let it never repeat itself!" After this she fell asleep, having forgot utterly her promise to meet Amabel downstairs.

Miss Stanton awakened her, however, in time to dress for dinner. The ball in honour of herself and Lord Wyborn was to take place that evening, and she did not think her mother would care to sleep through that no matter how fatigued she was. She was correct in this: Lady Stanton had no wish to appear eccentric to Lord Wyborn, and it would have looked very odd indeed not to attend her own daughter's festivities. She begged to take dinner upstairs in her own rooms, but assured Amabel she would join the others for tea. Amabel ought really to wear the white sarcenet gown, with the Brussels net; she looked a perfect angel in it, and no one at the castle had seen it as yet. This suggestion agreeing entirely with Amabel's own plans, she ran off to her room to meditate upon the remainder of her toilette. The duchess, who remembered more of her youth than one might have suspected, made certain to have a wreath of red and white roses sent up to Miss Stanton. This Amabel wore like a crown, looking excessively pretty (in spite of her continuing unease at the very thought of Lord Wyborn) when she finally appeared in the doorway of the ball-room.

It was really just a ball, like any other—lavish, but no more so than any the duchess might have given. The walls, in complement to Amabel, were festooned with red and white roses, and the sconces and chandeliers equipped with red and white tapers. The ball-room itself was chiefly white and gilt, a spacious, elegant apartment with a long series of French windows on two walls and a ceiling recently painted after the manner of Angelica Kauffmann. A trio of musicians, retained by the duke whenever he and his mother were both in Nottinghamshire, played sweetly and correctly. Nearly everyone was obliged to dance in order to make the floor appear full; Her Grace had invited a few families from the neighbourhood, but there were not many nearby whose rank could justify such an invitation and the large ball-room did have—it had to be admitted—a tendency to look rather sparsely populated.

In spite of this a good deal of gaiety and merry-making went forward: it was the first opportunity most of the gentlemen had had to dance with the exotic Contessa di Tremini, and they did not allow it to pass unemployed. Lady Olney flirted furiously with anyone she could find; her husband gallanted the ladies with exquisite foppery; the duchess, discouraging offers of conversation from those round her, watched the proceedings in seeming isolation. An expression of displeasure, which grew to one of severe annoyance, might have been observed upon her handsome features as the evening progressed; she was watching her son in particular, and she did not care for what she saw.

As was proper (she thought), he had danced the first dance with Lady Henrietta. This lady stepped the figures very evenly, very nicely—much, indeed, as she played the pianoforte. The duke skipped and bowed round her with as much assurance as one might expect in a gentleman who had been trained to perform such offices since earliest childhood. They spoke but little while the music continued, and at its end neither wanted for energy or breath. Despite this, the duke led Lady Henrietta inexorably back to her mother, where he stopped but a brief time to chat, and then deserted them entirely.

"Apparently he feels he has fulfilled his duty to her," thought Her Grace, with deep dissatisfaction, as her eyes followed her son's steps. These last were bent, by a wandering but traceable path, in the direction of—the duchess saw it with extreme disapproval—Miss Lotta Chilton . . . Lotta, who wore the same blue gown everybody at Grasmere had seen half a dozen times already. "What has he got to say to the chit?" thought the duchess. "I've half a mind to turn her off without a character." She had an impulse, too, to send for Miss Chilton directly, and order her to stay next to her mistress all night, but she did not care to run the risk of further exciting Karr's interest by causing Lotta to appear cruelly victimized.

She should dearly have loved to overhear their conversation, but could not—which was just as well. The two talked privately amid the moving crowd, with the relaxed tone of friends. "My mother would like to kill me," Karr was saying to Lotta, "but she never acts rashly. First she will determine the most elegant means, and the most proper moment. Then she will do me in."

"One can hardly blame her," Lotta murmured. "You dropped Lady Henrietta as quickly as if she had been a kitten who scratched you."

"Lady Henrietta is not a kitten."

"That is not the point."

"You haven't been accepting bribes from my mother, have you?" Karr inquired. "You are beginning to sound remarkably like her."

"A mere coincidence, I assure you. But you are very hard on Henrietta."

"What would you have me do?"

"Whatever you chuse to do—only I would have you do it soon. She grows more fretful by the day; one can see it in her eyes. It is not kind in you, you know, to keep her in suspense."

"She put herself there, if she is in it," Karr snapped back, his dark eyes blazing suddenly.

"Only a few days ago you admitted you had not discouraged her!" Lotta protested.

"Yes, but I did not say I had encouraged her either. I have paid no more attention to her than I have to twenty young ladies," he defended himself, "most of whom are now happily married."

"It may be true that you have paid no more attention to her than to others," Lotta said carefully, "but if I understand the story rightly, you have paid it over a longer period of time. That increases the interest due, you know. You must be meting it out very thinly; I am told she has waited for you these two years and longer."

"If you are going to scold me, I shan't talk to you," said Karr, almost sulkily.

"What choice have I, when you look so guilty? If you would ask me to dance, I might refrain from talking to you altogether, but as it is . . ."

"Ah! I did not ask you to dance because—you will hardly believe it— because you look so very exquisite."

"It is a novel explanation," said she, while he paused.

"When one dances, one is obliged to share one's partner with whom- ever may be near her. When the steps of the figures demand it, one must abandon her, be it only so briefly. In conversation, however, it is possible to present so forbiddingly intimate an aspect that no one would dream of interrupting. That is why I sit here chattering with you, and hesitate to lead you to the floor."

"Very pretty," she smiled, her lucid complexion colouring just slightly. She kept her head averted but looked up at him with huge, lu- minous eyes, and continued, "Won't you change your mind, however? I should so love to dance."

"Ah, if that is the case—!" he cried. "You make me perfectly ashamed of myself." He began to lead her toward the other dancers, who were now forming for a new set, but checked suddenly. "It won't do," he said. "Sir Francis Olney has seen us, and I know he is angling for a place near to you. We must wait for the next set."

"Really, you are too silly. What is it to you if Sir Francis crosses a step with me?"

"What is it to me? Why, only all the world."

"Your Grace is quite extravagant."

"Your Grace!" he echoed. "No more of my Graces from you, if you please. You may call me Karr."

"Ah, now you are preposterous," she exclaimed, genuinely uncomfortable.

"Preposterous? Why? Is not Grasmere my castle? May I not set what forms I desire?" His eyes blazed up again, fairly piercing her.

"Has Your—has my lord been drinking?" she asked finally, alarmed at his unwonted enthusiasm.

"Drinking—yes, of course. But my inebriation stems from your intoxicating glance, not paltry wines and liquors."

He had spoke rather loudly, and she looked about in some concern. "My dear sir, what if your mother should overhear us?" she whispered.

"What of it?" cried he, his gestures growing wider by the moment, and his voice louder.

"She would be horrified—and very rightly, too."

"Horrified! Then it is her own fault! Damme, I feel wonderful. Let's be married—won't you?"

Miss Chilton simply stared. Something had snapped inside the duke; she could guess that much, but she could not be certain what it was. Perhaps Lord Marland had pressed him for a decision; perhaps it had been the duchess herself. In either case—in any case—he was behaving with a wildness she had never suspected in him. She felt herself somewhat to blame for it, since she had encouraged him to be free with her, to take her into his confidence. She hated to think what might be the consequences if he were to remain in the ball-room in his present state. She stared a moment longer, then acted abruptly, too swiftly even to allow herself time to reflect. "Come, my lord," she hissed, placing an importunate hand on his arm. "Come to—to the conservatory. I have mislaid my nosegay, and want more flowers."

The duke escorted her out willingly, heedless of where she led him or what, precisely, she had said. "Won't you marry me?" he repeated, while they passed perilously close to the duchess.

Lotta shuddered. "In the conservatory. Wait until we are alone."

"Ah, yes, to be alone with you—! That is what I want; that is *all* I want. Let us be married, and be private together for ever and ever."

"My Lord!" she exclaimed, hurrying down the corridor with him. She gained the conservatory with a sensation of excessive relief, and closed the doors behind them hastily. This last she did with the single thought of preventing anyone from hearing His Grace; what other results it might have she never considered.

"Alone," breathed Karr, drawing her to a lightly carved Confidante nestled among the roses. "Come, I can think again."

"Thank heavens," said she, hopeful at once that it had only been the music, or the lights, or the closeness of the ball-room which had rendered his conduct so peculiar. His breath was faintly tinged with liquor; she had noticed it at once—but then that was true of all the gentlemen, from dinner-time until they retired. So far as she had known, Karr had no more trouble keeping his head than had the rest of them, but it was possible his being just a trifle foxed, plus the pressure from Marland, plus the disapprobation of his mother, plus her own teasing . . . it was possible they had all combined to make him temporarily mad. She sat beside him on the carved Confidante, smoothing her velvet skirt and hoping devoutly this was true.

"Now I can say it properly," the duke began when he had been silent some minutes. He stood before her, bowed, and continued, "Miss Chilton, will you do me the honour to become my wife? I am thirty-six years of age, and have never admired or loved a woman as I admire and love you."

"Oh, dear," said Lotta, involuntarily. This was not at all the restoration to calm good sense she had been hoping for.

"Oh, dear?" he echoed. "Amorous though I am, I cannot pretend that you meant to call me 'dear.' Had you said 'darling,' I had been certain of it—but 'Oh, dear' sounds very like an exclamation of displeasure."

"My good sir—Your Grace—"

"Not that! I told you, not that! I command you," he added, as she failed to respond.

"Your command, of course, I am bound, as your dependent, to honour," she commenced, "but—"

"Ah, no," he interrupted, looking quite stricken. "Did I say command? I meant, entreat. Certainly I did not mean to remind you of your dependence here." With these words he knelt, took her transparent hand, and bent his head over it, brushing it with his lips.

"Your Gr—Dear sir, pray rise and sit beside me," she begged him, as it suddenly occurred to her that anyone might enter at any moment.

Karr obliged her, but again took her hand. "You make me no answer," he said. "As you reminded me just now, it is unkind to keep devotion in suspense."

"Dear sir," she commenced, "I know not how to say this . . . The impossibility of what you propose—so impossible, I do not really believe you mean it at all—is so evident as to render all answer superfluous. Imagine—well, for one thing, imagine what Her Grace would say to it."

"She will be delighted."

"Good sir—!"

"I will command her to be delighted."

"You really are quite drunk, you know," Lotta muttered almost inaudibly. "Perhaps you will be more sensible if we take a more likely example. Imagine, if you will, what Her Grace would say were she to hear me calling you Karr. She would be outraged—and understandably."

"But why?"

She perceived that her experiment had failed. "But because familiarity between a personage so exalted as yourself and a lady's companion rapidly approaching thirty is utterly beyond all bounds."

"All bounds of what?" he asked, as if automatically.

"All bounds of propriety."

"I hate propriety."

"Of decency, then."

"I hate decency, then," he answered promptly.

"My lord, you know that is not true."

He dropped her hand. "No," he agreed, after a moment. "It is not true." He fell silent, his dark brows drawn together as if he thought very seriously.

Lotta said nothing, but experienced a feeling of relief which almost immediately turned into regret. Karr's outburst had been hopelessly inappropriate—really, in bad form—but it had been rather exciting. She hated to admit it to herself, but what had just passed had been a fantasy of her own—a fantasy in which she did not permit herself to indulge, but one she was aware of nonetheless. How very wonderful it would be to be swept off by the duke, out of subservience and frugality and loneliness—! For Lotta was very lonely, and the necessity of living in the households of strangers, apart from the Chiltons, made it all the more difficult. Besides that, she had liked Karr from the moment she saw him. He was handsome, and good-natured, and entirely trustworthy, apart from being a duke. He had attracted her from her first glance of him. She had not troubled to deny it to herself, since the knowledge was certain to remain her own secret.

All that, however, was neither here nor there—as she sternly reminded herself now. She had had a brief moment of gratification; it was come and gone; she ought to be happy to have had any at all. She did not flatter herself that Karr would be otherwise than entirely embarrassed when he looked back upon this unexpected interview, but she did feel—giving herself her due—that he probably returned at least some of the regard she felt for him; if not, he would have chosen another woman, perhaps an abigail.

All these thoughts behind her, her confusion may easily be imagined when Karr spoke again. "I do not hate propriety, nor decency," he pronounced, very soberly indeed, as it seemed. "Nor am I in a position to defy convention, as it were, or to disregard it. Such a course would be ridiculous in a man in my position. You are quite right."

She smiled rather gravely. "Thank you, my lord," she murmured. "As for . . . all this . . . It will be forgot, I promise."

"Forgot? I beg your pardon?" he took up.

"This—this accidental episode," she said helplessly.

"Accidental? Providential, you mean! My dear Miss Chilton, kindly do not misunderstand me," he said earnestly. "I will confess to having spoke rashly—inaccurately, one might say—but never with the intention of letting it all be forgot! I desire to marry you, Miss Chilton. I desire it with all my heart. I *will* marry you, Miss Chilton, if you will be so good as to accept me. Only I will not inform my family of the event quite so flippantly as I pretended."

She literally gasped—there was no other word for it. Her throat seemed to constrict, and her mouth to go dry: there was no question in her mind now of Karr's entire sincerity, but the whole sequence had begun to take on the quality of a dream.

"I will not pretend, either, to wonder why you hesitate," he continued, as she found herself unable to say anything. "The prospect has many facets, some—I hope—attractive, but others certainly unpleasant. My mother will learn to tolerate you, but she will, in all likelihood, never do much more than that. You will probably be accused of scheming, and perhaps all your life hear the echoes of that accusation. And then, to be mistress of Grasmere, no matter who it is who carries that title, is a busy and trying occupation. You see what it has done to my mother; no doubt she was gay and easy in her time, but she has lost all that. I will not pretend, as I say, to wonder if you give me no answer as yet; but—will you permit me to hope?"

"My dear sir," Lotta began, after a very long pause, "I begin to believe you are in earnest."

"But of course I am. I have never been quite so much in earnest in all my life, I think. I admit, this is not a proposal I have thought long and hard about; on the contrary, it came to me all in a flash. But it came, when it came at last, with a conviction. I will not be a happy man unless you marry me. That is all there is to it."

"And Lady Henrietta?"

"It is most lamentable, this business of Lady Henrietta. One does not, however, marry to oblige one's father's old friends."

"One does, however, marry to oblige one's family," she pointed out.

"One does indeed. Evidently, I do not. I thought I would; but I don't."

"My lord, this is too complex a matter to be decided upon an instant's consideration."

"I grant you that," said he. "I only ask that you *will* consider it."

Lotta hesitated for a moment, thinking. All at once she felt as if she would like to cry. She bent her head and buried her face in her hands but raised it still dry-eyed. "Your Grace, the very briefest reflection satisfies me of the impossibility of what you propose."

"Ah—! You do not care for me!"

"Care for you—? But indeed, I care for you extremely," she contradicted him. "That is nothing to do with it."

"It is everything to do with it."

"In the case of the Duke of Karr, it is nothing," she insisted. "I am afraid you must count among the disadvantages of a great estate the fact that you cannot marry on a whim."

"This is not a whim," he said, displeased.

"Even if it were the greatest passion," she urged, "you must, for your own sake, renounce it."

"What dry, mad philosophy have you been reading, that you recommend renunciation with such a glibness?" he asked sharply.

At this juncture the deep division of her own feelings overcame her at last, and she did begin to cry. "It is no philosophy," she cried, huge tears splashing on her translucent cheeks. "It is only common goodness, common sense."

"You are guilty," he charged her, ignoring her tears, "of the same fallacy with which you charged me. The fact that renunciation is disagreeable does not insure that it is good. When you refuse my offer, do you speak from your head or your heart?"

"Both, my lord," she insisted. "It is wrong, wrong, all wrong."

"Both!" he spat out. "Rubbish. What do you *want,* Miss Chilton?"

"I want this to be finished," she said faintly.

"If there were no laws, no estates, no religions," he persisted, "what would you want?"

"I would want to marry you!" she cried, rather hotly. She faced him squarely now, feeling a flame of anger rise up within her. "Naturally I should like to marry you. What else can you imagine? Surely you don't believe me such a fool as not to have noticed what exists between us—the familiarity, the esteem, the understanding! You don't fancy, I trust, that I might *really* be afraid of obligations, of power! You besiege me as if nothing existed in the world save you and me, as if you had not a mother and I no mother at all, as if you were not a duke and I not in your employ. Naturally I should like to marry you," she repeated with scornful emphasis. "Do you think I am an idiot? But it *can not be.* Can not. Am I making myself clear?"

He stared at her, apparently unmoved. "Why are you angry at me?"

Her anger disappeared on the moment, and the tears began to fall again. "Because you insist on simple-mindedness where nothing is simple," she said. "Because you hold a carrot up before my nose and expect me to go forward as if I did not know the carrot was forbidden fruit. Because you forget I am an intelligent donkey."

"Not intelligent enough to know, it seems, that a carrot—if it is forbidden at all—is a forbidden vegetable, and not a forbidden fruit." He said it lightly, and she gave a laugh through her tears.

"Still," she said, "it is forbidden. I must hold to that."

"I begin to think your donkey metaphor is better chosen than it appears. You are going to be stubborn about this, aren't you?"

"I trust the privilege of obstinacy is not limited to the peerage," she said.

"Not at all," he agreed, bowing his head. "I have learned sufficient tonight, however, to know what I will do now."

She looked up at him almost timidly. "You will marry Lady Henrietta?" she guessed in a whisper.

"Ah, my dear Miss Chilton! No, of course I will not do that. I will marry no one but you."

"And since you will not marry me either—?"

"I will not marry," he said, with a shrug.

"And your name? Your family? You are content to leave things at that?" she inquired, as if fascinated.

His Grace the Duke of Karr held up a bejewelled quizzing-glass (an accoutrement he very rarely made use of) and scrutinized Miss Chilton through it. "Ah, yes," he said at length. "I thought I heard a murmur of it in the tone of your voice, but I could not be certain."

"Be certain—?" she prompted, as he stopped.

"There is a look in your eyes, my very dear Miss Chilton, which suggests you are not entirely without a kindness for dukes in distress. It confirms my suspicion," he continued, letting fall the quizzing-glass, "that I am not, for all you say, without hope."

She smiled at him. "But you are, for all that."

"Not according to your exquisite eyes."

"There is nothing in my eyes," she said carefully, "that I have not given voice to."

"It was in your voice as well," he reminded her.

"You make something out of nothing," Lotta began warningly.

" 'The lunatic, the lover and the poet,' " he cited, smiling warmly upon her, " 'are of imagination all compact.' "

"Which are you?" she inquired. They rose together as if at a signal and pursued their way back to the ball-room. Their interview—whatever its purpose or consequences—had lasted too long, and the duke, at least, was certain to have been missed.

7

The duke had indeed been missed, and the dowager duchess, at least, was displeased. She vented her displeasure on Miss Chilton, the following morning, as soon as the guests had scattered to their several occupations. "You will walk with me in the Glass Gallery," she said to Lotta, a deep scowl taking hold of her austere features the moment they were alone. Lotta said nothing, but rose and accompanied her formidable employer to the passageway she had referred to. This was a straight, rather narrow corridor which ran along one side of the castle and overlooked an interior courtyard. The courtyard contained a few examples of ancient statuary—representing mostly abbots and saints—and a crumbling colonnade of grey stone. At this season, for winter had begun early, it also contained a great deal of bleak, cheerless light. The gallery—called the Glass Gallery because the face of it which overlooked the courtyard was almost entirely window—was on the second story, which meant that Her Grace of Karr and Miss Chilton had a very considerable number of steps and stairways to traverse before they reached their destination; the journey, notwithstanding, was accomplished in utter silence, the duchess too angry to speak, her youthful companion too anxious.

They attained the Gallery at last, the duchess slightly short of breath as a result of both her exertion and her high wrath. The Glass Gallery was nearly always deserted, being spartan in its adornments (a few dull mirrors and a threadbare carpet) and not central to the principal rooms of the castle. It was deserted now, in any case, and this was all the duchess required. Though fatigued, she refused to be still, instead setting a course which ran straight from one end of the corridor to the other, then back again, with never a pause or a break. She began immediately to pursue this course, Miss Chilton naturally by her side, at a brisk, clipped pace, and repeated it innumerable times throughout their interview.

"Miss Chilton," she began, not looking at Lotta but always keeping her regard fixed at some phantom point before her, "your behaviour at last night's entertainment was unconscionable. I do not ask for an explanation since there can be none. I will only ask you to tell me precisely what occurred."

"Your Grace, I am desolate if I have distressed you," said the unhappy girl.

"Distressed me!" the great lady echoed, sharply sarcastic. "The affair hardly merits so delicate a term. What did you do with my son, Miss Chilton? That is all I desire to hear."

Lotta wished to defend herself, to explain the duke's insobriety (if it could be explained); to explain, at least, that she had had nothing at heart but the honour of the house of Karr. She saw, however, that the duchess would hear nothing but what she demanded, and so she addressed herself to the question as directly as possible. "His Grace and I went directly to the conservatory. We sat there in conversation throughout our absence, and returned as directly to the ball-room."

The duchess did not look at her, but took up scathingly, "In conversation? How very intriguing. And are you quite certain no other sort of exchange passed between you? Nothing you may, for its very smallness, have forgot this morning?"

"His Grace," she brought out with some difficulty, "ah . . . saluted my hand at one point. It was a formal and correct salute."

"And was your colloquy equally formal and correct?" the duchess pursued relentlessly.

"It was not," Lotta confessed, "not entirely so formal."

"Ah!" cried the dowager, as if the prisoner she tortured had at last let fall an admission. "You do well to tell me the truth. Now tell me," she continued, clasping her hands before her as she walked and pressing them together tightly, "exactly what was the matter of your not-so-formal talk."

Lotta blanched on the instant, but she continued to keep pace with her mistress, and spoke evenly. "I do not feel at liberty to discuss that,

Your Grace. I beg you will not press me to answer a question when, in order to do so, I must betray a confidence."

"My son makes confidences to you," the duchess said, in an extraordinary tone. It was flat, bland, neither shocked nor accusatory, but by its very lack of passion it seemed to indicate the effort it cost the duchess to speak.

"Begging Your Grace's pardon," Lotta murmured, "he does."

"This is very curious. This is most curious," said the elder lady, after a considerable pause. She had regained some of her acidity; her step quickened to an unnatural swiftness. "It distresses me to be no more obliging to you than you have been to me," she said, "for I hate to answer rudeness with rudeness—and even more, unscrupulousness with unscrupulousness. However, I *will* press you for an answer to my question; I will instruct you, on penalty of your post, to break that confidence to which you refer."

The duchess had spoke as if, with such stipulations attached, there were no doubt but that Lotta would bend to her. She did not bend, though, with the consequence that she left her interlocutress much startled. "My grief at having to refuse you is without measure," she said, "but I must refuse you nonetheless. I am all respect and admiration before you, and gratitude—but I cannot break my word when it is given."

The duchess broke out with a dry sound like the cracking of a stick. "This is a fine time to cleave to your honour!" she cried. "When you have thrown my son into disrepute, and all my affairs into confusion!"

"Good madam," said Lotta, not so much offended as surprised, "I cry you mercy! I had no notion of achieving such wonders with half an hour's colloquy. I knew of course that it was—it was an unfortunate time for a private interview; I pretend to know no less. But Your Grace must trust me—I beseech you will believe me—when I say it was the better of two unhappy choices."

"And what choices may those have been?" the other exclaimed shrilly. "Am I to believe my son has been issuing ultimata among the servants?"

"Your son issued no ultimatum, Your Grace, and yet a certain . . . intemperance . . ." she could not continue along this line, she found. "In spite of his having detailed no choices, I felt I must chuse between a public scene and a private one. I chose the latter, for the sake of Your Grace's service and, if I must point it out, to the detriment of my own."

"And in what way has my son acted to your detriment?" the dowager caught at this. "Am I to understand that you bring charges against him?"

"On the contrary, dear madam," Lotta hastened to say. "I only meant that in consequence of my decision last night, you behold me now suspected and threatened. By yourself, Your Grace. That is all I mean."

"Ah, you are very careful to maintain your own security," Her Grace observed sharply.

"I do not like to appear villainous when I have pursued virtue," she agreed, though in rather a muffled tone. The scene had taken on a doleful cast for her; she felt cruelly misunderstood, and yet at a loss to defend herself. "If I may add one boldness to the list you have already, it appears, compiled of my sins, I will suggest you take these questions to your son. He has my consent to repeat any or all of what passed between us last night. I am not, as you think, so careful of my own reputation as I am of his."

The duchess took this in slowly, and turned to regard her young companion for the first time since their interview had begun. Her look was dreadful, a commingling of ire and loathing. "Miss Chilton," she said, presently returning her eyes to their former, forward stare, "the honour of the house of Karr has been preserved unblemished for upwards of four hundred years. I think I am safe in saying that in that entire period, no master of Grasmere has ever been obliged to thank a servant for the maintenance of his reputation. Your concern for my son's good name is most—touching—but it fails somehow to persuade me. I am sorry to be obliged to dismiss a young woman like yourself on such unpleasant terms as these; it is a cold world, and you will have trouble now in finding yourself a place by another family's hearth. You leave me no alternative, however. Please be gone from Grasmere within four-and-twenty hours. That is all I have to say," she added, as Lotta neither spoke nor went.

"Your Grace does me inestimable wrong," she said, when she felt sufficiently in possession of herself to say anything. Tears stood in her eyes but she had too much pride to release them. "Pray God we shall reach a better understanding someday."

On these words Miss Chilton did go, forcing herself to keep a stately pace while the duchess's eyes were still on her, but fleeing headlong down the intricate corridors as soon as she was out from under them. She began to cry even as she ran, and hurried down a long stair-case toward her room, barely able to contain her sobs. Her vision was blurred by hot tears, her hair—which had come loose during her flight—streamed out in wisps behind her, and she kept her head down lest any chance passerby should see her face. She travelled her route mostly from memory, since she dared not look up, and so it was that when, while crossing the first landing of the great stair-case, His Grace of Karr observed her, she neither saw him nor heard his greeting but instead rushed blindly against him.

"What's this?" he asked gently as she jumped from him, and made as if to run away without a word in explanation. He put his strong, solid hands upon her shoulders and sought to look into her face. "My dear Miss Chilton," he cried, perceiving her utter discomposure, "are you well?"

"Am I—? Ah, God!" she exclaimed. She pulled away from him and buried her head in her hands. She had governed her misery before the duchess, but she could not bring herself to do so before Karr. She turned away from him, still intending to find the refuge of her chamber before sharing her distress with anyone.

Karr would not let her leave, however. He took her arm in a steady hand and led her firmly through a door a few paces away, a door which opened into an apartment he himself used for reflection on the affairs of his estate, and for consultation with his steward. It was a smallish room, very comfortably set up with a great deal of dark leather and even darker wood, and Lotta fell gratefully into an enormous arm-chair, where she proceeded to cry for a good ten minutes. The duke let her weep as she would, furiously impatient to know the cause of this uncharacteristic fit, but too wise to disturb her until she was ready to speak.

"I am very sorry," were her first words, uttered while still gazing, through her hands, at the ottoman near her feet.

"So am I, that anything to cause you so much sorrow should happen between my walls. What is it? Not bad news from home, I hope?"

"Oh no—dear no . . . Bad news *for* home, is more like it," she replied, with a feeble attempt at a smile.

"This is very mysterious," he said kindly, drawing up a chair near to hers and seating himself. "Won't you tell me what it is, then?"

"I may as well," she said, with a kind of recklessness. "If I don't you shall nose it soon enough, as Hamlet says."

"I trust you have not murdered anyone," exclaimed Karr, with a laugh.

"No, I stop at high treason," she assured him, rather obscurely.

The duke pondered this. "Treachery, is it? You haven't been talking with my mother just now, have you?" he inquired, as if he strongly suspected she had.

Miss Chilton merely nodded, too miserable again to speak.

"And she accuses you of treason. She has never trusted you, though I know not why."

"Never mind; she stops for no reason but convicts me on the spot," Lotta brought out, with some bitterness.

"You stand sentenced already?" asked Karr, taken aback.

"It was a brief trial. There were no witnesses and but one judge."

"I would pause to inquire the precise charge, but I hate to lag behind my mother. We will speak of that later; for now, tell me your sentence. Are you banished from the dinner table?"

She laughed, again with a nervous, reckless edge. "Banished I am, but not only from your board. From the castle, in short."

"I beg your pardon?" he said, genuinely surprised.

"From the castle," she repeated. She looked at him for the first time, and her face was very still. "I am turned off without a character."

His Grace heard this and his features seemed to turn to stone, so grim did his expression become. "Here is a sentence that wants reversal," he said in a low voice. "Excuse me; I will see my mother."

He began to leave the room on these words, but Lotta stopped him with a gesture. "We have had enough of rashness, my lord," she said. "Stop another moment and consider what you do."

"I correct an injustice. There is no need of consideration," he said, but he did linger as she requested.

"In your eyes, perhaps. In mine, certainly. In Her Grace's eyes, however, you prove yourself immoderately foolish. She interrogated me with regard to our interview in the conservatory . . . last night. I am afraid she is extremely displeased with you, as well as with me."

"I am not frightened of her displeasure," said Karr; but added, "what precisely did you tell her?"

"I said only that we spoke. When pressed, I admitted that you—you kissed my hand," she said, blushing at the indelicacy of such an allusion even under the circumstances. "I admitted that our talk was less formal than it might have been, but I refused to discuss its nature. That was what brought on my dismissal. She desired me to break my confidence with you."

"And you refused," Karr put in.

"Naturally. It is the only point wherein I am certain I acted rightly."

"I am certain you acted rightly on every point," said Karr, his anger mounting again. His powerful jaw was set and clenched in such a way as must have been damaging to his teeth.

"I beg you will take a broader view of things," said Lotta, though without much spirit. "So far as Her Grace is concerned, my little indiscretion—if it was such—may have ruined the prospect of your marrying Lady Henrietta. At least, I presume that is what disturbs her, though she did not mention her ladyship."

"If there were any indiscretions committed last night, they were ours," Karr observed, "not yours alone."

"Before you go, I may tell you one last thing," said Lotta, as he again turned away. "You have my consent to recount in detail as much as you like of what passed between us last night. You need not be afraid of betraying me. It is more your secret than mine."

"You are positive?" Karr questioned her. "My mother has no right, you know, to hear what is said in private."

"I have nothing to be ashamed of, and in her present mood I think it best not to stick at technicalities. What is more important than that, however, is this: if you will accept my counsel, my lord, you will not seek to confront your mother at all."

"I beg your pardon?" he said a second time.

"She has judged harshly, I think," Lotta continued, her tears beginning to flow again as she spoke, "but not without reason. I ought not to be here; it is difficult for both of us, and for her. Your affairs will go on better without me, and to grapple with her on this question will only bring further unhappiness and disorder."

"I believe I mentioned to you last night," said Karr, not appearing at all amused, "that my affairs, as you call them, are inextricably bound up in your sentiments. As for unhappiness and disorder, they will be the result if I keep my silence. Good men have only to do nothing, for evil to conquer."

"Your adage is inaccurately applied. There is nothing evil in Her Grace."

"This is quibbling," he said. "I appreciate the fineness of your scruples and I go to my mother not for your sake but for mine. Pray continue as you were before I found you; go to your chamber, if that is where you were going; and forget we have spoke, if it will comfort you. I should, as you say, have nosed this out with or without your information; and I should not, under any circumstances, have allowed the situation to pass unchallenged."

Miss Chilton would have kept him longer—at least until some of his wrath had subsided—but he bolted away at last without another glance at her. She was left with nothing to do, therefore, but to take his advice. Accordingly, she removed herself to her room, where she had a very long and difficult fit of weeping, and an even longer conference with her own conscience and sentiments. At the end of an hour a note was delivered to her door by a liveried page, a note which she tore open and read greedily.

"Dear Miss Chilton," it said,

"Your sentence has been overturned by a higher court, and I hope will someday be confessed to have been a grievous miscarriage of justice. There is this change, however: that you are to remain at Grasmere, so long as it pleases you, in the rôle of guest, not servant.

"The catastrophe which precipitated this morning's trial was not (at least not solely) our departure from last night's festivities but the intention on my lord the Earl of Marland's part to remove himself and his family from the castle. This news was imparted to my mother just previous to breakfast, and no doubt occasioned in her an acute and lamentable fit of indigestion.

"I do not pretend—you are too wise for such foolery—that Her Grace is very happy with the current state of affairs. I take the liberty of reminding you, however, that my own happiness utterly depends upon it, and of warning you that if you should chuse to quit Grasmere precipitously I will certainly follow suit.

"With the deepest apologies for the painful scene visited upon you today, and the tenderest hopes of your present recovery, I remain,

"Your most obedient and devoted servant,

Karr."

Lotta read this note, and re-read it, with the deepest division of feeling. It was a great relief, of course, to be rescued from the necessity of an obscure withdrawal from Grasmere—though, if she was saved, she did not for a moment believe she had been entirely vindicated in the eyes of the duchess. Her continued presence at the castle, she was certain, had been thrust rather violently down the great lady's throat, and she would take her time about swallowing. Moreover, while it was a fine novelty to be in residence at such a place as Grasmere on a footing equal to any of the guests, it was a dignity ill-suited to her needs. What would Mr. Chilton say when she wrote to him that she had lost the remuneration owing to a servant in favour of the honour due a guest? He would say, no doubt, that she had better find a place with less luxury and more cash attached to it. On second thoughts she knew he would not say quite this; his kindness to her and his delight in what would appear to him her good fortune would cause him to offer to support her again while she enjoyed her unusual windfall. Since this was a cost he could ill-afford, and his supposed decision taken with reference only to his good heart, and not to his purse, Lotta would necessarily refuse it . . . and then . . . where was she to find another post? Her reflections on this topic were interrupted by a knock at the door, which opened to admit Miss Jessica Cawley. Miss Cawley was in high form, excited and beset with a problem. Problems were among Miss Cawley's favourite things, and she had come to share hers with Lotta as another person might have come to share glad tidings.

"Great news, my dear," she said, skipping in and bouncing to a rather frayed sofa which, as not being fine enough for more stately rooms, had been exiled to Miss Chilton's chamber. "Lord Marland leaves today—had you heard? Henrietta goes with him; and you know what that means!"

"Do I?"

"Why, that we shall want another Foible for our play, of course," Jessica told her. "I know it is a far lesser part than Marwood, but won't you take it anyway? We shall make Cosmo Waitwell, and Karr—"

"Hold, hold a moment pray," cried Lotta, giving a genuine laugh for the first time that day. Miss Cawley's notion of what most signified in Henrietta's departure from Grasmere amused her no end. "Can you think of nothing but that play?"

"Is there something else I ought to think of?"

In as few words as possible, Miss Chilton recounted to her friend what had passed between herself and the heads of Grasmere that morning, touching only lightly on what exactly the duke had said to her, and concealing utterly the matter of her talk with him on the previous evening. "So you see, you may be out of a Marwood as well," she concluded, "for I do not see how I am to remain at the castle."

"This is most astonishing!" said Jessica. "This is most—though you strive not to make it so—mysterious as well. I can believe the duchess's annoyance at your intimacy with Karr, but what precisely—my dear girl, whatever *is* the state of affairs between you and His Grace?"

Lotta murmured an excuse for her reticence, which, though inaudible, provoked a strong reaction in the other lady.

"And I have been planning for you a destiny with Remington!" she cried; "Lotta, my dear, I had no notion you kept such large ideas!"

"I have no ideas," she insisted.

"Pooh!" Jessica dismissed this. "If you haven't, I'll wager Karr has enough for the two of you. Dear, dear, the duchess must be prostrate with dismay! Not that she doesn't deserve it, my dear," she added. "Pride *will* have its fall."

Lotta coloured slightly at Miss Cawley's rapid perception of her situation. "I never said anything to you, you know," she reminded her.

"Oh, goodness, no," Jessica replied; "you are guilty of no indiscretion. But I guess everything, everything! Unless . . . I am not to believe that Karr has offered to—has offered to stain . . ." she trailed off.

"My virtue? Dear heavens, no. Such an offer I should know how to answer in a moment. You recall the importunate nephew in Surrey."

"Vividly," Jessica agreed. "No, I did not think the duke was such a one as he. Karr has far grander notions—I protest, Lotta, I am positively ashamed of myself. Imagine living in the very midst of such an intrigue, and never suspecting a thing! Cosmo Remington indeed—you must have thought me an idiot!"

"Not an idiot, my dear; not at all," Lotta disclaimed. "Very kind, in fact. Believe me, what your idea lacked in grandeur it more than made up for in feasibility. As you will easily understand, His Grace has placed me in an entirely untenable position."

"Yes . . . for the moment, spiritually," Jessica mused; "but in practical terms, I do not see why you shouldn't stop on here a while longer. You will, won't you?"

Miss Chilton smiled gently. "There is a small matter of money," she said, with some reluctance. "My wants are few, but my father . . . is only a tutor of Italian, after all, and my sisters are many. I cannot in good conscience continue where no money is to be earned."

"My dear, what on earth could you want? If it is only a question of a few pounds pin-money—as it must be, for you have not expensive habits —you are more than welcome to mine!"

"Your generosity is most delightful," said Lotta, colouring again, "but not a little embarrassing. I really could not."

"Oh—fustian!" the other exclaimed, exasperated at once. "You really could, you know. In fact, you really ought to. Fancy your becoming the Duchess of Karr! You will make it up to me a hundred times, simply by the satisfaction of seeing it come about."

"I am afraid that particular satisfaction has a higher price than a couple of pounds," Lotta persisted, a bit sadly. "What it would cost the duchess in misery is more than I can reckon. Anyway, I do not care to lay such charges to her account; she was very good, you know, to engage me at all; I am sure she went over the heads of twenty poor relations to do so. And what is more, she has been exceedingly kind to me since my arrival here—excessively, as she would no doubt confess it herself."

"So you think it would be a very mean trick to reap the benefits of her liberality, eh?" Miss Cawley took up. "Dear girl, in the case of an emergency, one has sometimes to be just the tiniest trifle wicked."

"I do not think so," said Lotta softly, shaking her head.

"But if it is a grand passion—!"

"What is a grand passion, if you please?" Miss Chilton inquired, with some dryness. "Merely an attraction opposed. Remove the opposition and the attraction falls apart on its own. His Grace would not think near so much of me if I were not, though perversely, unattainable."

Jessica was silent for a moment. "Ridiculous," she pronounced.

"A thing is not the less true for being ridiculous," said Lotta.

"Perhaps not . . . but it makes it eminently negligible," Jessica insisted. "I will not see you run your life along principles of high silliness. Confound it, I *will* not!"

"Such swaggering talk!" said Lotta, in mock surprise.

"No, listen to me. This is a very important matter. It will determine the course of your whole life. You must—you do love him, don't you?" she broke off abruptly.

Lotta said nothing; it was not necessary that she say anything to answer the question. Her eyes filled with tears (they had done so so many times already that day, she thought to herself, they must be learning to like it) and her throat swelled so that she could not speak. The strength of her own emotions surprised even herself; she was grateful Miss Cawley could read her answer without waiting for words.

"Very well, then," said Jessica, matter-of-factly. "This is precisely my point. You will stop on at Grasmere for the winter; ignore the duchess; and apply to me in case of any need. That is all there is to it. If the Chiltons might object, do not tell them."

"I must tell them," Lotta murmured.

"As you like. The important point is that you stay. And as for the play—"

"Oh, the play!" Lotta broke in, on a gurgly laugh.

"Yes, naturally. As for the play, you will take Foible and we'll leave the duke across from you. The duchess will simply gag."

"Miss Cawley—" said the other reproachfully.

"Pooh for your scruples," Jessica retorted. "It will do her good to be taken down a peg or two. At least it will thaw that eternal frost she breathes."

"You may take delight where you will," said Miss Chilton, a bit stodgily, "but I beg you will exclude me from any exultations concerning Her Grace. I shall have enough to do when I begin to reconcile my conscience to prolonging my stay here."

"Off to the priest with you, then," said Jessica briskly, getting up and bustling to the door. "I wish you good luck when you endeavour to explain just exactly what your sins have been; it is more than I should undertake. Anyway, I need to find a Marwood now; I've a fancy to the contessa, you know."

"And who for Mrs. Fainall then?"

"Ah—" said Miss Cawley airily. "Lady Olney, I suppose. It hardly matters. My dear," she added, turning suddenly to embrace Miss Chilton, "I am very, very happy for you."

"I thank you for your good will," said Lotta, returning the embrace, "but let us remember that your happiness is entirely premature. I myself am all apprehension. "

"Ah, my dear, what am I to do with you?" Jessica cried in response to this piece of caution. She pushed Lotta away with a light, humorous tap and let herself out of the room. Miss Chilton (though she knew her friend had mentioned the priest as a jest) thought it rather a good moment to pray, and that is what she did as soon as she was left alone.

Dinner that day proved quite excruciating for her. The duchess refused to look at her, and pointedly directed the Countess Tremini to take the seat near her which had hitherto belonged to Lotta. Karr attempted to make it up by engaging her in some particularly high-flown chatter (he was customarily rather taciturn at table), and Mr. Longstreth, on her other side, filled in whenever the duke's attentions lapsed; but tension was in the air, and Miss Chilton tasted it with every morsel she ate. The gentlemen sat but briefly after the ladies had withdrawn, for Miss Cawley had announced that a meeting of her players was to take place first thing that evening. Everyone was welcome, she said, but it was mandatory for those who had been allotted rôles, and as that included more than half the company, most of the guests hurried after dinner to join her in the ball-room.

The stage was only just starting to be constructed, of course, but Miss Cawley did not allow this to dismay her. She seated everyone on chairs arranged in a circle, and led them through a reading of the first two acts.

At each change of scene the seated players would re-shuffle themselves, gathering or dispersing as the action demanded. It was a cumbersome process, resulting in much scraping of chairs and adjustment of positions, but Jessica remained enthusiastic throughout and her high spirits communicated themselves to the assembled company. Miss Chilton coloured noticeably when, at the very close of the second act, it was necessary for her to read, with His Grace of Karr, the lines of a pair of newlyweds. She rebuked herself soundly (though to no avail), reminding herself that no one but Jessica could guess how significant such a scene might be, and spared a pious thought for poor Lady Henrietta, banished by her proud papa from the neighbourhood of the duke. She coloured nonetheless, however, and Karr remarked the circumstance with pleasure.

In the ensuing weeks such meetings as this took place almost daily, the company moving—when such a move became possible—from their inconvenient chairs to the newly-completed stage itself. Her Grace, to do her justice, had spared no expense in the building of this temporary construction and its necessary accoutrements—in spite of the fact that she had noticed Miss Cawley's growing amity for Lotta, and had felt therefore the less inclined to oblige her. Lady Louisa Bridwell proved to be the wonder of the project, repeating her lines with a perfection none the less comical for being unconscious. Half the time, indeed, Jessica asked herself if Lady Louisa knew how very diverting she was in the part of the vain, foolish Lady Wishfort; certainly her ladyship did not laugh nearly so much as did the other members of the company. A number of rehearsals, in fact, had to be terminated during her scenes on account of uncontrollable hilarity among the *dramatis personae*. Lady Wishfort's catch-phrase in the play, "As I am a person"—became a trigger among the actors which, when pulled, released an explosive round of laughter; it might have been heard anywhere at Grasmere for months—at meals, on the grounds, at card-tables, and in shooting-parties.

The Contessa di Tremini, while taking very ill the novelty of having people laugh at her, managed her part (she had taken Mrs. Marwood after all) very gracefully, contriving to appear far more subtly treacherous than Lotta could ever have done. Poor Mr. Chauncey Stanton, who—at the insistence of his sister—had been given the part of an unnamed footman, continually missed what few entrances he had for want of concentration. Try though he would, he could not prevent himself from gazing in dumb awe at his violet-eyed queen: he would find himself, of a sudden, rapt in admiration, and (remembering his father's in-

junction) attempt to call himself sternly to attention. It was no use,
however. Five minutes later, invariably, he could be observed again in a
trance-like state of contemplation. He made rather an amusing picture
at it all: a steady watcher would see him go from slack jaw and misted
eyes to the impassive rigidity of a soldier, and then, a moment later, to
gaping mouth again. He could not help it, poor lad. The contessa
seemed to him a faerie figure, only one-quarter human, the other three
parts goddess. On the rare occasions when she deigned to look at him
he fairly melted with excitement; the scenes which referred to her secret
passion for Mr. Mirabell were very painful to him. He could not—pity
him!—separate the character she played from the person she was, nor
keep distinct, in his own mind, the magical properties with which his
imagination imbued her from her very real limitations. More than once,
when the contessa had noticed him gawking at her, she had whispered to
her neighbour (usually Mr. Septimus Faust; in any case, always a gentleman) that "she wished that cub would waken from his eternal rev-
ery." Chauncey, fortunately for him, could not hear these murmurs; if
he had they would surely have broken his over-wrought heart. Miss
Cawley found his inattention to herself exasperating, but she guessed
what was happening and became amused by it instead. "Young Mr.
Stanton's upper teeth are strangers by now to his lower," she observed
one day to Lotta. "Perhaps he hopes to air out the under-part of his
moustache, and so encourage it to grow faster."

She had reason to be gay. The project which was so dear to her was
proving an immense success. Everyone was diverted by it, whether because engaged in it directly, or at second hand. Her players had been so
obliging in learning their lines that she felt safe in scheduling the performance for mid-December, a scant six weeks after the practising had
been begun. Invitations were sent out by the duchess to the gentry of the
neighbourhood, and anyone who cared to was at liberty to send out private invitations of his own. What with one thing and another, an audience of some forty people might be expected, a prospect which Miss
Cawley contemplated with satisfaction. She was in a humour for pleasant thoughts: Mr. Longstreth, showing himself to be no better an actor
than one might have expected, took a great and obvious relish in his rôle
across from her. His was not, perhaps, an heroic figure; but it was neat
and trim, and looked very well upon the stage, she thought. She thought,
too, that she heard a possibly authentic ardour in his voice when he read
her certain lines, lines pertaining to his courtship of Mistress Millamant.

This circumstance, though she did not dwell on it, tickled her delightfully. Everything, it seemed, went forward very well.

Her only distress, in this period, was that her novel suffered for the play. Rehearsals, revisions, petty quarrels among the players kept her occupied from evening till late at night, forcing her to keep more and more advanced hours if she wished to make progress on her book. The book itself was well: Lotta had become the heroine, held captive in a castle discernibly similar to Grasmere, and tossed miserably between fear of her glacial mistress and suspense as to the mysterious sentiments of that lady's noble son. Despite the wealth of material, however, in the plot and in the people currently round its authoress, she came each night to her pens and paper already weary with exertion. Being a surprisingly strict adherent to discipline, she did not allow herself to set aside the Gothic enterprise while the more classical one went forward, but the strain of two considerable endeavours told on her sometimes, and she found herself singularly prone to fatigue.

She wrote, late each night, in the little room adjoining her bedchamber, kindly allotted to her for the purpose by her hostess. The gold ring which she still wore hampered her efforts to hold the quill properly, but she stubbornly refused to remove it, even when alone. Often, temporarily overcome by a weariness she was reluctant to admit, she would sit idle, staring out of the long window before her at the descending moon. The castle was full of whispers at night: dry branches brushed the window-panes, owls hooted into the darkness, and the wind sighed back as if in response. Thick vines of ivy had long since overgrown the intricately mullioned windows at the side of her desk; they admitted but the faintest rays in daytime, and none at all at dark. She worked by the light of candles, which flickered inconveniently in the draughty little room; it would have been more sensible to write by day, but she never could persuade herself to work alone when she might have the diversion of companions and conversations. Anyway, she had grown accustomed to the sounds of the sleeping castle—the little sighs and creaks, the unexpected cracklings of the fireside behind her, the sudden, noiseless shifting of shadows. She had laboured tranquilly among all these influences for two months now, and had come even to look forward to them; thus it was that when, in a deep midnight of early December, she became frightened nearly half to death, it was not from any spinsterish imaginings, nor any excess of fancy at all.

She had discovered, just after dismissing her abigail that night, that she had managed somehow to mislay her copy of "The Way of the

World." She was much in the habit of losing things, as she had mentioned to Miss Chilton, and it hardly surprised her; it was only very vexatious just now, for she had counted on reviewing a scene in the fourth act, a scene which her players could never seem to perform without an extraordinary amount of confusion. Inwardly berating herself for her carelessness, she rose from the desk and went in search of the wayward volume. She might have dropped it on her bed, she thought hopefully—but a quick glance at that piece of furniture assured her it was not so. Very well then, she told herself, a retracing of steps was in order. She had had it in the ball-room, of course; most probably it was there she had forgot it. She took a candle into her hand, for the house was asleep and the corridors but dimly lighted, and began to wend her way to the ball-room, looking in every likely spot she passed for a sign of her lost property. The ball-room was at a very considerable distance from her own apartments (she had noticed it before, when trying to run from one place to the other during a rehearsal) and her path to it took her through a perfect maze of rooms and hallways, winding stair-cases and suites laid out in succession. What an idiot she was to have left it behind! she reproached herself. She had never done so before—she had made a point, in fact, of remembering to keep it with her precisely to avoid such nocturnal meanderings as these. The whole process would take some ten minutes, no doubt—ten minutes which might have been expended a good deal more fruitfully. Such were her musings as she passed through the corridors, as swiftly as the flame of her candle would allow. She had lost so very many things in her time that the entire subject was grown annoying to her, and she came down very hard upon herself.

Almost the final passageway she had to traverse before reaching the ball-room was the picture gallery, a long, dim hall hung with the fading portraits of innumerable ancestors of the house of Karr. She entered this room in the act of resigning herself to the obvious: she had left her book in the ball-room itself, and would be spared no steps in retrieving it. The most ancient of Karr's line were hung at the end of the corridor nearest to her; a ghastly, time-stained countenance emerged from the shadows on her left as she hurried by, then another somewhat less ravaged, and a third only vaguely dusky.

It was as she was passing the fourth portrait that she brought herself up short all at once, and stood listening curiously. She thought she had heard footsteps. She turned about, peering into the dimness she had left behind her, then facing the entrance to the ball-room again and trying to see through its open doors. If anyone were astir, he did not seem to carry a light. If he did not carry a light, she reasoned, he could not be astir, for only a fool would attempt to make his way through the convoluted passages of the castle without a candle. There was no one, then, she concluded, and proceeded (a bit more slowly) toward the ball-room again. As soon as she had begun to walk, she heard it again. She could hear her own footfalls too: they were light, and clicked a trifle. What she had heard, if it were anything at all, was the heavy, deliberate tread of a large man. Who? Lord Wyborn? He was ponderous enough. But why should he be abroad at this hour—and without a candle? She looked up and down the gallery again. There was no one, nor the shadow of a shadow, save her own. Miss Cawley, though it was not like her, was beginning to feel just the slightest bit apprehensive. Aware of this, she straightened herself severely and resumed her march to the empty ball-room. A step! She had heard it, as clear as day, and though she stood still herself now, the steps continued. What was above her? Could someone be passing through a hallway over her head? She rather thought (though the castle was so strangely laid out, it was difficult to be certain) that a series of chambers for the guests occupied the space in question. If it were so, the unknown walker must have been passing through walls to pursue the course he did. She would look in the morning, she told herself bravely, as the steps, eerie and irregular, continued. What on earth—? Of a sudden there was a loud thump, and it was this that startled Miss Cawley so much that her heart seemed to jump into her throat. A silence ensued. She listened, and the footsteps resumed, passing inexorably to the very threshold of the ball-room. There they stopped, and she could hear only the beating of her own heart. Was it finished? A moment assured her that it was not, for the steps began again, this time moving toward herself. Miss Cawley suddenly decided that it was not, after all, so very important to recover her lost volume. She turned and moved away from the advancing footfalls, slowly at first, but then more and more swiftly. At last, giving in to a sensation of irresistible agitation, she ran from the ominous scene. Her candle blew out; still she ran. Her uneasiness gave way to a positive terror, and she reached the safety of her chamber gasping for air.

8

"I should die in such a case," Lady Stanton declared to her husband, while administering the final touch of her toilette with a mechanical gesture. She could not concentrate on her reflection, and entirely failed to notice that the eardrop in her right lobe did not match the one in her left. She would never have thought of going out at such a moment anyway, except that this was Sunday and one had—one wanted, in fact—to go to church.

Lord Stanton watched her, fully prepared to depart and walking the length of the room as was his wont. "My dear, things are impossible enough without your exaggerating," he said, as gently as he could. He was quite as over-set as Lady Stanton, and did not care to hear his own sentiments restated.

"I am scarcely exaggerating," she brought out, dropping her brush absent-mindedly and turning round to face her lord. "Could you go on living—would you wish to, after all—with such a disgrace as that upon our heads?"

"It is a case of the lesser of two evils," he muttered, pacing more rapidly. His aimless gyrations brought him alongside of a highly polished Pembroke table, on which lay a little note, neatly folded. He reached for it, did not quite touch it, hesitated an instant with his hand hovering in the air, then faced away from the table abruptly. He knew its contents—knew them perfectly, indeed. It was a second demand from the Contessa di Tremini; Lady Stanton had discovered it beneath her pillow when she retired the previous night. The contessa, it appeared, was not to be satisfied with a single payment: as Lady Stanton had feared, she saw no reason to desist when she had found so successful a formula. This time she wanted a good deal more money. The Stantons could pay it, Lord Walker had told his wife, without being obliged to liquidate their major holdings. However, if they paid the countess from such funds, they would not be able to give Wyborn Amabel's dowry as promptly as they had promised. The contessa, moreover, had made it clear that she was impatient: time was of the essence.

"Why is she so greedy?" Lady Stanton suddenly burst out tearfully. "To look at her one would never dream she wanted money! And I had understood the late count was very wealthy." A salty droplet rolled from her eye and down her pretty, fading cheek. She was too distressed to bother with brushing it off, and it fell from her cheek to her chin, and thence to her breast.

"I can't say, I can't say," her husband murmured, as puzzled as her ladyship. "Perhaps she loses at cards."

"Then she ought to stop gaming."

Lord Stanton made no reply.

"In any case, you will have to ask Wyborn to wait," Lady Stanton resumed. "It will put us in an odious position, but that is nothing, I suppose, to what Lady di Tremini's displeasure might do."

"Precisely," said Stanton.

"I do not know how I shall sit through church today," his wife took up fretfully. "I am half mad with hatred for that woman. It is almost blasphemous to enter a church with such sensations. Fancy her putting that note under my pillow! I nearly died of surprise and misery."

"At least, however, you were alone when you found it," Lord Stanton pointed out. "The note she dealt to you at that whist table seems to me to have been much more demoniacally conceived."

Lady Stanton did not answer, but rose and made as if to leave the room. "We must make it plain to her that there will be no payments after this," she said in a low tone as she passed out of the apartment. "If we are forced to sell Driscow Park, all the world will know something is amiss."

"Driscow Park!" his lordship echoed. "We *will* be forced to sell that, immediately. What we must hope is that we shall not be obliged to part with Baddesleigh!"

She was too dismayed to speak for a moment. Then, "Oh, Walker, is it as bad as that? I had not understood," she cried, and seemed almost to wilt visibly. His lordship would have liked to comfort her, but there was no time, even if there had been means. He administered a bracing squeeze to her arm, and the two marched soberly off to the principal drawing-room, where a party for church had assembled.

The reader will recall that the church attached to Grasmere stood at the top of a steep hill, just across the stream which ran through a part of its park. When the weather permitted, it was the habit of the duchess to walk across the grounds to a little bridge that spanned the stream and, crossing over the bridge, ascend the knoll afoot. Today was not a mild day—in fact, it was very cold—but the sky was open and the air brisk. The earth, already frozen, made a barely audible crunching sound as the party of church-goers bent their steps upon it. They went in pairs and little knots of people; nearly everyone chose to attend services, though more from habit than piety.

Lotta Chilton hung a little behind the rest of the company. Since her rupture with the duchess she had grown almost accustomed to attending services with the guests (instead of, as had hitherto been her custom, with the servants), but she felt awkward nonetheless—she felt awkward nearly all the time now, it seemed—and she straggled as far behind her unwilling hostess as was practicable. Karr escorted his mother; Remington and Longstreth went together, buzzing furiously over some piece of news; it was only natural, therefore, that Miss Jessica Cawley should eventually forsake her brother and fall behind to bear Lotta company. Besides, she had decided to share her strange adventure of the previous night with Miss Chilton, and could hardly wait to tell her what it was.

"You don't think it was a hoax?" Lotta inquired, when she had been put in possession of as many facts as Miss Cawley knew.

Jessica took her companion's arm and leaned her pert head close to Lotta's beautiful one. "You know, I am certain it must have been," she said confidentially, "and yet . . . I can't imagine how it was contrived. Whoever arranged it certainly did it well!"

"You say you looked upstairs this morning—?"

"Yes, I prowled about while the others were gathering in the drawing-room. It was just as I thought: three guest chambers, all in a row. There is a hallway in front of them, of course, but it is not nearly in the same situation as the picture gallery. Even if it were," she continued earnestly, "that does not explain how our prankster knew I would be in the gallery, at just that moment, on an errand only I could have known about."

"You had mislaid your book? Was that it?"

Miss Cawley nodded. "I had been talking to Mr. Longstreth just before I went upstairs—"

"Ah, Mr. Longstreth, was it?"

"I beg your pardon?"

"Nothing, my dear," said Lotta. "Pray continue."

Jessica paused a moment longer, then resumed. "I remember pointing out to him that troublesome scene, the one in which everyone seems invariably to step on everyone else's toes. I was telling him how I meant to go through it that night; I must have put the book down, somehow, while I explained. And then when I got to my desk, I found it was missing."

Lotta pondered this, frowning slightly. A sharp wind had brought the delicate colour in her cheeks to a high glow, so that even this unattractive grimace could not spoil her prettiness. "Are you quite positive you could not have imagined it all?"

Jessica glanced at her reproachfully, as a little girl looks at an adult who is talking excessive nonsense to her. "Really, my dear! You must give me some credit for knowing truth from fancy."

Lotta shrugged lightly. "Then it is one of those things which has happened, yet which cannot have happened. There are such things, you know."

"I beg your pardon?"

"Well, you know what I mean," she said, as they crossed the little wooden bridge and began to mount the hill. "For example—"

"Yes, an example is in order!"

"For example, suppose you close a window. You stand up, you go to the window, you take hold of the latch, you pull it to, you bolt it, you sit down again. Not only do you remember closing the window, you remember that the latch had grown warm standing out in the sunshine. You remember everything, including how it felt."

"And—?" Jessica urged impatiently.

"And yet when you look up again, there stands the window open! You know perfectly well you just shut it; you remind yourself of the warmth of the handle—and yet there is nothing to do but get up and close it all over again. It would hardly do to insist that, having done it once, it is too unjust to be obliged to do it once more."

Miss Cawley pouted, evidently unpersuaded.

"Another example, then," Lotta resumed. "Surely this has happened to you: you are looking for your work-box. You are seated at the worktable; you *know* you left it just there, just last night. But it is nowhere to be seen! You grow more and more annoyed; impatiently, you ring for the maid. 'Susan, where is my work-box?' you fairly shout at her. The poor girl curtsies and blushes. 'But it is right there, ma'am,' she says, afraid you are playing tricks with her. 'Right in front of you!' You look at the corner of the table where she points, and lo and behold—the work-box, which must have been there all along. Now don't tell me you have never lived through such a scene; I won't believe you. Certain things simply cannot be; and yet they are, as clear as day," Lotta concluded. "That is what I make of your footsteps."

Jessica's pout had deepened. "Well, I do not like it," she said stubbornly. "It seems to me that is a very poor explanation—though I do admit, such things can happen."

"If you find a better explanation, I hope you will tell me," Lotta said, not at all offended at being disbelieved.

"I have certain ideas," Jessica said darkly, staring very hard at Algernon Longstreth's back while they toiled after the others up the hill. "Mr. Longstreth," she said, in a low, breathy tone (the hill was rather precipitous, and she had to speak her words in little groups so that she could breathe between them) "seems to have the most . . . particular interest . . . in convincing me the castle is . . . haunted. He even had . . . Frant . . . tell me some cock-and-bull . . . story about . . . Robin Hood." The ascent complete, the two women stood for a moment at the door of the ancient stone church. "I mean to have a talk with that young fellow," Jessica continued, still panting slightly. "But I won't for the world admit I was frightened! If it was he who set the trap, it would give him too much satisfaction."

Miss Chilton smiled as her friend passed before her into the church. This postscript to the mysterious account seemed to her to clarify many things: Mr. Longstreth must have been ingenious indeed to baffle Miss Cawley so thoroughly. Though the sermon was long and tedious, Miss Chilton submitted to the discomfort of sitting through it almost gratefully. She had been enjoying the past few weeks far too much, she felt. It was the first time in all her life she had had no duties whatever to perform, except the most personal ones; she was unaccustomed to so leisurely an existence. It almost made her nervous, particularly as she found herself adapting to it so easily, and she did not think an hour of tedium would come at all amiss. Miss Chilton's family, being of lower rank than the families of her companions, had taken their religion a bit more sincerely, caring less for flourishes and more for sagacity in the sermons they heard and read. Some of that seriousness had rubbed off, inevitably, on Lotta, and though she did not care much for visions and miracles, she did have a deep sense of good and evil.

Miss Cawley, on the other hand, cared for religion about as much as she cared for the rules of precedence: she would never have thought of either herself (and if she had, she would have fashioned them differently), but so long as they were there, she was just as glad to have them. The sermon seemed to her interminable, and she very frankly said something of this sort to Mr. Longstreth, as they left the church together. She had made sure to gain his side for the journey back home, speaking of trifles until they had descended the hill, but addressing him carefully thereafter. "You know, Mr. Longstreth," she told him, nonchalantly availing herself of the arm he offered her, "I rather think I met your ghost last night."

"*My* ghost! I should hope not," he returned. "I should be dead, if you had."

"You know what I mean," she replied, rather crossly. "Frant's ghost, if you will. Grasmere's ghost."

"Oh! Robin Hood's ghost," he exclaimed.

"Hush!" She did not, for some reason, wish this conversation to be widely heard. "Yes, Robin—that one," she amended. It annoyed her to pretend, as he did, that such things could be.

"Did you *see* him?" Algernon inquired eagerly.

"You know perfectly well I did not. I heard him. Or rather, I heard whatever it was you contrived—"

"Miss Cawley, this is fascinating," he broke in. "Where did you find him? In your apartments?"

"Can't you guess?" she asked, with emphasis.

"Oh! You don't mean to say you went to the picture gallery and listened!" he cried. "That was very bold, but foolish."

"I did not go to the gallery to listen," she corrected quite harshly. "I went to fetch a book I'd lost."

"Oh! And the ghost was waiting for you there?"

"What do you mean, waiting for me?"

"Well, no doubt . . . if there is anything to that ring you found, you know—no doubt he is more interested in you than in anyone else."

"Mr. Longstreth—!" she said, in annoyance.

"Miss Cawley," he went on, ignoring her, "this is most astonishing. I don't mind telling you that—even while I insisted upon it so strongly to you—I had my doubts about the real existence of this spectre. I know I pushed it rather far, but I think you guessed that I was only half in earnest. If you did not, I apologize—" He broke off, as if waiting for her to murmur an acceptance, but she said nothing. "Anyway, I did feel a trifle sceptical about it . . . you know—so very superstitious! One does not care to give in to such, ah, Gothic notions . . . But this puts a whole new light upon the matter! So you actually heard him? Tell me about it, pray!"

Miss Cawley glanced at him askance; this was not the response she had expected to provoke. He did look, she was obliged to admit, very excited. "I can't but believe that you know more of it than I do," she said, after a moment. "Come, Mr. Longstreth—confess, won't you?"

"Confess? But . . ." He stopped as if bewildered.

"It was all your doing, now wasn't it?"

"Miss Cawley!" cried he, reproachfully.

"Do not play innocent with me, I beg you!" she said, in a tone which was far from beseeching.

"Miss Cawley," he repeated, still aghast. "I own, I am not above playing such a trick on a fellow; Mr. Remington would tell you that, if I did not. But to frighten a lady! For a joke! Miss Cawley, do you truly suspect me of such ungentle behaviour?"

She hesitated for an instant, then answered, "Yes. And besides, I wasn't frightened."

"My dear ma'am," said he, as if about to protest again. Then his tone changed abruptly and he continued, "Your suspicions grieve me, but are really neither here nor there just now. The chief thing is, you have actually heard the ghost! That is extraordinary. That is so extraordinary that—if you will do me the goodness to tell me just where and when you heard him—I will listen for him myself tonight."

"You will not hear anything."

"But you did!"

"Good sir, I think you know what I mean."

"Do I?" He mused for a minute. "Oh! This business of its all being a trick of mine. Well, dear Miss Cawley, *you* may be persuaded of that, but I am not."

"That *is* extraordinary," she said acidly; but the truth was, she was bluffing. Mr. Longstreth's surprise seemed so authentic, his curiosity so genuine, that she had begun to wonder if, after all, there might really be a ghost. It was very near to Christmastide; that was when, according to Frant, the ghost was wont to appear. Perhaps Mr. Longstreth was telling the truth! In that case she would be a fool not to investigate further.

Who could tell when she would have another opportunity to encounter a ghost? And it would not only be foolish to avoid the spectre; it would be cowardly as well. Algernon seemed aware of this when he spoke again.

"I would invite you to listen with me," he said, "but for two things. First a mid-night meeting such as that would have the look of a tryst between us. Secondly, I have no doubt the experience will be rather frightening, and fear itself can be hazardous to a lady, if the ghost is not."

If mere curiosity could not decide her, this did. Faced with the double threat of society's disapprobation and a reencounter with terror, Miss Cawley could not cry craven. "I will listen with you," she said, evenly and firmly.

"My dear ma'am, I entreat you," said Longstreth. "I only mentioned the possibility in order to dismiss it. I would not for the world expose you to such—"

"You expose me to nothing," she broke in, laying a heavy emphasis on the word expose. "I have not maintained my independence for nine-and-twenty years for nothing. If I do a thing, I do it. No one else does it for me, or to me."

"Ah! You are very wilful," he murmured.

"If you chuse to characterize it so," she assented.

They had been keeping up a brisk pace all this while, and had almost arrived again at the castle. "At what time precisely did you hear him last night?" Algernon asked, while they crossed a terraced garden made barren by frost.

"I imagine it was some time after two," she said. "Even the gentlemen of the billiard room had retired."

"Very good, then. I shall wait for you in the picture gallery at two."

"I will be there," she replied, but the boldness of this suddenly struck her. "Dear sir," she added, somewhat more softly, "do you think we ought to invite a third party? Merely for corroboration, as it were . . ." Her voice trailed off. She was lying, and felt that her companion knew it.

"Ah, that is a delicate thought," he said, "but I suspect we will scare off our—er—quarry if too many persons accumulate. Even as it is, with two of us, I am afraid he will hesitate to walk."

She blushed at this proof that he knew from what source her suggestion sprang. Miss Jessica Cawley was, at heart, a very modest and decent girl, but she would not for the world have Algernon know this. There was something about him which made her desire to convince him she was just as daring and reckless as any of his male companions. She had portrayed him in her last novel as a dreadful milksop; not for anything would she let him know she was just as mild, essentially, as he. "Very well, then," she answered, willing her colour to subside. "Just as you like. I suppose you can have no objection, however, to my apprising Karr of our plans?"

"Miss Cawley, is it possible you expect me to take liberties with you? I assure you, nothing is farther from my purpose!"

"It is nothing to do with that," she insisted, her flush mounting in spite of her efforts to suppress it. "It simply occurs to me that if there *is* a ghost, and if we are to watch for it, the master of the castle ought to know about it."

"And then your brother ought to know of it too," Longstreth took up, "and of course some lady or other should be informed—for balance, if not for propriety—and before we know it, half the castle will be crowded into the gallery, buzzing and humming . . ."

"I only meant to tell His Grace," she said, drawing herself up.

Mr. Longstreth shrugged. "As you please," he said indifferently. "I only note that such a course did not figure in my own plans."

"Oh, very well!" she exclaimed, exasperated, as she passed indoors at last. "Have it your way, precisely. The last thing I desire is to be charged, tonight, with having spoilt everything by chattering too much."

She glared at him with noticeable hostility, but Algernon declined to notice it. "As you like," he repeated smoothly. "I shall look forward to tonight with the liveliest curiosity and pleasure." With this he bowed, and took leave of her; they met one another at dinner, and again afterwards, but neither mentioned the projected tryst. When they did finally speak of it again, it was in the shadowy picture gallery, just before two o'clock.

Mr. Longstreth begged Miss Cawley to extinguish her candle; he had already done so to his light.

"I don't see that it could matter; I had one last night," she whispered. They both whispered, though without having agreed upon it in so many words.

"Even so," said Algernon, "it has always been my understanding that ghosts consider darkness more hospitable than light."

Jessica hesitated, but she blew out the little flame at last. The utter blackness that enclosed them had the effect of increasing her pulse and quickening all her sensations. It also made her quite scared. "You know," she said, feeling that it would be a comfort at least to hear Mr. Longstreth, even though she could not see him, "I rather wonder if today's being Sunday won't affect his walk. It is a holy day, after all; I should think ghosts would avoid it."

"On the contrary," his voice hissed back, all the stranger for being disembodied, "I believe it stimulates them—makes them more restless, I mean."

"Oh," said Jessica. She cast about in her mind for something more to say, something (preferably) which would draw an audible response from her invisible neighbour. Her suspicion that this was all a trick of Mr. Longstreth's had not been entirely forgot, but it had lost a great deal of its conviction. The oppressive silence of the long gallery, the deep darkness which reigned there, had done much already to persuade Miss Cawley that there might, after all, be unhappy shades at Grasmere. Certainly if a ghost did exist, and if he were aggrieved, this would be a very delightful spot to haunt. Such uneasy concessions to superstition took increasing hold of her thought, so that she could not find anything better to say (after a good deal of searching) than, "Mr. Longstreth?"

There was a silence, which seemed to her interminable. Then, "Miss Cawley?" he answered at last.

"Mr. Longstreth, can you see me?" she asked, at random.

"I can make out a greater blackness where you are," he replied.

"I can't see anything," she whispered back.

"Perhaps the light is better from here. Should you like to exchange places? Are you frightened?"

"Oh, no!" she answered automatically. "Not at all. I was only wondering . . ."

"If that is all, perhaps it will be best to keep silence between us," said Algernon. "Unless there is something significant to say."

"Of course," she said, ashamed of having manifested her unease. "I was about to suggest that myself."

"Very good, then," he answered, and for many minutes (as it seemed) a complete, ghastly soundlessness prevailed.

"Mr. Longstreth!" Jessica hissed suddenly. "Mr. Longstreth, did you hear that?"

No one answered.

"Mr. Longstreth!" she repeated, her eyes straining through the dimness in an effort to see him.

"Miss Cawley?" came at last.

"Mr. Longstreth, did you hear it?" she asked urgently.

"Hear what, dear ma'am?"

"Why, the step! Listen—here it is again!" Jessica forced herself to be quiet, though the dull, heavy sound had reawakened in her the terror of the previous night. All her muscles seemed to go rigid, and her throat constricted excruciatingly.

Three or four more steps reverberated clearly in the gallery before Mr. Longstreth spoke. "I hear nothing," he whispered finally. "Are you positive you hear it?"

"Nothing?" The meaning of this did not sink in for a moment; when it did, poor Miss Cawley's palms grew moist, and her knees began to tremble. "Dear sir, listen again," she said, most pathetically. "Surely you hear it."

Mr. Longstreth obligingly fell silent once more, but at the end of a minute he murmured, "Have you heard it again?"

"Yes—constantly! Haven't you?"

"Not a thing," he said, causing his companion deep distress.

"Mr. Longstreth, I believe we ought to—to go," she whispered, keeping her voice as steady as possible—which was not very steady.

No answer came.

"Mr. Longstreth?"

"I was listening."

"Can't we go?" she fairly pleaded, not even bothering to ask if he had heard anything.

"Oh! Yes, if you like," he replied, apparently unconscious of how near she was to fleeing with or without him.

She turned gratefully away from the miserable gallery, walking slowly at first but quite skipping as she neared a lit sitting-room. Algernon joined her after a moment, carrying his unlighted candle, his expression clearly disappointed, but interested nonetheless. If he saw how frightened she was, he gave no sign of it, a courtesy she appreciated. It would have been a blow to her pride to be seen behaving in cowardly fashion; pride was all that had kept her in the gallery once Mr. Longstreth had denied hearing anything. "Most extraordinary," were Algernon's first words, as he rejoined her. "Most extraordinary."

He had maintained a whisper, and so did Jessica. It was some time before either of them remembered they were now at liberty to raise their voices. "I am glad you were entertained," she said, her voice still shaking. Abruptly, she seated herself on a tufted ottoman; it was a great relief to her trembling legs.

"Oh, I was but—how can it be that you heard him, and I did not?"

All unwillingly, Jessica shuddered. "A puzzle," she murmured, afraid that any longer a sentence would necessarily reveal the tremor in her voice. She clasped her damp hands tightly in her lap, striving valiantly to govern herself.

"A puzzle indeed," he agreed. "You know, I see only two explanations possible . . ." He paused, waiting for her to ask what these were. As she said nothing, he continued, "First, it may be that because you wear the ring, you are privileged to hear him."

Jessica was too uncomfortable to weigh her opinions of this possibility just now. Algernon had gone to the fireplace, and stood leaning on the mantel, looking at her as if he did not really see her. "Second?" she prompted at last, squirming under his thoughtful gaze.

"Oh! Well, obviously, that it is in your imagination, Miss Cawley. With the greatest respect for you, of course, and with no intention of giving offence, that is the other logical conclusion."

"It is not my imagination!" she contradicted hotly, feeling alive for the first time since quitting the gallery.

"Ah, I am sorry to unsettle you," he said. "I see I have offended after all. But you know, it is hardly an insult. Novelists are expected to have high fancies; really, you might take it as a measure of your poetic ability."

"Mr. Longstreth, I do not fancy it," she insisted, with vehemence. "Perhaps it *is* the ring, if that is the only alternative—but I know it is not mere imagination, and I will not rest till I have proven it."

Algernon smiled, rather kindly. "I think you must do that, at least— rest, I mean. It must be near three by now. Tomorrow we will talk of this again."

He was right. It was too late—and she was by far too exhausted—to investigate any further. She was not too fatigued, however, to think, and the first result of this process was (it seemed to her) an inspiration. "Dear sir, I know how we ought to proceed," she said, as she gathered herself together to rise. "Tomorrow night we will meet again, just as we did tonight—but you will wear the ring."

Mr. Longstreth seemed to consider this, a faint half-smile round his lips. "Very well," he said, "but it cannot be tomorrow night. Tomorrow night I am engaged to Mr. Remington; I promised I should go over his financial papers with him. It seems they are rather in a muddle."

"Surely not so much of one as to keep you all night!" she protested.

"On the contrary, dear ma'am. I am afraid poor Cosmo has no head for numbers; you would scarcely credit the quantity of debts he owes. And then, we are to review my papers too. We do it every winter, when the dust of the season has settled thoroughly. It keeps us out of the sponging houses."

"Can't you do it alone?" she asked, pouting.

"Oh, no, that would never answer! It's a tradition, don't you see? Even if we could do it by ourselves, half the diversion would go out of it."

"It sounds like precious little diversion in the first place," she murmured, as they passed together out of the sitting-room.

"So it does, I suppose; but I assure you, we enjoy it hugely. We take a few bottles with us, you know, and whenever we find a bill we had forgot, each of us takes a swallow."

"I expect you are quite foxed at the end of it."

"Oh, under the table every year!" he assured her gaily. "But do not fret, I pray. You and I shall meet again the night after, and I shall wear the ring."

Jessica was obliged to be contented by this; but she found, on the following evening, that she could not leave matters hanging quite as they were. Instead, she begged Lotta Chilton (who already knew of the matter anyway—so Mr. Longstreth could not object, she told herself) to meet her in the picture gallery at two in the morning and listen with her.

"Two!" cried Lotta, smiling. She had a pretty good idea what would happen if they went that night, and though the whole thing amused her, she had no desire to keep such excessively late hours.

"Please," said Jessica; and, "You must."

Lotta's smile widened, but she said, "Well, if I must, I must." The ladies sat alone in Miss Cawley's sitting-room between mid-night and the appointed hour, to ensure that neither fell asleep, and proceeded down the shadowy corridors together.

"Mr. Longstreth says we ought to extinguish our candles," said Jessica, as they entered the gallery.

Miss Chilton shivered, but not with fear. The corridor was cold, and her fatigue caused her to feel the chill the more. "Then let us do so," she replied.

"But I don't think it's necessary," Miss Cawley informed her.

"Very good, then; let's don't."

Accordingly, they did not, merely standing with their flickering tapers and waiting to hear the steps. Silence reigned.

"Perhaps we ought to snuff them after all," Jessica conceded after some ten minutes of soundlessness.

Lotta smiled, as she had earlier that evening. "As you like," she

agreed, and blew her candle out. Jessica followed suit and the two
women stood, both shivering from their several sensations, in the black-
ened passageway.

Nothing happened.

"How long have we been here?" Miss Cawley whispered finally.

"Oh, half an hour, I should think."

"He ought to have walked by now," said Jessica. "Do you think we
read the hour wrong, before we came down here?"

"I doubt it," Lotta answered.

"Perhaps I should look again?" Jessica murmured dubiously. The
eeriness of the dark gallery had begun to disturb her again; she seemed
to feel the painted eyes of Karr's dead forebears upon her. Lotta knew
Miss Cawley was on edge, and took pity on her.

"There's no point in it," she said gently. "Shall we go to bed? I don't
think the ghost is coming tonight."

"Oh. If you think so," Jessica answered, a careless remark which was
meant to veil her deep relief. She felt much better as soon as they had
regained the lighted sitting-room, and questioned Miss Chilton eagerly.
"Why do you suppose he didn't come?" she asked.

Lotta yawned. "Perhaps he had to go over his accounts."

"I beg your pardon?"

"My dear, doesn't it occur to you this ghost is a creature of Mr.
Longstreth's making?"

"Frequently," Jessica said, "but I don't think it can be."

"Because—?"

"Because he should have to walk through walls to make that noise. I
went back and looked a second time, you know. Apart from that, his interest in our investigations seems to be most genuine. Of course," she
added, "he *is* a good dissembler. He plays Mirabell very well, don't you
think?"

"Ah, in that rôle he is inspired," said Lotta, giving a laugh.

"Do you think so?" Jessica looked at her, her round, bright eyes
sparkling at the possibility.

"Why certainly!" Lotta told her. "Mark my words, you shall have an
offer from him before next season, whether you want it or no."

Miss Cawley did not, as she had on a previous occasion, beg her
friend to desist from such speculation. Instead her bright eyes softened
to an almost dreamy quality, and she answered, "That would be
pleasant."

"Would it?"

Jessica returned her attention to Miss Chilton with a snap. "Oh, I suppose so. It is always agreeable to hear offers, I think."

"For a moment, perhaps," said Lotta. "It is scarcely agreeable when one is obliged to disappoint the gentleman, however."

Miss Cawley had made a complete return to her habitual attitude of impudence. "Poor Lotta, you would find it so. I positively revel in it. And if the gentleman is boorish, or stupid, I make certain to let him down with a thump."

"I don't believe it," Lotta said frankly.

Jessica shrugged. "Then don't," she replied. The two ladies exchanged their good-nights a few moments after this, and retired to their chambers.

Late the next night (Jessica ought to have been dropping with fatigue by this time, but her excitement kept her in motion), Mr. Longstreth found Miss Cawley awaiting him in the lighted sitting-room nearest to the picture gallery. "Good evening," said he, bowing. "I hope you rested long and well last night, to compensate for the previous one?"

"I did, thank you," she lied. To her surprise, this drew a grin from Algernon which might almost have been described as michievous; certainly the gleam in his eye could appropriately have been termed so, and his amusement was manifest. "You haven't been talking to Lotta?" she challenged him abruptly.

"Miss Chilton?" he said. He seemed to muse for a moment. "No, I believe not. Not today, that is. Why?"

"No particular reason," she returned, hardly caring for the uselessness of this answer. She was still suspicious, and meant to ask Lotta whether or not she had told Mr. Longstreth of their mutual exploits the night before. She had been begged not to; Jessica would think it very unkind in her if she had. "Here is the ring," she said in a moment, taking the heavy gold band from her finger.

Mr. Longstreth received it soberly, and slipped it on to the smallest finger of his right hand. "Are we set, then?"

"I am," said Jessica. She had a momentary desire to abandon the effort altogether—even to confess her apprehensiveness to Mr. Longstreth. She suppressed it at once, though, and bravely led the way from the sitting-room.

"I hope your affairs are in order now," she said, as they approached the gallery.

"Ah, very much so!" he replied, emphasizing his words as if they meant more than they appeared to.

Miss Cawley had no time to question him again, however, since they had reached their posts once more. "May I?" said Algernon, having blown out his own candle and offering to do the same to hers. Jessica nodded, and the long passageway was filled with darkness at once.

Almost immediately, Mr. Longstreth began to whisper. "I hear it!" he hissed. "I hear it!"

"No, do you?" she breathed in return. "Isn't it dreadful?"

"Dreadful, dreadful," he agreed. "Ah! There it is again."

Jessica was silent for a time, while Algernon emitted a series of poignant Ahs. Then, "You know, I hear nothing," she said.

Mr. Longstreth made no reply.

"Mr. Longstreth?" No answer. "Mr.—dear sir, please!"

"Most extraordinary," he said, after what seemed an eternity.

"Why did you not answer me before?" she asked, piqued.

"Astonishing," was all he whispered back.

"Then you admit it was not my imagination," she challenged. Somehow she had utterly forgot to doubt his word: if Mr. Longstreth said he heard the steps, then he heard them. Lotta Chilton might believe it was all a hoax of his, but Jessica could not believe he would carry the joke so far. He had not the stomach for it, she had decided; he was too much the dandy.

"Oh, dear!" he said, not answering her query. "He's turning."

Miss Cawley began to sense his excitement as well as her own. "Mr. Longstreth," she hissed suddenly, "let me take the ring."

"Oh, no—it is too ghastly!" he protested. "Ah! Another step."

"Let me, I pray," she repeated. "I want it. Oh Mr. Longstreth, I wish to hear it."

"No, no. So unearthly—!"

"Mr. Longstreth!" she said, stamping her foot with vexation. Of all things in the world, Miss Cawley could least bear denial.

"You do not really—" he began, but she interrupted him by making an abrupt gesture in the direction of his hands—or at least, in what she supposed was the direction of his hands. She ended up, however, brushing his elbow with her left hand, and clutching at the air with her right.

"Please," she begged, frustrated in her miscarried attempt to take the ring by force.

Mr. Longstreth still hesitated. "I do not—well, I suppose you may as well . . ." came out of the darkness, but the next thing she heard was a small, hard clink as the ring hit the floor. "Damme!" cried Longstreth.

"You haven't dropped it!" she exclaimed in dismay.

"Yes, I'm afraid I have." In an instant both persons were on their knees, brushing wildly at the surface of the polished wood floor in hopes of retrieving the lost treasure. This was scarcely the most sensible behaviour; what they ought to have done was light a candle, then look. Jessica instinctively felt, however, that to make a light would be to scare the ghost away, and so she simply crouched, arms extended, and swept the floor with her fingers.

"Stupid of me. I'm so sorry," Algernon hissed.

"Well . . ." she said. Her left hand found the wall; carefully, she felt along its length. It was excessively frustrating to be able to see nothing, particularly when time was so significant. Who could tell how long the ghost would walk? Perhaps they had already frightened him off for the night. Dimly she wondered where Mr. Longstreth might be; she could hear his breathing, but not clearly enough to locate his situation. Just as this thought crossed her mind her hand came up against something in the dark—not the ring, as it turned out, but something surprisingly agreeable. It was Mr. Longstreth's hand, and he grasped hers in it and held it warmly for a good long while.

Somehow the ghost was forgot.

9

"Dear lady," Mr. Septimus Faust was saying to his hostess a few days later, "you must at least allow she is charming."

The duchess, however, apparently did not feel compelled to allow this, for she turned her austere gaze from him and said nothing.

"Allow then, that she is intriguing," he pursued.

The duchess hesitated. "She is that," she brought out at last, not without some dryness of expression.

Septimus grinned. "So you seriously suspect her of scheming?" he took up. "What a compliment you pay her!"

"I? Pay Miss Chilton a compliment?" said she. "I am afraid I do not understand you."

Mr. Faust shrugged his bony shoulders. "To conceive of a really excellent scheme, to plot it, to execute it successfully—that requires extraordinary qualities. One must be shrewd, sensitive, pitiless, firm of purpose—oh, any number of things! Think of Lady Macbeth: would you endow Miss Chilton with her parts?"

Her Grace of Karr moved listlessly in her chair. "If there is a point to this, Mr. Faust, kindly arrive at it soon."

"Ah, I am sorry to say it, but you disappoint me, madam." Septimus sat (he had been circling vaguely round the dowager's chair) on a mahogany settee across from her, and leaned his elbows on his knees. "One ought never to judge rashly. One only plays into the hands of one's adversary by doing so. When you suspect a scheme, see first if there is a schemer involved in it. Miss Chilton, I must humbly submit, is not a schemer. Frankly, I do not think her pretty head capable of the necessary decisions."

"You are drawn in by that prettiness," said Her Grace warningly.

"Not at all," he disclaimed. "It is you, indeed, who are swayed by Miss Chilton's beauty. You allow it to prejudice you against her."

"Fustian," the duchess returned sourly. "You fancy yourself some sort of knight, defending your fair lady. You will do well to remember that this particular lady is in no need of your defence."

"To prove to you, madam, that I am not merely a gallant fool, I will tell you frankly that though Miss Chilton is capable of no grand deceptions, the Contessa di Tremini most certainly is. You once intimated as much yourself—do you remember? And if the contessa's is not a face to worship, I beg to know whose is. Not even Miss Chilton holds a candle to her."

"I don't suppose you are trying to tell me that it was the contessa who plotted the failure of Karr's courtship of Lady Henrietta. Are you? For if she did, she seems to have bungled it. Lotta Chilton has got the man."

"Good heavens no," said Faust. "If the contessa were to carry out a plot, I can assure you it would entail nothing so unpleasant as her being obliged to remarry. She must have been quite a trial to her first husband; I am sure nothing is more distasteful to her than the loss of her freedom."

"You seem to know a good deal about the contessa," said she sharply.

Mr. Faust smiled, not without modesty. "I know what I see," he said simply.

"And you see innocence in Lotta, and duplicity in Rowena. Very interesting. You must permit me to borrow your quizzing-glass someday; no doubt it has some very unusual ocular properties." And the duchess brought her heavy eyebrows very low. It was nearly time to dress for dinner; how many times, she wondered, had she dressed for dinner in her life? And what was the use of it, and the thousand other proprieties to which she had sacrificed her youth, her happiness, and time, if her son took to his bed a little piece of Italianate riff-raff—and made her Duchess of Karr to boot, for all anyone knew?

"It is not in the glass, but in the eye which penetrates it," said Faust, refusing to take offense. He drew out the article in question, first dangling it on its riband, then raising it to his eye. "I see an unhappy lady before me, for example," said he, surveying her. "That is not how she presents herself, however."

"Certainly not," Her Grace agreed. "If I am ever unhappy, you will kindly have the goodness not to observe it until I point it out to you. Otherwise it is like having a spy in one's own home."

"Ah! A spy! That is very good; I enjoy that immensely. A sentimental spy; that is my true nature."

"You are very pleased with yourself," the duchess remarked.

"And you are very displeased with everyone. No, Your Grace, for your own happiness, I must insist on your reevaluating Miss Chilton. Confess that she had no designs upon your son; she is not that sort of female. What is the use of bearing so fruitless a grudge?"

"One does not bear grudges for any use, as you put it," she informed him. "Your rather sordid past is showing, Mr. Faust. One bears grudges as an exercise of leisure, of liberty. An injury to one's honour costs nothing, in general, and the defence of honour is equally barren of reward."

"You feel your honour is injured?" Faust inquired, adding, "My past is in no wise sordid, by the by."

She smiled, but without humour. "I had always imagined it to be quite rank with vulgarity," she said.

"Then you oughtn't to let your imagination roam so widely of the mark."

"This conversation is taking on a distinctly unpleasant tone," Her Grace observed in even, careful accents. "Shall we terminate it?"

"Not before you have made me some reasonable answer about Miss Chilton," Faust said. "I must beg you to believe I have your own best interests at heart. You only wound yourself with this obstinacy. Karr is too besotted to mind your sentiments, and Miss Chilton—though I am sure she regrets your ill-feeling—must know herself to be innocent. She is the sort of girl to find great and sustaining comfort in such a thought."

"Phaugh!" was all the duchess said. She was really quite repulsed by Mr. Faust's tranquil self-righteousness. Who would have thought so dedicated a hedonist could one day have authored such nice little speeches? She did not know—truly she did not—why she had not sent him from her half an hour ago.

"'Phaugh' is all very well for you, but we cannot tell how painful it may be to Miss Chilton," he said.

"I thought you just told me she suffers no remorse."

"Not for her own actions, no—but for your displeasure . . ."

The duchess flared up suddenly, a thing she very seldom did except with Karr. "Will you have the courtesy to explain, please, precisely how Miss Chilton—if she is so profoundly good as you say—excuses her behaviour to herself?"

"What has her behaviour been?" asked Faust.

"Why, she entered this house as a dependent, estranged its master from his intended, and contrived to win his affection herself," the duchess snapped back, as if all the world knew. "Is more necessary before you will condemn a course of conduct?"

"She fell in love," Septimus said simply.

"Absurd. Girls of her class are not raised to fall in love."

"It explains a good deal, does it not?" asked Faust.

"What do you mean?" the dowager returned sharply.

"Simply that, if she were in love, the chain of events that you outline take on an irrefutable logic of their own."

"And what of Karr? Is it not necessary that he be in love? Mind you, I grant you nothing regarding Lotta," she added.

"Certainly he must be in love as well. Do you think it impossible?"

But the duchess chose not to answer this. She was silent for a while, then spoke at last. "Mr. Faust, are you familiar with the adage, 'Love laughs at locksmiths'?"

"I am," he said, his bright eyes trained upon hers in a curious stare.

"Well," said the Duchess of Karr, "I laugh at love," and so saying rose and ended their interview.

Faust walked away from it with a distinct sensation of failure. He did not often attempt to persuade anyone of anything—generally it appeared to him a quite useless occupation—but for a sufficiently moving cause, he could speak out. When he did speak he liked to be listened to. He could not delude himself into believing he had had any impact upon the duchess's opinion of Miss Chilton; it was a shame, really. She was a sweet, gentle girl—and such a complexion as that! Well, it was not met with every day. He went off to dress for dinner in a state of mind which was the mental equivalent of a shrug of the shoulders. Her Grace of Karr was a fascinating woman, he thought, but she was nothing if not stubborn.

Lady Anne Stanton, who—being neither so powerful as the duchess, nor so beautiful as Miss Chilton—took up very little space in Mr. Faust's consciousness, did not come down to dinner that day. She had made a second little visit to the chamber with the ivory knob on its door, a visit identical in every respect to her first one except that the sum of money she deposited with the abigail was a good deal larger. As before, she found the excursion quite exhausting, and lay, somewhat teary-eyed, on her bed while dinner was served to the others. She even declined an offer from her hostess to have that repast sent up to her room; she could not eat, nor could she rest comfortably. If a third demand for money should be made, she decided, it would have to be refused. She would sooner face any consequence than part with Baddesleigh: the relinquishment of her ancestral home would kill her, she felt. She said as much to her lord that night, who was very sorry to hear it, for he had had an encounter with Lord Wyborn during the evening which was anything but pleasant.

"He wants the dowry," Lord Stanton informed his wife. "Or at least a part of it. He will not discuss a date for the wedding until he has received something."

"What did you tell him?" asked her ladyship, stricken.

"I put him off, or tried to. It won't answer for very long, however. I'm afraid I must go down to Driscow Park, and see about selling it off."

"Ah!" cried Lady Stanton; and, "When?"

"Tomorrow, probably. Soonest is best."

Lady Stanton took this in. "I despise the very thought of it," she said finally, "but you will probably do best to offer it to Sir Hubert. He has had his eye on it these ten years, and will no doubt be willing to pay a good deal."

"That was my idea too," he agreed. Sir Hubert Tarpelow was their neighbour in Cambridgeshire, where Driscow Park was located. He and his wife were dreadful little people—so Lady Stanton had always thought—as narrow of mind as they were wide of girth, and barely kind enough to be called Christians. They were precisely the sort of people who would revel in the downfall of the Stantons, should their whole story ever come out. The thought of Lady Maria Tarpelow standing in the beautiful bay windows of the front drawing-room at Driscow, surveying what would then be her own lands, fairly made Lady Stanton's flesh crawl—but there was no help for it. She would be obliged to put the matter out of her mind altogether, to avoid going mad with rage. The following morning, when Lord Stanton had departed on his journey into Cambridgeshire (they devised a story between them of his having estate matters to settle there), Lady Anne Stanton made a private trip to the little stone church on the knoll. She went there, in fact, every day until her lord had returned, and prayed God to satisfy himself with the pun-

ishment he had already seen fit to visit upon her. "I am guilty, dear
Lord," she was wont to pray silently, "but I truly repent. And the
thought of Maria Tarpelow presiding at my breakfast table is my hair-
shirt. Truly, oh Lord, it chafes me as no shirt ever could!"

While this private domestic drama was being acted out, the other,
more public, theatrical was nearing the date of its performance. Miss
Jessica Cawley was still dissatisfied with a number of the scenes, but the
marvelous scenery the duchess had commissioned had arrived at the
castle at last, and it did wonders in improving the general effect of the
production. Hyde Park looked astonishingly like Hyde Park—everybody
said so—and the backdrops for the interiors were splendid. In any case,
even if Miss Cawley had been utterly displeased, there was little she
could have done: December 14th came as punctually that year as it ever
had before, and the play was to be performed on the 15th. Guests invited to make up the audience had already begun to arrive that afternoon, along with a spiritless flurry of snow. Miss Cawley excused herself
from their company however, and hurried away to the ball-room just before tea: there was to be no rehearsal that evening, as Jessica judged her
players would benefit more from a respite than from a second dress-
rehearsal. She had expected to be alone in the ball-room, but to her
surprise she discovered Mr. Remington there. He was standing upon the
stage, and started at her entrance as if he had been caught in a guilty act.

"I beg your pardon, Mr. Remington," Jessica said, seeing how she had
surprised him. "I had no notion anyone was here. There is no rehearsal
tonight, you know."

"Oh, I know, I know," he said, evidently agitated about something. "I
only came to s-see if all the pr-properties were in order."

"A very good idea," said Miss Cawley. Mr. Chauncey Stanton was
charged with the keeping of the stage properties, but he seldom did so
with any efficiency. In recent days he had grown even more careless
than usual: the termination of rehearsals meant the end of his opportunities for staring at the Contessa di Tremini, a circumstance which had
thrown him into deep despair.

"Th-thanks," said Cosmo Remington. As with many stutterers, his
difficulty with speech became more pronounced when he was worried, or
angry. On this occasion it was the former trouble which beset him, as
soon became clear to Miss Cawley.

"I came to count up the chairs," she told him. "Such a lot of guests
in front! More than one had expected, it seems."

"Are there?" he replied vaguely.

She had been counting seats, but now she turned and looked at him. "Yes. There are. Mr. Remington, is anything troubling you?"

Again he started. "No!" he said. Then, "Yes. Nerves, I suppose. The performance, you know."

"But you are an admirable Fainall," said Jessica, soothingly. "Is that all that worries you?"

"Oh, yes!" said he, giving a very nervous laugh. "Oh, no," he contradicted immediately, sitting down with an ungraceful thump on Lady Wishfort's divan.

"Would you care to share your difficulty with me?" asked Jessica, gently. She left the chairs and came up to the stage herself, seating herself near him. "I am your manager, after all, at least till tomorrow. Perhaps you find your wages insufficient?"

Mr. Remington tried to smile at the joke, but could not quite. Instead he regarded her morosely, his eyes large with perplexity. "I can't understand it," he said, after some time had gone by. "I simply cannot."

"May I ask what it is that puzzles you?"

"It's—oh, dear, Miss Cawley—this m-must be in strictest confidence."

"Absolutely," she agreed at once.

"You won't t-tell anyone?"

"Not a soul."

"It would relieve me awfully to speak to someone," he said.

She began to be curious, and assured him with some impatience, "Then speak to me; you are perfectly safe in doing so."

"It's Miss Chilton. Or rather, it's Algie. Oh, hang it all, it's both of them."

"Miss Chilton and Mr. Longstreth?" exclaimed Jessica. There was something in her which immediately disliked this conjunction of names.

"Yes. Oh, dear, Miss Chilton's a good fellow, but—marriage!"

Jessica gasped, just audibly. "Mr. Longstreth means to offer for Miss Chilton?"

"Does he?" Mr. Remington's eyes turned on hers in complete wonderment. "So that's what it is! And yet—no, that makes no sense."

"Dear sir, I am not telling you that Mr. Longstreth means to offer for her," Jessica clarified. "I am asking you *if* he does. Do you know?"

"Oh, no—I don't know anything," said the befuddled Mr. Remington. "I only know he's been talking a deuced lot about marriage lately, and he keeps telling me what a fine girl Miss Chilton is."

"Oh, dear," was all Jessica said, but she felt her cheeks go pink.

"And I haven't a thing in the world against Miss Chilton," said poor Cosmo, "but I don't want to marry her."

"Oh!" cried Jessica. "Then he means for you to marry her."

"I don't know what he means," Cosmo repeated miserably. "I don't know anything. He just keeps mentioning how even the best of fellows must settle down someday, and asking me if I don't want a wife. Then he turns the conversation to Miss Chilton."

"This is very mysterious," Miss Cawley brought out.

"It's more than that," said Cosmo. "It's damned unsettling. Begging your pardon," he added.

"How is it—why is it unsettling for you?"

"Well, I don't want Algie to marry, for heaven's sake!" he replied, as if this were self-evident. "Why, Algie and I have been on the town together for a decade and more. How should I live, if he were to marry?"

"To marry Miss Chilton, you mean," she suggested.

"Oh, no! If you want my true opinion, in fact, he means for *me* to marry Miss Chilton, so he won't feel so bad about marrying himself. I don't know who *he* means to marry," he added glumly.

"It couldn't be—it couldn't be me?" Miss Cawley blurted out, with an extraordinary, uncharacteristic lack of diplomacy.

"You!" At this Cosmo did begin to laugh. "Oh, I shouldn't think so, not with the tricks he's played—oh dear," he caught up suddenly. "Oh, dear, oh, Jupiter, oh, dear! Algie will throttle me."

Miss Cawley had found his laughter most interesting, but what he dropped after it did not escape her either. "Mr. Longstreth has been playing tricks on me?" she hazarded.

"Oh, my, please—I did not mean to say a word of that. I swore not to! Oh, my, Miss Cawley, dear ma'am . . ." Mr. Remington spluttered, in obvious dismay.

"Oh, he'll pay for this mightily," said Jessica, not forgetting Cosmo's laughter. How, precisely, did Mr. Longstreth speak of her to his friends? And after the other night in the gallery—! Miss Cawley was confused; she was hurt; she was distressed. What she was above all, however, was angry. All a hoax! She could scarcely believe it, after what had passed.

"Miss Cawley, I beg you, say nothing to Algie of this," Mr. Remington pleaded. "He'll have my head, I know it!"

She was silent a moment. "He'll know nothing of it from me," she then said, rather grimly. "Believe me, the very last thing I should do is confront him with what I've learned."

"Ah, thank you—Miss Cawley, you are so good," said Cosmo, excessively relieved. "And I do th-think—yes, I protest I do—if Algie doesn't think of marrying you, he really ought to! He couldn't do better, that's certain."

"Thank you," said the object of this compliment, rather tightly.

"But this doesn't clear up anything about Miss Chilton," poor Mr. Remington continued. "What I thought you might help me with is—Miss Cawley, do you know if Miss Chilton expects an offer from me?"

Jessica forced herself to listen to him, though her mind was already seething with schemes to avenge herself on Mr. Longstreth. "I shouldn't think so," she answered.

"Ah! I can't tell you how glad I am to hear that," said Remington. "Algie made out as if she did, you know. And though I do admire her extremely, you know—really, if I had the least intention of marrying, I would think of . . . I admit, I *did* even think of . . . but after all," he went on, confused by his very relief, "a fellow my age, you know!"

"Oh, indeed, a fellow your age—!" Jessica agreed, with heavy sarcasm. "After all, you are scarcely as old as Mr. Longstreth, and we know *he* is hardly more mature than a boy of twelve."

Mr. Remington began to grow suspicious. "You are not thinking of what I—pray, Miss Cawley, you must forget my little *faux pas,* you know."

Jessica smiled a tight, unpleasant smile. *"Faux pas?"* she echoed, "Which do you mean?"

"Why, about Algie and the gho— Oh. I see, you have forgot already."

"Entirely, entirely, Mr. Remington," Jessica stood abruptly and began to hurry away. "Mr. Remington," she said briskly, "I find all of the sudden that the number of chairs in this room no longer interests me. Would you be so kind as to count them?"

"I should be delighted," said poor Cosmo. "And thank you ever so much for—for letting me know about Miss Chilton."

Miss Cawley did not hear the end of this grateful speech, however; she had already gone. Time to think was what she wanted; in a few minutes she had shut herself into her chambers for the purpose of solitary contemplation, and at the end of an hour she had arrived at what she felt was a wonderful scheme. "Ghosts!" she murmured to herself aloud. "We shall see who is worried about ghosts now." With this private, and somewhat obscure, reflection, she rose again and made ready to join the other guests at supper. She rustled into the dining-parlour to find the others already assembled there, and went directly to Miss Chilton's side. Her first act was to break entirely the confidence into which Mr. Remington had taken her; it was excessively indelicate, but she was too angry to care. Later, armed with Lotta's indignation as well as her own (Miss Chilton's was mostly feigned, since she had had a fair notion Jessica was being taken in from the very beginning), she stumbled by chance upon an even more outrageous discovery. This disclosure came by means of Lady Eliza Longstreth, Algernon's mother, who had come down to Grasmere for the play.

"I hope you found the Stepneys well," said Jessica to this lady, for her wrath—great though it was—did not extend to the members of Mr. Longstreth's family.

"I beg your pardon?" said Lady Eliza, a homely, pleasant woman with an air of skittishness.

"Is that not the name of your friend? Captain Stepney?" Jessica replied, supposing she had got it wrong.

"Indeed, I have a friend called Captain Stepney," Lady Eliza told her, "or at least, I trust I have. Since I have had no communication with him these fifteen years, however, I may be mistaken."

It was Jessica's turn to beg pardon.

"I say, I do have a friend named Captain Stepney, but I have not seen him this age. Not that he and his wife aren't perfectly charming people," she hastened to add, lest Miss Cawley think she meant to cast doubt upon their name, "but they live dreadfully retired. How is it you come to know them?" she asked curiously.

"Know them?" the other repeated, vaguely. "Oh, no, I do not know them, but your son—mentioned them to me."

"Did he? Why, I'm surprised he recalls them at all. He was still a boy when last we saw them."

"Was he indeed?" asked Miss Cawley. "How very interesting."

"Oh, yes! I wonder what caused him to mention them."

"You know, it is very odd, but I was under the impression you had gone to visit them recently," Jessica informed her, in order to verify her suspicions. "You did not, after all, did you?"

"Oh, no, goodness!" said Lady Eliza, giving a little laugh. "Though it is an interesting suggestion, I must say. They live very near to here, you know. Perhaps I will write to them, and ask if I may stop there."

Her ladyship went on in this vein for some time, telling Miss Cawley a great many things she did not care to know about the Stepneys, their children, their lands, and their house. Miss Cawley was not listening, in any case; her mind was wholly absorbed in an effort to remember that day in October when she had gone to Goose-Fair. Mr. Longstreth had not come—she remembered it very well. And apparently, he had lied in order to excuse himself; why on earth should he have done that? If he had simply changed his mind, surely he might have said so! What could have been his point in fabricating—the gipsy! The image of the mannish old crone rose up in Jessica's imagination all at once, and brought enlightenment with it. Mr. Longstreth had been the gipsy, of course! Fancy his doing so much for the mere pleasure of disturbing her! So it had been going on since October, all the time since then—she had had no idea the scheme was so old as that. And come to think of it, hadn't Mr. Longstreth been with her when she had found the ring! Most certainly he had, and it had been he who—Jessica stretched back into her memory, striving to recall every detail of the ring's discovery—yes, it had been he who touched the old oak first. Why, he might easily have dropped the ring in when he stuck his hand into the hollow—and then feigned disinterest in order to urge her to investigate it herself. Might have? Did; did, no doubt of it! Miss Cawley could barely keep her seat, so furious was she at these deductions. Oh, Mr. Longstreth would pay dearly, see if he did not! And as for marrying him—she would sooner marry Frant.

Jessica excused herself from Lady Eliza, in particular, and from the company, in general, as soon as she could, and retired once more to the privacy of her chambers. There she stalked up and down the rooms for a while, exclaiming to herself ever and anon on the deceitfulness of men. When she had tired of this diversion, she sat down on her bed to think again, and the first thought that occurred to her was: why on earth had Mr. Longstreth gone to such lengths to harass her? Did he really dislike her so much? Miss Cawley could not believe that anyone could really dislike her; one might disapprove of her, or desire her to behave a bit more decorously, but . . . The answer to the mystery came to her at length: the book. Mr. Longstreth had not cared for her last novel at all; in fact, he had deeply objected to his portrayal in it. No doubt he had been teased about it by his friends—men were such boys—and had made up his mind to visit some of his own discomfort upon the person ultimately responsible for it. That person was Jessica, naturally—and everything followed from there.

Was he justified? This was the next question to present itself to Miss Cawley. She was not given to searchings of the soul, nor even to the most superficial of self-examinations, and yet even she had to own that he might, in some sense, be excused for his outrage. After all, she had done a masterful job of making him look ridiculous—it was what she did best in her writings—and so much of it was true (she thought to herself rather uncharitably) that it must have cut very deep. He *was* sentimental; he *was* foppish; all the more reason why he should object to being reminded of it. This much Jessica could understand, but her softened judgement of his plight did not affect her resolve to punish him. He had suffered, perhaps, but it would have been more manly to take his sufferings in silence. That is what she herself would have done (at least, she supposed that is what she would have done). In any case, she was far too stung to let him off without a penalty.

So Jessica reasoned to herself, and if it seems to the reader that her logic was imperfect, it must be said in her defence that she was truly very hurt by the discovery of his unkindness. Jessica could not bear enmity; it was not his having made a fool of her which piqued her, so much as his having disliked her sufficiently to do so. She had gone through life charming everyone; impudent as she had been (and she had been extremely impudent at times) no one had ever borne her a grudge. The novel experience brought her up short. And besides, Mr. Longstreth was a special case—though she chose to gloss over this now. She had been particularly under the impression that he liked her; as her imprudent question to Mr. Remington revealed, she had even supposed he might wish to marry her. There is no fury like a woman scorned, says the bard, and it must be supposed there is some truth to the proposition, since Jessica was, by the time she went to bed, utterly consumed by her plans to frighten Mr. Longstreth as he had frightened her. The final mystery, to wit, how he had managed to create the sound of footsteps in the picture gallery, she could only guess at now: it had not occurred to her before, but very likely those three chambers above the gallery had been allotted to Longstreth, Remington, and another confederate. They must have charted the course of the passage below them in their own rooms, and each walked one third of the way. Although, of course, Mr. Longstreth had been with her during one of the walks . . . perhaps there was a fourth involved . . . these thoughts drifted through her sleepy mind as she lay in bed, and she fell asleep at last without having resolved them. Tomorrow was important to her; she could not stay up all night fretting over the technical aspects of Longstreth's odious trick.

The play was an enormous success. Poor Mr. Remington, who had the dubious privilege of speaking the prologue, stuttered his first few words and completely forgot one of the couplets, but after this the performance ran smoothly, and most delightfully, through to the end. The numerous entr'actes gave the spectators an opportunity to remark upon the marvellous scenery, the hilarity of Lady Louisa's depiction of Lady Wishfort, and the surprising facility nearly all the players seemed to show for acting their rôles. The Contessa di Tremini was, naturally, the most stunning element of the piece; a general murmur of appreciation was heard throughout the audience on her entrance, and her distracting habit of turning her best side toward her viewers whenever she could was not even noticed by most of them. Their host the duke was accounted to do his part very creditably, as were Mr. Remington, Mr. Faust, and the others; so that when the audience was called upon to applaud, they could do so with whole hearts and a good conscience. The only persons who were aware of anything amiss were the performers themselves: they, who had seen the play rehearsed again and again, knew that Mr. Longstreth and Miss Cawley had not been wont to act precisely as they did tonight. Miss Cawley, the more observant noted, was distinctly more abrasive than she usually had been—more abrasive, even, than the part of Mrs. Millamant ought to be. And Longstreth (though the audience hardly remarked this) reacted with increasing wonderment: as Jessica raised her voice and grew more brisk, so too did Mr. Longstreth; but it was apparent to his colleagues that he did not know precisely why he was obliged to do so. Apart from this, however—and the audience did not, as I say, know this—all ran just as it was meant to.

After the performance there was a festive supper, and after that a kind of ball in the ball-room. The chairs had been removed, but the stage still stood, giving the great apartment a somewhat peculiar look; the musicians used the boards for their platform, however, and a good deal of merriment went forward.

His Grace of Karr was in particularly high spirits, as it appeared. He solicited Miss Chilton's hand not only for the first two dances, but the two next as well. Lotta's discomfort in receiving such marked signs of his regard was as keen as ever it had been; she accepted him reluctantly for the two first, and refused entirely thereafter.

"Lady Henrietta is no longer here, you know," he reminded her lightly. "You need not fret over distressing her."

"I am all too aware of Lady Henrietta's absence," said Lotta, her wide gaze drifting uneasily in the direction of the duchess.

"Ah, dear ma'am! I hope I am not to discern in that pronouncement an indication that you still regret her departure."

"Discern what you please," said Lotta, her ever-watchful conscience pinching at her.

"I never miss her at all," said Karr quietly. "I have never even thought of her, from that moment to this."

"From which moment?" Lotta inquired, with a hint of her old minxishness. She looked very beautiful in a gown of pale rose, veiled with Brussels net, and with a coronal of roses on her head. Jessica had insisted on giving it to her.

"From the moment—from the day my mother dismissed you from service," he said, rather unwillingly. He did not care to refer to that particular episode, as she well knew; he had not yet come to terms with the duchess about it.

"You know I think of that day frequently," she said, with a trace of wistfulness. "More and more frequently, in fact."

"And why do you think of it?" As he spoke he took her arm (they were both standing) and tried gently to lead her away from the others, but she resisted.

"I am too long unemployed for so poor a girl," she brought out. It was painful to her to be obliged to speak of this, and she added with supreme irrelevance, "You know, Miss Cawley is right. You are the only gentleman in all the fashionable world who still ties his hair *ailes de pigeon.*"

"What if I am, Miss Chilton? Will you disown me for that?" he asked.

"Do I own you?"

There was a silence between them.

"Most certainly my heart has been bestowed upon you," said Karr at last. "Whether you have received it is another matter. Miss Chilton," he continued, his voice growing urgent, "will you receive it? Will you answer me at last, once for all?"

He seemed unconscious of the milling crowd round them, but Lotta was all too aware of them. "I did answer you, you know," she murmured.

"Ah, but you said no! That is not an answer," he objected.

"What is it, pray?" she asked. She smiled, but felt uneasy.

"It is a refusal."

"And you want an answer. I see."

"Precisely. Won't you consider again—?"

He was meaning to go on, but she interrupted him hurriedly. Such was his involvement in their conversation that he had utterly forgot the existence of anyone else. He was about to sink to his knees when she stopped him. "Come, dear sir; we will have this talk another time," she suggested.

"I am sorry. When I hear you speak of employment, and poverty, I can scarcely govern myself."

"They are very real things," she reminded him. "Both of them."

"But you won't leave Grasmere now!" he broke in. "I couldn't bear it."

"It's nearly Christmas," she said. "I should like to be with my family, you know, since I have no duties elsewhere."

"Ah, but you must not leave!" he begged again.

"I must sometime," said she.

"Oh no, you really mustn't, really you must not," he said, his dark eyes focused persuasively upon her, his hand reaching instinctively to clasp hers.

She withdrew it as soon as he touched her. "Your mother is watching us," she murmured. "Sometimes I think she will die of vexation—truly, such things have been known to happen."

"You may be certain nothing will kill my mother until she has seen her successor safely installed," said Karr grimly, sending a glance toward his resolute progenitrix. "Her ghost would never rest."

"Ah! Speaking of ghosts," Lotta took up, "Miss Cawley has told me the most peculiar story." She went on to relate to Karr exactly what she had heard from Jessica, and included her own suspicions as she spoke. She concluded, "She is determined to avenge herself, you know."

"Someone ought to warn Algernon."

"You do not seem very surprised," Miss Chilton observed, ever quick. "I don't suppose you knew of the plot already—did you?"

His Grace of Karr produced something very like a blush. "I am afraid I did," he admitted, after a moment.

"Did you!" Miss Chilton was genuinely astonished: it seemed quite unlike Karr to condone such nonsense. "You did not—you can not have helped, can you?" she added an instant later.

His blush deepened. "I did," he said faintly.

Miss Chilton felt only the most authentic incredulity. "I protest, I don't believe I know you very well after all! I should never have thought it of you—in fact, I should have gone to my death denying it! First you ask me to marry you, then you play tricks at mid-night to frighten women—you really are mad, aren't you?"

"I hope not," said Karr, smiling. "Besides, it was the other way round."

"What was?"

"The tricks and the offer. I agreed to assist Algie more than half a year ago."

"Indeed? Has the scheme been so long in preparation?"

"No, not in preparation; but the sentiments which motivate it date from then."

"And those sentiments are—?"

"Why, Mr. Longstreth's response to his portrayal in Miss Cawley's last novel, of course. It appeared mid-season, you know, and caused Algie more embarrassment than anything else might have done."

She took this in. "I can see where it would be somewhat painful—a ridiculous portrait, and so forth—but so painful as that . . ." Her voice trailed off doubtfully.

"But you don't know the other side of the tale," Karr said. "Longstreth meant to offer for Jessica."

"I beg your pardon?"

"Oh yes; not many knew it, of course, but for the few that did . . . well, you may imagine how poor Algernon felt!"

Indeed, Miss Chilton felt that she could imagine. "You were among those who know?"

"I guessed, if I did not precisely know. I watched him calling on the Cawleys nearly every afternoon; he was supposed to be looking for Roger, but nothing was more evident to me than his affection for that gentleman's sister. He moved slowly, naturally, since Jessica's dislike of suitors is quite well-known—but he was preparing to offer for her, I am certain of it."

"And then her book appeared," Lotta filled in, speaking rather slowly.

"And then it appeared," her companion agreed, "and with it as unflattering a picture of Longstreth as anyone might have hoped to draw. Poor fellow, he scarcely kept his countenance the first time someone mentioned it in public. I was with him."

"And later he asked you to help him with his revenge, is that it?" she guessed.

"I am afraid so," Karr confessed. "Of course I was not acquainted with the precise nature of his scheme until two months ago."

"My dear sir, this is most interesting," said Lotta, tapping her chin in a reflective fashion with the end of her ivory fan.

Karr attempted to look contrite, but burst into a sudden laugh in spite of himself. "I'm sorry," he said. "It's only—well, it has been capital fun, watching Miss Cawley fall into the trap. She is dreadfully bold, you know—sometimes she fairly begs for such a trimming as this. Anyway, it does not appear to have injured her seriously; in fact, she looks brighter than ever. I shall tell you who really does worry me, however, and that is Lady Stanton. Lord Stanton too, for that matter. She has never seemed quite well to me since that night when she fainted at whist, and he is certainly preoccupied by something."

"Naturally it is difficult for me to guess at her health," Lotta replied. "I am unacquainted with her except in her present state. I will say, however, that she does not look like a well woman to me."

He nodded, his countenance troubled. "She is pale, is not she?"

"Rather pale. Of course, some women are naturally so," Lotta was silent for some while; then she added, very slowly, "Do you know, I have the strangest feeling . . . I feel as if I knew Lady Stanton well. I haven't a notion why—and yet . . ." She fell silent again, then roused herself with a little shake. "It's silly, isn't it? Though I suppose it is possible I met her somewhere before."

"Yes, perhaps," said Karr, who had not been listening closely. "In any case, Stanton is in some sort of a muddle. He nearly killed a beater the other day, when we were out shooting. The man was standing right before him, clear as day, but Stanton appeared not to see him at all! Decidedly, there is something on his mind."

"Miss Amabel, perhaps? If I were about to marry my daughter to Lord Wyborn, I should expect to be preoccupied," Lotta affirmed.

"You sound as if you disapprove of the match."

"Perhaps I do. I disapprove of throwing Christians to lions as well, you know."

"Lord Wyborn is not such a lion," said Karr mildly.

"Only because some of his teeth are falling out," said Lotta. "Otherwise he would be quite ferocious."

His Grace sighed. "Possibly you are right. And yet, if Lord Stanton did not favour the match, I wonder he consented to it."

"Maybe you only imagine something is amiss," said Lotta lightly, spreading out her fan. "The ways of women—and men—are mysterious," she added, smiling and looking up at him archly.

Karr smiled, but still appeared troubled. He was nearly certain that all was not well with the Stantons, and felt obliged to concern himself with their difficulties since they were under his roof. Lady Anne was not a fretful woman, so far as he had ever known; why then was she so afflicted with sudden fits and pallors? He was not to learn the complete answer to this question for some while; however, a scene upon which he happened that very night transformed his suspicions regarding the Stantons into positive conviction. It was after the ball was over; nearly all the guests had retired to their chambers. Miss Chilton had steadfastly refused to dance again with her gallant admirer. She had refused, similarly, to promise she would not quit Grasmere. Karr had succeeded, however, in eliciting from her a promise that she would discuss her plans on that head with him the following morning, before she had come to any decision. His Grace had watched reluctantly while she moved smoothly up the stairs, away from him and toward her unattractive little bed-chamber, then turned back to do his duty to his other guests, and to his mother (such courtesies as were necessary between these two were performed these days with the most rigid correctness possible). When at last everyone seemed to have been taken care of, His Grace took his own way up the great stair-case, musing, as he went, on just what he should say to Miss Chilton on the morrow. His thoughts were interrupted as he turned into a long corridor and perceived ahead of him a couple, proceeding very slowly, the lady seeming to falter and lean heavily upon the gentleman. He at once recognized the pair as the Stantons, and moved forward rapidly to see if he might assist them. As he neared them he heard Lady Stanton speak.

"She will squeeze us dry, then discard us!" she said. Karr scarcely knew her voice, so choked and bitter was her tone. He was on the point of saying something, to advise the Stantons they were not alone, when Lord Stanton forestalled him.

"My dear," he said gently, "you must try to maintain your tranquillity, truly. You will fall ill if—"

"She has no more pity than a stone," her ladyship broke in, and began directly to sob.

"No, she hasn't; no, she has not," Lord Stanton agreed sadly. His Grace by this time had changed his mind about approaching them: it was too late for him to make his presence known to them without causing embarrassment and dismay on all sides, and though it was equally true that he had heard much more (he was sure) than the Stantons could have liked, he decided to retire without notifying them of his having been there at all. Accordingly, he dropped behind, still silent. He heard the heavy door to their apartments open and close, then took himself off to his own suite. He sat many minutes there, puzzling vainly over what he had heard, before he at last went to sleep. His pondering had brought no solution, of course; he could not know that the Contessa di Tremini had marched boldly up to Lady Stanton that night, much less that she had pressed a note into her hand, still less that the note contained a demand for a ruinous sum of money. The contessa and her victims were the only ones who could know this—and the latter, Lord and Lady Stanton, felt that they knew it only too well.

10

The morrow dawned drear and chill, "Just the proper sort of day," as Jessica Cawley remarked to her breakfast companion, "for a haunting."

"I beg your pardon?" said Algernon Longstreth, who was the person thus addressed.

"I say, if a ghost were ever to walk a gallery, he ought to chuse to-day. Odiously cold outside—have you been out?" Jessica smiled—with some difficulty, it might be noted, since the very sight of Mr. Longstreth set her pride to aching—and desired her neighbour to send the butter down her way.

"Not this morning," said Longstreth. He watched, as if fascinated, while Miss Cawley buttered slice after slice of toast, briskly and methodically, ate each one with obvious relish. Mr. Longstreth himself ate very sparingly: it would not do for a man of his slight frame to grow corpulent and sluggish.

"Not even to say good-bye to your mother?" Jessica asked, her enunciation somewhat impaired by a mouthful of toast.

"My mother has not left yet."

"Hasn't she? How very fortunate! I shall adore to see her again; really, she is a most estimable woman."

"Did you meet her?" Algie inquired, somewhat uneasily, as he recalled his cock-and-bull story about the Stepneys.

"Oh yes! We had the most delightful conversation," she assured him.

She was silent for a moment, buttering still another slice of bread; then she added abruptly, as if struck, "Perhaps she will watch for the ghost with us tonight! Do you suppose she might?"

Algernon eyed her warily. "I believe she means to depart before dinner," he said.

"Ah! What a disappointment, don't you agree?" cried Miss Cawley. "I know she must take a vast interest in spirits, or else how should you have done so? A belief in ghosts is something one inherits from one's progenitors, don't you think? Like the ghosts themselves."

"Actually, I am not the least bit certain my mother—ah—thinks of ghosts one way or the other," said Algernon, who was beginning to suspect something was up. Cosmo Remington had told him nothing of Jessica's discovery: he had sworn to her he would not. His Grace had likewise been silent, out of deference to Miss Chilton. Mr. Longstreth, therefore, could know nothing—but he could sense some new element in Miss Cawley's attitude.

"Really? Then I must ask her about them as soon as she comes down."

"I don't believe she means to come down, as it were," said Longstreth nervously. "She despises to talk to anyone in the morning; it quite oversets her. She always takes breakfast alone—as you see, she is not here—and prefers to make her entrances and exits without fanfare."

"What a shame!" exclaimed Jessica. "But she must come down sooner or later, if only for a moment. And I so long to speak to her again—at least to say farewell." Of course it was utterly indifferent to Miss Cawley whether she ever saw Lady Eliza again or not; she only insisted upon it because she could see it distressed Mr. Longstreth.

"Ah! Well then, you—ah . . . might I find some more toast for you, Miss Cawley?" Algernon replied in confusion.

"Oh, please!" said she, who had continued to eat ravenously. "I adore a bit of toast!"

Miss Cawley was so fortunate as to have further opportunity to annoy Mr. Longstreth a few hours later. By a simple process of hovering continually near the great front hall, she was able to make an unheralded appearance in that imposing apartment just as Lady Eliza was leaving. People constantly came and went at Grasmere; very little formality was attached to such movements by the owners of the castle. In consequence only Mr. Longstreth and his mother—besides the servants—were there for Jessica to interrupt; and interrupt them she did.

"Ah, Lady Eliza," she cried, coming forward with a gay, light step.

"How sad that you are leaving so quickly! I hope nothing displeased you here?"

"No, indeed, my dear," said her ladyship, in her slightly anxious, high-pitched voice. "Not at all. The play was splendid. Only I must go."

"What a pity you have not a more beautiful day for travelling, too," said Jessica. "Not but what you will be very safe—I am certain it is a fine day for driving—only the vistas will not be half so pleasant as they might have been on a sunnier morning."

Lady Eliza gave a quick smile, but said nothing.

"Oh, my dear!" said Jessica suddenly, clapping a neat hand to a round mouth. "Here I am chattering on and on when Mr. Longstreth was just telling me—how *can* I have forgot?—you detest to be spoke to of a morning!"

Lady Eliza looked in mild surprise from the lady to Algernon. "Indeed?" she murmured vaguely.

"Oh, you needn't pretend for my sake," Jessica assured her. "I quite understand; some people are like that. Only do forgive me, pray—I'll run away directly, I promise."

"Miss Cawley, I'm afraid you must have misunderstood my son," said the good woman. "I am always at my most cheerful at the start of the day. I quite wilt at sunset, and am invariably fatigued in the evening. Algernon, what have you been saying to Miss Cawley?"

"Dear ma'am—dear Miss Cawley," said Algernon, much discomposed, "this is some misunderstanding, as you say, ma'am." He inclined his head toward his mother, then toward Jessica. "Truly, you mustn't think my mother is—"

"Pray, I pray you!" cried Jessica, making a gesture as if to refuse all explanations. "It is enough, it is sufficient. I am honoured to know you, Lady Eliza, and I shall take the liberty of hoping to see you again." And with this, and a curtsy, she bounded away, leaving Longstreth to explain to his mother why he had been telling Miss Cawley such tales.

The master of the castle, having made certain early that morning that Lady Eliza's coach and horses would be properly prepared in time for her departure, was now free to pursue his affairs, the most interesting of which was the interview promised to him last night by Miss Chilton. They were to meet in the Oval Saloon, and Lotta rustled into that apartment to discover His Grace sitting idly at the harpsichord, running his fingers over the keys at random, though not striking any one of them with sufficient force to produce a tone. She nodded to him and seated herself immediately in a cream-and-gilt armchair, her fingers toying with a gold locket suspended on a narrow red riband round her neck. Karr turned round to face her; his expression was anxious. "You are charming to look upon," he said. "You warm the room as much as the fire in the grate—more, indeed."

"More, forsooth?" she echoed dryly. She tilted her chin up, causing her plaited hair to glint richly in the fire-light.

"More," he affirmed, with a slight bow. "And that beautiful, intelligent light in your eye—surely that is intended to tell me you are too wise, too good, too kind to leave Grasmere?"

"Surely not," said she promptly, "since that is precisely what I think I must do."

"Ah!" he cried, genuinely dismayed. "You promised you would take no decision until we had talked today."

"I have not taken a decision, precisely . . . and yet none needs to be taken, I may say. It is Christmas; I am not employed; I ought to go home. You will not find purer reason than that."

"I am not looking for pure reason," he told her. "On the contrary, in fact, I am looking for sentiment, for passion."

Lotta met his gaze with her own. "You seem to be forever looking for things in the wrong places," she said gently.

"Oh, no—you will not persuade me you are the wrong place to look for sentiment!" he answered. "That is my mother's mistaken belief—not mine."

"Your mother's conviction is deep," said Lotta. "I am afraid she feels I am entirely heartless."

"Do you desire to make me join her in that belief? You have only to abandon me here as you threaten to, and I will."

Lotta paused for a moment. "It would be better for you to believe me heartless than to persist in this ill-advised romance," she brought out at length.

"Ah, not this again!" he exclaimed, throwing up his hands in a helpless gesture.

"This always," she contradicted. "This continually, this eternally. No matter how I think of it, no matter how I twist my heart, my thoughts, my conscience, I cannot pretend that a duke (that is you) and a servant (that is me) do well to fall in love with one another. I am very sorry, my lord; I am more sorry than you know, indeed; but I must go home." Miss Chilton spoke evenly, quietly, and yet with a distinct fierceness. His Grace regarded her soberly.

"You pretend to be better than I am," he accused her at last.

"I pretend to be nothing of the sort," she denied. "If you look into your own conscience, you will see what I have said writ precisely as large."

"I look into my conscience," he retorted, "but I see no such thing. I only see that love is not given to many, and that it is shameful to refuse it when it is bestowed. Do you deny we are in love?"

Her delicate cheeks went crimson. "No," she murmured.

"And when do you expect to love again?" he pursued.

"Not . . . soon," she said, barely audibly. "Perhaps not ever."

"And yet you feel you have the luxury to push this opportunity away?" he demanded. "This is very madness!" His whole countenance had become cloudy and storm-like; she would have been frightened indeed if she had not known how much he cared for her.

"If it is then I chuse to be mad," she flung back at him. Tears sprang into her eyes and rolled hotly down her cheeks. "What do you know of poverty anyway? You have had ease all round you, from birth. The only luxury I can afford is an easy conscience. And that I shall insist upon, I do insist upon. You may not rob me of it, for all your wealth and all your power!"

Her sharp defiance brought him up short. "I suppose we have nothing more to say to each other today," he muttered after some minutes.

"The less we say the better," she agreed, and though her tone was hard and cold, her tears were not.

"You will return to Grasmere?" he said, as if this were inevitable.

"I shall consider it," she said quietly. "I must reflect on what is best to do, and I shall do that more easily at home."

"If you do not come back, I shall come after you," he warned her.

"I trust you will not attempt to capture me and carry me off," she replied, her voice somewhat muffled by the handkerchief she was now applying to her nose.

"So long as you are careful not to force me to such extremes," he answered. He smiled at her, but it was a very sad smile. "When do you expect to be going?" he inquired.

Miss Chilton said she hoped to leave as soon as possible, in a day or two at most.

"I shall arrange a coach for you," he said.

"I shall travel by the mail," said she.

"Ah, that I will not hear of!"

"An employe who has been turned off is not sent home in state," she reminded him.

"If you do nothing else, will you at least do me the kindness to forget you were ever in my employ?" he begged. The argument as to Miss Chilton's method of travel continued some while; the duke, in the event, triumphed. It was a sorry victory however, for him, since it only brought home to him all the more the fact that Miss Chilton would soon quit Grasmere. He was determined that she would return after Christmas—he *would* carry her off by force, if necessary, despite what she thought—but he could not honestly say to himself that her return then would settle anything. Certainly it would save him from despair, for a time at least—but he could not oblige her to marry him, and it was only her consenting to be his wife which would make him happy. His Grace was really convinced of this: never once, since the night of the ball in honour of Amabel Stanton and Lord Wyborn, had he ever contemplated the possibility of finding happiness without Lotta Chilton. It had grown to be a kind of mania with him; he was obsessed with the notion of making Miss Chilton his duchess. The dowager duchess's fury with him, terrific though it was, scarcely disturbed him. She would come round, in time; the major issue, the crucial point, was to obtain Lotta's hand. If he did not absolutely forbid her to leave Grasmere for Christmas, it was only because a few shreds of sanity still clung to him.

Lotta did not come down to dinner that day; she passed those hours alone, occupied in writing to the Chiltons. She wrote to advise them of her imminent return, a task which she did not find easy. Twice she was obliged to begin afresh, since twice her tears fell on the paper and caused the ink to blur. The scene in the dining-parlour downstairs was very different from the one where she wrote: the company, deprived of rehearsals and with no positive festivities to look forward to, was already growing restless. How they should amuse themselves through the Christmas season became the general topic of conversation at table, and it was continued when the assembled party had all regained the drawing-room.

"I think we ought to have a murder," said Lady Madeline Olney, with a tiny yawn. "Somebody kill somebody in a jealous rage—yes, that's it! How exciting that would be," she added, and returned, eyes sparkling, to Roger Cawley for confirmation.

"Doubtless very exciting," said he politely, "but a trifle inconvenient for the victim, I should say. Jessie, haven't you any ideas for diversion? We all rely on you for that sort of thing, you know."

"My profoundest apologies," said Miss Cawley, "but I must cry off this time. My bubbling springs of creative invention have gone quite dry, after my recent, strenuous efforts. Someone else must create an entertainment."

"Surely you cannot expect us to believe so much as that!" objected Mr. Septimus Faust, who sat by the duchess on the other side of the fireplace. "If nothing else, I trust your novel-writing still goes forward."

"Ah that!" she cried. "Indeed—but that is like breathing to me. I should not know how to live, were it not for that."

"So it would appear," said Faust. They had developed a shallow, bantering, slightly abrasive relationship during the time when the play was being rehearsed. Now he spoke to her lightly, but with a purpose. "Spinning tales is as natural to you as spinning webs is to the spider."

Miss Cawley nodded assent, her tight curls bouncing with the movement.

"Won't you tell us a story, then?" he said.

"I beg your pardon?"

"A story," he repeated, leaning forward. "After all, it is nearly Christmas Eve. We ought to have a few ghost stories, at least; we always did when I was a child."

"So did we," said Lady Louisa Bridwell, who sat on his other side. Her eyes grew misty almost at once, and she went on, "It was my favourite time of year. We all gathered by the fireside, while the wind howled out of doors, and munched on Christmas comfits, and went to bed scared half out of our wits. It was splendid! Don't you recall it, Sarah? Sarah passed many a Christmas with my family," she added, for the benefit of those who did not know.

"I recall it," said the duchess, but without the mistiness of feature or sensation that Lady Louisa suggested. Lady Louisa was the only person still living who called her Sarah; she did not enjoy that, nor did she like being reminded of happy days fifty years before.

Mr. Faust (as he frequently did) leapt in to fill up the conversational lapse. "That's what I say," he explained to Jessica. "We ought to have some ghost stories. And who will tell them better than yourself?"

"Ghosts," Jessica remarked, largely to herself. "You haven't been talking to Mr. Longstreth, have you?" she asked Mr. Faust. The idea of ghosts and the idea of Mr. Longstreth had become so intertwined in her mind, she could scarcely think of one without the other.

"Not as much as I should like to," said Septimus politely.

"Hmmph," Jessica returned. "Well, as for your stories—why don't you tell them? Roger and I grew up with no such tradition; we should be very green at it, no doubt, while you must be a master."

"I'll tell one," said Faust, a trifle reluctantly. "But someone else must tell another."

"Well, I trust someone else will," said Miss Cawley. No one said anything in reply; all sat gazing at her. "Pray, do not look at me that way! I am weary of amusing you all. Let . . . let Lady Louisa tell a story; she must remember some from her youth."

"Ah, my dear," that good lady protested at once. "It is long since my youth!"

"Surely not!" cried Septimus Faust immediately, as if deeply shocked.

Lady Louisa, never averse to flattery, produced a foolish smile. "I am older than you think, it is clear," she told him.

"Ah, were you twice as old as I think," said Faust outrageously, "you should still be young!"

"My good sir," she objected, though flushed with pleasure, "I will never be twice as old as I am."

"Be still my breaking heart!" he exclaimed, causing a general hilarity among the company which, though hearty, was not cruel. Lady Louisa was a woman whom it was almost impossible to offend, and she laughed good-naturedly along with the rest. She was also a woman who could be coaxed to do nearly anything, and before half an hour had gone by, she had agreed to regale the company with as thrilling a ghost story as she could devise. Mr. Faust was to take his turn first, though, in order to clear the way for her, as it were. There were those among the company who desired him to begin that very evening, but he resisted them, claiming that his story would not be a fabrication but a true, horrifying incident from his own life ("I knew your history was sordid," the duchess remarked) and that he must brace himself for the reliving of the event before he began to tell it.

"You will kindly remember there are ladies present," said Her Grace, when Faust had made this declaration.

"Dear ma'am," said Faust, with a bow; "I cannot forget you when you are absent! How then shall I forget you when you are not?"

"Under this unlikely exterior," said the duchess, waving a vague hand at Mr. Faust's bony skeleton and emaciated countenance, "beats the hard heart of a practised trifler. Ladies, I give you fair warning."

"He has already practised some of his arts on me," said the Contessa di Tremini, who had happened to stroll over to the group near the fireplace just as the dowager said this. "I resisted, of course—but who can say if I should withstand a second siege?" She lifted her chin and narrowed her gorgeous violet eyes, resting their extraordinary rays on Mr. Faust.

"*I* besiege *you!*" exclaimed Faust at once. "Dear madam, be kind, be just, I implore. The light of your eyes is liquid fire, and melts such paltry arms as I can muster."

The contessa laughed and appealed to the company round her. "Have you ever seen arrogance masquerade so convincingly as humility?" she asked.

"Or experience tricked out so neatly in the trappings of innocence?" Septimus countered at once.

"Ah! Impertinent!" cried the voluptuous widow. She lifted to her cheek a thickly beplumed fan, pretending to hide a blushing countenance behind it. Everyone knew there was absolutely nothing behind this teasing exchange of innuendo between herself and Mr. Faust, but the contessa enjoyed such flattering nonsense, and she sought to prolong it by exclaiming, "Will no one defend me?"

A general smile went among the company, but there was one who did not share it. This was Mr. Chauncey Stanton, and he—so far from smiling—shouted out at once, "I will! I will, madam; I am at your feet."

The party, vastly amused, turned toward him at once.

"Thank you, sir," said the Countess Tremini to him, mostly in order that someone should say something. She strived to look as amused as the others at her young admirer's awkward gallantry, but she was in fact secretly annoyed. She did not like to have ridiculous figures share the same tableau as herself; she was extremely vain, and felt she took too much trouble with her toilette to have it ruined by the chance appearance of a clown by her side.

Chauncey visibly trembled; this was the most encouraging phrase he had ever had from her lips. "Do not thank me, prithee," he brought out, his voice quivering. "Your own comfort is enough for me; I have no need of your gratitude."

"Indeed," murmured the contessa, and retired again behind her fan—this time for a purpose. She had a scowl to hide.

Lord Walker Stanton had been seated at some distance from his son (Lady Stanton, mercifully, was in her own apartment) and had missed the opening of Chauncey's public conversation with the countess. The silence which had fallen over the group attracted his attention, however, and he looked up to discover his son and heir in an attitude of abject worship toward the magnificent contessa. In a trice he was on his feet and beside Chauncey. "Go up to your mother," he said, in a low tone, but with a good deal of emphasis.

Young Stanton stood still. The company gazed with interest.

"Go up to your mother, I say," his lordship repeated, in a hissing whisper.

Chauncey managed to detach his eyes from the countess, and to turn them upon his father, but he could not say anything—he was too excited.

"My son, are you mad?" Lord Stanton demanded. He regarded the interested onlookers for the first time, saying, "You must excuse my son. He is too young to know what a spectacle he creates."

Chauncey found his tongue. "I am not too young for anything, Father," said he. "Madam, am I too young to be devoted to you?"

The contessa, who had the distinction of being addressed in this wise, hesitated. "Too young to be devoted, no," she said at length. "Too young to know what to do about it—perhaps."

Chauncey, though he was not very bright, began to perceive that his ardour was not entirely appreciated. "Father, you do not understand," he said, in spite of his growing suspicion. "Someone has offered Lady di Tremini an insult."

"I am sure she was too wise to take it, if so," Lord Stanton returned, with difficulty. The reader will easily understand how abhorrent it was to him to be obliged to deal politely with the contessa.

"Father—" Chauncey began again, hotly.

"It was a jest," Jessica Cawley put in suddenly. She had begun to feel rather as if she were attending a bear-baiting: young Stanton was awkward, he was unattractive, he was foolish—but it was cruel to encourage him to even greater folly merely for the sake of diversion. "I fear Mr. Stanton arrived too late upon the scene to understand the humour in which Mr. Faust spoke to her ladyship."

Lord Stanton bowed briefly to Jessica. "Many thanks, madam. Now, sir, will you go to your mother?" he added to Chauncey. His face had gone utterly red, and he could but barely govern his temper.

Chauncey looked from his father to his idol. "Must I?" he whimpered.

"Good God, yes, young man! How many times shall I say it?"

This was delivered so sternly that it penetrated even to Chauncey's addled consciousness. "Dear ma'am," he said, with a crooked bow to the countess, "I am obliged to depart. I beg you will remember me should you be in—in need of . . . in need of . . ." He wanted to say, a true knight, but this struck him as perhaps a bit overdone. "In need of assistance," he concluded at last, and bowed once more—even less gracefully than before, if such a thing were possible. His father nodded quickly to the company and left the drawing-room directly, shepherding his straying lamb before him. The whole scene, painful and yet so amusing, continued to be talked about for half an hour. It was thought by some that Lord Stanton was needlessly harsh with the boy; others (the duchess was among these) felt that Chauncey oughtn't to be permitted into society until he had learned to conduct himself more reasonably.

"I felt sorry for him," said Jessica Cawley to Mr. Longstreth, several hours later, when most of the inhabitants of Grasmere had gone to bed. They were in the little sitting-room near the picture gallery; Jessica had insisted upon their watching for the ghost that night. Algernon had been much disinclined to join her, but Jessica (by far the better debater) had prevailed.

"I don't think it's worth the bother," he had said, when she announced her resolve. "I doubt he'll come round tonight."

"And why not?" said Jessica, perceiving at once the nervousness beneath his careless tone.

"Oh, I don't know," he returned, with an effort at nonchalance. "It just seems the wrong sort of night, that's all."

"Oh, I couldn't disagree more heartily," she had answered, thoroughly enjoying his discomfiture.

"But . . . well then, all right—but you must allow me to wear the ring," he had said. Poor Algernon had been forsaken by his friends: Karr had agreed not to give the plan away to Miss Cawley, but he had also refused to assist any longer in making the footsteps (he and Remington had done this together in the past, Cosmo running silently from the first room to the third while Karr traversed the middle one). Remington, though he had not positively refused to help, was not keen for it either. He had intimated to Longstreth that he preferred to play billiards or sleep at such hours, rather than frighten young ladies. Longstreth knew, then, that the ghost could not possibly walk that night. Jessica, though she could not know, guessed as much from his discomposure.

"No, indeed," she had protested promptly. "Last time you took the ring we lost it, and I did not hear the ghost at all," she reminded him. "I shall not be so foolish again."

"But Miss Cawley—"

"If you insist, you may take it from me, after I have heard him begin to walk. And do you know, I think tonight we must begin to speak to him."

"Speak to him?"

"Indeed! What use is it to make the acquaintance of a ghost, if one does not ask him any questions?" She smiled at him, supremely delighted at his horrified expression.

"What—what should you like to ask him?" he inquired faintly.

She shrugged. "Oh, anything. About dead things, and the after-life, and hell . . . and whether he really is Robin Hood, of course. Imagine the mysteries we can clear up! We shall straighten out his legend once for all."

Mr. Longstreth had given up apprehensivensss and was now going in for despair. "I suppose you know how to communicate with spirits?" he said morosely.

"Certainly. One puts the question, and tells the ghost to knock once for yes, twice for no."

"And suppose the ghost can't knock?" he asked dismally.

"Well, ours can certainly stamp, if nothing else. We shall tell him to stamp, if necessary."

"Oh, very good. That is fine," he answered, glummer every moment. "I am vastly relieved now."

"And so you should be," Jessica had replied, nodding brightly. This conversation had taken place before dinner; by the time they met in the little sitting-room, Longstreth had sunk firmly into hopelessness. He almost stopped Miss Cawley before they had begun: the game was off, and she might as well know it sooner as later. He did not feel quite equal to the admission however, and so he merely agreed with her that young Stanton had been pathetic, and consented to follow her into the gallery. It was understood that she would address the ghost as soon as he had taken his first few steps.

They observed the same rituals as they had previously, creeping softly into the gallery with their candles lit, then extinguishing them. Jessica was rather sorry, all things considered, to be alone in the dark with Mr. Longstreth on this occasion (for she no longer trusted him for anything), but it was necessary to her revenge, and she steeled herself to it. Longstreth did not seem in a humour to take liberties anyway; on the contrary, she had never seen him so saturnine. She was obliged to conclude that he knew he had been found out—though why he did not confess it she could not guess. It was imperative, in any case, that she make her first move before he had time to own the truth to her.

She did so as soon as was feasible. "Mr. Longstreth, I hear him!" she hissed out of the darkness.

Algernon was too startled to keep his voice low. "I beg your pardon?" he said loudly.

"Shh!" she said, furiously. "I hear him. Mr. Longstreth, do you hear him?"

"I hear nothing," he replied, dumbfounded.

"Oh, no, of course not. I've got the ring."

"Miss Cawley, are you certain you hear him?"

No answer came out of the blackness.

"Miss Cawley, are you there?"

She savoured the anxious edge on his voice. "Yes," she said, after a long pause. "Why?"

"Are you certain you hear the ghost?"

"Shh!" she repeated, for he had spoke aloud again.

"Naturally. Why shouldn't I be?"

This time it was Algernon who gave no reply.

"Do you want the ring, Mr. Longstreth?" Jessica inquired at length. "Or shall I speak to him first?"

"Give me the ring," he murmured. They groped toward one another in the darkness; Jessica placed the ring in the curve of his palm.

"Do you hear it?" she whispered, leaving go his hand at once. He was silent. Then, "I hear nothing," he said.

"Nothing?"

"Not a thing."

Both kept still a while longer. "And now? Still nothing?" Jessica asked, as if this were incredible to her.

"Miss Cawley, there is nothing to hear," he muttered.

"Give the ring to me again," she instructed him. "Perhaps he has stopped walking."

"Miss Cawley, this is futile . . ."

"Please!" she insisted, making a grab for his hands. She found his wrist, which was near his ear (he had cupped that organ as if straining to hear something) and took the cherished band from him.

"I suppose you still hear it," he ventured after a few minutes.

"Oh, yes," she replied, as if in thrall. "I will speak to him."

"Miss Cawley, really," he began, sounding pained indeed.

"Dear sir, please be quiet!" she commanded, rather sharply. "I am addressing the spirit! Spirit!" she called softly. "Spirit, can you hear me? Knock once if you can hear me."

Algernon twisted his hands together. If his companion were not teasing him, she must be mad. Had he driven her mad? It seemed dreadfully plausible. He wished to stop her, to draw her from the gallery and quiz her severely as to what she had really experienced, but he could not think how to do it.

"He rapped! Did you hear him?" Jessica fairly squeaked in feigned excitement. "Mr. Longstreth—it is happening!"

Algernon could think of nothing to say.

"Mr. Longstreth?"

"Yes, I hear you."

She hesitated. "But you don't hear the rapping?"

"I hear nothing," he said, for the third time that evening.

"It is most extraordinary," she breathed. "One can only suppose he favours me over you, though I should not know how to explain it. It is true, though, that spirits reveal themselves only as they chuse, you know. Think of Hamlet."

"I have thought of Hamlet," poor Mr. Longstreth groaned. Indeed, he felt precisely as Gertrude must have felt when her son heard the voice of his dead father—which is to say, very poorly. He was certainly well punished for his trickery, he reflected, whether Jessica was truly persuaded she heard the ghost or not. These were his reflections as she continued her interrogation.

"Spirit!" Miss Cawley had called out again. "We hear you, we are grateful to you for speaking to us. Please tell us, are you really the ghost of Robin Hood? Rap once for yes, twice for no."

Mr. Longstreth was verging on hysteria by now. It was all too bizarre, the blackness, the hallucinations his friend apparently experienced even now, the suspense of being held in wretched ignorance.

"Yes!" Jessica cried abruptly. "Did you hear it? He is Robin Hood—he is!"

"Miss Cawley, I think we ought to come away from here."

"Come away? Now!" She made an impatient click with her tongue and addressed the ghost again. "Robin Hood," she called, "are you happy? Is that why you walk? Knock once for yes, twice for no." While she waited for the answer she added in an aside to Algernon, "I don't suppose one would call him Mr. Hood, do you think?"

Algernon did not know what to think.

"He knocks twice! He is unhappy!" Miss Cawley hissed jubilantly. "Robin Hood, we hear you! We are grateful for your answer, and grieved for your grief."

"Oh, for goodness' sake, Miss Cawley—" Mr. Longstreth muttered at last. He felt an overwhelming brew of sentiments rising within him, not one of them pleasant in character.

"Mr. Longstreth, I shall be obliged to ask you to leave if you can be no more helpful than that . . ." Jessica commenced.

Mr. Longstreth interrupted her in very rude fashion. What he did, to be precise, was to grab her by the arm, face her toward the end of the gallery, and shove her by main force until they had arrived at the lighted sitting-room. This was not accomplished in silence, as may be imagined; there was a good deal of protest from Miss Cawley, and quite a number of Go on, go on's from Mr. Longstreth—not to mention a lot of heavy breathing on both sides. When, as he thrust her into the sitting-room and shut the door behind him, Algernon finally released her, Jessica turned on him in a fury.

"Are you mad?" she upbraided him. "Look what you have done! I have left the ghost without so much as a farewell, without—it will be a miracle if he speaks to me again. They offend so easily, everybody knows that! You—you . . ."

But Algernon did not wait to hear by what epithet she was about to call him. "There is no ghost!" he shouted at her, feeling as though he were relieving himself of a mighty burden.

She stared at him. "No ghost?"

Still with his back pressed against the closed door, he shook his head. "None."

"No ghost?" she repeated, sitting down slowly on a tufted ottoman. "Mr. Longstreth, that is absurd."

"It is *not* absurd," cried the poor fellow. "It is true and you know it. I invented the ghost—I did!"

"You did not," she contradicted at once. "Frant knew all about him."

"Frant was—" he broke off in confusion. "Of course there *is* a legend of a ghost at Grasmere," said he finally, "and that is where I got the idea. But the steps you heard the other nights were Cosmo's, and Karr's! Oh dear!" he added immediately, as he realized he ought never to have divulged the identity of his co-conspirators.

His error had the virtue of bringing Miss Cawley up short, an advantage for Longstreth. Jessica was so taken aback by this news of Karr's complicity that she forgot (for a moment) to refuse to believe anything he said. "Karr?" she echoed, astonished. "His Grace?"

"Ah! So you admit there is no ghost! You admit you knew it to be a plot, don't you?"

Jessica saw her mistake. "I . . . perhaps it was. That does not explain what I heard tonight, however."

"Still!" he cried, exasperated.

"Still?" she took up. "What should have changed it?"

He regarded her, extreme annoyance in his features. "Miss Cawley, you are determined to punish me, I see."

"Nonsense," she replied, her face as innocent as his was piqued. "I only know better than to give up a ghost when I hear one, that is all. If you invented the first steps for me . . . well, then, that was very cruel. Though I might add, by way of digression," she went on, "that I cannot believe you could do such a nasty thing to me! I know you—and Mr. Remington, and Karr above all—are much too gentlemanly ever to think of such a plot, let alone actualize it merely to harass me. Why should you?"

"Merely to harass you," said he, with a return of his former dismal tone.

"Ridiculous," she dismissed this. "You had no cause. Anyway, regardless of what you did or did not do, you will admit that you simulated no ghostly sounds tonight, will not you?"

"I—if I must," he agreed reluctantly.

"Then I conclude that what you pretended to cause to happen in order to disturb me has actually come to pass now. It isn't much of a wonder anyway; Frant said the ghost comes round at Christmastide, and we are now closer to that time than we were before."

Mr. Longstreth said nothing, but gazed at her miserably.

"You don't believe me?" she inquired.

He still stared at her wordlessly, his wretchedness evident. So sorrowful, indeed, did he look, that Jessica scarcely knew how to continue her mischief.

"Whether you do or not," she forced herself to announce, "I am going back to the gallery tonight. I will not leave the ghost on such a rude note as that."

"Ah, Miss Cawley!" he exclaimed, dropping his head and running his hands through his fair hair.

Jessica was having more and more difficulty being unkind to him, but she reminded herself how she had been played for a fool and continued, "You may come or not, as you like."

"Miss Cawley," he said, raising his head, "not only will I not accompany you—you will not go at all."

"I beg your pardon?"

"I will not permit you to return there," he said simply.

"Indeed? And how do you propose to prevent me?" she asked.

Since Mr. Longstreth was still planted firmly against the door to the sitting-room, there really was no need of his speaking in order to answer her question. He was already demonstrating his means.

Miss Cawley's bright brown eyes opened wide as she understood him. "Dear sir, surely you are joking!"

"Not in the least," said Algie, not budging.

"Let me pass."

He did not move.

Jessica bustled up to him and faced him squarely. "Let me pass," she repeated.

"I am sorry madam, but I cannot do so until you promise you will not go back to the picture gallery."

"Why this grows more ludicrous every minute!" she cried. "Very well, sir; I shall not go to the gallery. Only let me leave."

"Do you promise?" he asked sternly, looking down at her from his not very superior height.

She hesitated. "I promise," she muttered finally.

"On your word as a lady," he stipulated.

"For heaven's sake, on my word as anything you like!" she told him. "Just let me go!"

Mr. Longstreth moved aside.

Miss Cawley ran immediately to the gallery.

Mr. Longstreth followed.

11

"Robin Hood!" Jessica was hissing when Mr. Longstreth caught up to her. "Sir, dear sir!"

"Ah, Miss Cawley, I pray you—!"

"Shh! Robin Hood?" she called again.

"Miss Cawley, I shall be obliged to silence you if this goes on any longer," said poor Algie. "You are driving me mad."

"Robin Hood!" she called a third time.

"Forgive me," he murmured, and in a trice had clapped his hand over her mouth. A moment later he was moaning with pain, cradling his fingers against his chest. Miss Cawley had bitten him.

"Dear spirit, tell me please—are you really the ghost of Lord Huntingdon? Rap once for yes, twice for no."

"Oh . . . oooh . . . Miss Cawley, please," groaned Algernon. He could hardly have said which caused him more pain—his injured hand, or Jessica's refusal to give up her nonsense.

"He is! He is!" she was crowing gleefully. "Did you hear it? He is the Earl of Huntingdon!"

"Miss Cawley!" he fairly shouted. "There is no ghost!"

"Lord Huntingdon," she persisted. "Lord Huntingdon, are you there? If you are there, kick Mr. Longstreth in the shins once; if you are not there, kick him twice." And with this Miss Cawley turned round to her companion and administered two very sharp kicks to his leg.

"Ooooh!" he shrieked.

"How do you like that?" she asked him, letting loose her anger at last. "Lord Huntingdon, if Mr. Longstreth is a miserable, ungentlemanly, cold cold trifler, kick him thrice!" And she proceeded, of course, to deliver this beating herself.

"Oh! Oooh!" said Mr. Longstreth, turning from her and beginning to hobble toward the end of the gallery.

She went after him. "Lord Huntingdon, if Mr. Longstreth has wilfully and for no cause whatever persecuted an innocent young woman, kindly box his ears once." They were nearing the end of the passageway now, and she could see well enough where the top of his stiff white collar was. She reached just above here with both hands, and cuffed his ears with a will.

"Aah! Oooh!" he screamed, feeling as if a host of imps and devils had settled upon him and tormented him on every side.

"There's for your cruelty!" Jessica was saying as they emerged from the dark hallway. "There's for your nasty little meanness. There!" she concluded—but the tone of her voice had gone rather strange, and Longstreth (even in his pain) noticed it.

"Miss Cawley," he said tentatively, turning to face her. They were near the threshold of the lighted sitting-room, and he could see her face, though dimly, in the glow. "Miss Cawley, are you crying?"

She averted her face and said nothing.

"Miss Cawley?" he repeated, with gentle urgency.

She sniffed.

"Miss Cawley, you *are* crying! Miss Cawley, why are you crying?" The unexpectedness of this was so great as to make him forget his aching ears and shins; all his attention was upon her.

Jessica sniffled again. "Why did you do it?" she demanded, in a muffled voice.

"Why did I do—what?" he asked, sincerely confused. "Come, let us sit down in here," he suggested, holding open the door to the sitting-room. "Sit down, please, and tell me what is troubling you."

She went in and sat again on the tufted ottoman. She hated herself for it, but now she had begun crying she could not stop. "Why did you do it?" she pouted. "Why did you pretend there was a ghost?"

"Oh dear!" said Longstreth, dismayed. "I had no notion it disturbed you so profoundly."

"It was mean," she told him. She did not in the least desire to tell him that it was not the scheme itself but the sentiments she was obliged to believe Mr. Longstreth entertained for her which caused her so much distress.

He blushed a little but regarded her steadily. "Perhaps it was," he said.

"It was. Why should you be so unkind to me? What have I done to you?"

"You mean besides doing your best to hobble me for life?" he inquired, with a brief, sudden grin.

She smiled as briefly. "Yes; before. What made you start the whole thing?"

"Miss Cawley, may I remind you that you . . . you put me into your novel? I did not appear to advantage there, you know."

She took this in. "But no one does!" she objected. "A caricature is not intended to be flattering."

"That may be," he conceded, "but I felt mine to be particularly malicious. You made me out an idiot—a sentimental idiot."

She drew her back up straighter. "If I did I am sorry," she said, in a small voice. "But I don't see how it should have mattered to you so deeply. According to Mr. Remington you don't care a straw for me," she blurted out suddenly. "Why do you care for my opinions?"

"According to Mr. Remington I what—?" he queried.

"You do not care for me. Mr. Remington . . . he laughed when I said . . . never mind that," she broke off. "Mr. Remington gave me to understand that you held me in very low esteem."

"I cannot imagine why Cosmo should have said such a thing," Algernon replied flatly. "That is perfectly wrong."

"It is?" she asked, looking up. Her tears stopped at once, but her face retained that vulnerable, childish look which it so often had when she was hopeful, or fearful.

"Of course it is. I could not hold you in higher esteem. I hold no one in higher esteem than I do you. *You* are the one who thinks little of *me;* your last novel demonstrated that quite clearly—not only to me, but to the world."

A first glimmer of understanding penetrated to Miss Cawley's mind. "My dear sir, you did not . . . you were not . . ." She could not think how to frame her question, but Mr. Longstreth rendered it unnecessary anyway.

"If you want to know," he flung at her rather roughly, "I had hoped to ask you to marry me. I suppose that will seem entirely risible to you, but perhaps it will show you why your portrayal of me grated so specially."

"Dear sir!" said she, stunned.

"I expect you feel fully justified now, in having painted me a fool. Fancy it! I believed myself to be winning your heart, while all the time you were sitting up through the watches of the night, composing a grotesque little depiction of me for your novel."

"Mr. Longstreth, I had no idea of your sentiments. I beg you to believe—I thought you came to see Roger!"

"If you had no idea of it, you were one of few. Half London saw what I was up to; in fact, there were wagers laid on my success at White's. Karr knew it, anyway; that's why he agreed to help me."

"And Mr. Remington?" she asked.

"Oh, dear, Cosmo . . . well, he is another case," said poor Algernon. "You know, we have been so close to one another all our lives—I'm afraid the dear fellow would feel it an abandonment if I married. I was trying to work him up gently to it . . . but then your book appeared."

"And you gave up hope?"

He laughed with an edge of bitterness. "Incredible though it will seem, I did not," he told her. "I felt it a set-back, a wound . . . but even while we have been here at Grasmere, I have hoped . . ."

"Even while you tormented me?" she inquired.

"I did not think it was torment. I only meant it for a joke," said he ruefully. "I had no notion how hard you took it till tonight."

Miss Cawley, strangely, began to cry again.

"My dear ma'am," said Longstreth, going over to her and reaching a hand out toward her, "I really do not know how to apologize sufficiently. I thought you would take the ghost nonsense as . . . merely mischief, you know. It was all a joke, after all, and you do like a joke, don't you? I mean—my dear Miss Cawley!" he broke off, sincerely at a loss for what to say, while Jessica sobbed harder and harder.

"It did not torment me!" she choked out at last. "I liked it, I like it! It was very clever, really it was. You are right, I enjoy a good ruse." But in spite of what she said, her tears fell more thickly even than before.

"If that is the case then—may I ask what distresses you so profoundly?" he begged.

Jessica looked up at him, red-eyed. "It's what . . . what Mr. Remington said," she confessed all at once. She began to sob again, but managed to add, "He said you did not like me."

Mr. Longstreth sat down abruptly. "Cosmo said I did not like you? This is most extraordinary!"

"And I m-mentioned m-marriage to him, and he laughed!" Jessica burst out accusatively, still weeping plentifully.

"I beg your pardon? May I inquire under what circumstances these interesting depositions were made?"

Jessica regarded him a bit shame-facedly; she despised going over each of her sentiments and actions so thoroughly, but she had gone so far she could hardly stop now. "It was a few nights ago—the day before the play. Mr. Remington was worried about Miss Chilton," she continued with a sniff. "For some reason he thought she wished him to marry her."

"Doesn't she?" Longstreth broke in.

"Good heavens no!" said Jessica, her tears beginning to dry on her cheeks. "Karr has offered for her."

"Indeed?"

Miss Cawley clapped a hand to her mouth. "Oh, dear," she said, through it. "Swear you will say nothing of that to anyone. It is the greatest secret, as you may imagine."

"I will say nothing," he promised, but with wonder in his voice.

"In any case, Mr. Remington thought he was meant to marry Lotta, and I assured him he was not. He said he thought you had meant him to—that was how your name came up, I think—and I said I couldn't think why. Mr. Remington couldn't either, but he said you'd been talking of marriage more and more frequently. And that was when I suggested . . . I suggested . . ."

"You suggested I might be proposing to marry you," Longstreth filled in helpfully.

"Mr. Longstreth!" she cried, as if offended.

"Didn't you?" he asked mildly.

Her face burning, she nodded assent.

Algernon rose and came closer to her. "I'm so very glad you thought of it," he told her gently.

She looked up at him, her face covered with crisscrossed tear-stains and a fading blush. "Are you?" she asked at last.

"Oh, very glad!" said he, and paused to swallow against the emotion which seemed to be swelling in his throat. He possessed himself of her hands (not a difficult feat, since she offered them to him) and seated himself next her on the little ottoman. "Miss Cawley, will you do me the honour to become my wife?" he asked.

Jessica's face broke into a bright grin; the reader may imagine her answer. Within an instant they were standing together, Mr. Longstreth's arms round Miss Cawley. They stood thus somewhat longer than an instant, to the mutual satisfaction of both. It would be difficult to say, indeed, when they would have broke from this attitude, had it not been for an unexpected entrance which startled them considerably.

The door to the sitting-room was ajar, so that their unasked-for visitor could not precisely be called an intruder (though both lovers felt her to be one). After her initial surprise, in any case, it occurred to Jessica that if there were anyone she wished to see at such a moment, it was Lotta Chilton, and so she welcomed the newcomer (who was equally startled at finding her fellow inmates abroad at such an hour) into the sitting-room.

"I should be happy to vanish," Lotta assured the pair, as she perceived that something extraordinary must be afoot between them. "In fact, I was only looking for my work-basket, and I see it isn't here—"

"Don't be silly, Lotta," said Jessica, going over to her. "We are delighted to see you—aren't we delighted, Mr. Longstreth?" She brought Lotta over to a chair while Algernon nodded his assent.

"Is something . . . is anything . . ." Lotta fumbled helplessly. "You weren't . . . er . . . ghost-hunting, were you?"

"As a matter of fact, we were," said Miss Cawley, looking askance at her betrothed, and breaking into a laugh. As succinctly as possible, she informed Lotta of what had passed between herself and Mr. Longstreth. Lotta, who had suspected such a match to be in the making (though she hardly supposed it would come about just at that juncture), felicitated her friends lavishly, and showered kisses on the bride-to-be.

"But why are you prowling about at such an hour as this?" Jessica finally thought to ask her. "Even if you had lost your work basket, what on earth could you need it for now?"

"Oh, that," said Lotta, dropping her beautiful eyes so that her wide gaze was directed at the floor. "Well, that will keep till morning."

"Oh no, my dear—never! all is not well with you; one sees that in a moment," Jessica objected firmly. "Sit just where you are, and tell us what it is."

"It is not a calamity," said Lotta, essaying a laugh (without too very much success). "It is only that . . . I shall be quitting Grasmere tomorrow. I must go home."

"Trouble there?" asked Longstreth.

"Poor dear," breathed Jessica, with quick sympathy.

"Oh, no, no trouble," Lotta assured them. "Only . . . I must go home for my sake. For the sake of . . . my life, as it were. This stay at the castle is very pleasant—it is wonderfully pleasant, in fact—but it is a *cul de sac* for me, as it were. It leads nowhere."

"Do you call becoming Duchess of Karr 'nowhere'?" Jessica demanded.

Miss Chilton glared at her.

"Oh, Mr. Longstreth knows," said that gentleman's affianced bride. "I dropped it by mistake. I am sorry, Lotta."

"I've already promised not to breathe it to a soul," Algernon put in.

Miss Chilton continued to look dissatisfied. "In any case," she said slowly, "there is no question of my . . . becoming the duchess. Her Grace the dowager duchess is no more reconciled to that notion than she was two months ago, as I am certain you will agree; in fact, she may be considerably less so. Karr is furious with me; he says he will come after me. I hope he does not," she continued, "but it is an eventuality I am prepared to face. You and I must say good-bye, my dear," she said to Jessica, taking her hands gently in her own, "for though I will send you what I owe you in time, I fear we may never meet again."

"Good heavens, Lotta," cried the other woman; "I shall do no such thing! Say good-bye indeed—it's preposterous, isn't it?" she added turning to Longstreth for confirmation.

"Entirely," said the gentleman. "Miss Chilton, I think you ought to know there is not the slightest chance of Karr's giving you up. He's the most tenacious fellow I know. Why, he would be dead right now if it were not for that!"

"I beg your pardon?" Lotta inquired.

"He was wounded once, you know," Longstreth explained, "as a result of an . . . ah, affair. The doctors informed him they could not save him. Nothing on earth could save him, said they—he must send for the priest at once. But Karr would not hear a word of it; it made him so angry to be consigned to certain death that he resolved on getting well—and he did get well, as you see. He is perfectly sound today. No, you'll never get rid of him now—not if he's really got his heart set on having you."

Lotta took this in silence. "Well, I know how to be tenacious myself, if it comes to that," she said at last.

"Oh, Lotta!" cried Jessica in exasperation.

"May I inquire, Miss Chilton, what it is precisely that makes you so averse to His Grace's suit?" Mr. Longstreth asked her. "You will forgive me for feeling—a friend's fond partiality, you know—that Karr is the most unexceptionable young man in Christiandom."

Lotta smiled sweetly. "I can hardly argue with such an opinion as that," she told him. "In fact, it is because I agree with you that I refuse him. He is an extraordinary prize—too extraordinary for me."

Mr. Longstreth mulled this over. "I must point out," he said after a time, "that his judgement is generally accounted to be as good as any of his other parts. If he chuses you for his bride, does that not reassure you of your own fitness?"

"Mr. Longstreth, you defend your friend's case with admirable form and fervour; he is happy who has friends to take up his causes so diligently. Nonetheless, it is not in His Grace's best interests to marry me; so I have told him and so I am resolved. Now my dear," she went on to Jessica, "I leave tomorrow early, so embrace me now."

Miss Cawley went to her and put her arms round her, but said, "This is not good-bye. I shall come to visit you, whatever else happens." Tears again crept into her eyes, and she clasped Miss Chilton closely.

"Good-bye," said Lotta, weeping freely. Poor girl, she had been disappointed so many times before, she did not honestly believe that Miss Cawley would make good her word. That Jessica believed now she would visit her Lotta was sure of; but that she would not, in fact, ever really come seemed equally clear. In consequence she said her farewell even more earnestly than did Miss Cawley, and cried a good deal more. Their embrace finally at an end, Miss Chilton shook hands with Mr. Longstreth and again wished the couple very happy. With that she retired to her bed-chamber, to try to sleep.

In the morning she rose before any of the other guests, drank chocolate in the kitchens (she had no abigail to bring her her cup, and the dining-table was not yet laid), and begged Frant to have a footman fetch her baggage downstairs. She stood waiting in one of the smaller front parlours until this task should be performed, dressed warmly in a thick travelling-cloak, when Karr found her. He had not slept on the previous night any more than she, as the haggard expression of his dark eyes showed. He greeted her in a jocular tone, but soon sank into obvious melancholy.

"So, Miss Chilton!" he said. "Sneaking away without a word of warning, eh?"

She smiled weakly in response to his feigned good humour. "Look at yourself," she replied, "prowling about while the sun's hardly risen. One would think you had a bad conscience." She was not feeling at all well, though she would never have said so to Karr. Even before his arrival, her knees had been weak and her head ached; now everything seemed to throb and burn twice as much.

"Not a bad conscience, but a very bad night," he told her soberly. "Miss Chilton, you do me wrong."

"Please," she murmured, finding it difficult to say more.

"But we will meet again soon enough," he continued.

"I hope you will not . . . force another such scene as this upon me," she brought out. Her knees threatened to give way beneath her, and she sank suddenly into an arm-chair.

"I shall force you to an hundred such, if necessary," he told her. "Painful as it may be to you to grant me my happiness, I shall make it a thousand times more painful to refuse it."

"This is very cruel in you," she observed.

"There is nothing gentle in denying a man his deepest desire," he replied. "If you disliked me, of course I should not press. But that is not the case, and I will press upon your scruples till they break."

"They are not fragile," she told him, while a tear escaped her and trickled down her beautiful, translucent cheek.

"Ah, Miss Chilton!" he cried, perceiving the tear. Abruptly he knelt before her, reaching for her hand. "Miss Chilton," he murmured.

He knelt there, his head bent over her hand, for some moments. "I must go," she said at last. "I hear the footman on the stairs."

"My dear!" he exclaimed one last time, letting go her hand reluctantly. Lotta rose at once and hastened into the entrance hall. She was grateful to discover, once she had done so, that Karr did not follow her. He, in spite of his determination to win her eventually, found himself overcome by his emotion. Preferring to cry privately, he permitted Miss Chilton to quit the castle without his watching her.

"Mr. Frant," Lotta was saying, with what little self-possession remained to her, "will you be so good as to give this to Her Grace?" She handed a sealed note to the butler; it contained such thanks and apologies to her erstwhile hostess as her pride would allow. This done, she turned resolutely toward the front door, passed through it and across the porch, and rushed (weeping again) into the waiting carriage. It was not until she had passed through the great iron gates that she realized Karr had tucked one of his handkerchiefs into the pocket of her cloak:

she pulled it out, recognized the initials on it, and put it to good use at once.

Momentous as this scene was to certain of the inhabitants of Grasmere, it came and went almost without notice where others were concerned. Lady Rowena di Tremini, for instance, neither knew nor cared that Lotta had gone: she had, as the reader is aware, other things on her mind. Her third demand had not been met, as yet, except for a note begging her to have patience. The Stantons were hardly to be seen about the castle, which seemed to their persecutor an indication that they were at least taking her seriously, but they gave no positive sign of being either willing or able to pay. This displeased the contessa deeply; her sentiments when Chauncey Stanton imposed his presence upon her, during the afternoon of the day of Lotta's departure, may therefore be guessed.

She was in the Rose Saloon, reading a rather thick novel by a Mrs. Corinna Thwaite, and pondering between the lines how to move next if the Stantons did not come through. The heroine had just found a key which fit the mysterious lacquered chest when the doors to the Rose Saloon burst open and Mr. Chauncey Stanton tripped (quite literally) in. He had stood outside those doors deliberating on whether or not to enter for a good ten minutes (a footman had informed him that the countess was within, and alone). Though he had taken a decision at last, he had unfortunately forgot to prepare anything to do, or say, once inside. Consequently he only stood and gawked at the gorgeous countess, while she sat and gazed wearily back.

"I—I'm sorry," stammered the young man at last. "I ho-hope I do not in-intrude?"

The contessa looked infinitely bored. "Was there anything in particular you wanted of me?" she asked.

He advanced a little farther into the room and stood, his hands thrust into his pockets, staring at her. "No," he announced.

She hesitated. "Was there anything you wanted at all?" she pursued.

"Oh, never!" cried young Stanton. "What you desire—that is what signifies. My wants are—are no matter. Never ask what I want, I beg you. Was there anything *you* wanted; that is a better question."

"If you did not care for my question, you need only have said so," she answered. She was quite weary of reading, and to toy with the lad, it now occurred to her, might be amusing—clumsy though he was. The only diversion that really interested her was gaming, and (though the play was deep enough at Grasmere when it did take place) she could find no one in the castle to play with her before dinner.

"Not care for your question!" he echoed, horrified. "My—my dear ma'am," he exclaimed, blushing at the word dear, "there is not a thing about you for which I do not care. Not a thing, I swear it."

"Indeed?" said the countess, setting her book aside. "Do sit down, sir, and tell me of this."

Chauncey, ecstatic and frightened at the same time, started across the room.

"Dear sir!" the countess said. "Pray do shut the doors first! How else shall we have a private interview?"

Mr. Stanton gulped but went obediently to do what his goddess told him. He then sat down across from her, stroking his new-sprouted mustachio with what he hoped was a sophisticated air.

"Now tell me all about your devotion to me," the countess resumed, fairly purring. "When did it start?"

"Oh, the very first time I set eyes on you," Mr. Stanton affirmed whole-heartedly. "Ages ago."

"Ages?" she took up archly. "I was not aware I had been alive for ages—let alone adored so long!"

"Oh, my, dear lady—I hope you do not misunderstand me," Chauncey pleaded. His voice, which was in the process of changing, took a disastrous upswing as he added, "I only meant it *seemed* ages—er, seemed ages," he repeated, having cleared his throat, "since my affection is so unrequited."

"Unrequited!" she returned at once. "Heavens, Mr. Stanton! How can you speak so cruelly? Is it possible you do not know?"

"Know?" he asked hoarsely.

"Know my . . . ah, sentiments for you," she said, endeavouring to summon up a blush but not quite succeeding.

Chauncey's eyes went round. "You have—sentiments for me?" he asked incredulously.

"Sentiments? By the dozens!" she assured him.

"Oh, Jupiter!"

"Oh, Jupiter indeed," said she, with assumed solemnity. "Do you mean—when you spoke up for me in the drawing-room the other night, you had no notion . . . how I felt for you?" She looked up at him shyly —at least she hoped she appeared shy (she was quite out of practice)— and caused her heavily-lashed eyelids to flutter delicately.

"I must be truthful with you, my lady," said he dramatically, as if he were making a dreadful confession, "and say no. I did not know—I never guessed! I only knew how I—may I say it?" he broke off, feeling very mature indeed.

"Say it! Say it!" she urged breathlessly.

"How I love you!" he brought out at once.

The contessa turned her violet eyes heavenward. "Ah!" she sighed.

"I have not offended you?" he hastened to ask.

"Offend me? Never," said she, dropping her eyes to the carpet. "Alas, how cruelly women suffer," she murmured.

"Madam, I hope you do not suffer!"

"Ah, no more, no more . . . But I did—ever so terribly—before you spoke today."

Chauncey was both astonished and emboldened by this information. "I shall never be happy until you have forgiven me, my lady. Tell me, can you forgive me? Can you ever?"

She gazed at him languidly. "I can . . . since we are . . . we are," she faltered.

"Yes, dear madam? We are—what?"

"We are to be married!" she brought out at last.

His eyes flew open. "I beg your pardon?"

"But good sir—surely that is what you intended when you began this declaration to me? Is it not?"

"It is . . . er—well, indeed I should adore to mar-marry you," he said, stammering wildly, "but my . . . er . . . my family! My parents! They will never allow it," he cried, delighted to think of such a solution. He had considered doing many things with the contessa, but walking to that altar was not one of them.

The contessa (practiced in this art) forced a few tears into her eyes. "And you allow them—you permit them—to ruin our happiness?" she reproached him.

"Allow . . . ? Never!" he replied stoutly. "Only—" he floundered about, searching desperately for something to say, "only I think we must wait until I have attained my majority," he concluded, inspired by necessity.

She pouted. "You don't love me," she accused him.

"Oh, but I do, I do!" he contradicted, tugging nervously at his cravat. His neck, his forehead, his palms—everything, it seemed to him—had gone damp and cold. This was not turning out at all well.

"Then come and kiss me," she wheedled, presenting a rose-tinted cheek for this purpose.

"Oh, but—oh, dear," said he, utterly at a loss. Full of misgivings, he minced awkwardly over to her and bent to peck at her cheek.

"My darling!" she said suddenly, throwing both arms round him as soon as he had come near. He pulled away from her, but she held fast, apparently trying to draw him down onto her lap.

"Help! Oh, help!" cried the poor lad.

"Help?" she echoed, as if shocked.

"Oh, no, I mean—oh, help! Somebody, help ho!" he cried again, struggling as desperately as any maid in a ballad.

"You do not wish to kiss me?" the contessa inquired, maintaining a firm grip on his shoulders.

"Ju-Jupiter! Let me go," said he, for all reply.

She released him at last, giving him a push onto the sofa opposite. "You will not kiss me, you will not elope with me, you do not love me," she summed up, magnificently. "I do not love you either, then."

"Oh, dear! My good lady—"

"No," she broke in, tossing her head. "I'll hear none of it. Go from me, and never speak to me of this again."

"But madam," he hedged, disliking to retreat in such disorder and disgrace.

She turned her splendid head away from him. "I could almost believe, sir, that you intended to—to put a stain on my virtue," she told him. "How should you like it if someone behaved so to your sister?"

Chauncey considered this question and recognized (though just in the nick of time) that it was rhetorical. He *had* been going to say—truthfully—that he would murder the man who thought of Amabel so dishonourably. "If I have displeased you so, madam, I am profoundly sorry," he answered finally. Actually, the only thing that made him sorry was that he had ever made her acquaintance at all. In light of what had passed between them, moreover, his fondest wish now was to remove himself from her presence at once.

"Oh, la!" sniffed the contessa. "That is so like men. An apology will repair any injury—that is what you all believe. Mr. Stanton, I must beg you to depart."

Chauncey bowed, gracelessly as usual. "Your desire is my command," said he, feeling that he was getting off easily.

"Go, go, go, and not another word!" she shrieked all at once, as if in a sudden fit of temper. Startled at her violence, the youth scrambled out of the Rose Saloon, and never stopped running till he had reached his own bed-chamber. Once there he took a vow that he would never—

never ever—speak intimately to a woman again until he had learned how to judge better whether or not she cared for him. He could have sworn Lady di Tremini despised him—he had never been so overset in his life as when she informed him otherwise.

Mr. Stanton's sister Amabel had undergone a romantic interview during the same hour as the one he spent with the contessa, but hers was rather different in tone. She was with Lord Wyborn, of course; he had begged her to meet him, at a certain hour, in the conservatory. There was something on his mind which he wished to say to Miss Stanton, and the sooner the better.

In point of fact there were two things on Lord Wyborn's mind, but one of them was of such a nature as to forbid his mentioning it to Amabel. This was the problem of her dowry; it had become a problem, indeed, since his receipt of it had been delayed for many weeks. Lord Stanton promised it was coming, and Wyborn did not disbelieve him. However, he would be careful not to tie the knot with Amabel until he had seen the sum in full.

The point which he did wish to discuss with his betrothed had to do, as he soon told her, with the difference in their ages. "Many people," he informed her, striding heavily up and down the room, "will believe I have been unkind in marrying you. Many people. They will believe you are too young for me, consider that your parents sold you off, pity you for your plight. You will excuse me if I speak bluntly," he added, staring down at her with his heavy-lidded green eyes.

"Yes, indeed," said she earnestly, as he waited for a response. Now that she had got accustomed to the idea of marrying him, Amabel was not quite so frightened of him. He did seem to her rather large, however; he had always seemed rather large to her.

"Very good then," he continued. "You must attempt to take no notice of such whispers. You and I shall be very happy together, so long as we do not regard those murmurs. I like you, Miss Stanton; I tell you to your head. You are very pretty, and very docile. That is well in a young girl. I like you very well."

Amabel coloured. "I beg your pardon, dear sir," she said, "but if I may be so bold—for what reason is it that you never smile when we are together? Since you like me so well—as I believe you must, to have offered for me . . ." Her voice faded as the conviction grew upon her that she had spoke too daringly.

But Wyborn, far from being displeased, laughed aloud. "Very good, missy; that is very well asked! If I like you so well, why do I not smile?"

His raw, ruddy complexion brightened as he chuckled over this. "Damme if I know," he told her at last, turning warmer eyes upon her than he had ever done before.

Miss Stanton's blue eyes, on the other hand, grew large and round.

"What is it? Oh, my, doesn't your papa say damme?" he guessed.

Amabel swallowed. "In fact, sir, I do not believe he does," she told him timidly.

Wyborn laughed again. "I will tell you a secret, my dear. Your father does say such things—he does indeed. Only he does not do so where you may hear him. That is very good between a father and his daughter, but I do not like it between husband and wife." He paused, musing. "Miss Stanton, could you grow accustomed to hearing such words from me? Only when we are alone together, of course—and naturally you will never employ them yourself."

Amabel rather enjoyed this notion. She had never thought much about the freedom that might exist between man and wife (she was not given to thinking overmuch, as we know), but now that it was brought up to her, she found it quite appealing. "That will be perfectly acceptable, sir," she said sweetly, adding, "I am very glad you like me."

Lord Wyborn surveyed her. "Damned if I wouldn't marry you *without* a dowry," he muttered, mainly to himself. He went on, more audibly, "My dear, now I have told you I like you, I think you ought to tell me if you care for me at all? How do you feel toward me? It will not alter our plans, whatever you say," he added rapidly. "You may be as honest as you like."

Amabel, whose colour had begun to recede, flushed again. "Well, if you truly wish to know—"

"I do," he interrupted; "and not such pretty speeches as we made to one another when I offered for you. That was form; now we are betrothed, we can be plain and straight with each other. That is what I want."

"Oh, dear, sir. Well then, since you ask . . . I am just the—just the smallest bit—you will not be angry with me, my lord?" she broke off abruptly.

Wyborn promised her he would not be angry.

"In that case, sir, I may tell you I am just the slightest bit frightened of you. Though not so much as before," she hastened to add. "When I first made your acquaintance I was terrified." Having said this, Miss Stanton went quite crimson.

"You were?" Wyborn took up, surprised. "And what was it—or is it—that frightens you so? My manner? My title? My—"

"Your proportions, sir," said she, in a tiny voice.

"My—! Damme, if that don't beat all!" he burst out, laughing hugely. "You're a woman in a million, that's all there is to it. Where else should I find a girl to tell me such things?"

"Then you aren't angry?" she asked.

"Not a bit of it," said he. "But there is one thing I should like to know yet, and that is if you like me at all in spite of that. Do you? Just a trifle?"

"Oh, dear, yes sir!" said she truthfully. "When you laugh I like you very much; even when you smile. I hope you will laugh a good deal after we are married."

"How could I fail to do so, so long as you are my bride?" he countered. "And if you learn to like me better—at other times, perhaps . . . Will you tell me?"

Amabel nodded affirmatively.

"Right away," he stipulated. "No delaying. I want to know how you feel the moment you know yourself. And I do hope you will like me better; do you know why?"

"So we shall be happy together?" she hazarded.

"Because I am becoming tremendously fond of you," he told her, and though Amabel could not quite return his feelings just then (she would be unable to do so for some while), she did begin to feel a very great deal happier about her impending nuptials from that moment forth. She felt safe when she thought of Wyborn, and for so meek a lamb as Amabel, to feel safe is no light matter. As time went on she grew to love Wyborn more and more, and she thought her father a perfect genius for foreseeing how this would be.

Her father, in the meantime, was learning to think of himself as a very poor protector indeed. Naturally it was not his fault he and his wife were being blackmailed, but he seemed to himself to deal with it rather ill. After much discussion, he and his lady decided to implore the countess to wait for her money until after Christmas. What advantage this delay would give them neither could have said, for eventually they must either sell Baddesleigh or throw themselves upon Lady Tremini's mercy (if she had any, which it appeared she did not). There was something comforting to both of them, however, in the idea that no matter what happened, it would happen after the great holiday, and Lady Stanton's relief was so palpable that she even managed to come down to dine with the others during the next fortnight.

12

Miss Cawley and Mr. Longstreth announced their betrothal the day after it was contracted—privately, at first, to Roger, and then publicly at dinner.

"Someone is missing," Lady Stanton murmured to her husband while healths to the happy couple were being proposed and drunk. "Who is it?"

Lord Stanton considered. "Lady Louisa?"

"No, she is there—to your left," said his wife. The absence made her feel strangely uneasy, though she could not for the life of her recall whose absence it was.

"Lady Stickney?" Stanton suggested.

"No, Walker—you are not even looking," said Lady Stanton, mildly annoyed. "Lady Stickney is right there—across from us. Who can it be? How vexatious this is!" she added, lifting her glass with the others, and obligingly donning a smile.

"I think it may only be your fancy, my dear," said his lordship. "Everyone seems to be here that I can remember."

"Miss Chilton!" cried Lady Stanton suddenly, though not loudly. "I knew there was someone! How extraordinary, that she should be absent now. She and Miss Cawley are particularly intimate; I've noticed it."

"Perhaps she is indisposed," said Lord Stanton, who was not in a position to know, yet, that Lotta had left Grasmere entirely.

"I don't think so," said his lady, abruptly; then, "Why did I say that, I wonder? How on earth should I know?"

"That is more than I can guess, my dear," said Stanton.

"But I have the most curious feeling . . . I am certain she is not ill. In fact, I am fairly sure she is not even in the castle tonight."

Lord Stanton shrugged. "Do you like her very much? If not, it makes no difference where she is."

"Like her?" Lady Stanton echoed vaguely. "Oh, I don't know. I suppose so. She is agreeable."

"Well, then, perhaps she is only abed with the headache," her husband said soothingly. "She will be down soon enough; you'll see."

Lady Stanton shook her head slightly while they drank the next toast, as if to indicate that Lotta Chilton would *not* be down, but also that the circumstance had little importance to her ladyship. The healths continued a long while (Miss Cawley was very well-liked by all the party), and the duchess announced, at the end of them, that a ball in the couple's honour was to be held Tuesday week, just a few days before Christmas.

The ball came and went with little to mark it out in the minds of the merry-makers. Jessica sparkled and teased, Algernon constantly at her side; Lord Cawley made a speech in his sister's honour. Lady Madeline Olney flirted madly, as did Sir Francis Olney; the Contessa di Tremini persuaded Sir Isaac Bridwell to gamble at cards with her, and left him nearly five hundred pounds the poorer—but since she did something of the sort almost every night, this was hardly remarkable. His Grace of Karr strove valiantly to enjoy himself, but Jessica (if no one else) could see he thought longingly of Lotta. He was not alone in this, for Miss Cawley (affectionate friend that she truly was) thought of Lotta too. There was a third person at the ball, indeed, who thought of Miss Chilton, but she thought very differently than these first two. This was the duchess herself, of course, and she mused upon Lotta's removal from the scene with deep satisfaction. It vexed her to be uninformed of Miss Chilton's precise reasons for withdrawing from Grasmere (Karr continued reticent on the subject), but even without knowing why she had gone, Her Grace was glad to reflect that she was, in fact, gone at last. She hoped now to persuade the Earl of Marland to return—or at least, to send Lady Henrietta back—and though this seemed a difficult project, she had effected greater miracles of diplomacy in her day. She meant to write to the earl at the start of the new year; for now, it was sufficient that Lotta had vanished.

The evening following the ball was the one marked out for the beginning of Mr. Faust's recital. This event had been anticipated by many among the company with extreme impatience; Mr. Ralph Hightower, in particular, grew increasingly jubilant as the appointed hour approached. "He looks like he could tell ghastly stories if he wanted to, don't he?" Mr. Hightower inquired, that day, of Cosmo Remington.

"Who's that?" Mr. Remington had asked. "Septimus Faust?"

"Yes, indeed," said Hightower, his eyes asparkle. "I could swear he's grown thinner this past week; I've been watching him. It comes of brooding on something grotesque—that's what it is. I tell you, he'll chill us all to the bone!"

"Mr. Faust?" repeated Remington. "Chill us to the bone?"

"Gracious, yes! I expect it will be gruesome, don't you?"

"Gruesome?" repeated the thin-blooded Cosmo. "Well, I should certainly hope not!"

Mr. Hightower stared at him, his eyes round in his otherwise blank face. "But what is a ghost story if it is not gruesome? It must be gruesome . . . and grisly . . . and gory . . . and—"

"Dear sir, please," Cosmo interrupted him. "If that's what it's to be I shan't listen. Grasmere Castle is peculiar enough, without allowing someone to wear one's nerves raw simply for a lark!"

But Mr. Remington did listen—everyone listened, almost. Mr. Faust had been so silent about the tale he meant to tell (he had said no more than those few remarks he made when the history was first requested) that everyone's curiosity was piqued. Even the duchess, who generally retired early now that the short winter days had come, sat up near the fireside to hear him. Mr. Faust himself sat directly next the hearth; the others drew as close to him as they could. He had arrayed himself in the most sombre hues—on purpose, no doubt—and eyed his assembling audience soberly, as if warning them that they were about to hear horrors, and ought to decide now whether to go or stay. His complexion, never rosy, was almost as dead white as the high points of his collar: not even the sharp heat of the fire could bring any colour to his cheeks. His dark eyes, catching the glow of the blaze, reflected its light almost feverishly. He did not smile, let alone grin, from the moment he entered the great drawing-room.

"Going to scare us, eh, Faust?" Sir Isaac asked him, seating himself in a comfortable chair.

Mr. Faust merely nodded, slowly.

"Not a very civil thing to do," remarked Sir Francis Olney. The atmosphere in the drawing-room had already become a bit nervous, and his comment was prompted by a desire to deny the tension.

"I make no claim to civility," said Faust evenly. "I pretend only to be truthful. Those who listen must understand that."

"I think we understand," said Miss Cawley, smiling. She was looking forward very much to this recital; it was very much the sort of thing she relished.

"The ladies particularly," Faust added. "This is not a pretty tale."

"Oh, good!" cried Ralph Hightower, while Miss Amabel Stanton stirred excitedly in her seat. Three months ago her parents would have judged her too young to hear such a story as this one; now, betrothed as she was, the decision was left to her own discretion.

"I have one request to make before I begin," said Septimus, addressing himself to Karr. "I should like to have all the lights in the drawing-room extinguished, save the fire, of course. I generally speak and think as little as possible of this period in my life; it is difficult for me. It will be even more difficult if I must look into the faces of my listeners. I had rather not see them, if you please."

Karr hesitated, exchanging a glance with his mother. "As you like," he said presently, giving the order to a footman. The lamps and candles which had previously made the drawing-room bright were put out one by one; they were left, in the end, with only the red firelight and a few pale, cold beams from the moon. Most of the guests were cast into shadow, and could see one another but dimly. They could see Mr. Faust very well, however, and an untoward sight he made indeed. The flickering fire caused weird shadows to travel upward on his face, and made great hollows of his eyes; his cheeks sank into deep cavities, and his wide brow beetled out sternly.

"If we are ready," he said quietly, "I shall begin." As no one answered he commenced his narrative, and did not cease speaking until he had done. "It was in London," Mr. Faust said, in the dull, flat, penetrating tone he was to maintain inexorably during the next two hours. "I was nineteen. I had just come up to town from Devonshire, my first time there, armed with my father's reluctant consent, a few pounds, and the idiotic dreams every young man takes with him to the great city. I had only been there two days when I met her: I was green as a winter ocean. My father, as I say, had been unwilling to let me depart; my mother was even more so. I pleaded with them, though—I begged, and complained, told them I suffocated in Devonshire, was half-mad with the pure rusticity of my birthplace—in brief, assured them I should commit some desperate act if they did not allow me to go. In the winter of 1788, therefore, they at last yielded to my importunities, kissed me well, bade me lead a Christian life, and promised to forward me a modest sum each month so that I might lead also a gentlemanly life. They knew very little (honest people as they are) of London, and could never have guessed how insufficient were the funds with which they had endowed me. I had that foolish pride so rampant in young men, and would not (even when I had reached town, and learned how severely they miscalculated) request more money of them; instead I took rooms in a cheap, disagreeable lodging-house near the Thames and resolved to make do with what I had or starve in the attempt.

"I knew no one in London at that time: I had no letters of introduction, no family, no one at all in town. I wished—and expected, may God forgive my impudence—to make the acquaintance of Mr. James Boswell who, I was positive, could know no greater delight than to make mine. Upon my fourth day in the great metropolis, therefore, I congratulated myself on the progress I had already made toward this aim, and set out cheerfully to achieve what little remained undone. With a sanguinity I have never recovered since, I bent my steps toward Mr. Boswell's residence, intending fully to call upon him and enjoy with him a comfortable chat.

"The day, most unhappily for me, happened to be damp. Before I had gone an hundred yards, a hideous fog began to drift off the river, obscuring landmarks and utterly robbing me of any sense of direction. Within minutes I was quite as lost as I have ever been before or since. Being possessed, as I have mentioned, of a young man's pride, I had of course scorned to carry a guide book with me, so that by the time the fog cleared I was as much at sea as I had been in the thick of it. It had begun to rain, not furiously, but with a sort of mizzling languor; the sky hung too low and leaden to permit of my seeing any great buildings, any orienting light. The only guide I had was the Thames itself, from which I had at least taken care not to wander too far. Unfortunately—very unfortunately, as you will see—I had lost track completely of north, south, east, and west: I could follow the river, but I could not know whether it took me closer to or farther from home. I was not sure which bank I was on—I suspected I might have crossed a bridge unknowingly while blinded by the fog.

"And so I wandered. The air was heavy with cold and damp; it seemed to press upon me as I went, and I drew up the collar of my coat against it. I saw scarcely anyone; the few whom I did see were as lost as I. I took a decision to walk as quickly as I could, for if it got me no-where, I reasoned, at least it would keep me warm. I accelerated my steps, therefore, and hurried onward, clinging always to the Thames. I had begun to experience the queerest sensation of dislocation—of forget-ting why I was abroad, where I had been going, what city I roamed—when, without a sound or any other warning, she knocked into me. I jumped away (I perceived her only as a solid grey mass in the viscous grey drizzle), expecting her to do the same—but she grasped my arm and held it. Even through the sleeve of my coat, her hand had the feel of a claw to it—it was that bony, that compelling in its grip. Instinctively, I shook my arm to cause her to leave go of me. Still she clutched. I could feel the moisture condensing on my forehead, my neck, while I stood there; I could feel the chill creeping steadily into me while I stopped with her in the rain. She drew me closer to her, lifted her face to look into mine. 'You must help me,' she said. 'I know you will help me.' "

Mr. Septimus Faust paused. He sighed profoundly. "What is it in youth that, failing utterly to help itself, finds the notion of helping an-other irresistibly seductive? Why, when we ourselves are drowning, is another's cry for help so poignant? I have often asked myself such ques-tions: the year which followed this chance encounter gave me reason to wonder—and leisure to wonder. In any case she asked for aid, and I was all desire to serve her.

"I must break here the flow of events to sketch for you, if such a thing may be sketched in words, what met my gaze when I turned it upon my petitioner. Maria was a girl of sixteen—seventeen, perhaps, at the oldest. She was small, slight, frail. Her features had a delicacy, a subtlety of expression as precise and as beautiful as that of any Renais-sance Madonna. In the rain that day, her complexion shone forth as if each droplet of water had been a crystal, magnifying, clarifying what lay beneath it. I have seen complexions as pure, but none purer. Her whole face, the great green eyes, the fragile nose, the tremulous mouth, was drawn up into a portrait of helplessness; her very breath and attitude implored. I could not look into such a countenance then and refuse as-sistance; I could not do so now, I am sorry to say. Those clouded eyes, that troubled brow! And yet, with all this, I would not have you believe she was beautiful. She was not. Her every trait was at variance with all the others . . . her countenance was a puzzle, threatening to fly apart into little pieces at any moment. And her clothes were drab, ill-kept, mended again and again. Her little form was lost in the great dark cloak that enveloped her like a shroud; the hood fell back as she looked at me and revealed a mass of dark, shapeless curls. If she wept I could not have known it: both our faces were wet with rain and exertion. And still, I do not think she was crying. She was not a sort to cry; her despair was too acute.

"She never ceased to clutch my arm, but drew me ever closer to her. 'I am Maria Chandler,' she said unsmilingly. 'My father is in league with Satan. You will help me.'

"'But my dear ma'am,' said I, quite astonished at this announcement, 'how should I be able to help you?'

"'You must take me home,' she replied. She shuddered suddenly, her frail frame quivering from head to toe. Even her voice trembled as she added, 'Please. If you do not, I am lost, and my mother and my sisters with me.'

"'I have hardly a home to go to myself,' I told her, while the mist rose all round us. I tried to smile in kindly fashion. 'I am sure your father cannot be in league with the devil. You ought to go home to your mother. Your father will be calmer now.'

"'Ah, but my father is not back yet!' she cried. 'He is still in gaol, until tomorrow.' She told me this as if I ought to have known, as though these were facts all the world was acquainted with.

"The scene began to take on the curious isolation of a dream. She spoke to me as to her only friend in the world, and I began to feel I was. 'But how will it help if I take you home?' I asked.

"'You are cruel,' she accused me at once. 'Pray do not be cruel! Take me home and I shall tell you everything; I promise, you will understand. Please,' she added urgently. 'Your eyes are gentle and say yes; why does your tongue resist?'"

Mr. Faust paused a moment. "I took her home," he resumed, speaking quietly, "and though the porter stared I brought her into my rooms without a second thought. Naturally it was some time before we found our way there, but she—born in London, as she told me—knew the city well and proved most helpful. When we reached my apartments at last she stood there, lost in her threadbare, voluminous cloak, staring mournfully at me.

"'I am very hungry,' she said at last. 'Have you anything to eat?'

"'I am sorry,' I told her, 'but I have not.'

"'I should not mention it at all, except that I fear I shall faint if I fast any longer,' said she, and sounded very weak and pitiful indeed.

"'Come,' I answered, 'you must sit by the grate and warm yourself.

I shall go to the baker and fetch you some bread. Should you like some bread-and-butter and tea?'

"She smiled and nodded, but not as if she relished the idea of eating. It was more the nod of one who approves a project which is nothing to do with him. In any case, I settled her by the fire—though I could not induce her to take off her mantle—and went out again in search of provisions. I was so fortunate, this time, as not to lose my way. I returned an hour later to find my visitor half asleep, her thin cheeks bathed in the glow of the fire. 'Are you in need of rest?' I inquired, as I set out the tea things and sliced the bread.

" 'I am in need of everything,' said she.

"I smiled at this dire assessment, but she did not smile back. Instead she waited solemnly until the tea had been brewed and the bread buttered; then she gulped the one and wolfed the other. She had been famished, it was clear. She never thanked me for the repast; she never thanked me, indeed, for anything. When she had done she began to stare at me again, intensely, scrutinizing my every expression and movement. 'Will you tell me how I may help you?' I asked her at length.

"She hesitated. 'I will tell you my story,' she answered, 'but you must never repeat it to anyone. Do you swear it?'

" 'I swear it.'

" 'In the name of Jesus Christ our Lord and Saviour,' she stipulated. 'Swear it.'

"I took the oath. You wonder, perhaps, why it is I break that vow by repeating her words to you now. The oath was broke long ago, as you will see—less than a se'ennight, indeed, after it was taken.

" 'My mother is a very holy woman,' said Maria—and I, looking at her daughter, who seemed so spiritual as to be unearthly, could believe it—'and a woman who suffers much. Her father believed that she was a love child, that my grandmother had conceived her while she lay with another man. This was false, you understand, but my grandfather believed it, and hated her for it. When she was sixteen he forced her to marry a bestial man, a man known everywhere for his cruel brutality. It was his revenge on her for reminding him of my grandmother's supposed infidelity.'

" 'My mother was repelled by my father, as was every honest person, but she went with him dutifully. She is a saint, I know it: she has never uttered a moan nor a cross word once in her life. And my father . . . my father was infuriated by her goodness. He took to drink, to gaming, to all manner of low behaviour. My mother bore him three daughters;

I was the third. He left her to provide for us, which she accomplished through menial, degrading labour. She proved indefatigable; her strength annoyed him. He began to beat her, more and more often, and still she never cried out against him. She only prayed more fervently to Mary.'

" 'My father is wicked beyond believing. Hearing her call upon the Virgin, he called upon the devil—and the devil (so evil is my father) came. They communed with one another . . .'

"Maria choked as she reached this point in her history, and was some time in recovering her voice. She had got very passionate in her narrative; it was evident she believed every word she told me. 'Did you—did you see him commune with Satan?' I asked her.

" 'No,' she told me, 'praise God. I should have died before such a spectacle. But he told us, and we knew at once it was so. It was visible in his eyes, in his smile. They were . . . hideous,' she whispered at length.

" 'He went out again that night, and when he came home he told us he had stabbed a man. My mother could not control a gasp—for which my father was delighted. At last he had provoked her—but it was not enough for him. He described to us each detail of his crime. He forced us to listen. And each time my mother cringed, he slapped her. We knew the man he had assaulted: he was a tradesman in the neighbourhood. My father had found him in the street and knifed him in the back, for the sole purpose of grieving my mother.

" 'When the night had passed my mother stole out of the house and went to Bow Street. She sent the runners after my father, and they came to investigate. They found that the tradesman had not died, but they took my father away to prison. He had a trial (my mother went to see it—even then she could not abandon him!) and was sentenced to ten years in gaol. His term expires tomorrow,' Maria concluded, 'and though I have prayed a thousand times that he might never return to us, he is coming back. Now you understand why I stopped you.'

"So Maria said; but I did not understand. That her father's impending return would frighten her was only natural, of course—no doubt the man had vengeance on his mind. But I still had no notion what she could want of me. When I asked her again she only stared, and said I must let her stay with me. 'But I cannot keep your sisters and your mother too,' said I. 'I cannot keep *you* much longer, indeed.'

" 'But you must!' she gasped.

" 'My dear girl!' said I. I had begun to suspect she was a trifle mad, after all. Perhaps her father was a brute; perhaps he had been in prison, and was coming home; but this business about the Virgin and Satan seemed to me a bit overdone. She appeared, furthermore, to be obsessed by the notion that I ought to help her, that my patronage guaranteed her security. The only point I was quite certain about was, as I have said, that she firmly believed every word she uttered. Her conviction was quite apparent. 'Miss Chandler,' said I, 'if you are frightened you ought to go to Bow Street for help. Or enlist the support of a neighbour: do not stay alone with your father.'

" 'Do you suppose Bow Street can stop him?' she demanded, her eyes huge and reproachful. 'He is possessed by the devil—by the Evil One!'

" 'Ah, Miss Chandler,' I said, discouraged in my attempt to reason with her. 'You must understand, please, that I am only just come to London myself. I have very little money, and no friends . . . and I shall lose my room if the porter reports my having guests for any length of time.'

" 'So,' she said, slowly; 'the Evil One whispers to you too.'

" 'Miss Chandler, really—pray be reasonable—'

" 'Let me sleep here tonight,' she interrupted me.

" 'But my dear Miss, the impropriety . . . the porter . . .'

" 'One night only,' she pleaded. 'One night and I shall be gone. If you turn me away now I must sleep in the streets, for I shall never find my way home in the dark.'

"And indeed, night had fallen while she told her story. The moon was hidden behind swollen clouds, and the damp crept in at the windows. 'Miss Chandler, I shall give you money for a link-boy,' I suggested, but feebly, I fear.

"She refused my offer. 'One night, one night for pity's sake,' she wailed, and at last I gave in. Idiot that I was! I had no thought, not the hint of a premonition how profoundly I would regret it someday. I gave her my bed and sat up myself by the dying fire. The night seemed to me to go on forever, but the dawn came at last.

"The moment the sky began to lighten, I woke her. I gave her what was left of the bread-and-butter, and poured her a last cup of tea. Then I told her she must go. She protested, begged, pretended I had promised more. I was genuinely frightened for myself by then: if I were to be turned out of my rooms I should be obliged to leave London altogether, for I had no means to hire other apartments. I stood fast, though I was sorry to do it. I may tell you now that if taking her home was an error, turning her away was an even graver one. She gazed at me one last time, her green eyes full of bitterness, reproach, disappointment. I will never forget that look. It was the last time—no, I cannot say it was the last time I saw her," Mr. Faust interrupted himself. "It was the last time she saw me.

"For three days I heard nothing of Maria, though I remembered her often. I thought of her as one would expect a romantic young man to think: I hoped she was well, hoped she thought of me, hoped she might revisit me someday. On the third day after she had gone a knock sounded on my door—the first, so friendless was I then, since I had come to London. I had gone to Mr. Boswell's residence and left a card; I was so ridiculous, now, as to believe he might somehow be returning my call. When I opened the door, however, I found—so far from that distinguished, illustrious gentleman—two distraught, ill-dressed young women, who regarded me angrily.

" 'What have you done with Maria?' the elder demanded.

" 'I beg your pardon?'

" 'Maria,' the woman repeated. 'I am Miss Victoria Lowell, and this is my sister Clara. Maria told us she had been here; she told us all about you. In the name of heaven, Mr. Faust, tell us what you have done with her!'

" 'Miss Lowell,' said I, stepping back so they might enter my parlour, 'I am dreadfully sorry but—though I am acquainted with a Maria, her surname is not Lowell. It is Chandler,' I added, as they regarded me suspiciously.

" 'Chandler!' they cried in unison. 'That was Mother's name, before she married.'

" 'Indeed?' said I. 'Then perhaps I do know your sister. And yet I am obliged to disappoint you again, for I have not seen her these past three days. You do not mean to tell me that . . . you have not either?'

" 'She has vanished,' said Miss Victoria Lowell, still surveying me with distrust. 'We have been frantic.'

"I invited the Misses Lowell to inspect my rooms, if they cared to, but assured them they should find no sign of Maria. They declined this courtesy, however, and removed themselves from my parlour almost immediately. Maria's disappearance was all they could think of, and if she was not with me, they must go elsewhere.

"Again I heard nothing, this time for two days. Then, as before, there came a knock at night. This time I thought it must be the Misses Lowell, perhaps Maria herself. I was mistaken again. Two gentlemen stood in the corridor, demanding to know if I were Mr. Septimus Faust. I told

them I was. 'Then you must come with us,' they told me, and very
sternly indeed. They were Bow Street men. It was near mid-night, but
I followed them obediently, my mind full of questions as to what they
could want with me. They refused to say anything. We reached a squat,
ugly house and entered it; I was handed into the custody of other
officers. In a very little while I learned the ugly edifice was the home
of the parish constable, where a body had recently been laid out.

"I was brought into the presence of an unclad corpse, a female. I
will not describe in much detail how it looked: it was bloated, distended
everywhere, the skin blue. I could look at it for a moment only; then
I turned my eyes away in horror.

" 'Do you know who this is?' inquired an officer.

" 'It is Maria Lowell,' said I, faint with disgust and distress.

" 'You are the first to have been able to identify her,' said the officer
straightway. 'I arrest you on the charge of murder, in the name of the
King.' "

13

Several among Mr. Faust's audience stirred at this juncture. "Mr. Faust," said Miss Cawley, who was far more frightened than she had expected to be, "I thought this was a ghost story. Where is the ghost?"

"There are two ghosts," said Faust. "There is the spirit of Maria Lowell, which haunts me; and there was her father's ghost, which haunted her. I learned later," he went on, turning to the rest of the company and resuming his former flat tone of voice, "that Maria Lowell had been found at the bottom of the Thames. Evidently she had thrown herself in in despair—though I ought not to say evidently, for it was far from being obvious to Bow Street. The King's agents were convinced I had drowned her; both her sisters had come to see the body, but neither had been sure it was Maria. The fact that my identification was so positive and so rapid led them to believe I was aware she had been drowned; and the only means I could have had to that knowledge was to have committed the murder myself.

"How, you will wonder, had I been so certain? I cannot say. I can only tell you that, swollen and decayed as that body was, I knew at once it was the mortal remains of Maria. Perhaps it was the pathetic angle of her limbs . . . perhaps . . . no, I had rather not speculate on it. It must suffice you to be told that I did know, and knew immediately—although this explanation did not at all satisfy the government officers.

"They imprisoned me that night and kept me there three days, until my father had been sent for and arrived. I was released into his custody but enjoined to stay in London until the inquest had been completed. They would have preferred to keep me incarcerated, but the evidence against me (even they were obliged to admit it) was thin. My name was printed and whispered everywhere in London in connexion with the bizarre, gruesome story; as often happens, what the coroner only suspected, the press and the people took for fact. I was turned out of my rooms; wherever I was recognized I was pointed at and shunned. I would have given much to have been able to quit London, but that freedom was denied me. I spent an entire year in miserable isolation, communicating only with my parents, strangers, and of course the gentlemen investigating the death of Maria Lowell. They seemed to have no qualms at all about harassing me for something I was only suspected to have done; indeed, they seemed to think I should be grateful at having been let out of gaol. They appeared so convinced of their generosity that I began to feel as they did; there were times, in that wretched, unthinkable twelve-month, when I almost suspected myself of murder.

"I ought to go back a bit and tell you what, precisely, were the facts of the case as I came to know them. Maria Lowell was the daughter of a fish-monger, a quick-tempered fellow who had taken part in a drunken brawl during which a man had been stabbed. Lowell was not the one who had stabbed him, but he had been tried for creating a public disorder, and had been kept in gaol some eight months. He had died there of a fever before his term ended. It was true, apparently, that he had been a rough man, and no one denied he was in the habit of striking his wife when he was drunk or angry; however, the idea that he was deliberately vicious, or that he pretended to be intimate with the arch-demon, was a queer fancy which had somehow taken possession of his daughter's brain. Outside of her mind these extraordinary notions had no validity, but inside they were profound and certain truths. She was, in short, a trifle mad.

"She had met me on the eve of what would have been (had he lived) her father's return from gaol. She had quitted her mother's house early that morning, secretly, convinced no doubt that she must find shelter elsewhere. She had returned the next day, after I turned her away, waiting until she fancied her father had gone out before she entered. It was then she recounted to her sisters the story of her visit to me. The tale she had given them was, it would seem, a little confused. She represented me to them first as an angel, later as a demon; first as having proffered help, later as having lured her into my rooms for the purpose of harming and shaming her. Confused as it was, she had got my name and my direction correctly. These proved useful to the Misses Lowell when Maria again disappeared. Nothing could induce her to stop where she believed her father was bound to come, and she went out again almost as soon as she had come home. This time she never returned.

"On the second day of her fresh disappearance Maria Lowell came to me. I was not at home, however. The porter saw her enter and leave; that was all. She had left no message, so he said nothing to me. He testified to the coroner, though. How prone we are to think ourselves the masters of our own fate! We feel strong, courageous, full of our own wisdom and pride, until such a chance mishap as this comes along and alters everything! Had I been in that day—had I only been in!—I believe Miss Lowell would never have killed herself. I could have spoke to her, aided her, taken her to her home myself, made certain all was well. As it was, her visit brought her no assistance whatever; as for me, it became a part of the evidence against me. No one—save my father and mother, for which a thousand blessings on them—believed my acquaintance with Maria to have been what I insisted it was. Her daring to visit my rooms alone and uninvited increased the doubt and prejudice against me yet more. And even if it had not, the porter knew she had stopped the night with me. That alone was enough to establish my guilt in certain minds. I dareswear there are those among you now who do not believe my account of that night—and you meet me as a guest of Her Grace the Duchess of Karr! Imagine, if you will, how strong your sentiments might have run against me had we met at a coroner's inquest.

"The third day after her second disappearance from home was, apparently, the day she committed suicide. It was not possible to be certain, of course, but from the state of the corpse the doctors judged her to have been two days dead on discovery. I was called in and interrogated any number of times in the following year, and the question of where I had been on that night was invariably raised. I had been at the theatre, I was obliged to tell them. Not a soul remembered to have seen me there; the porter had seen me leave, but he had fallen asleep before I returned. I had no alibi.

"Why did she kill herself? One can only guess, of course. Sometimes I feel, rather oddly, that I am the person best equipped to speculate. I believe she was terrified. She was convinced her father was alive, a criminal, and on his way home to avenge himself upon his wife and children. Her mother would not listen when Maria warned her of the danger; her sisters would not listen. No one would listen, indeed; even I pushed her into the streets and into her imagined jeopardy once again. She was afraid to go home; she had come to me and found me away; she went to the Thames and leapt in. I know she must have been deeply desperate to have done so, for she was devoutly religious even in her madness, and suicide is a mortal sin.

"She is buried ignominiously in an unmarked grave near London. I went to visit it once, a little time after her death, but my legal counsellor suggested I ought not to do so, since it looked ill for my defence. Of all the names connected to the case, Maria's is the only one which does not stir bitterness in me. She was pitiful—bedevilled and pitiful—and had no idea how much anguish she eventually caused me.

"I will not draw out this narrative any longer than need be. My ordeal ended, officially, a year after it began, when the charges against me were dropped for lack of sufficient evidence. In the interim I had been haunted continually by the image of Maria Lowell—it still haunts me, indeed. I had awakened in the dead of night, shuddering, having dreamt of my own hanging; or seen in a night-mare flash Maria's distorted face. I had pled for my innocence and my life scores of times, to hundreds of people. I had endured the undisguised hatred and mistrust of my fellow men, and all through no fault but the folly of youth. I may add one curious postscript, however, before I close entirely. Some three years after Maria's death, I chanced to see the Misses Lowell in Covent Garden. Their fortunes seemed to have improved somewhat, for they dressed a bit more luxuriously. In any case, I approached them, and bowed. They stared at me. I spoke to them, calling them by name. This did not persuade them to answer me. It was impossible they could have forgot who I was, yet I sought to remind them a little. They drew positively away from me, closer to each other, turned without a word and hurried off. I did not follow them, of course. Evidently they still believe me guilty."

On these words Mr. Faust ceased to speak, though he gave no other sign that his tale was over. A few moments of silence passed; then the company began to move, rustling and murmuring and making trivial, nervous jokes. Karr gave orders for the lights to be illuminated once more; the duchess, meanwhile, addressed Mr. Faust.

"If that was a true story, dear sir," said she sublimely, "I am a Siamese shop-keeper."

Septimus laughed, but he appeared gaunt and haggard, and his laugh sounded hollow. "As you chuse to believe," said he, indifferently.

Her eyebrows lifted slightly. "I think I must write to your mother. She will tell me."

"If you are kind, you will not broach the subject to her. It is an unhappy one for my family."

"This sounds like an evasion," said the duchess dryly.

"Things are not always what they seem," Miss Cawley interrupted suddenly. "If we did not know that before Mr. Faust told us his story, I think we ought surely to know it now."

"Ah, dear lady," Septimus addressed Jessica, with a bow and a hint of his wonted grin. "We never know from which quarter help is coming. Did you enjoy my tale?"

"Oh, yes, rather," Jessica replied. She tried to employ a careless tone of voice, but an involuntary shiver which ran through her as she spoke gave her away utterly. "Oh, dear," she laughed, "it was awfully chilling. How dreadful for you!"

"Mr. Faust seems to have survived it intact," observed Algernon Longstreth, who sat next to his betrothed. "Fortunately," he added.

"Thank you for that postscript," said Faust jocularly to Mr. Longstreth. "Now, Lady Louisa," he went on, turning to her, "I have done as I promised. It is abhorrent to me to remind a lady of an obligation, but you *do* owe us a story, you know!"

"Good heavens!" cried the plump old woman. "I had nearly forgot, I was so scared. I declare I thought I was a child again. Are you certain you desire me to tell my story? It is not nearly the match of yours."

A chorus of "Please"s broke out among the company.

Lady Louisa's pasty cheeks flushed pink. "Now? Directly?" she asked her eager audience.

"After tea, perhaps," said the duchess, a trifle severely. "We are all panting to hear you, Louisa, but I think we are also thirsty."

Tea was accordingly rung for and drunk. Lady Louisa felt a bit ashamed at not having realized the company must want a pause before she commenced (whenever Her Grace of Karr reminded Louisa of anything she felt sadly reprimanded—it had been so since their earliest childhood), but a few thickly buttered muffins taken with her tea soon consoled her, and by the time the dishes had been cleared away and the party re-assembled before the fire, Lady Louisa Bridwell was in fine spirits. "This is a story my grandfather told me when I was ever so little," she began, while through the window behind her a peaceful fall of snow might have been observed in the moonlight, "and which I have never forgot. Sarah, you may recall it. It is about Susan, the shepherdess, the smallest lamb of whose flock strayed away one Christmas Eve. Her poor family could ill afford the loss of so valuable an animal—and besides, Susan was a gentle girl, and her good heart fairly ached when she thought of the sweet woolly thing all alone in the snow. In any case, she went out after it, and that is how her adventure started.

"There was but half a moon that night, and the snow fell swiftly. None of you has ever looked for a lamb in the snow at night, I trust, but I may tell you it is no easy task. Lambs being white and snow being white, one may look long without reward. Susan looked long indeed: she walked over the nearer pasture, then the farther; she went through a frozen apple orchard and across an icy brook. No lamb was to be found. Miss Susan thought of turning round, but then she remembered again the pitiful lamb and continued. She had entered a rolling meadow when she thought, at last, she heard the bells of the lost sheep. She had been listening for them from the first, indeed, but their jingle was so soft and the wind so high, she had little hope of hearing them. Still, she seemed now to hear, through the whistle of the sharp wind, a faint jangle. She followed it. It receded. The sound grew fainter, then clearer, fainter, then clearer, while Susan travelled many miles. At last, far across the fields from her father's cottage, she came to a small stone dwelling. No smoke issued from the chimney; the door stood ajar to the chill of the night. Within, Susan thought she heard the bells of her lost lamb. She stood upon the threshold of the cheerless cottage, peering into the darkness. She could see nothing. The place seemed so strangely deserted, she almost turned away in fear, but she thought her lamb might be there, so in she went. Besides, the snow had begun to fall thickly, with small, icy, stinging flakes, the moon was obscured behind clouds, and Susan was not at all sure how to find her father's house again.

"In she went then, calling for the lamb. The cottage had only narrow slits for windows, and these did not emit enough light for her to see. She was certain she heard the bells, though—first in this corner, then in that. Hither and yon she went in the dark, her hands reaching out to the poor little beast, but nothing did she touch but the cold stone of the inhospitable hovel. She found the hearth, but no fuel lay near it, and no fire. By now she was very cold indeed—nearly frozen—and she would have been glad to find her lamb only for the warmth they might have shared. She discovered nothing but the stone walls, the straw on the floor, and the ever-shifting jingle of the bells. She was weary, numb with cold, and mystified at her failure to touch the lamb when she could hear him so clearly. Finally, reasoning that the cottage, dreary as it was, could afford her some shelter (whereas if she endeavoured to make her way home, she was likely to die of the cold) Susan curled up in a corner on a heap of straw, and waited till the day had come and she could see.

"While she waited she slept, and while she slept she dreamt. She dreamt of a star that appeared in the sky just over the roof of her father's house. This star sent a beacon to her, guiding her home. So vivid was the dream that she woke and ran to the door, to look at the heavens. There was no new star, however. Disappointed, she returned to her corner. As she fell asleep this time, she heard the jingle of the lamb's bells coming toward her. She felt his woolly warmth as he came and nestled against her. She could not see him, but she leaned her poor head upon his soft coat, and wrapped her arms round his body. When she woke again it was morning.

"What did she find when the sun's rays crept at last through the slits in the walls of the cottage? Not the lamb she had lain against last night— no, indeed. The lamb had gone, and its jingling too—and when Susan went home that morning her father told her the lost sheep had returned only minutes after she had left to look for it. But this was only the first of the mysteries, for when Susan awakened in that little cheerless cottage on Christmas Day, she found beside her a heap of passion flowers, bright and pure upon the straw-strewn floor. Unlearned as she was, she did not even know the name of these exotic blossoms; certainly she had never seen such things before. And yet their beauty touched her; she cried, while she gathered them up, for their sheer loveliness. She knew it was miraculous for such flowers to appear, from nowhere, in deep of winter, and she told the story often to her children (as she grew older) and her grand-children (as she grew even older). She did not know, however, that the flowers she found were tropical blooms, and never grow in England—but we know, and we ought to remember it on Christmas Day."

This was the end of Lady Louisa Bridwell's story, which—though mysterious—will be seen by the reader to have been rather more sweet than frightening. Lady Louisa had not desired to scare anyone anyway; they had had enough of that, she felt, through the offices of Mr. Faust. Apparently the remainder of the company shared her sentiments, for they thanked her very sincerely indeed for the tale, and talked of it afterwards quite as much as they talked of the earlier one.

Christmas itself came upon them pretty swiftly, and was celebrated with much wassailing and other merriment, as well as several visits to the stone church. A troupe of mummers appeared from Stirnby, playing out the tale of St. George and the Dragon, and were much admired by the guests at Grasmere (who had by now some notion of what amateur theatricals entailed). New Year's came and went in its turn, and was observed with those traditional festivities which had been the rule at Grasmere Castle for centuries. Miss Jessica Cawley was pleased to note (as was Mr. Longstreth) that if Robin Hood's ghost was heard to walk, it was heard by the servants only. *That* nonsense, at least, had been laid to rest where she and Algie were concerned.

The early days of January passed, bringing with them snow and winds so forbidding as to persuade even the hardiest sportsmen to stop indoors for the time being. Karr, who found it more difficult to pretend to be cheerful with each passing day, began to be noticeably restless. Even the duchess (who ordinarily did not bother with such trifles) observed it, and she brought it up to him one day when they met by chance in the library.

"Are you quite well, my son?" Her Grace inquired.

"I am sufficiently well, thank you, madam."

"You seem listless," she told him. "You are in need of diversion."

"The society of some twenty-odd people is adequate diversion, I think," he said. He was still very much out of charity with his mother, as she knew.

"So it would seem," she agreed, "but apparently it is not. I am going to suggest something, Karr—don't bite my head off," she warned him, "but I should like to invite Lady Henrietta to return to Grasmere this spring."

This brought Karr up sharply; he glared at his magnificent interlocutress. "To what end, if you please?" he asked in a low voice.

"I—I am fond of her," said the duchess, in a fashion rather too indirect to be worthy of her. "I thought you were too. Are not you?"

"Madam, I have not the least intention of offering for her. I suppose that will answer your question."

"Intentions often go astray," the duchess observed.

"This one will not," he said, rather grimly. "In fact, I will make it a point never to offer for her—as a matter of policy, if nothing else. And I will offer for no one else you wave under my nose; is that the kind of information you seek?"

"If you mean to be obstinate to so outrageous a degree," she answered evenly, "I suppose it is best you tell me."

"Then I have told you," he said, with perceptible bitterness in his tone. He bowed and made as if to leave her.

"One moment," she said. "I want to know one thing more. Do you hear from—from Miss Chilton?"

He gave her an icy, unpleasant glance. "I do not," he replied, striving to keep the disappointment and hurt this circumstance caused him out of his voice and his expression.

"Good," Her Grace responded, with customary candour. "It will be better for you not to hear from her, believe me."

"So she said," Karr observed.

"Did she?" asked the duchess, surprised.

"Yes, she did. Do you imagine it was my idea for her to leave Grasmere? It was hers and hers only. I promised her, in fact, to go after her and fetch her whether she wishes to come or no."

"I see Miss Chilton had more sense than I gave her credit for," Her Grace remarked.

"What has sense to do with it?" asked her son.

"She saw how foolish it would be for her to stop longer near you. I am only sorry you were not the one to perceive that."

Karr found it infuriating that his mother should insist upon Lotta's "sense" and ignore utterly the goodness which motivated her removal from the castle. Karr had sent Lotta any number of letters, but not one of them had been answered. He had been on the point of travelling to her father's home a few days ago, for he had been serious about following her and fetching her back if it were necessary, but something had caused him to delay. For the first time he had begun to see how inane—how cruel, indeed—such a course of conduct would be. Lotta had made her decision; what right had he to tease her, to hammer at her, to pester her? It would only—as she had said—cause her more pain. These were the thoughts that had stayed him, then, and now they caused him (some days after his unpleasant interview with his mother) to write her one more letter. This one informed her that, miserable as he was, he had come to understand finally that he ought not to pursue her against her will. He still did not expect to marry: she could return to him at any time. He begged her to think of him kindly, and not to forget that his happiness remained in her hands, but he saw the ungentleness of his harassing her even through the post, and he would send her no more letters for a while. After despatching this, poor Karr found himself more miserable even than before, and it was indeed a great strain on him to act the part of the pleasant and sociable host.

Despite the difficulties, he was playing that rôle on a certain evening in mid-January, two days after he had sent Lotta Chilton the missive mentioned above. It was an evening like any other—a bit more inclement than most, perhaps, since the snow had gone rather soft and wet—and the guests at Grasmere were just finishing tea. As was his custom, His Grace was seeing to it that each of his visitors found some sort of occupation to divert him during the remainder of the evening: the Countess Tremini, magnificent in a gown of crimson velvet and a sumptuous set of rubies, had begged him to set up a whist table for her, and Septimus Faust had expressed the hope that one of the ladies might be persuaded to play upon the harpsichord. Karr was in the act of convincing Sir Francis Olney (who protested that he had already lost too much money to the contessa) that he desired to play whist again that evening, when a piercing shriek was suddenly heard that brought everyone up short. It was Lady Stanton who had screamed, just as she had so many months before, alarming all the company. This time she did not faint, however. She merely stood in the middle of the drawing-room, her hand clapped over her mouth, her eyes huge and terrified, staring round at the others as if she had been a rabbit and they the hunters.

14

For a long moment everyone stood as if frozen. Lady Stanton had gone quite white; the Countess Tremini, who stood near her, was as flushed as the other was pale. The long, still moment was broke when Lord Stanton, and Amabel and Chauncey after him, rushed up to her lady-ship. "My dear!" cried her husband.

"Mamma!" cried her children.

"Lady Stanton!" cried Lord Wyborn, who (as her future son-in-law) felt it his duty to see to her health with the others.

Lady Stanton stared at these solicitous people as she had stared at everyone else. Abruptly she began to cry. "That woman is going to be the end of us," she exclaimed passionately, so that everyone could hear her. "She is going to expose us, Walker—she just said so! I want to do it myself—now. Please, Walker, let us have done with it at once—let it be over before I die of misery and suspense!"

It may be imagined how much curiosity was stirred by these words in the breasts of the listening company. Interest was heightened even further when the Countess Tremini, in quite an audible tone, said urgently to Lady Stanton, "Do not give it all up now—you have come so far! Certainly," she added, lowering her voice, "you will find the money."

"I will not, I will not!" Lady Stanton answered piteously. "We have no more money—we have nothing, you—fiend! We have given you Amabel's dowry; we have sold off Driscow Park . . . We own nothing more but Baddesleigh, and I will not part with Baddesleigh, I will not, I will not!"

Lord Stanton and the others (except Lord Wyborn, who had removed himself just a few paces when her ladyship happened to mention Amabel's dowry) had sought all this while to calm Lady Stanton, but to little avail. "Don't you see, Walker—she's just threatened us again," her ladyship pleaded with her husband. "Pray, let it be done with; I cannot bear another hour of it."

The onlookers, as was quite natural, were entirely mystified by this extraordinary spectacle, and no one knew what to do. At last His Grace of Karr came forward and put out a steadying hand to the distraught lady. "Dear Madam," he said, "I do not know what can have happened to cause you such keen distress, but your evident pain disturbs me deeply. Might I beg you to come with me, away from . . . her, where we may speak privately of this matter?—you and Lord Stanton, I mean. I am certain we can resolve the . . . problem, whatever it is, if you will only allow me to assist—"

But Lady Stanton interrupted him. "No," she said firmly. "I thank you, but this is far beyond anything that may be resolved in such a fashion. There is but one resolution possible," she went on boldly (though not daring to look at her husband, who might be signalling his disapproval to her) "and that is for me to make a clean breast of it—now, here, in public." She looked round the drawing-room appealingly. "Will you hear me out now? I pray you will; it is desperately important."

"If there is something you desire to say to all of us, I am sure—" Karr began, but again she broke in.

"This will take some time to explain," said her ladyship, addressing herself to the party in general. "Lord Wyborn, I am afraid you must prepare yourself for a dreadful shock . . . and my poor children," she added, gathering her son and daughter to her, "I fear you will think very ill—oh, very ill indeed!—of your pitiful mamma."

Her children clung very prettily to either side of her, but it was obvious they were excessively frightened. Lord Stanton himself, indeed, seemed none too confident; the only one quite in control of herself, it appeared, was (strangely) Lady Stanton. Now she had made up her mind to tell all, an overwhelming sense of relief had come to her. Swiftly she seated herself on a sofa near the centre of the large apartment, inviting the others to range themselves round her, so that they might hear what she had to say. They complied eagerly enough, for even the most jaded of them was consumed with curiosity by then.

"I am about to reveal a set of facts which I had never thought to breathe a word of. No one living knows these things now but myself and Lord Stanton, the Contessa di Tremini, and one other. I see you are surprised at my mentioning the contessa," said Lady Stanton, glancing briefly and without expression at that lady, "but you cannot be more surprised than I was when I learned she was privy to my secret. How she came upon it I still do not know, but that she knows she has proven to me. I am speaking to you now because—excuse me one moment," she broke off suddenly. "Your Grace, if you would truly serve me, you will have somebody constrain the contessa. Believe me, there is a possibility she will attempt to flee Grasmere at any moment; I am telling her secrets as well as my own."

"Lady Stanton, this is somewhat extraordinary—" said Karr, in a quiet, serious tone. He kept an eye on the contessa even as he spoke, however, and could not help observing that she looked very uncomfortable indeed.

"I will not run," said the countess, as all eyes turned to her. "I give you my word," she added, as Karr continued to regard her carefully.

"Her word is worth nothing," Lady Stanton said bluntly. "She has been blackmailing Lord Stanton and myself since October. Your Grace, I beg you will force her to stay."

A general gasp was heard at the word "blackmail." His Grace stood finally and went to the great doors of the drawing-room. He whispered a word to the footmen outside, then shut the doors himself. "We will all stay," he said quietly. "We will hear you out, then listen to the contessa."

"Thank you," said Lady Stanton, resuming her story. "When I was a girl—a very green girl—I had a drawing master, a young Italian nobleman whose family was so impoverished that he was reduced to giving such lessons."

"My dear," Lord Stanton interrupted, "I hardly think it is necessary for you to tell every detail. Surely a simple sketch—"

"No. I wish to make a clean breast of it. Everything," insisted her ladyship. "This drawing master was very handsome, and very gallant—though not, as it later developed, overly scrupulous. He paid court to me in my father's house—without, of course, the knowledge of my father. Had he known, the drawing master would have been out upon his ear in a trice—but we kept it a secret, the . . . two of us," said Lady Stanton, stumbling over the word "two." "I was only fifteen. I was persuaded I was in love, that I would never love another, that I must be with this gentleman forever. The man—Lodovico was his name—felt similarly, or said he did . . . Even to this day, I believe he was sincere in his affection for me: he was not foolish enough to believe my father would ever accept him, I think. In any case, we decided to elope."

"Mamma!" cried Amabel Stanton suddenly, half horrified, half charmed with the romance of this.

"Shhh!" said Jessica Cawley. She hadn't meant to, but it escaped from her, so intrigued was she by the story. Her interest, though she could not have said how or why, was somehow greater even than she might have expected it to be. Whatever the reason, she was listening very carefully.

Lady Stanton looked at Jessica with mild, sad eyes, and continued. "We went to Italy and were married. We dared not go to Lodovico's family, for we felt certain my parents would look for us there. Instead we settled alone in a little town near Florence. We were very poor, and quite friendless. In no time at all we were both miserable. When we had been there some ten months, I gave . . . gave b—" At this point Lady Stanton burst into a freshet of tears, which she overcame only with effort. "I gave birth to a child," she said, in a barely audible voice; "a girl. Her name was Charlotte."

"Dear God!" Miss Cawley suddenly exclaimed.

"I beg your pardon?" said Lady Anne.

"Nothing—go on, pray go on," said Jessica, gesturing impatiently. "This may be . . ." but her voice faded away as she murmured the rest of her words to herself.

"By now a year had gone by since I had left my family. I had never written a word to them (miserable though I sometimes was). I was too proud to admit I repented of my rashness; I fretted over them, and longed to hear from them, but I did not let them know where I was. Naturally they had been looking for me all this while. We had covered our trail so efficiently that it was half a year before they discovered we had gone to Italy; it was even longer again than that before they learned precisely where. They did find us at last, however, when the baby was only a few months old.

"I was suffering dreadfully from a nervous complaint. The baby was healthy but small. Lodovico was prepared to stand by me to the end, but I knew he regretted our marriage as profoundly as I did. He was a very sweet man, really—a good man," said Lady Stanton, restraining a sob, "but he was just as foolish as I. In any case . . . my parents persuaded him to go to his family and acquaint them with what had hap-

pened. At the same time, I was to return with them to England, until I
had regained my health. The baby, being weak, was to remain in Italy.

"Accordingly, I said good-bye to my . . . my husband and child, and
set sail for England. Lodovico was to write to me there as soon as he
reached his family—but he never wrote. We could not imagine what had
happened; I was beside myself with worry. After two months of silence I
returned to Italy with my father—but we could find no trace of my husband. His family said they had never heard from him, not since he had
been in England. He and the baby, in brief, had—" and at this point
Lady Stanton did choke, "quite vanished."

Her ladyship wept for a few minutes. "We never found them. We sent
out agents—the same ones who had looked for the two of us before—but
they turned up nothing. They had disappeared into thin air; that was all
there was to it. I did not know—I still do not know—what happened to
them. It is possible that Lodovico, recognizing how unhappy we must always be together, had thought it best to remove himself and Charlotte
from my life. It is possible—though this appears not to have been the
case, since the contessa must have learned of all this through Lodovico—
that he and the baby were somehow . . . killed on their way to his parents. I do not know," she repeated simply. "I have never known. After
three or four years, however—remember, I was only sixteen when I returned from Italy—some of the urgency had gone out of my sorrow and
confusion. I began to think of that episode in my life as something very
remote, as something someone else had done, almost—a story about a
girl I hardly knew. God forgive me, but when my parents encouraged
me to put the whole, terrible memory behind me, I listened to them. I
resisted at first, but I listened to them."

At this juncture Lady Stanton cried again, and this time not a few of
the ladies of the party joined her. Certainly Amabel's sweet little face
was wet with tears; even Algernon Longstreth (in contrast to his betrothed, whose countenance was all impatience) might have been seen
raising a linen handkerchief to his moist eyes.

"Five years after my return from Italy—when I was twenty-one—Lord
Stanton . . . paid me the honour of showing me a marked attention. I
had been living very retired, partly to avoid the possibility of just such a
difficulty as this. Lord Stanton, however, pursued me even in my re-
tirement, cultivating an intense friendship with my father. My father had
never had a son, of course: I was an only child. I believe he found in
Walker's company what he had missed in my mother's and mine; in any
case, he favoured his suit. My father—God rest his soul—had by this

time made up his mind that I ought to marry; if I did not, his estate as
well as his title would pass to his cousin, whom he had never held in
much affection. As for the fact that I was already married . . . I suppose it seemed to him that Lodovico had disappeared so fortuitously,
and so completely, that it would have been mere quibbling and nonsense
to insist upon remembering him. Moreover, if it seemed unlikely that
Lodovico would reappear after so long a time, it was even more improb-
able that the baby should . . . and so . . . I was advised to accept my
lord's suit.

"This I was not unwilling to do," said Lady Stanton, for the first time
giving a semblance of a smile, and extending a pale hand toward Lord
Stanton. "I was sufficiently mature by then, at least, to recognize
Walker's excellence of judgement, his evenness of temper—in short, all
those qualities which have drawn me closer to him with each passing
year. I knew he was not as wealthy as we, nor quite as exalted in the
peerage, but I also trusted he would never marry merely for pecuniary
or social advantage. And indeed, he has never done anything to prove
the contrary: when my father informed him of my history, assuring him
that he was free to rescind his offer for me, Walker never faltered, but
(after a reasonable period of reflection) thanked my father for his
straight-forwardness and held to his original purpose. He agreed to bear
equally with me the burden only I was truly responsible for—I mean the
threat of a reappearance of Lodovico or little Charlotte—and we were
married with all due ceremony.

"Until very recently, we lived like any other married pair. I bore him
a daughter and a son," (Lady Stanton hugged each of these as she
named them) "my lord looked after the estate my father had given us,
and later (when both my parents had passed away) he managed Baddesleigh itself. There was never a breath heard from my past—never the
slightest whisper. Those few servants and relations who were in a position to know I had once run off had never been told exactly where I had
run to, or with whom . . . About the absence itself they were good
enough to keep silent, I suppose out of loyalty to me. Neither Amabel
nor Chauncey ever knew a word of this before today—poor things! And
so, feeling uncommonly blessed by fortune (for our lives have been so
serene that whole years have passed without my thinking once of my
dreadful, youthful folly) we accepted Her Grace's invitation to winter at
Grasmere.

"I will not deny—it would be absurd to do so—that we had in mind,
when we came, the idea that my lord the marquis of Wyborn might be

encouraged, both by his own inclination and by her near presence, to offer for Amabel. He did offer, as you know; and it may fairly be asked of us, I think, why we did not share with him the history I am now recounting." Lady Stanton paused to look long and sadly at Wyborn. "It was because, I must confess, of my own cowardice. I was afraid that he might baulk if he were told; and if he were to cry off, I should be obliged to explain it to Amabel. And, as I say, I did not desire ever to teach my poor children their own mother's disgrace. Therefore, my lord Wyborn, I said nothing—but now I may speak, and I offer you my profoundest, my most desolate, apologies for my former silence."

Lady Stanton had been about to continue, but Wyborn—moved by her glance and tone—interrupted her. "I have no intention of crying off," he declared, with the utmost gallantry. "I hold your daughter—and indeed, all your family—in the highest esteem, whatever your private history or your troubles. The house of Wyborn is not so proud that it cannot forgive, and if your sins are no more than the youthful ones you have narrated, then in my eyes you have already—by your gentleness and your suffering—obtained absolution." Lord Wyborn, having said this, approached his betrothed and kissed her tenderly on her forehead. The extraordinary generosity evidenced by his brief speech, meanwhile, brought tears into many pairs of eyes, and provoked in Lady Stanton a most beautiful, though tremulous, smile.

"So worthy a sentiment as that," she said in a low tone, "I feel unfit to answer. I will only finish my story, which is near its end already. I suppose you will all recall the evening when I fainted so dramatically in this same apartment, while I sat at whist? I fainted because I had been dealt (with my cards) a note signed by the dealer. The dealer was the Contessa di Tremini, and the note was to the effect that she knew I had been married as a girl in Italy, and knew I had another child. She later demanded to be paid for her silence."

Fascinated, horrified eyes turned upon the countess at this disclosure. "It is a lie," said the contessa faintly, but she looked wildly frightened, and no one believed her.

"I have notes in her hand to prove what I say," Lady Stanton resumed quietly. "We conferred with one another—Lord Stanton and myself, I mean—and concluded we would do best to pay her. She promised to demand no more; but she did, and very soon after. I no longer recall how many notes there were, but it came to three demands, two of which we have met. The latest demand, a reminder of which provoked the scream you heard from me this evening, we could not have paid without ruining ourselves entirely. Lady di Tremini, as the tale has it, has killed the goose that laid the golden eggs. Now it is all out, I hope we will be able to put her in gaol for her crimes. I do not know the penalty for extortion—perhaps it is even death. She has proved herself so cruel these past few months, I almost hope it is," cried her ladyship, on a sob. She embraced Chauncey very firmly. "You see, my dear, why your father was so displeased with your . . . your admiration for the contessa," she said, weeping. Master Chauncey could not only see; he could not prevent himself from crying with his mother.

"Of course we are ruined," Lady Stanton added by way of conclusion. "Lodovico must still be alive, or must have been when I married Lord Stanton, at least, or how else should the countess have learned my secret? She lived long in Italy, of course . . . they must have met . . . And so I have lived in sin all these years, and my children are b . . . are bas—" but Lady Stanton could not pronounce this last word, and she yielded completely, at last, to her tears.

At this point Karr felt it his duty to stand up and take hold of things. "Lady Stanton," he said, "though what you have told us comes as a shock, I think I speak for everyone here when I say that our sympathies are with you. Lady di Tremini," he went on, "I am afraid I must ask you to answer these charges. It is difficult to believe, indeed, that a lady of your rank and reputation could be reduced to such criminal activities —and yet, if you have not threatened the Stantons, I am even more at a loss to understand why her ladyship should have told us what she just did. If you please, I think we have a right to know how on earth you discovered her—her secret, and what, precisely, let you turn it to your own advantage."

"Dear Karr, no more speeches!" begged Jessica Cawley suddenly. "More hangs in the balance than you can guess—believe me. Only make the contessa tell all at once, pray!"

"There will be no necessity of coercion," the contessa said, addressing Miss Cawley. She lifted her sublime head as proudly as she could contrive, and regarded the younger woman with what dignity was left to her. If she was found out, the contessa had decided, she would at least not cower or cringe. She had always lived magnificently; she would continue magnificent as long as she possibly could. "I discovered Lady Stanton's buried past without subterfuge, and I had excellent reasons for demanding money. I am—or was before the Stantons paid me—stupendously in debt."

"Ah, Sarah! I *said* you would regret inviting her," Lady Louisa murmured to the dowager duchess.

"You see," Septimus Faust whispered triumphantly into her other ear, while the countess spoke. "I told you she was the sort who schemed. Of course this is doing it a trifle brown, I think," he added with a grin. The duchess, meanwhile, was doing her best to maintain her tranquillity in the midst of all these scandalous revelations. At the moment she was managing to look rather better than she felt.

"My husband left me without funds," the contessa was saying, not a little bitterly. "The notion that his death made me a woman of means is a fairy-tale I invented. I have always had my pride," she added, with a flicker of something angry in her violet eyes. "I might have fared well enough," she went on, "if it had not been my penchant for gambling. The first thing I did after my husband's interment was to sell all my jewels—these are paste," she explained, fingering the fabulous rubies round her neck and wrists. "They are imitations of the ones I was obliged to part with."

The countess sighed deeply. "I do like gaming," she admitted, ruefully but now shame-facedly. "I am, as one says, addicted to deep play. Unhappily, the cards do not often run in my favour. The number of debts I incurred last season in London would stagger an ordinary person. I never allowed them even to break my stride. When I arrived at Grasmere it was with the consciousness that unless I made enormous winnings here, things would go very badly indeed with me when it came time to return to London. And indeed, luck has gone my way this winter . . . but I have not needed it. Thanks to the Stantons, I have been able to discharge all my debts of last year. This last demand—" her voice dropped a little, the first indication that she was at all ashamed, "was to set me up a little for the future. I am tired of wearing paste; any woman would be. And if there is a woman who thinks otherwise," she added defiantly, "she ought to try it herself."

"Lady di Tremini," Jessica Cawley interrupted urgently, "forget, if you can, your jewels! Go on with the story."

"All in good time; all in good time," said the countess, who did not care to be prodded. "I happened upon Lady Stanton's secret by chance, in Italy, many years ago. I had just been married—against my will, I may add—to a fat Italian clown whose very voice I have always despised. In any case, I was young. I had gone on a journey, a visit to a distant cousin of mine then living in Milan. My husband's family were Romans; on my way from Rome to Milan, I stopped in a little town

near Florence. I took a room in an inn—it was a dismal little hostelry,
but I was feeling ill, and preferred to stop anywhere than to continue
just then. I was lying on the bed—I had just sent my maid out to fetch a
doctor, I recall—when a knock sounded. A messenger—a ragged little
boy—handed me a letter and ran off. I could not imagine how anyone
could have found me at that obscure inn, but I tore open the missive
and began to read it. It was addressed to My Lord the Earl of Baddesleigh."

The contessa paused while everyone exclaimed at this first recognizable connexion between the two stories. "I looked, then, at the super-
scription on the envelope—for the first time. Indeed, it was for his lordship. The hotel was the same; I concluded that the ragged boy had got
my room wrong, and that the earl, whomever he might be, was my
fellow guest. I was ill, however, as I have said, and peevish. At another
moment I should probably have folded up the letter without reading another word of it, attached a note explaining the mistake, and sent it
along to its proper destination. Being fatigued and rather lonely, though,
I decided to read the note first for whatever interest it might hold. It was
written in a very pretty hand, and referred to the earl's daughter—the
penman's wife—and the earl's granddaughter Charlotte. It was brimming
with explanation and apology; I gathered that the earl's daughter, Lady
Anne (as the letter told me) had run off with the author of the missive;
that they had been absent a long time; and that the son-in-law (my unconscious informant) ranked greatly below his new father. He expressed
his willingness to do whatever the earl thought wisest—stay with Anne,
leave her be, take the child, or part with her—anything at all. I do not
recall every detail, but I remembered enough of it to have known, when
I met Lady Anne here, that there might be more to her than met the
eye. In truth I did not recollect everything at once; it was not until she
admitted to having been in Italy many years before that I began to put
things together. When I heard Lord Stanton mention Baddesleigh one
day, however, the whole situation became clear. So far as I knew at first,
Lady Anne's first husband had died, and the child too, before she even
met Lord Stanton. I suspected somehow that this was not the case, however, and her ladyship's spectacular faint when confronted with my
knowledge confirmed my suspicion. If you had kept your countenance,
my lady," she went on, turning to her erstwhile victim, "I might never
have thought of it again. Perhaps that will teach you to maintain—"

"Dear God," Jessica Cawley suddenly exploded, "will neither of you ever say it? What is his name?" she cried, jumping up. "His name, his name—your first husband's name!"

All the company stared at her in wonderment. "Lodovico," said Lady Stanton mildly. "So I told you. Lodovico del Silandro."

"Ah, yes!" Jessica shrieked, grinning suddenly ear to ear. "Yes, yes— did you hear it?" she appealed to Longstreth, and then to Karr.

"My dear ma'am!" said His Grace, who felt that the very last thing he needed was for Miss Cawley to go mad.

"You do not know?" she asked him. "No, I see you do not. My dear good man, ring for your fastest courier! Send him to Lotta Chilton at once. My dear Karr," she went on, as he only stared at her the harder, "Lotta's father was Lodovico del Silandro!"

15

If the previous portion of the evening had been unsettling, what followed was simply chaotic. Miss Cawley was plied with an hundred questions, the answers to most of which she did not know.

"I am afraid it is a long time since she told me," she apologized. "It was the day we went to Goose-Fair. I am certain del Silandro is dead," she told Lady Stanton, who inquired repeatedly, "but I cannot say precisely when he died. You must ask Lotta—oh, Karr, do send someone for Lotta!"

"But was she young when he died?" Lady Stanton begged. "Was she young enough so that my second marriage was binding? That is what I must know."

"Is it of no interest to you at all to discover that Lotta Chilton is your lost daughter?" Jessica inquired of her, her bright eyes round with wonderment.

"Dear me yes . . . but—"

"If Miss Chilton is Lady Stanton's daughter, and her father was an Italian lord . . ." Karr suddenly interrupted, addressing Miss Cawley.

"Then you may marry Lotta," Jessica filled in joyfully. "Yes, yes; that is precisely why it is so important. Karr, *do* go and ride for her, or send someone, won't you?"

"I will in a moment, only . . . why does she not call herself Charlotte?" he asked, while Lady Stanton nodded her head vigorously to indicate that this had troubled her too. "And why does she use the name Chilton?"

"Good heavens, Karr, I don't know," Jessica replied impatiently. "I suppose Lotta was a childhood abbreviation. As for Chilton, she took it from her adoptive father. She knew her father's right name—she told me, after all—but she never used it. I think she feared it would injure Mr. Chilton's feelings. They treat her very much as their own."

"Walker," said Lady Stanton slowly, "remember what an odd sensation I had the day Miss Chilton left the castle? No wonder! She is my own flesh and blood."

Lord Stanton began a reply to this, but he was interrupted by the dowager duchess—who, indeed, curtailed all the anxious conjecture which had been going forward. "Hold," she said imperiously; "hold, just one moment."

"Yes, madam?" said her son.

The duchess rose slowly and assumed rather a regal pose. "It is very interesting to learn that Miss Chilton is the long-lost offspring of our dear Lady Stanton. It would be even more interesting to me—with all due respect to Miss Cawley—to learn precisely how she came upon this bit of intelligence."

Jessica took this in, and when she had done so her cheeks flamed up noticeably. "Am I to understand that Your Grace does not believe me?" she inquired deliberately. "Do you suppose I heard the name Charlotte and decided to take advantage of the situation in order to provide noble parents for my friend? I presume that is what you insinuate—that I fabricated the whole business."

The duchess regarded her steadily. "I should prefer to say, my dear," she answered, "that you are, perhaps, the victim of your own imagination. Perhaps Miss Chilton is Charlotte del Silandro; perhaps she is not. In either case, what I desire to hear is how you came upon your information. That is all."

Miss Cawley was furious. The duchess was doubting her word, no matter what she pretended. "If this matter were not so critical," Jessica declared, "I would refuse to answer you. In view of the circumstances, however . . . Miss Chilton told me her father was named Lodovico del Silandro, that she was born in Italy, and that she never knew her mother's name. Ever since she can remember, she was with the Chiltons."

"Ah! That is very good," said Lady Stanton, catching at this even while she coloured at the thought of her own eagerness. "Then she must have been young when he left her. Did he die? Is that why he left?" she appealed eagerly to Miss Cawley.

"I should think so," said Jessica. "Of course, she told me her mother had died young too—but I expect she was only told that by the Chiltons . . . so that she shouldn't feel deserted, you know."

The duchess spoke again. "This is very interesting," she said; "very interesting indeed. As the matter is so extremely crucial, however—as you say, Miss Cawley—I wonder if we oughtn't to devise a little . . . test for Miss Chilton. In view of the circumstances—as you say, my dear—I think it only proper that no one speak to Lotta on this matter until she has been summoned to me. When she has come, and only then, I shall ask her the name of her father. If she says del Silandro—"

"If!" cried Jessica, outraged. "My dear ma'am, this is a trifle overdone. Do you persist—"

"Ah, please, Miss Cawley," Karr broke in suddenly. "I know how unpleasant it is to be doubted, but my mother—in all fairness—has some reason for making her demands. After all, a great deal hangs upon Lotta's birth, for if she *is* Lady Stanton's daughter, I trust Her Grace will give her blessing to us . . . That is what you intend, madam, is it not?"

All eyes turned to the duchess, whose expression seemed to grow even more austere on the spot. "It is," she finally brought out. "If she says del Silandro, you may marry . . . with my blessing." These last words were produced with so much difficulty that when, immediately after saying them, the duchess sat again, it appeared to be because she had exhausted herself.

"Ah! Dear ma'am!" cried Karr, and ran up to her to kiss her. He would have kissed her cheek, but she extended a hand to forestall him, as she frequently did.

"Kindly do not make a spectacle of this. I am only behaving according to the dictates of logic. A bride chosen from the populace cannot be welcomed into the family of a duke. A bride who is the daughter of an Italian peer and the grand-daughter of the Earl of Baddesleigh is another matter. Mind you, I have heard of more illustrious matches—with all due respect to Lady Stanton . . . but this one will serve."

Karr turned to the assembled company, a broad smile upon his handsome lips. "You see how perfectly my mother has learned diplomacy? She yields, yet contrives to sound as if she yielded nothing." And with this, he saluted her hand once more. "And now, if you will all pardon me, I think I must set out upon a journey."

"At this hour, my son?" the duchess objected at once.

"This moment," he replied, and turned to leave the room. Just as he did so, however, a knock was heard at the drawing-room doors. The servants, of course, had been instructed to allow no one to leave; so the footman who now entered did so carefully.

"Your Grace," he said, going up to Karr directly. He murmured something to the master of the castle, then stood back respectfully.

"Providence!" exclaimed Karr; "the hand of Providence is in it. Yes, yes, man—let her in. Beg her to come in at once, I pray you."

The footman went upon this errand while everyone stared at the duke. "One moment, one moment," was all he would say. "You will see who it is." And before five minutes had gone by, indeed, another knock was heard at the door, and Lotta Chilton passed in to the drawing-room.

"Dear sir," she said, going up to Karr at once. "I had asked to see you alone."

"Ah, my dear, how beautiful you are!" said Karr, fairly transported by her sudden reappearance. And she did look beautiful, in truth: she wore travelling clothes, and had evidently come a good distance; but the excitement of seeing the duke again had brought an exquisite, delicate flush into her translucent cheeks, and a deep glow into her eyes. "Forgive me, but I could not greet you alone—you will see why in a moment. Mother, if you will be so good as to ask Miss Chilton your question—?"

Lotta, weary from her journey and with a score of emotions in her breast, hardly knew which way to turn. She had told the footman to beg for a private interview with His Grace; now, instead of that, she was faced with all the guests at Grasmere. Moreover, Karr appeared to wish her to submit to some sort of interrogation by the duchess. It was rather perplexing, but she did as the duke desired. "Your Grace?" she said, curtseying to the dowager.

"Miss Chilton," said the duchess, without any sort of prologue, "what is your father's name?"

"I beg your pardon?" asked the surprised young lady.

"Your father's name," repeated the duchess, glancing briefly at Miss Cawley. The suspense in the drawing-room was painful.

"My natural father?" asked Lotta.

"Good heavens yes, girl!" exclaimed Her Grace impatiently.

"Lodovico del Silandro," Lotta answered at last, wonderingly. "But I don't see—"

But Miss Chilton—or rather, Miss del Silandro—never got to finish this sentence. She was swept off her rather fatigued feet by His Grace,

who rushed upon her with an unearthly whoop of joy. He was so excited
that it was some minutes before she understood what significance her response had to their mutual future. "You *will* marry me, won't you?" His
Grace demanded abruptly, suddenly realizing that for all he knew, Lotta
no longer desired to be his wife under any circumstances.

She spoke in a low tone, so that only he could hear her. "That is why
I came," she said. "I could not bear it any longer—I had to be near you.
Will you forgive me for not answering your letters?" she added. "I was
trying to forget you altogether, but as you can see, it was no use."

Karr nodded a hearty affirmative, and took hold of her hand.

"And now, my dear," Lotta continued, "try not to think me a simple-
ton, but I did not quite understand what you said about my parents.
Why, exactly, am I now permitted to be your wife?"

His Grace regarded his betrothed in silence, then led her to where
Lady Stanton sat. "Will you explain, madam?" he asked.

"Ah, my dear!" cried Lady Stanton, whose sentiments of pain and
pleasure had never been more confused. "My dear, an explanation in a
moment. But first—tell me when your father died. Do you know?"

Again, Lotta's confoundment was as manifest as it was under-
standable. "When I was an infant," she replied. "He was killed in an accident when I was two or three."

"Two or three?" the other lady took up. "Not five? You are quite
certain it was before you were five?"

"Quite certain," said Lotta mildly. "Why?"

"Thank God, thank God," rejoiced her ladyship. "Walker—can you
imagine? Do you hear? It is all settled now; it is all done, and well done.
Dear Amabel—dear Chauncey—your mother did not wrong you so terribly after all!" And after Lady Stanton had embraced both these children, she stood up and embraced her eldest (who was, reasonably,
rather startled by the action). She asked Lotta to come out of the drawing-room with her and grant her a private interview; which having been
accomplished, Lotta was informed of her own history where she could
hear it without an audience. Karr, who could not bear to be away from
his betrothed for very long, followed the two ladies half an hour later,
and discovered them in the Rose Saloon, their hands joined and both
pairs of eyes shining with tears. Lotta, who had thought her mother long
dead, had never even considered the possibility of such an encounter as
the one she now experienced, and the whole thing maintained the tenor
of a dream for her for a number of days.

By the close of the following se'ennight, however, a good deal had
been sorted out, and her sense of reality had returned to her. She ex-

plained to her new-found mother that her father, del Silandro, had left the baby with the Chiltons one day while he went on a brief excursion. The Chiltons, it seemed, were people whose acquaintance he had made after Lady Anne had quitted Italy. Though the journey he took was not long, the accident that befell him in its course was fatal. The Chiltons, having expected to keep the child several days, ended by keeping her twenty years. Whether del Silandro had run off with the infant in order to spare Lady Anne the discomfort of an ill-conceived marriage, or to spare himself, or for any other reason, Lotta could not say. She doubted indeed if the Chiltons knew, for it did not seem the sort of information del Silandro would have been likely to share.

Lady Stanton, to say truth, did not care a very great deal. It was enough to her to know that her daughter was alive and well, and to know that she had committed no sin through her second marriage. This latter fact had an interesting effect on the fate of the Countess Tremini: since the Stantons found (to their surprise) that in spite of everything they were *not* ruined, they rather lost their desire to press charges against the contessa. To bring her to justice, after all, would be to expose the irregularity of Lady Stanton's youth to a public to whom she disliked to reveal such intelligence. It was decided, then, to allow the contessa to resume her adventuring as best she might. She was cautioned, though, that if any one of the guests then at Grasmere ever heard of her pursuing such criminal activities again, the Stantons would be informed of her relapse and would assuredly reveal the scheme she had worked against them. Unhappily, it was impossible to demand that she return the money she had extorted; she no longer had it. On the other hand, as Lady Stanton reflected contentedly, the Stantons were about to acquire a very wealthy son-in-law. "And the way Wyborn spoke, you know, about not crying off," said her ladyship privately to her (second) husband, "I don't think we need fret about the dowry."

"My dear," said his lordship, "we are about to acquire *two* very wealthy sons-in-law. Surely you don't think Karr will let us starve!"

Lady Stanton looked at him, puzzled. "Karr? But he is to marry—oh dear! You are very right; I never even thought of it! And I never welcomed him to our family . . . How dreadful of me. Excuse me, my dear," she smiled, rising. She gave Lord Stanton a light, gay kiss and tripped happily out of the room upon her errand, as glad and bright a girl again (in her heart at least) as either of her daughters.

THE END

793765

Fic
Hil

Hill, Fiona

The love child